"You're st ... investiga ...

"Oh yeah?" She got in Jack's face. "Is your name Parker Lord? Do you head up the FBI? Do you currently serve as president of the United States? Because unless you can say yes to any of those questions you have no control over whether I stay in this investigation or not. Got that? You don't control me." Evie's voice came out in a lethal whisper.

Jack took a step toward her and grabbed her wrists. This time she didn't let that touch soften her. One knee to the groin. Or an elbow to the gut...

But she must maintain calm and absolute authority in front of her team.

"Officer Hawes." Evie dipped her head to a uniform standing in the doorway. "Please cuff Mr. Elliott and take him downtown..."

ACCLAIM FOR *THE BROKEN*

"Coriell's Apostles series launch is a true roller-coaster ride of romantic suspense...The gradual attraction between Hayden and Kate is believable and intense, as their flaws make them all too human. And the suspense is top-notch, with so many twists and turns that even the most astute reader will be riveted to the stunning conclusion."

—*Publishers Weekly* **(starred review)**

"4½ stars! Top pick! Coriell's latest grips the reader from the first page. An engaging, intriguing plot...a definite must-read."

—*RT Book Reviews*

THE BLIND

Also by Shelley Coriell

The Broken
The Buried

THE BLIND

SHELLEY CORIELL

FOREVER

NEW YORK BOSTON

Forever
Hachette Book Group
1290 Avenue of the Americas
New York, NY 10104

www.HachetteBookGroup.com

Printed in the United States of America

First Edition: July 2015
10 9 8 7 6 5 4 3 2 1

OPM

Forever is an imprint of Grand Central Publishing.
The Forever name and logo are trademarks of Hachette Book Group, Inc.

The Hachette Speakers Bureau provides a wide range of authors for speaking events. To find out more, go to www.hachettespeakersbureau.com or call (866) 376-6591.

The publisher is not responsible for websites (or their content) that are not owned by the publisher.

To Darlene Taylor

ACKNOWLEDGMENTS

A world of thanks to those who've enriched my life and this story: Liz Munoz for sharing your language and culture; Bev Pettersen for your horse smarts; Stacey Goitia for your artistic eye; Erin Jade Lange for a peek into the newsroom; and especially Colonel Jim Smith, public safety director, Cottonwood Department of Public Safety, for technical and tactical expertise on explosive situations. Any mistakes are a product of my imagination—and a main character—gone wild.

Some books require a bit more birthing assistance than others. A heart full of gratitude for the extraordinary midwifery of editor Lauren Plude on this one. Continued thanks to the Forever team at Grand Central for not giving up on, and "getting," my Apostles, particularly publicist Marissa Sangiacomo and cover designer Elizabeth Turner.

Finally, to my aunt Darlene. Thanks for letting me borrow all those mystery and suspense books from the bookcase in your spare bedroom during my summer vacations and igniting my love for all things dark and twisty.

THE BLIND

CHAPTER ONE

Tuesday, October 6
10:42 a.m.

Wake up, sleeping beauty." Carter Vandemere kissed the smooth, warm curve of the woman's shoulder. "The clock is ticking."

Tick tock, like a clock, ready, set, go!

Maria moaned but didn't open her eyes. He didn't know her name, but he called her Maria. Mary. The Madonna. Beautiful. His lips brushed the two-inch square of raw, rippled flesh on the back of her shoulder. So, so beautiful. His lips trailed along her throat. Soft. The tip of his tongue slid along her jaw. Sweet. His cheek brushed hers. Warm. Like heated cream. He nibbled her ear, then bit. Hard.

Her eyes flew open, and she tried to scream. The duct tape held, a scream-catcher of sorts.

He gave her shoulder a reassuring squeeze. "Don't worry, Maria. Soon the entire world will hear you." With a grin, he settled onto the edge of the futon that reeked of body fluid stew. His fingers sifted through the thick fall of honey-colored hair, and his nails dug into the raw flesh on the back of her shoulder. Her eyes bulged and cheeks flushed. So much color and texture. She was his finest work yet.

"So here's the deal, Maria." An electrified heat pulsed through his fingers as he picked up an eighteen-gauge wire. "Tiny little thing, isn't it? But with it you have the power to live or die." He attached the wire to the mercury switch secured to the fanny pack he'd belted around her exquisite hips. The pack disrupted composition and led the eye astray. Definitely not beautiful, but necessary, the final brushstroke. Hot sparks shot down his arms and across his chest.

His fingers lingered over the corner of the duct tape at her mouth. Pain was part of art, part of the artist.

Riiiiiiip!

"You son of a bitch. You sadistic, fu—"

Smack! How dare she ruin his work with such crudeness? He pulled in a breath, cooling the electric firestorm. In his art, timing was everything.

"Such ugly words from such a beautiful mouth," he said with a soft cluck as he taped the wire to her bottom lip. "Now let's talk about that beautiful mouth. From this moment on, if you open your mouth, the wire will trip the anti-movement switch. After a thirty-second delay, enough time for me to get away, an electric loop will close, setting off the initiator and starting the firing train. The train will activate the primary explosive, which will detonate the main charge. And boom!" His fisted fingers fanned out, but he didn't see the paint-smudged digits. He saw the spark, the gritty puff of air, the exquisite shattering and scattering of metal and Maria. Breathtaking.

"Bottom line, Maria. You open your mouth, you die. Understand?"

She sat before him, a still life. There was beauty in everyday, inanimate objects, but masterful art lived and breathed. And in his case, died.

"Blink once for yes. Twice for no."

Maria gave him one blink, one terrified, beautiful blink.

* * *

11:27 a.m.

Freddy Ortiz loved the ponies, fast ones that could win a race with the wind. Unfortunately, he hadn't found many winners lately.

Bang, bang, bang! Which was why Skip Folsum was banging the shit out of the front door of his West Hollywood studio apartment.

Freddy tore off the covers and groped under his bed for jeans until he found a pair that wasn't too crusty. He knew the drill. Kind of hard not to when you spent the past ten years swimming with sharks.

"Dammit, Freddy, I know you're in there. I want my money."

He thrust his legs into the jeans and threw on an L.A. Kings T-shirt. Essentials only. He grabbed his camera. On second thought, he scooped up his boots.

"Open this damn door!" The door handle rattled, and the wooden frame shook as if terrified. Smart door. Skip carried a .38 Special. Freddy'd seen it last week.

With sweat-slickened palms, Freddy threw open the window and squeezed out onto the landing. He half-climbed, half-free-fell down three flights of fire escapes until he landed with a thud in an alley that smelled of cat piss. Above him, Skip poked his head—and .38—out the window.

Crack! A chunk of alley exploded.

Freddy ducked a hailstorm of asphalt and hauled ass to the car lot at the end of the alley and his late-model Ford Mustang. He fumbled with his key fob.

Crack! The right taillight shattered.

He dove into the car, gunned the pony, and squealed out of Cat Piss Alley. His hand shaking, he dug into his shirt pocket. Shit. Nothing but lint and the hammering of his heart. He took three quick turns and checked the mirror. No Skip. One hand on the wheel, he dug through the glove box. Shit, *shit*. No cigarettes. He groped under the driver's seat and found one bent stick of gum. He was a gambling man, but today was not his lucky day.

With another check of his rearview, he popped the gum in his mouth. Skip needed money, which meant *Freddy* needed money. He could head to LAX or the Brentwood Country Mart, good places to shoot Hollywood stars coming and going, but with Skip's .38 now aimed at his not-so-small ass, he needed more than Hollywood ho-hum. A few deadly sins would be nice. He'd always been a big fan of lust and greed. Again he checked the rearview. He was also a big fan of staying alive.

Lately, downtown L.A. had been his honey hole. Last month he snagged some photos of a soap opera actor shelling out money to a prostitute for a bit of dirty, and prior to that he shot a pro ball player getting hauled into the downtown station for disorderly conduct following a game at the Staples Center.

Ca-ching.

As usual, downtown traffic was a bear. He crawled through the snarl of cars toward the police station. Near the library, a scream split the sunshine cutting at sharp angles through the high-rises. The library was hardly a paparazzo's playground, but he grabbed a parking spot because in his business, screams usually meant money.

Looping his camera around his neck, he bulldozed through a cluster of gawkers near a grassy area and found a woman in a shiny white robe reclining at the base of a thick tree. He let out a soft whistle. A real beauty. Creamy skin, waves of golden hair, big, brown eyes. Not an actress, at least not one he recognized. Too bad. The rags paid big for Hollywood hotties doing dumb shit. He snapped off a series of wide-angle shots and elbowed his way to the front.

Up close he could see her body shook and lips trembled. Was she drunk? Cranking? Or was this some kind of reality TV show or B movie publicity stunt? The woman shifted, the front of her robe opening and framing a pair of *tetas*. Niiiiice.

He fired off another round. Damn, she was a beauty. Especially those lips. He zoomed in and spotted a wire snaking from her mouth. A mic? His viewfinder followed the wire to her waist circled by a piece of nylon webbing attached to a bulging pack. He zoomed tighter, focusing in on a metal prong at the end of the wire. His fingers froze. His blood, too.

"Holy shit," Freddy said on a strangled cry. "This is one of them Angel Bombings."

En masse, the crowd lunged back. Some ran. Others pushed. The guy at his right was punching 911 into the face of his cell phone. Freddy backed away. No one could save her. And even if there was a way, he wasn't a hero, not by a long shot. But that didn't mean he was without a weapon. His fingers shaking, he aimed his camera back on the woman.

Click. Click. Click.

His work was all about the story, and in this moment, Freddy knew that was all he could do for this woman. Tell the story. A siren wailed. Tears streamed down the woman's face. Her body jerked in silent sobs. Then one escaped, high-pitched and fast, like an animal caged too long. Her cry clawed at his chest.

Pop.

The world as seen through his lens exploded. The ground rocked. A roar tore through his head. Bits of twisted metal and earth rained from the cloudless blue sky. He ducked a flaming tree branch and stumbled toward the street, his chest curved around his camera.

A little girl with pigtails swatted at the ashy air, screaming, "Daaaaaddy, where are youuuuuu?"

Somewhere glass shattered. Freddy looped his arm around the screaming kid and dove behind a car. His head low, he hauled in deep breaths but froze when he spotted a gelatinous, veiny glob on the toe of his right boot. The world spun a second time, something hard and heavy churning in his gut. The kid whimpered. He cradled her pigtails and turned her face away from his boot. Then he forced down chunks of horror clawing up his throat.

Freddy had some killer shots, literally, which might help track down a serial bomber. But he also had a little change in luck. One hand resting on the pigtails, he steadied his other hand on his camera. Then he aimed the lens at his foot, zooming in on the chunk of the beauty's brain.

Click.
Sick bastard.
Ca-ching.

CHAPTER TWO

Wednesday, October 28
7:55 a.m.

Evie Jimenez hauled her emergency response duffel from the back of her truck and hoisted sixty pounds of Kevlar and ceramic plates onto her back. Despite the load, she felt she could fly.

Her helmet cradled under her right arm, she pushed her way through the bodies gathered in the high school parking lot, her zigzag gaze canvassing the crowd. So far no one triggered her internal radar. No loner high school boy with mischief or a mission on his mind. No disgruntled or disenfranchised type showing too much glee. Although there was the ginger in the nice suit leaning against a white sedan. Too relaxed to be a parent or teacher. Too well dressed to be a media parasite. Her arm tightened around her helmet as she jogged past the section roped off for camera crews and news reporters.

"Look! Isn't that Agent Jimenez?" a man with a handheld mic called out.

Evie blinked off a salvo of blinding flashes and kept her pace steady.

A woman from a news station in Bangor thrust a microphone in her direction. "Agent Jimenez, has your suspension following the debacle in Houston been lifted?"

Keep walking.

"Agent Jimenez, is it true that the president of the United States asked for your resignation?"

No talking.

"How do you feel about putting a dark mark on the arguably miraculous record of Parker Lord's Apostles?"

No punching anyone in the face.

"One more question, Agent Jimenez. Since you're back in the field, do you plan to go to L.A. and work the Angel Bomber case?"

Her boots slowed for a fraction of a second. *That was the* plan.

But right now a clock was ticking. She ducked under the crime scene tape.

As she rounded the hazardous devices truck, a uniformed officer grabbed her arm. "Hold up, young lady. You can't go back there. We have a bomb on the premises."

Evie reached for her creds, but the officer snapped back her arm. Having long ago resigned herself to life at five-foot-two, she craned her neck so he could see every inch of her face. "I'm not young, and right now I'm not feeling very ladylike, so get your fucking hands off me so I can defuse that bomb." The officer dropped her arm as if she were on fire.

At the inner perimeter she found the lieutenant in charge of the scene, a grandfatherly type who scrubbed a thumb across his chin after she introduced herself. "You're Parker Lord's guy?" the lieutenant asked.

They could talk about the difference between male and female later. "Yes sir. Has the bomb robot been unloaded?"

"Five minutes ago."

"Excellent." Evie slipped off her pack. "Has the area been evacuated and perimeter set?" Preservation of life was key. It was the first tenet in her manual, and in her world, it was the beginning, end, and everything in between.

The lieutenant gave her a grave nod. "Teachers are currently getting a head count to make sure all students are accounted for, and the homes on the street behind the gym have been evacuated."

Because at this point she was working with unknowns. Unknown charge. Unknown material. Unknown ticking clock. Pulling her hair into a knot on top of her head, she secured it with a rubber band. In the hazardous devices truck, she took a seat behind the monitors and reached for the control panel that guided a one-armed robot with an orange body. "What's his name?"

"The bomb squad boys call him Lobster Claw," the lieutenant said.

She powered up the camera and set the robot in motion. "Okay, Mr. Claw, it's time."

Evie and the robot went to work with a surgeon's precision. X-rays. Infrared readings. Sensors checking for biological, chemical, and nuclear agents. All transmitted to her workstation. When the last of the vitals flashed on her screen, she pulled in a deep breath. They were down with an IED. It would be a simple blow and go, the type of stuff she could do in her sleep.

Approach with caution.

Clear debris.

Set charge.
Detonate.

She flexed her fingers, the knuckles popping as if charged with little bursts of electricity. Then she reached down and unzipped the duffel holding her bomb suit.

* * *

12:38 p.m.

"That was some mighty fine work, Agent Jimenez." The lieutenant slapped her back.

Evie set her helmet on her duffel and gave her head a series of hard shakes, droplets of sweat flying across the high school's practice field. Damn, that felt good. And it *was* good. Textbook perfect. "Thank you, sir."

"We're thrilled Agent Lord agreed to send you."

The skin on the back of her neck cooled. Technically her boss hadn't. She was still on suspension following the botched IED disrupt in Houston, but when the assist call had come in from Bar Harbor PD, Parker had been on a flight to San Francisco and the Maine State Police Hazardous Devices Unit had been tied up with a threat at the airport. Her butt had been conveniently nearby, glued to her desk chair at The Box, home base for Parker Lord's Special Criminal Investigative Unit. "Glad to be of service, sir."

"How about lunch at Max's to celebrate?" the lieutenant asked. "First beer's on me."

"Make it a shot of Knob Creek Rye, and you're on."

Lines crinkled the older man's eyes. "Need a ride?"

"I'll walk." She plucked at her sweat-soaked tank. "I need a cooldown." She always did after a disrupt. The three layers of protective materials ratcheted up her body heat, and of course there was the fire inside. Plus she needed to tell Parker about the high school job. The president would probably blow a fuse, but Parker would stand behind her, just like he had two months ago in Houston when the president had tried to make her the scapegoat.

Save the baby!

Her finger traced the new scar dissecting her right eyebrow. She'd done just that.

She took out her cell phone and texted Parker Lord two words: *Call me*.

Slipping on her shoulder rig and denim jacket, she ducked under the crime scene tape and darted between cars, keeping a wide berth between herself and the media slugs. Parker could deal with them. He was less likely to use swear words or hit something.

Her blood still amped with heat and adrenaline, she raised her face to the flurry-filled sky and caught a snowflake on her tongue. Damn, she loved being back in the field. Her stomach growled. She also loved lobster rolls.

One block into her walk, she spotted the tail. The ginger with the fancy suit. Evie took a quick right and headed down Main but slowed as she passed a shop selling frou-frou scarves. Within seconds, the ginger turned onto the street. He was five and a half feet and a buck thirty, tops. That suit screamed designer. She ambled to the other side of the window, pretending to be captivated by a display of bedazzled handbags, and got a full view. His face didn't match any of the FBI's most wanted posters or anyone in her personal gallery of bad boys who played with bombs, but he had slick shoes, too slick for coastal Maine.

Every cell in her body on heightened awareness, Evie ducked down an alley and slipped behind a Dumpster. Seconds later, along came the ginger. Like a tightly wound spring, she pounced. He shifted right and spun. She adjusted in midair and slammed into his midsection.

"Oomph!" Ginger down.

One hand around his neck, she jammed her knee into his groin. Ice crystals formed on the air between them as she lowered her face to his. "Would you like to lose one testicle today or two?" She expected a wince, groan, or a few well-chosen expletives.

His shoulders jiggled with a laugh. "They warned me about you, but I didn't believe them. Oh, God, this is going to be fun."

Fun? Who the hell was this bozo? More important, did he have anything to do with the IED planted at the high school? She hauled her service revolver from her shoulder holster. "You want fun?"

He stopped laughing.

"Who are you?" Evie asked. He reached for his pants pocket, and her knee dug deeper. This time he winced. "I said, who are you?"

"Brady Malloy of Elliott Enterprises. Card's in my pocket."

She dug into his wallet and withdrew a California-issued driver's license. Home address in Los Angeles. Organ donor. Excellent. If he had anything to do with that backpack of C-4 in the high school gym, she could help him part with a few organs. She pulled out a fancy embossed business card. "Okay, Mr. Brady Malloy of Elliott Enterprises. Says here you're a public relations guy."

"I'm good with people."

Unlike her. She climbed off his midsection but did not holster her firearm. "So what the hell is a public relations specialist for a"—she checked the card—"an equity investment firm from Los Angeles doing at a bomb disruption at a high school in Bar Harbor, Maine?"

"Following you," he said with wide-eyed sincerity.

Her fingers tightened around the card. The honesty surprised her. So did the fact that he got the jump on her. "And now that you've found me?"

He stood and dusted the snow tufts and dead leaves from his jacket. "I'm here on behalf of my employer, Mr. Jack Elliott. He'd like to hire you to deal with . . . an incendiary situation."

This time Evie laughed. Clearly this guy had no idea who she was. "I'm no dick for hire."

"Mr. Elliott doesn't want a private detective. He wants you. He wants an Apostle."

She wasn't surprised he knew who she was. Thanks to the Houston job, anyone who watched the nightly news knew she was the bomb and weapons specialist for Parker's team, but like all of the Apostles, she was too busy catching this country's most vile criminals to take side jobs. Malloy's boss was probably one of those guys who threw money around and expected others to hop and skip. Too bad for Mr. Jack Elliott that as a kid, she never got the hang of girly games like hopscotch.

She holstered her sidearm. The rumble and tumble with the ginger had left her thirsty. "Wish I could say it's been a pleasure, Mr. Malloy, but frankly, this chitchat is keeping me from a much-needed shot of whiskey." She headed for the mouth of the alley. "*Adiós.*"

Malloy cleared his throat. "Mr. Elliott has information on the next Angel Bombing."

An invisible hand yanked Evie to a stop, and she spun toward Malloy. For three months investigators from LAPD, ATF, FBI, and an alphabet soup of other agencies had been hunting for the bomber responsible for a series of explosions that had killed seven, maimed or injured 105, and scared the hell out of 3.85 million residents of the City of Angels.

Thanks to her suspension, she wasn't officially on the case, but she'd been all over it, poring through case notes, collecting images, and keeping everything in a folder she took out every night and read like a bedtime storybook.

"What kind of information?" Despite her shackles, she couldn't back off from a lead.

Malloy once again settled that earnest gaze on her. "Mr. Elliott would prefer to tell you in person."

She bowed, sweeping her hand through the alley. "Tell him to come into my office."

"He's in Los Angeles."

"Then get him on the phone."

"He'd prefer to tell you in person."

Evie pushed a wayward curl off her forehead. "And I prefer a little less bullshit." The Angel Bomber had been consistent in creating chaos. His bombs went off the first week of every month for the past three months, and they were just days away from November first. "Exactly what does your boss know about the bombings?"

Malloy shuffled his feet, kicking at airy snowdrifts, before finally looking her squarely in the eye. "Mr. Elliott believes the next victims will be a brown-haired woman in a red dress and a baby with blond curls."

The image slammed her like an M120 mortar.

"That's all I know," Malloy continued. "He insists on telling you the rest in person. He has his private jet ready to fly you to L.A."

And she had a presidentially mandated suspension hanging over her head like a two-ton anvil. She shifted from one boot to the other. In bomb investigations forensic evidence didn't solve cases, people did. This guy's boss could have a tip that could lead them to the deadliest bomber in the country, or hell, this guy's boss could *be* the bomber.

Again Malloy motioned to the alley. "Are you ready, Agent Jimenez?"

Mr. Elliott believes the next victims will be a brown-haired woman in a red dress and a baby with blond curls.

Save the baby!

"Hell, yes."

CHAPTER THREE

Wednesday, October 28
7:24 p.m.

Ding.

Ding.

Two voice mails had come in while Evie had been flying from Maine to Los Angeles. She brought up the call log. One from her teammate Hatch Hatcher, the other from—

"Shit," she said under her breath.

"Everything okay?" Brady asked as he guided the car out of LAX.

"Yes." Although her answer might be different after she listened to the second voice mail, the one from the president of the United States, but she wasn't going to do that until she talked to Parker. She checked her texts. Still no word from her boss, but that wasn't surprising as he'd been in San Francisco all day working a case.

Evie had spent most of her day on Jack Elliott's private

jet. Plush leather recliner seats. Fully stocked minibar. Hi-def movie theater with a state-of-the-art sound system. She'd been most interested in the jet's in-flight Internet service, which she used to run a background check on Jack Elliott. Evie was impressed with what she found. Elliott was the proud owner of a Harvard MBA, ran a legit equity investment business in So Cal, and had money coming out his ass. No record. No ties to extremist groups. Not a hair out of place. So why the hell did he allegedly know so much about the bomb investigation of the decade?

As Brady exited the freeway and aimed the car at L.A.'s downtown financial district, the bomber's fallout was everywhere. Three billboards so far: *Angel Bomber Hotline 1-555-NO-BOMBS*. Handbills with a similar message were taped to light poles and plastered on bus stop benches. On a marquee outside a church off Olympic Boulevard was the message: *Pray for our fallen angels*.

Brady pulled the car into the Elliott Tower parking garage, and the parking attendant slid open the glass window of his booth.

"Evening, Mr. Malloy," the attendant said. "I'll need your—"

Evie reached across the car and flashed her badge. The parking attendant took down the number.

Inside the Elliott Tower, a thirty-six-story high-rise, she jerked to a stop before a display window in a fussy boutique on the bottom floor. A mannequin in a slinky gold gown rubbed noses with a fake Chihuahua wearing a gold-and-diamond collar. Another mannequin in a red sweater-y thing cradled a fake poodle dressed in an elf outfit.

"Really?" Evie asked.

Brady Malloy grinned. "Welcome to L.A."

"More like welcome to another planet." Despite the late

hour and heavy cloud cover, the city wasn't completely dark. A warm, soft light hung over downtown L.A. like a golden halo.

They made their way through the marbled entryway to a guard station where Brady signed her in. Once again a security guard took her badge number, adding in the margin "red boots." He also snapped a photo for a visitor's pass.

"Would you like a pint of blood with that?" Evie asked the guard, who took a plastic card rolling out from a printer and attached a clip to the top.

"We're very serious about security," the guard explained as he handed her the ID badge, her mug shot emblazoned on one side along with a bar code.

"Even more so since the bombings started," Brady added. "All businesses downtown have stepped up security, and police have increased patrols." Because the bomber would most likely strike in a matter of days.

Near the elevator, Brady motioned to a ladies' room door. "Do you need to use the restroom or anything?"

"I'm good."

Frosted doors of an elevator etched with the giant letters EE slid open. A face with one eye where an ear should be stared at her. The face had no nose. She read the brass plaque on the bottom of the painting. *Picasso.* She knew little about art, but even she recognized that name. What kind of man put Picassos in his elevator? She flipped over her visitor's pass. The same kind of guy who put flowery reprints of Vincent van Gogh on ID badges.

Brady escorted her to the thirty-sixth floor, where she strolled through a lobby lined with artwork from Bellini and Vermeer, and she'd bet the college funds she'd started for each of her seven nephews that these were the real deals.

"Your boss likes fancy paintings?" Evie asked.

"My boss likes," Brady quirked his mouth, "collecting."

She pictured the artwork on her refrigerator door back in her rarely used condo in Albuquerque, all originals by her nephews, but unlike the art in her home—finger-painted landscapes and portraits made with crayons—these paintings did nothing to warm the offices. The top floor of the Elliott Tower was cool, almost cold.

A woman in a beige suit, beige lipstick, and beige hair greeted her with a short nod. "Good evening, Agent Jimenez. Mr. Elliott is wrapping up an overseas call. Can I get you a cup of coffee, tea, or mineral water?"

"I'm good."

"Or perhaps some heated towels to, uh, freshen up?"

"I'm good."

"Are you sure?" Her nose wrinkled.

"Yes." Evie wasn't one to check in with mirrors throughout the day, but her newly minted ID card showed a serious case of helmet head, sweat stains on her tank, and alley grit on her denim jacket.

"Please have a seat. Mr. Elliott will be with you shortly."

Evie had been sitting way too much today. With the door to Elliott's office closed, she paced the length of the room. She checked her phone again. Another message from the president's office and a media alert on the Angel Bomber investigation. Ignoring the president, she clicked on the link to a breaking news report from a Los Angeles television station.

"In the latest move to track down the Angel Bomber terrorizing downtown Los Angeles," a news reporter was saying, "authorities announced today that a twenty-five-thousand-dollar reward is being offered to anyone providing information leading to the capture of the bomber. According to Captain Vince Ricci of the LAPD, the bomber will most likely strike within the next week and may again target heavily populated areas."

Evie stopped in front of the secretary's chrome-and-glass desk. "Can you please tell Mr. Elliott I'm here?"

"As soon as he wraps up his call," the woman said. "He's finishing a very important business deal with associates in Germany."

The nameplate on the woman's desk read *Claire Turner, Executive Assistant.* Her title should have read, *Guard Dog.* "More important than stopping a serial killer?" Evie asked.

Claire's polite smile didn't crack. "Mr. Elliott will be with you as soon as he finishes the German deal."

Or not. Evie headed to the door beyond Claire's desk.

"You can't go in there!"

Says who? Evie side-stepped a beige arm and threw open the door. Elliott's inner sanctum was the size of the ice rink where her oldest nephew played hockey. Centered in front of a wall of glass overlooking the dark skies and bright lights of the downtown L.A. skyline sat a shiny glass desk the size of a small country. Behind it was a man who reminded her of a European prince. Dark-haired and angular, he wore a snow-white dress shirt with a dark, pin-striped vest, monogrammed cuff links, and an air of privilege. She'd personally drop to her knees and kiss his royal ring if he could help her nail a killer. And if he was the bomber, she'd do her damnedest to make sure he got himself fancy new duds, the kind with black and white stripes.

"Good evening, sir." She squared up in front of him, her back and resolve ramrod stiff. "I'm Special Agent Evie Jimenez. I'm here about the Angel Bombings."

Keeping his gaze on a computer screen, he showed her his palm.

She clasped her hands behind her back and shifted from one boot to the other. She made it fifty-seven seconds before she cleared her throat. "Mr. Elliott, I'm sorry to interrupt your business, but if you have information on a killer, I need to know as soon as possible. There's just three more days until the first of November, which means he could right now be scouting out or abducting his next victim."

Without looking up from his computer screen, Elliott extended a single index finger and jabbed it at her and then the door.

Claire's lips thinned. "If you'll come this way, please."

"No, I don't *please*. Mr. Elliott and I have business to discuss." She dropped her bag on the floor, hiked her jeans, and climbed across Elliott's desk. Raising her index finger, she pushed, End Call.

Claire gasped. Brady, who'd followed them into the office, groaned.

Evie shimmied back across the desk, her boots thudding to the marble floor. "Now we can talk."

Jack Elliott's gaze finally snapped to her. She'd expected slate gray or obsidian or even sharp green. Instead he had faded blue eyes, the color of worn denim.

"Who are you?" His words, on the other hand, came out hard and sharp.

Amazing. He'd been so intently focused on his phone call that he hadn't heard a word she'd said. He would make a great bomb tech. She took out her business card. "Special Agent Evangelina Jimenez. I'm here about the Angel Bombings."

He took the card, his fingers curving around the paper as he brought a fist to his chest for a heartbeat before slipping it into a pocket on the inside of his vest. "Thank you for coming, Agent Jimenez." His voice was strangely calm.

If she were him, she would have yelled, that is, after body-slamming anyone who crawled across her desk. Disconnecting his phone call had been bold and borderline rude, but it had snagged his attention. Score one for Team Stop-the-Serial-Killer.

He slipped off his Bluetooth and shut down his computer. "Claire, get Germany back on the line and ask Heinrich to send our contracts division the new addendum. Then forward all docs to legal and accounting. Brady, call Roy at the Lakers office and get a pair of courtside tickets for a game this weekend and send them to Heinrich's liaison in New York."

"The waterfront deal went through?" Brady asked with a catch in his voice.

"We're scheduled to close tomorrow." The cool denim of Elliott's eyes warmed. "Heinrich sweetened the deal with a hundred-thousand-dollar donation to the Abby Foundation."

Brady whistled. "Congrats, boss, on the biggest deal of your career." Brady saluted the man behind the desk.

Elliott clicked a button on his phone. "Darryl, please bring my car around." He pushed a button under his desk, and a wooden panel in the wall slid open and revealed another shiny glass-and-chrome elevator. "My apologies for the delay, Agent Jimenez. This way, please."

She kept her boots firmly rooted on the front side of the desk. This was a man who gave orders and expected full compliance. Too bad. "Exactly where do you want to take me?"

"To an art exhibit. It's just a few blocks from here in the warehouse district." Facing the mirrored elevator door, he adjusted his shiny platinum tie tack so the oval was vertical, then pushed the elevator's Down button. The silvery doors parted with a muted *ding*.

"What does an art exhibit have to do with the Angel Bomber?"

"Everything." He delivered the single word as if it were an undisputable fact. "It will make sense when you see the exhibit."

She had infinite patience with bombs but not with people. "It will make sense if you tell me exactly what you know about these bombings."

Jack Elliott blinked, as if genuinely surprised she wasn't jumping to attention. He slipped a hand in his pocket, a soft jangle sounding. "The bomber's first three bombings have been re-creations of the first three paintings in the exhibit."

Evie's fingers twitched. Investigators had nothing on the bomber. If Elliott was onto something…She wiped her palms along the thighs of her jeans.

Approach with caution.

"I've been studying this case for months and never heard any mention of paintings or art exhibits."

"The connection wasn't obvious in the first two bombings because the post-explosion damage had been so extensive, but the tabloid photographer's shots in the third bombing clearly show a connection."

A money-grubbing tabloid photographer had been on-scene at the third bombing and snapped photos of the terrified victim before, during, and after the IED detonated. Then the slug held a bidding war and sold the gruesome images to a gossipy online news rag in the U.K. Evie didn't admire his motive, but she knew the value of those images.

Clear debris.

"Those photos were released three weeks ago, hours after the explosion," she said. "Are you telling me you just now made the connection?"

"I was single-mindedly focused on the German deal."

She could believe that. She'd had to disconnect his phone to get his attention. Jack Elliott was a guy buried in and married to his work. No ring on his left hand. No family pics on his credenza. No office supplies made from recycled juice cans on his desk.

Set charge.

"And no one else has seen these disturbing similarities?"

"It's a private collection." The jangling stopped, and she pictured that hidden hand tightening into a rock-hard fist. Something flashed in his eyes, but it was so fast and fleeting that she couldn't make it out. "And I'm the owner."

Detonate.

"Show me the artwork."

CHAPTER FOUR

Wednesday, October 28
8:22 p.m.

Her Glock still at her side, Evie slipped out of Jack Elliott's sleek black Audi and followed him down a buckled sidewalk to a narrow, red-bricked, three-story building in the heart of L.A.'s old warehouse district. A sign on the oversized green door with shiny brass handles read, *Abby Foundation*.

The old warehouse had been converted into a hip gallery with a few stylized benches, edgy paintings, and funky sculptures. Madison Avenue Jack looked sorely out of place.

His face a polite mask, Elliott opened a door leading to a staircase. "This way, please."

"After you, *please*." She and her Glock were so much more comfortable bringing up the rear. Again she wondered if he could be the bomber.

She frowned. At heart, serial bombers, like long-range assassins, were cowards, and there was nothing cowardly about Jack Elliott. When he spoke, people jumped. Nor did he have poor impulse control. To the contrary, Elliott was a man in charge and in control.

When they reached the third floor, her nose twitched. A tinny, oily odor hung on the air along with something base and loamy. Chemicals. Her fingers tightened around her Glock.

Elliott flicked a switch, and soft light poured from half globes hanging from poles extending from exposed rafters of the high ceiling. The loft had been divided into work areas, the nearest one filled not with wiring, timers, or propane cylinders, but blocks of marble.

"Artist's studios?" Evie asked.

"The Abby Foundation hosts artists-in-residence programs." At the far end of the hall, he swiped his ID badge along a magnetic strip reader and punched a series of numbers and letters into a keypad.

She held her breath as he opened the door. Was the key to stopping the most wanted bomber in America within her reach? He switched on a light. She made a small *o* with her lips, the air rushing from her lungs. She knew squat about art, but she knew the paintings on the walls before her were very fine and very old, and were most likely very, very expensive. More than that, they tugged at her, calling her closer. "They're beautiful."

The corners of Elliott's lips shifted. If she were generous, she'd call it a smile. "I call it *Beauty Through the Ages*. It's a collection dating from the fourteenth century to today."

She drew up in front of a portrait of a smiling dark-haired woman with generous curves bathing in a lake set aglow with silvery moonlight. "You think these are tied to the Angel Bombings?"

He pointed to the third painting. "In the Titian, the

woman is stretched out on a white blanket beneath a tree, similar to the third victim, who'd been lying on a white robe at the park outside the library."

A wave of gooseflesh inched across her arms. The similarities were chilling.

"Now look at these images from the second bombing." With his phone, he showed her a photo of a dark-haired woman, a gold-and-pearl choker embedded in the mangled column of flesh that had once been her throat, the choker similar to the second painting. "And here's a photo from the first bombing." The next photo showed a twisted piece of metal, which in its pre-explosion state would be a dead ringer for the cross the woman in the fourteenth-century painting held. "What do you think?" For the first time since she'd met him, Elliott did not ooze calm and confidence.

The blood racing through her limbs heated. "How long have you had the collection?"

"I purchased the first piece a year ago. Three months ago I secured the final portrait."

"Did you personally buy every piece?"

"Yes. I paid fair market value and then some for these specific pieces."

Jack Elliott was starched shirts and pin-striped suits. He did his wheeling and dealing from a throne of icy glass in a corporate castle that sliced the sky like a blade. His life seemed cold and calculated. Except for his paintings. "Why these pieces?"

"They're beautiful."

She tore her gaze from the art. "They're beautiful?"

The lines around his mouth softened. "Since the beginning of time, there's been a good deal of ugliness in this world: war, famine, natural disasters, hatred. But through it all, pockets of beauty survived. The collection celebrates the enduring power of beauty."

This guy was all about power. A jolt of electricity rocked her chest. And he was right. "You'll need to step out of the gallery, Mr. Elliott. I'm officially declaring this a crime scene." Because some sick SOB was using these portraits to create powerful messages.

Elliott let out a long breath but in no way appeared deflated. If anything, the intense look, the one he'd been wearing when he was on the phone with Germany, was back. "I'll call Captain Ricci and have him meet us at the downtown station."

"No."

"Excuse me?" Affront stiffened Jack Elliott's already starched suit.

"Chasing after serial bombers is best left to those who do not have Harvard MBAs. I will contact Ricci and brief the task force."

Elliott jabbed a hand at the wall of beauties. "I'm clearly involved. You need me."

"Agreed, and I'm sure we're destined to have some nice, heart-to-heart chats." Right now Elliott was key, but he was also an unknown.

"We need to get moving on this." Urgency edged his words.

"That's the plan." Elliott opened his mouth, but she held up a hand. This guy may be king of his universe, but not hers. "Mr. Elliott, exactly why did you send Brady and your jet across the country to pick me up?"

"You're the best." Another cold, hard fact neither of them could dispute.

"Exactly, Mr. Elliott. Now please let me do what I do best." She flexed her fingers, placed her fingertips on the broad plain of his chest, and nudged. The element of surprise—because she got the feeling no one shoved Jack Elliott around—must have worked for he backpedaled out of the gallery.

Then she reached for her phone. She had to contact Vince Ricci at LAPD, dig up background information on Elliott and these portraits, and get details on who had access to this collection, but first she needed to take care of a not-so-minor detail.

She punched in Parker Lord's number to tell him she had just defied presidential orders and inserted herself into the Angel Bomber investigation.

* * *

9:42 p.m.

Jack stood on the balcony of his penthouse just down the street from the Elliott Tower and held a glass of bourbon up to the moon, hidden tonight by streaks of clouds. The liquid was too dark. He waited until the clouds shifted, leaving the moon to set the night aglow. The whiskey warmed and brightened. There, *that* was the color of her eyes. He turned the glass, the ice clinking. The color was right, but the ice was all wrong. There was nothing cold about Special Agent Evie Jimenez.

This morning when he'd seen the tabloid photographer's gruesome images and made the connection to his *Beauty Through the Ages* collection, he'd immediately called an associate who worked for the FBI and asked for the best bomb investigator on the planet.

He took a sip and set the glass on the ledge, the ice bobbing and sending fractured bits of caramel light across the balcony. He dipped a hand into his pocket and took out his phone.

"Jack," the voice on the other end of the line said. "Good to hear from you. How did things go this evening?"

Jack checked a laugh. Like Parker Lord didn't know. "Your Agent Jimenez is quite impressive."

In his office, she'd stood before him, her flushed cheeks as red as the cowboy boots on her feet. A pile of wild, dark brown curls hung askew from her head, and fire shot from her eyes. For a moment Jack wished he were a painter of great art instead of a mere collector, but even with the skill of one of the masters, he would not be able to capture on canvas the fire inside Agent Jimenez.

Jack had seen the all-consuming passion, felt it rolling across his office. "I showed her the paintings and the crime scene photos your man got for me. She agreed that there's a connection. I'm surprised she hasn't called you."

"Oh, she has." Parker did not check a laugh. "Four messages within the past hour, each louder than its predecessor."

"And you haven't returned her calls?"

"I'm waiting on word from the president."

"Not sure if that's healthy for the state of California. If she blows, she'll go hard."

"That's my Evie." Parker's fatherly tone was not lost on Jack, but it surprised him.

Except for her size, there was nothing diminutive or childlike about Agent Jimenez. With those red boots, tight jeans, and wild hair, she could pass for a teenaged street walker, but she had plenty of impressive miles on those boots. The background check he'd run on her showed a woman with an exceptional and decorated service in the U.S. military and a storied career with Parker's FBI team. Nothing about her past gave him pause until the bombing two months ago in Houston. She'd been the lead officer overseeing the disposal of a bomb at a Houston medical clinic when the bomb exploded, injuring a toddler, Agent Jimenez, and another officer. "The fallout from Houston didn't in any way compromise her ability to do her job, physically or psychologically?"

"Absolutely not," Parker said. "She took a hit from some shattered glass, but she's been released by medical. Like I told you, Jack, she's the best. She lives for her work and, despite what the president says, doesn't make mistakes. If it were me or anyone I cared about strapped to one of those bombs, I'd want Evie working the scene."

Which is why he personally brought Evie on board. Jack always worked with the best. He took another long sip of bourbon, the ice clinking at the barely there tremble in his hand. On this one he needed the best.

After he finished the call with Parker, he dialed up the investigator he'd hired this morning, a former Navy SEAL who'd been running a private investigation firm in Los Angeles for more than thirty years.

"Any news?" Jack asked.

"We found a possible match at the third bomb scene, but nothing definitive at this point."

"Keep me posted." But Jack wasn't about to sit back and let others do the work, even good ones like Agent Jimenez and his PI. He took his computer from the patio table, set it on his lap, and called up the photos of the third crime scene. With the moon shining overhead, Jack began to search for the sun.

CHAPTER FIVE

Thursday, October 29
7:16 a.m.

Evie had been in her share of war rooms, but none with so many naked women on the walls. This morning someone on the Angel Bomber task force had made enlarged prints of each of the paintings in the *Beauty Through the Ages* exhibit and hung them on the walls of one of LAPD's case conference rooms. Images that inspired a three-month killing spree were now inspiring a team set on capturing that killer.

And she was a member of that team.

After a near-sleepless night at a cheap motel north of the Arts District, she finally got a call from Parker.

"The president wasn't happy about you taking the high school disrupt in Maine," Parker had said, his tone crisp and factual.

"Bullshit," Evie had argued. "He wasn't happy that I was on TV. I'm the face of a botched bomb disrupt that has the American public doubting *his* administration's ability to control both foreign and domestic terrorist activities. This is all about him covering his ass."

"And he will continue to do so until next year's election."

Something akin to a growl clawed up Evie's throat. "Officer Gilley took full responsibility for his actions in Houston, and Internal Affairs cleared me of any wrongdoing or negligence."

"The president finally read the IA report, and he agreed to lift your suspension."

Yes! She'd fisted her free hand and punched the air. *It was about time.*

"But you need to keep your nose squeaky clean on this one." A laugh had rumbled on the other end of the line. "Well, at least as clean as you can keep it." Parker's voice had softened. "Remember, Evie, your job is to preserve life, all life, including yours."

And with that Parker had assigned her to the multi-jurisdiction task force investigating the Angel Bombings. Less than fifteen seconds after hearing those beautiful words, she was on the horn with Vince Ricci and told him about the *Beauty Through the Ages* collection. Within minutes, Vince had mobilized his team and called a task force meeting.

She stood in front of a copy of the fourth painting, the portrait of the woman in the red dress and child with a halo of golden curls. She'd held enough of her nephews to know that cheek. Soft and warm, powdery and sweet. "You are not going to die." She ran her finger along the cheek. "Do you hear me? You will not die."

"Took you long enough," a deep voice said from behind her. Vince Ricci gripped her shoulder and gave her a one-armed squeeze. She'd met the LAPD bomb squad captain two years ago at a special FBI training session on weapons of mass destruction for large, urban police forces, and she'd been impressed not so much with the big man's brawn but his brains. He'd proven to be one of the session's more contemplative students with a knack for creative problem solving and well-thought-out tactical ops.

"I called Parker after the second bomb requesting your services," Ricci said. "Where the hell have you been?"

"In time-out."

Vince chuckled.

"It wasn't funny."

Vince's lips thinned. "I'm sorry about Houston, but I'm glad you're here. Everyone's anxious to hear about your pretty pictures."

"According to Jack Elliott, *beautiful* pictures." She turned from the beauties and rested her butt on the conference table. The portraits were key, and so was the holder of those keys. "Have you talked with Elliott yet?"

"No, but I have a unit securing the gallery."

"Good. I want to get a tap put on his phones and get someone digging into his past."

"You're not thinking Elliott's the bomber, are you?" Ricci ran a hand through the snowy-white waves of his hair. "He's a pretty big deal in this town, a real mover and shaker."

Honestly, she didn't know what to think about Jack Elliott. He was intense and focused, and he had the first solid tip in an investigation that had been stymied for three months, but he was also a control freak, doling out critical information on his own terms and oddly determined to insert himself into the investigation. "I don't think he's flipping the switch, but his interest in these bombings is far from casual."

When all of the task force members had gathered, Ricci clapped his hands, then rubbed his palms together. "Okay, Evie, show us what you have."

Bill Knox, the LAPD homicide detective who'd been working the third bombing that killed Lisa Franco, smirked. "Can't wait to see what she has under wraps," he said loud enough for even her to hear.

Evie had put up with this crap all of her life. Guys like Knox didn't see the soldier who exploited unexploded ordnance in Somalia or served on a team of international peacekeepers hunting down weapons of mass destruction in Syria. When they met her, guys like Knox couldn't get past the X chromosome. But eventually they came around. Every one.

Evie pulled a stack of reports from her bag and plopped them on the table in front of Knox. "Take one and pass them down." She went over each bombing, showing with painstaking detail the similarities with the first three paintings.

Quiet hung over the war room until Steve Cho, one of her colleagues from the FBI, let out a soft whistle. "This changes everything."

"Especially given that for the first time we have an idea what the next victims will look like and a hint as to where the bombing may occur," Evie added. In the fourth painting, the mother, who was holding a rosary and the child, sat on some kind of wooden bench, possibly in a church.

Ricci closed the report. "Where do you plan to go from here?"

"I'm finding out who has access to the Abby Foundation gallery and tracking down the names of anyone and everyone who knows about the collection. Right now it's all about people."

"Oh, goody," Knox said with a lift of his unibrow. "A touchy-feely type."

Captain Ricci opened his mouth, but Evie stopped him with a quick shake of her head. She'd been in the trenches before; she knew the battle tactics that worked best for the entire team. "Cho, can you remind everyone in the room what type of forensic evidence we have collected on the three bombings."

"No DNA," her FBI colleague said. "No errant fingerprints, not even a partial, and no witnesses to any of the bomb and victim drops."

"What about the IEDs?" Like the old saying, to know the artist, study the art. Likewise, to know the bomber, study the bomb.

Cho reached into his briefcase and dug out a series of diagrams. "Pipe bombs, and not of the Average Joe persuasion. Both ends welded with metal caps. A metal rod inserted into a pipe and bolted into place. Makes for a structurally strong housing that delays the explosion."

"He took significant pains to optimize explosive force," Evie said with a shake of her head. "He wanted pain, and he knows enough about the science of explosions to know how to cause it."

"We're thinking someone with a tech background, possibly ex-military," Ricci said. "The bombs are carefully and consistently constructed, indicating a meticulous, methodical maker."

Evie took out her notebook. "What about the initiation device?"

"Remote controlled. Thirty-second delay."

Evie shuddered. "Nice. He's a watcher. Got an official profile worked up yet?"

Ricci tapped the tips of his fingers. "With so little to go on, we're looking at a standard bomber profile."

She opened her notebook. "A white male with above average intelligence in his prime. Age thirty to fifty. College educated but underemployed. He's a loner with overwhelming feelings of inadequacy. He came from a broken home and has a strong desire for revenge, either against real or imagined perpetrators of wrongs against him."

"You're right on target," Ricci said.

"No one's come forward to take credit?" Evie asked. From a criminal perspective, these bombs had been wickedly successful. Each caused death and considerable destruction and garnered the bomber media attention. This guy had one of the largest cities in the United States trembling in its glittery shoes. Makes for a happy, happy bomber. Someone, somewhere, was gloating.

"We got rumblings from a quasi-militia group, but nothing came of it," Cho said. "A few crackpots and crackheads piped in, but no go."

"Have you figured out what statement he's trying to make?" Evie asked. Many serial bombers were terrorists, mercenaries, or organized crime operatives. Some were disillusioned idealists or psychopaths. All were on a mission. They had a statement to make, and they wanted the world to hear it.

"Nothing," Ricci said.

"Until now," Evie added as she spun her chair and faced the wall of beautiful, mostly naked, women. "We're looking at a guy re-creating art." She remembered the powerful pull of the images in Elliott's gallery. "But art also makes a statement."

"Could be an attack on Elliott Enterprises or corporate America in general, whiffs of Occupy Wall Street movements," Aaron Jarzab of the ATF said.

"Or perhaps it's an attack on Elliott himself," Ricci said.

"He has his fingers in a lot of pies, and my guess is not everyone at the kitchen table appreciates his brand of business."

"Could be someone with mother issues."

"Or a misogynist determined to publicly show his rage at women."

"Or it could be an ultra-conservative fanatic who considers nudes pornographic."

Ideas flew through the room like birds scattered by gunshot. Evie jotted down notes. There were so many ways this thing could go, and it could go at any time.

A woman with brown hair shaped like a helmet popped her head through the doorway. "Excuse me, Agent Jimenez, but a Mr. Jack Elliott is here to see you."

Her pen stilled. She was not surprised he was here but surprised it had taken him two hours to insert himself into the investigation.

Captain Ricci tucked the report under his arm and stood. "You all have your assignments. We'll meet first thing tomorrow morning, sooner if anything pops." To Evie he said, "Keep me posted on Elliott."

Captain Ricci had given her a temp office on the second floor of the downtown station, where she'd done her unique style of decorating. Along one wall she'd taped a photo of each of the seven victims. Jack Elliott stood before that wall, unblinking.

"Good morning, Mr. Elliott."

He gave her a crisp nod. Everything about the man was crisp. The crease in his trousers, the knot in his tie, the sharp angles of his hair. She brushed at the grime on the right sleeve of her jacket, compliments of her alley run-in with Brady. Last night before moving into her motel, she'd picked up a few T-shirts, an extra pair of jeans, underthings, and a box of laundry soap, but she'd been too busy putting together her report to do any laundry. Still was.

"What brings you here this morning, Mr. Elliott?"

Reaching into the pocket on the inside of his jacket, he took out a small piece of paper. "It's a reward for information leading to the arrest of the bomber."

She unfolded the paper, a business check with the EE logo. "*Dios mío!*" In investigations gone cold, a big chunk of change could heat up things. Promises of riches turned brother against brother, husband against wife, minions against mastermind. "A quarter of a million is a shitload of money."

"And here are some individuals you'll need to talk with." He handed her a thumb drive. "That includes security and access records to the Abby Foundation and every piece of paperwork I have on the *Beauty Through the Ages* collection."

Elliott was so generous, handing over gifts like Santa. She pressed her palms into the sides of her jeans. What the hell was up with this guy? She took a seat on the edge of her U-shaped desk. "Let me guess, you wanted to be a cop when you were a kid."

His brow wrinkled. "I wanted to be a horse jockey."

She sputtered out a laugh. "You're kidding." The guy was six-feet-plus with shoulders twice the width of hers. Shoulders used to carrying heavy loads, she couldn't help but think.

"I don't kid," he said with a straight face.

She shifted her legs, her boots swinging. She could do serious, too. "Did you know many serial killers insert themselves into an investigation?"

"I am not your bomber, Agent Jimenez." No blink. All cool and control.

"Then who are you?"

He turned back to the victim's photos, but not quick enough to hide the twitch in his jaw.

"I said, who are you, Jack? And why are you here?" She hopped up and waved the check in his face. "And why do you care so damn much?" She stood still, the small piece of paper hovering between them.

Seconds gave way to minutes, and he finally pointed to the photo of the first victim. "I may not be your bomber, but I am a killer. I'm her killer." He stabbed a finger at the next two photos. "And her killer and her killer." One by one he pointed to the other individuals who'd been killed because they'd been within the IEDs' deadly reaches. "I may not have abducted those three women, I may not have planted and detonated those three bombs, but I am responsible for those seven deaths and for the terror gripping my city."

Guilt etched his face, carving pain, sculpting sorrow, chipping away at a block of marble. That stirring in her gut wasn't wrong. In Jack Elliott's mind, he was guilty. Her own gut jackknifed. She knew what it was like to hold another's life in her hands and have it yanked away. Horror pummeled your gut, anger exploded in your chest, sadness swelled in your throat, choking off words. The kicker was, the guilt never went away. It became a part of you and everything you did.

With a sharp nod, Jack clipped toward the door. She dashed after him, settling her hand on the arm of his suit coat. Silky smooth and rock hard but unexpectedly warm. Jack Elliott was human and hurting. "The secret to dealing with guilt is keeping the SOB in a corral until it can serve you and the mission." She lifted the check and flash drive, holding them squarely in front of his face. "Thank you, Jack. These *will* make a difference."

He pulled in a deep breath, his chest pressing against his pin-striped vest, today a deep blue, almost black. "I hope so." He exhaled and left her office.

After the echo of his shiny dress shoes died away, she sat at her computer and popped in the thumb drive. Jack had given her a valuable hit list, names of every individual who had access to the *Beauty Through the Ages* collection. As she scrolled through the files she was thankful Jack Elliott was a control freak. The records listed every individual entering the secured gallery along with day, time, and duration of stay. Claire of the Kingdom of Beige clocked in monthly visits, probably to make sure things were "freshened up." Foundation director Adam Wainwright stopped by about once a week as did Brandon Brice, who was the foundation's current artist in residence.

She reached the final page. That was it. Only three distinct visitors.

She tapped her thumbs on the keyboard. Something wasn't right. Again, she read through the list. No one raised any red flags. No dates or pattern of entry seemed significant. She closed the file and scrolled through the other documents created by the uber-efficient Jack Elliott. And then it hit her. She went back to the *Beauty Through the Ages* access records, and there it was, clear as the brilliant sun shining today. With the exception of last night, Jack Elliott had not stopped by to see his multimillion-dollar art collection. Odd, but on a deeper level, sad. Jack Elliott collected beautiful paintings but didn't take the time to look at them.

CHAPTER SIX

Thursday, October 29
9:33 a.m.

Evie ducked under the splintered wood railing and side-stepped a pile of horse manure, her boots slapping the concrete that separated the barns at Hollywood Turf. A brisk breeze stirred up the scent of fresh hay, sweaty horses, and grease, the latter emanating from the man with slicked-back hair sitting on the bench in front of the last barn. She parked herself at the end of the bench.

"If Skip sent you, tell him I'll have his next payment a week from Tuesday," he said without looking up from the playbook in his hands. "And if you're looking for a tip, I recommend Waltzing Matilda here to show in the eighth." He took the highlighter from behind his ear and ran it across a line in the book. "She's forty-five to one 'cause she's really a miler, doesn't like the long halls, but she loves running in sunshine."

Evie placed a single dusty boot on the bench. "We need to talk."

His gaze snapped to her, not a single greasy hair moving out of place. "For a filly with great legs, anything." He ran the side of his highlighter along her booted calf.

She kicked away the pen. "You're slimier than I thought, Freddy Ortiz."

"My reputation precedes me." The tabloid photographer placed his fingertips on his chest and bowed. "You must be a fan. Want my autograph?"

"Your stench precedes you." She flashed her creds. "I want answers."

He curled the playbook into a column and aimed it at her. "So you're Agent Jimenez. Police scanners are all abuzz about you this morning. I was gonna hunt you down."

"Beat you to it." She snatched the playbook. "So talk. How did you end up at the library at the time of the bombing killing Lisa Franco? Someone tip you off?"

"I already did this dance with Captain Ricci, but because I like your hooves," he jutted his chin toward her red boot, "I'll take to the dance floor again. Nothing on my tip line. I was trolling the streets of downtown looking for lewd and lascivious and lucked out."

"Some luck." The side of her mouth curled in a snarl. "Having a woman's brain explode and land on your shoe."

"Yep, that was my money shot. Pretty artistic, if I do say so myself. But I'm no different than you, Lady Feeb. We're like souls, both earning a living off these sickos."

Her hand clenched, tightening around the playbook until it was the diameter of the barrel of her Glock. She aimed it at his chest. "But unlike you, I'm attempting to stop them."

He raised both hands to his chest. "Hey, it's not like I want a psycho bomber on the streets."

"But until he's stopped, you have no issue exploiting him for personal gain."

"A got no issue with making a little money." He held out his hand for the playbook, but she slipped it in her back pocket.

She slid her boot off the bench and ground her heel into the straw scattered across the floor. Criminals used media slugs to further their missions, but so did people on her side of the law, and for now, this slimy mass of humanity was important to her case. "Has the bomber contacted you since the bombing?"

"No."

Reading people wasn't her strong suit. She took a step toward him.

"I swear on the grave of my sweet *abuela*." He made a sign of the cross, then ran his fingers along his crumpled brow. "Why would he?"

"Most bombers have a burning desire to share a message. Your photos were picked up worldwide and shared for days. He got unprecedented attention, all thanks to you. He most likely sees you as an ally."

"Yep, that's me, a guy with friends in low places." The rolls of flesh on Freddy's upper body shuddered.

"Which is why I'm going to put a trace on your phone. It's possible this guy could reach out to you."

"Whoa, there. Not my tip line. If folks find out the Feebs are listening in, they won't do no more talking. I gotta protect my sources." He waggled his finger at her. "You can't touch my tip line."

"I can." She slipped the subpoena from her bag.

"You move fast." A smarmy grin slid across his lips. "I like fast women, but I also know my rights. The only stuff you guys are allowed to act on is anything related to Bomber

Boy. Anything more, and I'm calling foul. Learned that in J School."

She feigned shock. "You went to school?"

Freddy took a bright green pack of gum from his shirt pocket and popped a square into his mouth. Even from three feet away, the too sweet, too tangy odor made her gag. "I studied photojournalism back in the nineties," Freddy said. "I was gonna chronicle in pictures the big stories. The fall of communism. The clash of cultures in the Mideast."

"Lose your passport?" Evie asked.

Freddy grinned. "Found a gold mine. The dirt rags pay big, especially for a guy willing to dive into the mud and muck. Despite all the dirt, I'm still a news guy at heart. Everything I do is about the story." With a wink, he lifted the camera at his neck.

Click.

Evie blinked away the blinding flash. "What the hell are you doing?"

"Chronicling the story. Something tells me you, Lady Feeb, are going to be in a few chapters."

Evie reached for his camera, but Ortiz, surprisingly fast for a guy of his girth, spun away. "Hands off, cowgirl. This here's my lifeblood."

"That photo you just snapped has very much to do with my blood." She held out her hand. "I'm a federal agent involved in a murder investigation, and you will not sell any photos of me to anyone, anywhere." She jabbed her outstretched hand at Freddy's chest. "So hand over the camera, or the next race you see will be the one of me hauling you off to jail."

Ortiz puffed out his bottom lip in an exaggerated pout. "You're no fun. A woman who wears red boots should be fun."

He handed over the camera. She deleted the shot, then scanned the thumbnails. Tons of photos from the downtown branch of the L.A. Public Library. "You've been shooting at the bomb site."

"Yep. I stop by every day and snap a few. Two days ago I got some great shots of a Girl Scout troop hanging paper cranes from the trees. I'm planning a photo essay called *After the Boom*." He waggled his eyebrows. "Should rake in some serious money, maybe even get me a six-figure book deal."

The guy was a slug, but even slugs had a place in her world. "You haven't noticed anyone hanging around the crime scene, have you? A white male between the ages of thirty and fifty, loner-type, neat appearance, little uptight?"

He rubbed his hands together. "That the profile on the bomber?"

"Just answer the question, Freddy."

"No, no one like that comes to mind, but I'll keep my eyes open."

She tucked her business card in the playbook and handed it back to him. "Yeah, I get it. The bomber's your trifecta."

His slick grin slid away, along with the toasty color of his skin. Waltzing Matilda nickered and shuffled her hooves. The tabloid photographer said nothing, but he didn't need to. Evie smelled his fear. The bomber terrified him. Good. She could work with fear.

* * *

10:02 a.m.

"Nice day, huh?"

Carter Vandemere raised his face to the brilliant sun streaming through the glass. "Beautiful," he said. Today the light was unfiltered by clouds or a veil of the ubiquitous L.A. smog. He flexed his fingers, the knuckles letting out happy pops. Perfect for working.

His right nostril lifted as he reached for his hard-sided lunch box. Not this work. Work that mattered. Work that fed his soul. "I'm going to lunch."

"Isn't it a bit early for that?" his colleague asked.

"I'm hungry." For the light.

Outside, downtown L.A. buzzed and beeped and whirred and whistled. So many people coming and going. Businessmen in suits, the homeless wearing bits and pieces of the street, a tiny oriental woman with a large sunhat. A good place to get lost. He hurried down an alley to the fourth building on the right. Abandoned earlier in the year, the building's sunny rooftop was perfect for working.

Once on the roof, he opened his box and took out the tiny canvas, a work of art in itself. He'd taken a chopstick and broken it into four pieces. Then he'd smoothed the ends with fine-grit sandpaper and secured them in a tiny square. Then came canvas preparation. Scraping. Cleaning. Drying. Stretching. Tanning.

He poked through the tubes of oil paint in his box. So many colors, but always the same subject. A sun. His fingers slid over a tube of Cadmium Red Deep. He dabbed the tip of his tiny brush into the swirl of paint and added a burst of color to Maria's beautiful flesh.

CHAPTER SEVEN

Thursday, October 29
11:07 a.m.

Evie sank to her knees and ran her hands through the scarred earth outside the L.A. Public Library.

Her lungs filled with warm morning air still tinged with smoke and the odor of melted plastic, charred metal, and dust. The smells were always the same. Sounds, too. The pop of the ignition switch, roar of an explosion, screams of innocents. She sat on a bare patch of ground, her fingers digging into the crumbled earth, and felt the ground shake.

Bombs had no nationality, no politics, no religious preference. They were conduits for destruction, and the more times she dug her hands into the jagged scars they left behind, the more she hated the hands that made them.

The trees to her right shivered. Was it the breeze? A feral cat? A bomber revisiting ground zero? And then she smelled

him. Fine leather, opulence, and a hint of citrus. She took a
deeper breath.

"You really shouldn't sneak up on people who carry
guns," Evie said.

Jack stepped out of the leafy cover of trees. "I needed to
see you."

She swatted the dirt from her palms. "If you keep this up,
I'm going to think you have a thing for me."

"Not a thing, a who." His lips remained stick straight,
his gaze intense. "Brother Gabriel North. He's the leader of
a religious group with a sizable church in Topanga Canyon
and a mission outreach north of Bunker Hill." He pulled a
folded piece of paper from his pocket. "After I purchased
the Titian nude, he sent me an e-mail politely asking me
to rid the downtown area of the sinful work, and after his
signature, he included a quote from scripture: *If any man's
work shall be burned, he shall suffer loss: but he himself
shall be saved; yet so as by fire. 1 Corinthians 3:15-17.*
I ran across the e-mail when I was reviewing correspon-
dence associated with collection acquisitions. North and
his crew later held a public protest outside the foundation
gallery."

She hopped up from the ground and snatched the paper.
The date on the e-mail was one week prior to the first
bombing.

"My research team's been digging up information on
North," Jack said. Of course they have because Jack was digging out from a shitload of guilt. "I forwarded their reports
to you and contacted the Topanga Community police station
to find out if they've had any issues with North or at his compound. I'm waiting for a callback from the captain."

She pressed the heels of her boots into the earth to keep
from kicking Jack's butt back to his shiny corporate tower.

She appreciated his astute observations, contacts, and piles of money, but he wasn't trained to deal with explosives and the mutants who found great pleasure in using them for criminal activity. Few people were.

"Jack, I'm not the sensitive type, but I get it. Guilt is a big dog with sharp teeth, and it's got you by the ass. But the thing is, you made the deal. You brought me here and got me on board. Now it's time to let me do my job. A clock is ticking." She picked her way across the scarred earth.

Jack fell in step beside her. "What's your plan of action?"

This guy wouldn't let go, which is probably one of the reasons he raked in the millions. She puffed a lock of hair hanging across her forehead. "Contact North for a little heart-to-heart."

"He won't talk to you. He has a serious distrust of authority figures and the media, as both groups are keeping watch on him and his almost cult-like organization. Apparently he's quite charismatic with loyal followers from all walks, many quite fanatical and some handing over their life savings or moving onto the compound. According to my sources, he doesn't let many into his inner sanctum."

Most of these zealous, out-of-the-mainstream groups rarely did. "A subpoena will change all that."

"Subpoenas take time." He leveled a hard gaze at her. "Which you don't have."

Jack must be a brute in the boardroom, but he was right. "You have an alternative plan." She didn't phrase it as a question. She could see that every inch of him was ready to take off and take charge.

"I'll contact his executive assistant." Jack's confidence bordered on arrogance.

She had no problems with arrogant men. She worked damned well and often with men who thought they were one step removed from God. "Executive assistant. Like your Claire. That's your secret weapon?"

"Do not doubt the power of the Claires of this world. The guard at the gate, who has been trained to fend off outsiders, especially those seeking Brother North, will patch us through to his assistant without hesitation. When we get the assistant on the line, we'll tell her we're here with a significant donation, cash in hand, earmarked for North's pet mission project near Bunker Hill. Wanting to be the harbinger of such great news, the executive assistant will deliver the message and get us in the door. It's a matter of netting the little fish to use as bait for the big fish." Spoken like a man who knew a thing or two about rods and reels.

"I'll buy into your smooth moves," Evie said, not bothering to hide her skepticism, "but do you honestly think North is going to talk to you, the man behind the Abby Foundation and its offensive nudes?"

"No, which is why I won't be using my real name." He motioned to his car parked on the street.

The guy had an ego, but he also had a history of successful million-dollar deals. If this deal went down, they could shave hours off an investigation where seconds mattered. "Okay, Jack, let's see if the fish are biting."

* * *

1:19 p.m.

Evie's boots kicked up fine, silty dust as she and Jack followed their escort, a short man with arms like hams, along a footpath snaking through the twenty-acre True North Retreat and Renewal Center to Brother Gabriel North's private residence.

"Why the gun?" Evie asked their escort. She'd seen the bulge under his jacket the minute he met them at the front gate of the fenced compound.

"Lots of undesirable critters in the canyons," the escort said.

These grassy hills and scrub canyons an hour northwest of downtown L.A. were home to mountain lions, coyotes, and rattlesnakes, maybe even a few dangerous critters with two legs. This area, close enough to L.A. to house plenty of rich and famous, had its share of rundown shacks, hippie vans, and hand-written *Keep Out!* signs.

The spiritual center looked more like a summer camp that stopped having fun thirty years ago. The main building, a long block structure with a chipped tile roof, sat on a hill surrounded by scrappy bushes, a few bent sycamores, and an ancient white school bus. There was a fire pit circled by felled logs and a half dozen small outbuildings with sagging roofs.

They reached a small hacienda-style house with a red-tiled roof and a large courtyard. North's executive assistant met them at the door. "Right this way, Mr. Ellis."

Deal done. Evie tipped an imaginary hat to Jack. Jack managed a half smile.

Brother Gabriel North was a man in need of a shave and a haircut, or maybe he was trying to rock the Jesus look. Despite his ragged appearance, he wore an air of superiority. The pastor held out his hand and asked, "Seeking True North, Brother Ellis?"

Jack shook his hand. "Bearing gifts." He patted the breast pocket of his jacket where his checkbook extended. "And seeking the truth. I'm hoping you can help my friend here." He slipped his hand along Evie's back, the touch warm and firm. "This is Special Agent Evie Jimenez of the FBI's Special Criminal Investigative Unit."

The pastor, blinded by Jack's checkbook, blinked as if noticing her for the first time. He snapped his fingers at their escort. "Brother Jenkins, please show Brother Ellis and his friend out. A good day to you both. God bless."

Evie gave props to Jack for being a straight shooter. They didn't have time to waste on this one, plus she had a feeling a man like Brother North knew all about bullshit. "I'm FBI," she said. "Not ATF, and I'm not interested in the weapons you are stockpiling in the outbuilding on the northeast end of the property."

Brother North and Brother Jenkins shared a panicked glance. Jack shifted, inching his body in front of hers.

Evie none-too-gently nudged Jack aside with her shoulder. "You can talk to me now, Brother North," she continued. "Or I can come back later and bring one of my good friends who does happen to own one of those snazzy blue ATF jackets." She paused, taking time to read the Ten Commandments, which were emblazoned on the wall behind North's desk.

The pastor's shoulders stiffened, and he sucked in a sharp breath through flared nostrils.

Bull's-eye. Evie took out her phone.

With pinched lips, Brother North invited them to sit at a group of chairs before an unlit fireplace. "What is it you need, Agent Jimenez?"

"I need you to tell me why you threatened to blow up the *Beauty Through the Ages* art exhibit."

"That's not art but the devil's work, and we were within our First Amendment rights to stage that protest. It was a peaceable assembly."

"There was nothing peaceable about the note you sent to Jack Elliott threatening to set fire to his art collection."

A light fired in the preacher's eyes. "God's words are so

much more powerful than man's. The Lord wanted to be heard; I was merely His vessel."

"Yes, you certainly got our attention." Evie needed to keep this guy talking. North took issue with the content, had a mission downtown, and didn't shy away from explosives. "So why protest this particular collection?"

"It's pornography, degrading to women, poison to men, and detrimental to families."

Next to her Jack shifted, the fine fabric of his suit making whispery noises.

"I'd been preaching on the sanctity of the body at the same time one of the newspapers reported that Mr. Elliott had purchased the nude painting for more than one million dollars. All this while just blocks from the exhibit on Skid Row men and women and children were living on the streets and starving. I felt this was a real-world exercise in living out our faith and getting this important message out to others."

"But you didn't get much media attention, did you?" According to the reports from Jack's people, not a single reporter covered the protest.

"The devil's got hold of the media." A vein popped out on North's forehead. "Bunch of liberals who talk about truth but are well off the path."

"This lack of media coverage upset you." Because guys like North craved attention. They longed to have their messages heard.

"Agent Jimenez, you and I both know that the more witnesses the better," North went on. "However, our efforts were not in vain. We shared our message with hundreds of people walking by. Some stopped long enough to hear about True North, and others took our literature."

"So you'd label your protest a success?"

"Anytime a single follower turns to True North, we have success." He pressed his palms together in front of his chest, his fingertips pointing to the heavens. "Simply put, just like you, Agent Jimenez, I want to save lives."

"Yet you stockpile guns and explosives."

"Strictly to protect the flock. I have a clear set of rules to guide me, including that one." He pointed to the section of words behind his desk: *Thou shall not kill.*

Clearly this guy was giving off mixed messages. "What were you doing around lunchtime on Tuesday, October sixth?"

North ran a hand along his scraggly beard. "We have healing services for the aged on the first Mondays of the month, so I spent all day on Tuesday following up with prayer calls."

"Can anyone verify that?"

"My assistant can give you my phone records."

Yes, the almighty assistant and right hand of God. "Please have her send them to me." This guy may have an alibi, but he also had plenty of minions to do his will. She tossed her business card on the coffee table. "I'll be in touch."

When she reached the office door Jack still sat near the fireplace, his checkbook on his knee. He tore off a check and gave it to North, who flinched when he saw the name on the check but pocketed the money.

The guard escorted them past the gate, and once they reached Jack's car, she asked, "You actually gave a donation to a man who all but called you and your art collection an enemy of the family?"

"Makes good business sense, especially in this deal, because after that exchange I'm sure you're not done with North." He reached for the door handle but didn't open the door. "How'd you know about the munitions?"

"I didn't."

Jack laughed, the sound so unexpected and bold, it sent gooseflesh racing across her skin. "You were bluffing?"

"Don't look at me like that." She popped him on the upper arm, the flesh rock solid. "I'm sure you bluff all the time."

"Of course, but I'm dealing with money, not life and death."

She lifted her shoulders. "All the more reason to bluff."

Jack remained motionless, only his eyes moving as he studied her with slow precision. Thirty seconds. One minute. Again she marveled at his steely control. At last he stepped from the car door. A half smile curved his lips as he tipped an imaginary cap.

CHAPTER EIGHT

Thursday, October 29
7:29 p.m.

By the time they fought traffic back to downtown L.A., darkness had set in. Evie had spent most of the drive researching the victims who'd been strapped to the first three bombs. One was a student, another an exotic dancer, and the last a waitress. While she tried to find links between the victims, Jack had spent much of the drive sneaking peeks at her laptop.

"Don't you have work to do?" Evie had asked him.

"I signed off on the German deal today, and right now, I'm focusing my energies on these bombings."

Evie no longer bothered arguing with him. It was like arguing with a brick. Or herself, she realized with a smile.

Jack drove toward the library where her car was parked, but the police had blocked off the street. Hundreds of men, women, and children holding tiny flickering candles marched down the street in front of the L.A. Public Library where the third bombing had occurred, singing a song about hearts holding on until the end of their troubles.

She breathed in the song, let it seep through her body. That's why she was here, to end the troubles. When they reached a roadblock, Jack turned into an alley.

"You can drop me off here," Evie said. "I'll walk the rest of the way."

"You can't just take off in the dark in the middle of downtown Los Angeles."

"Jack, what part of *federal agent* do you not understand?" She unlocked the door. "Anyone who looks crossways at me should be worried."

"True." He pulled into a loading dock, which was empty at this time of night. "I'll walk you to your car."

She hopped out. "You really are a control freak."

"Also true." He spoke with an unabashed authority that grated against her spine.

"Do you ever lose an argument?" she asked with a snap.

"Only when I choose to," he said with a flash of white teeth.

She raised her hands but fought back the urge to strangle him. Jack Elliott was cut from the same cloth as her boss, Parker Lord. He was the self-proclaimed master of his universe, which right now intersected with hers, and she was grateful. Not only had he made the art connection, he offered a sizable reward and expedited her meet and greet with Brother North.

The night was cool, and she wrapped her denim jacket tighter about her as they wove through the concrete maze of the downtown financial district, a graveyard at this time of night. No business suits or messengers on bikes. No hot dog vendors offering a quick lunch. No—

Crack! Something hot whizzed past her right shoulder. A chunk of the squat office building behind her shivered and exploded. She ducked and lunged at Jack just as he threw himself at her, curving his body around hers.

They slammed into the pavement. Her cheek ground into dirt and rock. Slivers of concrete and wood rained down on them. Jack's chest pressed against her back, his heart booming as fast and hard as hers.

When the dust cleared, she pushed herself to her elbows, simultaneously pushing him off.

"What was that?" Jack asked.

"A bullet." She scrambled to her feet and hauled out her Glock.

Jack bolted to her side. "What are you doing?"

"Going after the guy holding the gun."

He grabbed her arm. "You're running after someone who shot at us?"

"Yes, Jack. That's what I do. Chase bad guys." She pried his fingers from her arm and took off down the alley, calling over her shoulder, "Call Ricci. Tell him what happened and get me some backup."

She sprinted down the alley and onto the street and swiveled her head. Key was finding someone moving fast. There. Big man. Brown bomber jacket.

"You're mine, buddy."

Evie sprinted down Olympic, her cowboy boots pounding. Bomber Jacket took off at a dead run. He hopped over a concrete bench and ducked into a small side street. She followed. The pavement grew uneven; the skyscrapers gave way to gray block buildings and deserted storefronts.

Footsteps clacked behind her. Her backup? The gunman's buddy? She shot a glance over her shoulder and cursed. "I told you to call Ricci."

Jack slipped his cell in his pocket. "Done."

"Dammit, Jack, I don't have time to look out for you."

"Then don't."

She bit her bottom lip to keep from unleashing on him. Nothing could hurt this guy because he was padded with too much ego. She hopped the concrete wall and took off around the corner. A man selling *mariscos* wheeled in front of her. She leaped, diving through swirls of shrimp-flavored steam.

The shooter wove in and out of thick bolts of fur and fabric. He jammed his shoulder into a box of bolts, which spilled across the sidewalk and into the street.

"Hey!" a shopkeeper yelled.

Evie hurdled over the bolts. She could make out blue jeans and a black baseball cap. And she smelled him. Man did she smell him. Ripe sweat.

She shimmied between cardboard boxes of ribbons and bows. The shooter crouched and disappeared into a sea of mannequins with fancy party dresses. She batted at lace and ruffles and darted through wide stiff skirts with hoops.

A good foot taller than her, Jack swiveled his head left and right. "Across the street."

A blur of brown disappeared across the street behind a row of poufy bridesmaid dresses on headless mannequins. She pushed her way through a group of teenage boys. The shooter shoved at the mannequins, which fell like a set of human dominoes. He slipped into a crack between buildings.

She clawed her way over the downed plastic bodies. The crack was a narrow alley filled with metal garbage cans. And bad news for him, a wall of chain link topped with barbed wire spanned the far end. This close she could smell not just ripe sweat, but raunchy, ripe sweat. And this sweat ball was hers.

He ran at the fence and grabbed at the barbed wire. "Aargh!"

She grabbed his foot and yanked. The shoe slid off, and she fell on her ass. Silver flashed above her. A bullet zinged past her and into a garbage can. She ducked behind another garbage can as he threw his body over the barbed wire.

On the street, sirens blared and feet shuffled. Two uniformed officers ran into the alley.

"That way," she told the officers between huffs of breath. "Bomber jacket, blue jeans, black baseball cap." She held up the sneaker. "One shoe." She kicked at the trash can. He was in her hands and slipped away.

* * *

8:01 p.m.

Evie slammed the shoe on the hood of Captain Ricci's unmarked car, the sound louder than the gunshot still ringing in Jack's ears.

"That's one big shoe," Captain Ricci said.

"He was one big guy," Evie said. "Six-foot-one, two hundred fifty pounds."

"You get a look at his face?"

"No. Nor did I make out hair color, skin tone, or any distinguishing characteristics. *Someone* knocked me to the ground, delaying pursuit." She turned to Jack. "What the hell were you thinking?"

"About someone putting a bullet in your head." Jack felt every degree of Evie's heated glare. Pulling her body to the ground had come from a place of pure instinct.

"I'm the one with the gun and shiny badge and more than a decade of training."

"And you were the one who almost took a bullet." Jack aimed a finger at her right temple to underscore his point. "If you were a half foot taller, you would have a bullet in your brain."

"You . . . this . . ." She sounded like a sputtering match.

Ricci held up a hand. "You see anything, Jack?"

Unlike Evie, he'd been facing the entrance of the alley and got a good look at the shooter. "Caucasian. Wide face. No facial hair. Close set eyes. Wide nose."

"If we pulled some guys into a lineup, think you'd be able to ID him?"

"Absolutely."

Evie's hand fisted at her sides. "If you hadn't gotten involved, there would be no need for a lineup."

"If I hadn't gotten involved, you may be dead." His words were as hot and sharp as hers.

Evie searched the sky, as if looking for a bolt of lightning to strike him.

Ricci squatted and peered at the hole blown in the garbage can. "You've taken a few shots before, Evie. Any sense if this was a random shooting, mugging gone awry, a gangbanger?"

"More likely D, none of the above. That guy could have been our bomber." Evie pushed back a tangled wave of curls. "I've been doing a good deal of poking around today. Maybe I poked too hard and riled a big bear."

Jack agreed. "The shooter wasn't wearing gang colors, and he didn't look like he spent much time on the streets. Clean-cut and clean clothes."

"So time for a little bear hunt." Evie dipped her head to the chain-link fence, then to the uniformed officer. "Have crime scene techs check up there for blood and skin scrapings between the third and fifth poles. Then get a rush put on the slugs from the garbage can and the alley near the road block. I want ballistics ASAP."

The officer nodded.

She pointed to the other uniformed officer. "Get on the other side of this fence and check for a blood trail. He's shoeless and probably cut the hell out of the bottom of his foot on those rocks."

She left the alley but spun on her boot heel. "And Ricci, get some guys door to door. If he did hurt his foot, he might have been forced to hide nearby."

"Anything else, Agent Jimenez?" Ricci asked.

"Probably. It'll come to me at one or two in the morning."

"At which time you'll call me," Ricci said with a tired smile.

"Of course."

As she made her way over to a squad car that just drove up, Jack asked Ricci, "Is she always like that?"

"Like what?" Ricci said.

"Like a performance engine firing on all cylinders."

Evie yanked open the door and dove in, her phone already to her ear.

"Yeah," Ricci said. "I don't think she knows any other speed."

Fast and furious and fiery. That was Evie. And Jack wasn't sure if he found her infuriating or fascinating.

CHAPTER NINE

Friday, October 30
6:58 a.m.

Cinnamon? Evie pulled her head out of the five-gallon bucket. She swatted at the air, pushing away the odor of charred metal and melted plastic, and sniffed again. Definitely cinnamon.

Without turning, she waggled her fingers at the door behind her. "Morning, Hayden."

Footsteps from polished, expensive Italian shoes sounded behind her. "Morning, Evie," Hayden Reed said. Hayden was the SCIU's head guy, their criminal profiler, and he had a thing for cinnamon candy.

She dug into the bucket and pulled out the remains of a metal rod. She'd arrived at LAPD at the crack of dawn and planned to spend most of the morning going through debris. She was hoping to get a lead on where the bomber's materials came from. "You can report back to Parker that the shooter was a crappy shot. Tell him I didn't break a finger-nail."

"What makes you think I'm here to check up on you?" Hayden asked.

"Aren't you?" Sometimes she got tired of being the little sister. She placed the mangled rod on the tarp and dug out a melted pipe. Her teammates and Parker respected her, but there were times when they pulled the big brother cards. Like now. Someone had taken a few pops at her last night, and Parker had sent Hayden to make sure she was all right.

"That's the excuse I gave Smokey Joe," Hayden said.

Evie's head snapped up. "Smokey's here?" She hadn't seen the old man since this summer when he'd helped the team track down a serial killer known as the Broadcaster Butcher.

"He stopped at the vending machine to get a coffee."

Evie wiped her hands on her jeans. The right side of her teammate's hair was unusually ruffled, and he looked like he could use a coffee. "What's up?"

Before he could answer, a door slammed somewhere down the hall. "Dammit to hell! I may be blind, but my feet still work."

Hayden closed his eyes and sank into the chair behind her computer.

A man with sprigs of gray hair, a white cane, and a cagey smile stepped into the doorway.

"Smokey!" Evie hopped up from the floor and wrapped her arms about the old man. He was definitely thinner than the last time she saw him. Shorter, too, as if his bent old body was curving into itself. She tightened her hug.

Smokey Joe landed a kiss on her cheek. "How's the most brilliant bomb tech in the world?"

"Sniffing out bombs and the assholes who plant them."

He patted her cheek. "That's my girl."

She stepped back, eyeing the bandage on his forehead. "What's up with the head wound? You didn't go after another serial killer again, did you?"

"Little accident."

Hayden crossed his arms over his chest. "Concussion, lacerated forehead, three broken ribs, and a collapsed lung."

"A *little* accident?" Evie asked.

Smokey Joe shuffled his feet. "Fender bender."

"He drove his car off a cliff," Hayden said.

"Correct me if I'm wrong, Smokey, but aren't you legally blind?"

Smokey grumbled something that sounded like, *Last time I checked.*

"Chair's three steps forward, two steps to the right," Hayden said.

Smokey Joe didn't move. "Tell G-man here I don't need no babysitter."

Evie sat back down on the floor next to her bucket of bomb debris. "Hayden, Smokey doesn't need a babysitter."

"And tell him I'm not stupid, that my brain still works."

"Clearly functioning brain, Hayden."

"And tell him to make Katy-lady back off." Smokey was so mad Evie could see the steam coming out his ears. Strange, as the battle-hardened old soldier had a soft spot for Kate Johnson, Hayden's fiancée, who was the Broadcaster Butcher's ultimate target.

Hayden's eyes plunked closed, and he rested his head against the back of the chair. She could imagine how tired he was of being caught between two personalities as strong as Kate and Smokey Joe. Poor guy.

"Mr. Bernard." A uniformed officer popped her head

through the doorway of Evie's office. "The coffee machine's been fixed. Do you want me to get you a regular or decaf?"

"No, thanks." Smokey spun and, leading with the cane, tapped his way out of the office. "I can git it myself."

Evie leaned against the wall and crossed her ankles. "Sounds like you have some bombs going off in your corner of the world."

Hayden opened his eyes and shook his head at the ceiling. "In the past five months Smokey's run off three aides, and Kate's ready to lock him up in a home for cantankerous old men. Last week she told him she would do just that if he fired another aide, which was about the time he hopped in his car and drove off the side of the mountain."

"Are you serious? He was driving a car?"

"Down the road to the mailbox. Apparently he's done it before with great success. He listens to the sound of the tires on the gravel, cattle guard, and rough grade, but during his last attempt he had a head cold and wasn't hearing too well."

Evie's gut tightened. She knew the Colorado mountains where Smokey Joe lived, and he was lucky to be alive. "What's Kate going to do?"

"Not sure yet. Smokey can't find an aide he likes, and he refuses to move in with us. Right now she's trying to track down his closest living relative, some cousin in Florida, because it looks like for his own safety, he may need to go into an assisted living facility."

Evie winced. "Tell Kate I have a bomb suit if she needs it. Size x-small."

Hayden gave her a wry smile. "To give both warring parties a break, I invited Smokey Joe to join me for a few days. He left his mountain only when I told him about the bomber and you getting shot at last night. He agreed that we needed to check on you, make sure you're okay."

"You really are one of the most brilliant human beings I know."

Hayden gave his cuffs a tug and motioned to the bits and pieces that had once been a bomb. "So what are your bombs telling you?"

She picked up a half-inch-wide piece of rebar twisted into a question mark. "Clearly constructed by the same individual. He's unsettled but not completely snapped. Things are too meticulous and well-planned. He's not an amateur or experimenter. High level of skill and complexity." She handed the rebar to Hayden, like one of those talking sticks her nephews used in Cub Scouts. "What do you see?"

Hayden weighed the chunk of metal on his palm, then swiveled the chair so he faced her growing office art collection, which now included photocopies of the *Beauty Through the Ages* exhibit, diagrams of the bombs, and a giant map of downtown Los Angeles, the bomb sites and last-known whereabouts of the abducted victims marked with red and yellow dots. "All three bombings occurred within a ten-mile radius, and all featured victims from the same area," Hayden said. "The bomber works close to home. He doesn't have the confidence, sophistication, or means to go too far. I'm aging him down. He's between twenty and thirty-five years old."

Then he turned his chair to the copies of the *Beauty Through the Ages* portraits. Still holding the twisted rebar, he walked to the far corner of her office, never taking his gaze from the beautiful images. He moved to another corner and then to the doorway. As a profiler, Hayden looked at the evidence, crime scenes, and victims from hundreds of different angles. "This guy's also not making a statement," he finally said.

"Come on, Hayden. You know these guys. Bombers are always making a statement, even if it's, 'I'm bored' or 'I have mother issues.'"

Hayden shook his head. "He's not a typical bomber. These bombings are not about the message but the medium. We're not looking for a bomber making a statement but an artist making art."

* * *

9:37 a.m.

The server at the swank coffee cart on the bottom floor of the Elliott Tower handed Evie the small box and two dollars and forty-one cents in change. "Would you like a cup of coffee to go with that?" he asked.

"It's not for me but a little gift for a, uh, friend," Evie said.

"In that case"—the server took the pen from his pocket and drew a bow with twisting ribbons on the top—"here's a little gift wrap."

She plopped a two-dollar tip in the jar and hurried to the elevator with the frosted *EE*s.

"Excuse me, ma'am, but you'll need to check in." The security guard, the same skinny young man she'd met two days ago, waved her over.

She showed him her visitor's badge. "I'm here to speak with Mr. Elliott."

"Do you have an appointment?"

She didn't blink. "Yes."

The guard scanned a clipboard. "I'm sorry, but I don't see your name on the list." She snatched the pen from his desk and wrote her name on the paper. The security guard seemed stunned at first, and then he smiled. He tipped his chin at the box under her arm. "What's in the box?"

"Cake." Technically it was a peace offering, similar to the check Jack had handed to Brother North, something to keep the lines of communication open. She'd been livid with Jack last night after he'd tried to *protect* her, but her reality was this guy was integral to this case, and she needed him on her side, especially right now. After learning from Hayden that the bomber was an artist, Evie went straight to the Abby Foundation to talk to Brandon Brice, the artist in residence who visited the collection weekly, but Adam Wainwright, the foundation director, wouldn't let her through the door. She flipped open the box, and the guard nodded.

She headed for the elevator.

"Agent Jimenez," the guard called out. "You'll find Mr. Elliott in the north stairwell. He'll probably be there awhile."

Evie heaved open the heavy utility door to the stairs, wondering what kind of businessman hung out in a stairwell. Footsteps pounded above her along with a deep, rich voice echoing through the vertical corridor. "I want a list of every employee with every company that was involved with the transport of any of the *Beauty Through the Ages* paintings." She craned her neck. Two flights above her Jack powered up the stairs in black jogging shorts, T-shirt, and a pair of white running shoes. "Send a copy to me along with Agent Jimenez and Captain Ricci."

At least Elliott was being consistent. The guy never stopped working. And for better or worse, he was working on her case. She slung her bag over her denim jacket and pounded up the stairs.

When she caught up to Jack on the fourth floor, he was still talking. "Clear my schedule for the rest of the week.

Tell Brady to call Matsumoto's bluff and walk. When Mats comes back begging for the six-point-five-percent interest rate, have Brady tell him it's now six point seven-five. As for the Seattle project, send it to the city's zoning commission. That should put everything on hold for a while."

She waggled her fingers at him and matched her pace to his. He frowned but didn't slow. Even without the suit, he looked like a million bucks, with interest. A monogrammed towel hung around his neck, and not a single bead of sweat marred his brow.

"Do you always do business in stairwells?" Evie asked when he finished the call.

"It's an efficient use of my time." And Jack liked efficiency.

So did she. "I need to talk with your artist in residence, but your pit bull at the gate is baring his teeth. Your Abby Foundation director wouldn't let me in the door."

"Adam's very protective of the program and the artists. I'll give him a call. You can expect his full cooperation."

Jack talked. People jumped. She stood there shaking her head. Incredible.

"Is there anything else, Agent Jimenez?"

She was about to take off when she remembered the box. "Here."

"What is it?" Jack asked.

"German chocolate cake." She whipped open the lid, and a wonderful puff of chocolate, toasted nuts, and coconut filled the stairwell.

He frowned. "You brought me a cake?"

"To celebrate the biggest deal of your career, the one with Germany."

His fingers dug into the ends of the towel at his neck. His frown deepened.

"It's a cake, Jack, a freakin' cake."

His eyebrows narrowed and lips scrunched, like her second-oldest nephew when he was trying to work long-division problems. "A clock is ticking, a serial bomber is on the loose, and you brought me cake?"

"That's the ideal time to eat cake. We need beauty when there's so much ugly, right?"

For the longest time Jack stared at her with his long-division face. At last he took the box. "Thank you, Evie." His voice tapered off, as if searching for words but not sure where to find them. He cleared his throat. "This is thoughtful."

"No, Jack, this is *necessary*. According to my nephews, no celebration is complete without cake." And something told her Jack Elliott was the type of man who needed more cake.

* * *

10:34 a.m.

"Let's make this quick." Adam Wainwright, the executive director of the Abby Foundation, slipped from behind his desk and headed for the stairs. He smelled like one of those cucumber and melon candles her sister-in-law liked to burn after her four boys went to bed. He wore an argyle cardigan, slim hipster jeans, and the scowl of a junkyard dog.

As they walked up the stairs, Evie noticed a smudge of red on the fleshy side of Wainwright's right hand. Her team-mate Hayden was sure they were looking for an artist. "Do you paint, Mr. Wainwright?"

"Excuse me?"

She pointed to his hand. "Are you a painter?"

He twisted his wrist and studied the red mark, his mouth arcing in a grimace. "This is from a few hours of accounting work this morning, which is clearly not my strong suit."

"You're an artist?"

"Was." They reached the third floor. He was about to reach for the door handle, when she wedged herself between him and the door.

"What happened?" Evie asked.

"I thought you wanted to speak to our current artist in residence."

"Right now I want to speak to you."

Wainwright tapped his shiny brown shoe.

She tapped her pointy red boot.

He took a cloth handkerchief from his pocket and wiped the red from his hand. "The muse died."

"But not your love of art."

"No. That kind of thing is in your blood." He shoved the cloth back in his pocket.

Evie studied the executive director, a smallish man with a soft voice. Not the ex-military type they were looking for, but Wainwright had a sharp edge and fit the age of Hayden's new profile. "Are you seeing someone?"

"I beg your pardon."

"Dating? Are you dating anyone right now?"

"You're hardly my type, Agent Jimenez."

The quiet, mousy administrator wasn't her type. She liked her men strong and confident and served up with a chaser of no commitment. Like Jack. She was drawn to power. Jack Elliott in a single word.

Adam smoothed the cuffs of his sweater. "My partner and I broke up earlier in the year. Still hurts. I haven't jumped back in."

A man who loved hard and fell hard. And hard falls usually left big bruises called resentment. "Where'd you go to college?"

"Stanford."

"Impressive. You must be a pretty smart guy."

"I like to think so."

"Do you own a gun?"

"Heavens no. I abhor violence." But he clearly loved art.

"Where were you around lunchtime on Tuesday, October sixth?"

"Is there a reason for this line of questioning?"

"Should there be?"

He took out his phone and jabbed at his calendar, and she got the distinct impression he'd love to be jabbing her ass out the door. "I was in a foundation board meeting. All day." Snapping his phone shut, he nudged away her hand and opened the door.

In one of the third-floor studios, she found a man standing before a block of black marble, his hands sliding across the stone in a lover's caress. A golden-haired dog sat in a dog bed in a circle of sunshine before the wall of windows.

She knocked on the door. The dog turned to her, but the man did not. She cleared her throat. "Excuse me, Mr. Brice. I'm Evie Jimenez with the FBI." Brice was the Abby Foundation's current artist in residence, and he visited the top-floor gallery weekly, clearly a man familiar with the *Beauty Through the Ages* exhibit.

His fingers traced a coppery-orange vein streaking the stone.

"Mr. Brice." She settled a hand on his arm, and he jumped, as if she'd taken a dagger to his flesh. She held up her hands. "I'm with the FBI, sir, and I need to talk to you."

"Now is not a good time." Once again, Brice closed his

eyes and ran his hands along the stone. He swayed, as if music were coming from the stone.

"Mr. Brice—"

His eyes flew open. "Didn't you hear me? Not! Now!"

Wainwright let out a chuffing sound. "Mr. Elliott says you'll need to talk with her."

The artist's hands dropped to his sides. "It appears I have no choice." Because Jack, the man who controlled the foundation, controlled this man's career.

Once again Wainwright tapped his shoe. He was another one of Jack's loyal and dedicated guard dogs.

"Can you excuse us, Mr. Wainwright?" Evie asked.

The foundation director tapped a dozen more times before he finally left. Evie reached out and scratched the dog's head. "She's beautiful. What's her name?"

"What do you want, Agent Jimenez?" Brandon Brice asked.

She was trying to take a few lessons from Jack. He was the kind of guy who knew how to work with people. Not her. Her teammate Hatch Hatcher, a crisis negotiator and master interviewer, accused her of skidding into these interviews at warp speed with limbs flailing. True. Words were hard. She had an easier time working with bombs. "According to security records, you visit the *Beauty Through the Ages* collection at least once a week. Why?"

"I appreciate good art."

"Good art is important in your world?"

"Good art is important in any civilized world. Art separates man from beast. It connects souls. It creates a feeling in both the artist and the viewer. And good art endures. That's really what makes that particular collection so amazing. Even after centuries, those paintings still live and breathe and speak."

This was a man passionate about his art, but was the passion twisted enough to sanction murder in his mind? "Where did you go to school?" Evie asked.

"MIT."

"You studied *art* at MIT?"

"Engineering. My parents thought I should have a practical degree in case I couldn't make a go of it with my art."

Bomb enthusiasts by nature have more than a layman's knowledge of mechanics and chemistry and basic engineering. "Are you making a go of your art?"

"This is my second commission this year."

"Are you married, Mr. Brice?"

"To my art."

A loner with limited success. "Do you own a gun?"

He laughed, a snort so loud and hard it blew a puff of marble dust across the room. "You're kidding, right?"

"*I* don't kid."

A rumble rocked his chest, and his shoulders heaved. Peals of laughter filled the room, and tears rolled down his face. "And this, ladies and gentlemen, is our U.S. tax dollars at work."

"Mr. Brice, do you own a gun?" Evie kept her tone firm and even.

"No, Agent Jimenez, I do not. Nor have I ever shot a gun." He wiped the tears streaked down his face. "You really don't know?"

"Know what?"

Another laugh gripped his body before he managed to get out, "I'm blind."

Her eyebrows shot up. She would never have guessed, but that didn't exclude him from the bombings. Look at what Smokey Joe managed despite his blindness. The old man ran an online jewelry business with Kate and had—at least for a while—successfully driven a car. Evie would never underestimate a person with a physical handicap.

"Where were you around lunchtime on Tuesday, October sixth?"

"Where I'm at every afternoon. Here in my studio. All my comings and goings duly noted with this." He saluted her with his access card and turned back to the chunk of marble.

CHAPTER TEN

Friday, October 30
1:37 p.m.

Jack Elliott was blind. Or stupid. Or possibly both.

It was a good thing for Jack that Carter Vandemere was neither.

The elevator doors parted and Carter entered the executive offices of Elliott Enterprises, a plain brown box under his right arm. He double-checked the time. Twenty-three minutes until Claire would return. She really was like a dog to Jack Elliott, loyal and obedient.

Carter could count on her, too. Claire liked order, probably because before landing with Elliott, she spent ten years with an alcoholic husband who made her life a chaotic living hell. Carter had learned that six months ago when he'd noticed the scars on her arm and showed her his. The scar along his jaw where a surgeon had had to rebuild the bone. The faint white line above the cartilage on his nose that hadn't healed straight. The puckered scar at his temple from the final blow of his father's fist. In hushed tones, he'd told Claire about his own hellish war. Battle wounds made for solid comrades.

So every day from one thirty to two, Jack's order-loving executive assistant would go downstairs to the coffee cart, pick up a caramel macchiato—passion fruit iced tea if it was summer—then take her brown-bag lunch up to the garden atop the Elliott Tower.

Plain brown bags, like plain brown boxes, were just that. Plain. And brown. But there was something about an unadorned box that drew one's eye, something that screamed, *Open me and look inside.*

Carter shifted the plain brown box to his left arm and took a pair of gloves out of his pocket. He slipped them on and swiped the key card in the magnetic reader. The red light flashed green, and he pushed open the door of Jack Elliott's office.

People who knew art realized the art experience wasn't just about the image on the canvas. Setting and framing were equally important. The wrong frame could ruin a brilliant painting. The wrong backdrop could take away from a magnificent sculpture.

He considered Jack's desktop, a large, cold piece of glass, but the proportion was all wrong. The credenza in front of the window? Too much light. Of course there was the display shelf in the corner that held some exquisite pieces, a nice piece of Murano glass and a beautiful celadon jade Chinese vase, but Jack didn't look at his beauties. He simply collected them. That is, when he was not destroying people's lives.

Carter opened the top drawer of Jack's desk where he kept his fancy pens in velvet-lined cases. Indirect lighting.

Nice backdrop of dark-grained wood. The perfect display place for his latest creation.

Carter placed the plain brown paper box in the desk drawer and set the switch.

Beautiful.

He checked his watch. Claire would be back in thirteen minutes.

* * *

5:06 p.m.

"What are you looking for?" Jack motioned to the mangled and charred material spread out across a tarp on the floor of Evie's office. It looked like the wreckage of a small plane, and given the smudges of black on her cheek and jacket, she'd been digging through the wreckage for some time.

"Don't you have business to do?" Evie asked from the floor of her office.

"It's Friday after five." Jack had spent most of the day here at LAPD going through mug shots and trying to finger the shooter from last night. He'd found no one, which is when he'd taken to the streets, walking for miles, poking his head in alleys, talking to street people. Double nothing. He was hoping Evie had something on her end.

"Like *after hours* means anything to a guy like you," Evie said.

"I'm in good company." Jack sat in the chair behind her desk. Parker was right. Evie lived for and loved her work. Sitting amidst the bomb wreckage, she radiated light and energy and showed no signs of slowing down for the night. He rolled the chair toward her. "What are we looking for?"

She tossed a charred piece of white fabric in a bucket

and whisked soot from her hands. "Each bomber utilizes supplies and a method of construction that are uniquely his. He sets up and detonates the bomb in a way unique to him. He selects specific locations and targets important to him. It all adds up to something greater than trace evidence, a signature."

He thumbed through a stack of sketches on her desk, which consisted of pencil drawings of each of the bomb sites, with before and after images. "You drew these?" Jack asked.

"Sorry they're not in color." She gave him a wry smile. "One of my nephews borrowed my box of crayons."

"They're not half bad."

She snorted out a laugh. "If you weren't you, I'd accuse you of hitting one too many happy-hour specials this evening."

He tilted one of the drawings, changing the angle of lighting. "I'm serious. This has no artistic value—"

She clutched her chest. "Ouch."

"—but value to collectors of true crime or even Los Angeles memorabilia."

"How do you know all this?"

"I'm a collector."

"You collect more than priceless pieces of art?"

"I have a few collections."

"Like?"

"Stuff."

Evie cocked her head. "If I were the suspicious type, which I am, I'd be checking into your past. You can save us both a lot of time and trouble and tell me what I'd find."

Another thing about Evie was she didn't have a filter. She spoke her mind, wore her heart on her sleeve, and ate cake. He'd never met anyone like her inside or outside the boardroom. "Not much. I'm just a guy who works hard to make a buck."

"A buck?"

"A few bucks." He held up the sketch so the image faced her. "Enough that I would like to purchase this. I'm starting a new collection of crime memorabilia, and this will be my first acquisition."

"What if I don't want to sell?"

"Everyone has a price."

She leaned back onto her palms. "Not everyone."

"Four years' college tuition for your oldest nephew. Any university in the country, including those with ivy." He pulled out a pen. "But you must sign it."

"Are you..." She gave her head a shake, a curl of hair slipping from the banded bunch on top of her head. "You don't kid." She took the pen and signed her name with a flourish, tossed the pen in the air, then held it out to him with a saucy tilt of her head. So much passion in the simple act of signing her name. Was it possible to be too passionate?

He reached for the pen, but she didn't let go.

"You're not holding out for two nephews, are you?" he asked.

Her lips flattened, then turned down at the corners.

"What is it?" Jack asked.

"A signature." Evie hopped up and angled her thumb, booting him from her chair. She sat before her computer and called up a folder with hundreds of photo files. "Every bomber leaves a signature, as do artists, and my team's criminal profiler said this guy is an artist first, bomber second. So if the bombings are indeed re-creations of the original paintings, it's possible the bomber signed his work in the same place as the original masters."

Jack planted himself at her side. "Titian signed the original in the lower right-hand corner."

"What color?" Evie asked.

"Red."

She clicked through the thumbnails and called up a wide angle shot.

Jack pointed to the concrete path that wound through the library grounds. "It would be in this area. Zoom in."

"Must you always do that?"

"Do what?"

"Order people around."

"Okay, *please* zoom in."

Some of the path had been blown away. "Look, there," she said. "See the red?"

"Could be blood."

"Could be a signature." She grabbed her bag. "I need to get to the bomb site."

He slipped his hand in his pocket, his keys jangling. "Good thing one of us has a collection of fast cars."

This time Evie didn't argue.

* * *

6:03 p.m.

"Let's make a frame." Evie handed the end of the crime scene tape to Jack, her hand rocking with anticipation. "Take this and go stand near the library."

She motioned to three boys riding their bikes. "Hey, you wanna play FBI agent?" They slowed, and she took out her wallet and flashed her shield.

They stopped, and a boy in a surfer hoodie picked at the grip on his handlebar. "Is this about the Angel Bomber?" Even in the dark, she could see the tremble of his lips.

"Yes."

Bits of foam from the grip floated to the ground like bits

of ash. "You think he's, uh, gonna come back here and blow up someone else?"

Her gut twisted. Kids out on bikes worrying about bad guys was wrong. It was all so wrong. But she could ease the boy's mind on this account. "You and your friends are safe." However, a woman in a red dress and blond-haired child were not. At least not yet.

The kid kicked the toe of his sneaker at his bike tire. "I hope you catch him."

Evie put her hands on the handlebars. "I will."

The boys hopped off their bikes and with Jack marked off a giant square frame with crime scene tape. She looked from the photo of the Titian painting to the crime scene. "Hoodie, take two giant steps back," she called out. "Perfect. Gray shirt, five steps to the left. One more. Good. And Jack?" Evie paused. He looked so serious and intense. The boys, too. "Take two steps back, one step right. There. Now do the hokey pokey and turn yourself around."

The boys broke out in laughter. Even Jack cracked a smile. She thanked the boys and sent them off. Jack jogged back to where she stood at the "base" of the painting. "If we use the actual portrait as a guide, the signature should be right there." She pointed to the section of earth below the tree, which had at one time been a concrete walkway, but was now a gouge in the earth.

"Damn," Jack said under his breath. "They already cleared away the rubble."

Evie rolled up the sleeves of her jacket. "Cleared, but didn't haul off." She climbed onto the lip of a construction waste container.

"What are you doing?" Jack asked.

She hooked a leg over and jumped in. "Looking for puzzle pieces."

Jack grabbed the ledge of the container.

Evie hauled a flashlight from her bag. "What are *you* doing?"

"Helping." He took out his phone and turned on some kind of flashlight app.

She tilted her head. She understood that he felt guilty, but he was dogged, as if this case was personal. Balancing on the debris, she cupped her hands over his. "Jack, I can do this."

"I am in no way doubting your ability." He swung a leg over the container.

"You're going to ruin your fancy suit."

He hopped inside. "I have others."

After fifteen minutes of toeing through dead branches, mud clods, and construction debris, Jack lifted a hunk of concrete. "Found one."

She studied the streak of red, which looked like a small letter *t*. "Where?"

"This pile."

They worked side by side and after two hours found three more pieces with what appeared to be red letters. An uppercase *C* and lowercase *r* and *e*.

Jack tossed the last chunk of concrete back into the pile with more force than necessary. "We need more than four letters."

She wiped her hands on her jeans and smiled. "We have them." She sat on a tree stump in the middle of the waste container and hauled out her phone.

* * *

8:38 p.m.

Fake fog rolled along the weathered concrete of L.A.'s Old Bank District. Evie squinted past men in fedoras carrying fake Thompson submachine guns. "There he is," she told Jack. "Guy across the street standing at the mouth of the alley."

Jack double-parked his car, this one a svelte red Porsche Spider, in front of the barricade blocking off Main Street, and they wove their way through the crowd gathered in front of century-old buildings to watch late-night filming of some big-budget gangster film. According to Freddy Ortiz, the lead in the film was an aging Hollywood A-lister who'd been happily married for forty years but was now boinking his nineteen-year-old co-star. Freddy was hanging out in the wings hoping to get a shot or two of the alleged boinkers.

"Friday is one of my busiest nights," Freddy said as he downed half a Corona. "You're messing with my bread and butter."

"After we're done," Evie said, "I'll bake you a cake."

Freddy laughed. "I like you, Lady Feeb. You got spark."

"Good, consider me lighting a fire under your ass. I have a job for you."

He downed the rest of his beer and tossed the bottle in a battered metal trash can covered with swirls of paint, more art than graffiti. "Lead and I shall follow."

"Holy shit," Evie said when Freddy stepped out of the shadowy alley. "What happened to your lip?"

Freddy slid a finger along a swollen hunk of flesh. "Skip Folsum's fist."

"I take it Waltzing Matilda didn't do too well at the races?"

He let out a grunt. "Nor did Sizzling Sam or Rockabilly Sue."

"Your luck's about to change. Tonight you're going to be a winner."

Freddy leaned closer, his sickly sweet breath fanning her neck. "Got some insider info?"

"I *need* some insider info," Evie said. "I have a lead and need to see all your shots of the crime scene, including those *after the boom*."

"How bad do you want to see them?" The tabloid photographer's already beady eyes narrowed.

Evie turned her gaze heavenward, praying for patience to keep from splitting this guy's other lip. "We're trying to catch a killer."

Freddy stroked the camera slung around his neck. "Me too. In my wildest fantasies, I catch him, 'cause that catch is going to pay for a beachfront condo in Maui."

For the first time, Jack spoke. "What's your price?"

Freddy rubbed his palms, the friction igniting a spark in his eyes. "A man who speaks my language."

Evie had to give it to Jack. He and his mountains of money were nice to have on her side, and to his credit he was letting her do her job and take the lead, but damn if this wasn't a great move at just the right time.

Jack reached into the inner pocket of his jacket.

Freddy waved off the checkbook. "No money. I want in."

A groan slipped from Evie's mouth. First Jack. Now the tabloid photographer. The entire world wanted to play cop. "Freddy, this isn't a day at the track," she said. "The Angel Bomber has already killed seven people, and I don't want you to be number eight."

"Ain't gonna happen. I'm made of armor." He grabbed a roll of fat at his waist and jiggled. "So here's the deal. You can get another one of those subpoenas, but that'll take time, and frankly, I know you want these photos now. As for me, I want a story. I want to be there when you nab this guy."

"Not gonna happen. My job is to preserve life, and I can't have you underfoot on a takedown."

"Come on, Lady Feeb, hotshots like you make deals all the time. What can you do for me?"

The criminal justice system was full of deals: payments to lowlife confidential informants with the lowdown on the lowest of the lows and plea bargains and deal downs in the pursuit of the greatest good. Jack wasn't the only one who could work a deal. "You give me full access to your photos right now," Evie said. "And when we collar this guy, I'll give you a call from the scene, and you can shoot the take-in and lockup. Exclusive."

Freddy's puffed lip lifted in an attempt at a grin. "It's a deal."

CHAPTER ELEVEN

Friday, October 30
10:01 p.m.

Should I be disturbed that you have photos of eight little girls on your refrigerator?" Evie stood in the kitchen of Freddy's apartment, a one-room walk-up dive in the part of West Hollywood that was anything but glamorous, Jack at her side.

"Those are my nieces." Freddy fired up the computer on his kitchen table. "The one in pigtails is Lilliana. She's twelve years old and already knows she wants to be a great photojournalist like her old uncle."

"Eight nieces? I have seven nephews with one on the way."

"Maybe someday we should introduce 'em." Freddy called up an ungodly number of file folders. "Who knows, we might end up with a match or two. I can be the wedding photographer, and you can bake the wedding cake."

Evie rolled her eyes and parked herself at his right shoulder. "Let me see what you got."

Unlike his person, Freddy kept his work files in meticulous shape. He had thousands of photos of the bomb scenes, all sorted and labeled with descriptive titles. "Where do you want to start?"

She pointed to the photos before the bomb detonated, the ones of a living, breathing, terrified Maria Franco, the third bombing victim. "Let's try these." She didn't see him, but she knew the minute Jack stepped up behind her. Tonight she felt an odd heat generating from his body.

Freddy scrolled through the photos.

"Stop there," Jack ordered when Freddy brought up a wide-angle shot that showed the concrete path below the tree.

Her heart beat triple time. "Can you zoom in on that bit of red?" The spot became a giant red blur. "Damn, it looks like a bunch of fuzzy squiggles."

"Not for long." Freddy flexed his fingers. "Time to work a little Photoshop magic. First I'm going to isolate and enlarge." He zoomed in on the blur. "Now I'll decrease shadows and increase highlights." His mouse scampered over the red. "I'm going to sharpen a few angles and clean up a few curves." All the while the squiggle of red darkened, and shapes became more distinct.

"Looks like he's had some practice in Photoshop magic." Evie jabbed Jack in the ribs.

Jack didn't seem to notice. He was fixated on the screen. A thin layer of sweat glistened on his forehead. Jack sweating? She did a double-take.

"Now it's pixel playtime," Freddy said. One by one he moved blocks of red and gray. Sweat beaded his forehead.

"Okay, my friends." Freddy pushed back the mouse and held up both hands. "Looks like we got something. Carter Vandemere."

Evie stared at the signature, a bold splash of red, taunting her like the red cape of a matador. She grabbed Jack's arm. "It's him."

"Probably a pseudonym," Jack said with a frown.

"Probably, but at least it's something." She hijacked Freddy's mouse and printed out a copy. Then she took the printout and smacked it against her lips.

"What? No kisses for me?" Freddy puckered his lips.

She thwacked him on the shoulder and turned to Jack. "I need to get this to Ricci. *Vámonos!*"

* * *

11:54 p.m.

"County data sources records?" Evie asked.

"Nothing," Ricci said.

"State?"

"*Nada.*"

"Federal?"

"Zip." Ricci slid his mouse across the desk so hard, it slammed into the wall. "Carter Vandemere does not exist."

Evie paced the length of his desk, her boots itching for a chase. "He does, just under a different name."

"I'm going to widen the search and start knocking on doors," Ricci said. "We'll look for variations on the name. I'm calling a press conference for tomorrow."

Evie had been waiting for this particular bomb for two days. "You know a press conference will play into his hand, right? He wants the world to know Carter Vandemere created those horrific scenes and killed those people. That kind of attention will just empower him."

"Tomorrow is the last day of October," Ricci said.

"Things could blow any day after that. It's possible he already has his victims."

A woman and a child. Evie's back teeth ground together.

"Giving a man who has the gall to sign his name to a murder a turn in the spotlight may not be a bad thing," Jack said. "He clearly has an ego."

"True," Evie admitted. "With power comes confidence, and in some cases, cockiness. With cockiness comes carelessness, and with carelessness comes a better chance of a collar, but don't forget we're not dealing with a standard bomber here. Hayden says he's an artist first, which means he's an unknown entity, and unknowns are a bear to work with. You don't know what's going to set them off and how bad the fallout will be."

Would increased media attention feed Vandemere's ego and escalate efforts? Would he strike faster or harder? Was the clock already ticking? Had he already abducted a woman and child?

After Ricci and his men disbanded, Evie took off for her office.

"You're up to something," Jack said as he caught up with her, his tie loose and leaves still in his hair from their trek through the waste hauler. He'd been a calm, steady presence all evening.

"I'm not done with Carter Vandemere. I have one last Hail Mary." Evie fired up her laptop and logged into her team's video conference room. "Technically it's a Hail Maddox. He's my team's cyber intelligence specialist. I called him a few hours ago and asked him to do some digging. If Vandemere has a trace of a fingerprint online, Maddox will find it."

Moments later, Maddox appeared on-screen.

Evie clicked on the audio button. "*Hola, amigo.* Sorry to keep you up so late."

Maddox's fingers flying across the keyboard, he looked up from his screen and grinned. "Never a problem." His hair was more unkempt than hers.

"I take it you found something?" Evie asked.

"I did some tunnel work and poked my nose into a few private online art communities. I didn't find anything anywhere by a Carter Vandemere. So I focused on what's really important."

"The images," Jack said, dragging his chair next to hers.

Maddox's forehead lined, but Evie made room. "This is Jack Elliott. He's the owner of the collection."

The crevices along Maddox's forehead deepened.

"You can speak freely," Evie assured her teammate.

Maddox tapped his thumbs on the keyboard seventeen times before finally nodding. "I performed image searches for well-known works by some well-known artists and came up with thousands of hits," Maddox said. "Then knowing you're looking for a twisted mind, I more or less twisted the images, adding blood and mutilated elements. Eventually I found this artist who signed his work with a *V*."

Her breath caught in her throat. A single letter, but it had the same sharp tails on the top of the *V* as Vandemere's signature at the bomb site. Could this be him?

The screen split in two, and on the right-hand side appeared a series of paintings in thumbnail. Most were females, all young and beautiful. She squinted at the splashes of color. All grotesque. She touched the screen, calling up the first portrait of a young woman with soulful brown eyes, her head in her lap. The second portrait showed a woman with the skin removed from her chest and blood pooling in a heart shape on the floor.

Evie forced herself not to recoil. Worse than the blood and gore were the faces. Mouths twisted in pain. Eyes glazed

with terror. She closed her eyes and pictured the same pain
and terror on the third bombing victim's face in the photos
by Freddy Ortiz. She breathed in the char of twisted rebar,
hot smoke, and metallic tang of blood. This had to be the
work of the same twisted mind. Work of a killer.

"There's more," Maddox said. "The IP address this guy
used in this forum was from a coffee shop in L.A."

Evie reached out and set her hand on Jack's arm. "Jack,
you know the L.A. art scene. Does any of this stuff look familiar?" When he didn't answer, she turned to him. His face
was as pale as bleached marble. "Jack?"

"Enlarge the portrait of the woman in the blue dress,"
Jack said. Maddox must have heard the urgency in Jack's
voice, because he moved swiftly. "Zoom in on her purse.
There."

Maddox zoomed in on the purse clasp, a silver sun with
intricate swirls forming a smiling face. Evie's skin prickled.
She'd seen something like that. Before she could say anything, Jack pointed to a portrait of a woman standing on a
balcony with fancy ironwork. "Now get a close-up of the
balcony."

Centered in the ironwork the artist had painted another
sun, same smiling face. Maddox quickly scrolled through
the gruesome images, and each one featured a smiling sun.
"Appears to be a recurring and significant motif for him."

Evie pushed back from the computer and paced. "I've
seen that somewhere before."

"The second bombing," Jack said, his voice couched in a
hush.

"Yes! The woman wearing the bomb wore an earring that
looked something like that, but it had been damaged in the
blast."

Jack was now inches from the computer, watching as

Maddox scrolled through and found the sun motif in each piece of art. "It's the same design."

Warning bells, the ones that had been echoing strong and steady at the back of her head ever since Jack Elliott planted himself in the middle of her investigation, clanged faster. "How can you be so sure?"

"I've compared it to this." His gaze still glued to the screen, Jack dug into his pocket and pulled out his key ring, the metal jangling. On his key ring was a small silver sun with intricate swirls forming a smiling face, the same sun that appeared in the gruesome online gallery by a man named *V* who used an IP address in L.A.

I'm guilty, Jack had said. But there was more.

She took the keys, the points of the silver sun digging into her palm. "Jack, where did you get this?"

"At an art fair in Pennsylvania. I bought it for my—stop!" Jack's voice was so loud, she jumped. "Click on the girl in the white dress."

Maddox called up a portrait of a girl in a white sundress sitting on a yellow chair.

Still, stoic Jack was shaking so hard she swore she could hear his bones rattling.

"Jack, what's going on?" Evie asked. "Who is the girl?"

"Abby. My sister."

Abby, as in Abby Foundation. Jack had been so passionate about this case. The reward. The leads. The laser-beam focus. Her gut tightened.

"Jack." She grabbed his hands, two blocks of ice, but that could be because fire was running through her veins. He stood granite-still, his gaze transfixed on the girl in the white dress. His sister. Who was linked to the bomber. "Where's Abby?"

His hands tightened around hers, two frozen manacles. "She's dead."

CHAPTER TWELVE

Saturday, October 31
12:42 a.m.

When it came to doing business, boardrooms were over-rated. Jack slid back the front passenger seat of Evie's red convertible Beetle, slipped his knotted hands behind his head, and stared at the sky.

"Are you ready to talk?" Evie's voice was unusually soft, almost whispery, like the breeze blowing off the Pacific. In a brilliant tactical move, she'd dragged him from LAPD and that computer screen with a portrait of his dead sister and images of all of those suns.

He pulled in a long breath of briny air. "Yes." He hadn't planned on having this discussion with Evie because he thought Abby and his personal quest had no bearings on the case. He ran a hand down his face. "I have no idea where to start."

"The beginning."

He closed his eyes and pictured his hometown in Pennsylvania fifteen years ago. That was the winter of snow drifts that closed highways, ice that toppled trees, and a sun that refused to shine. That was his last winter at home, his last winter with Abby. "The story begins with ice cream." Something hard and heavy settled on his chest. He opened his mouth, but pressure trapped the words.

"I love this story already. What flavor?" Evie leaned toward him, so close he could feel the warmth of her breath on his cheek. "Is there cake?"

A scrappy laugh crawled up from under the boulder on his chest. The sound must have dislodged the tangle of memories. "Vanilla." He attempted a half smile in Evie's direction. "No cake."

"I'll survive." She slid back, resting her cheek on the seat and giving him her full attention. Because Evie didn't do anything half-assed. Which meant he'd have to give her the full story.

He stretched his neck, trying to loosen the muscles along his throat. "When I was seventeen and Abby was sixteen, we drove to town to get a pint of vanilla ice cream. Crazy thing to do on a sunless, below-freezing day in February in Pennsylvania, but my sister had this crazy idea. She wanted to make root beer floats and sit on the front porch pretending it was the Fourth of July and that the air was hot and steamy and filled with smoke from barbecues.

"Abby hated the cold. She hated our small steel-mill town in southwestern Pennsylvania. But most of all, Abby hated the weeks we'd go without sun. Mom never had Abby diagnosed, but looking back I'm sure my sister suffered from some kind of seasonal depression because she craved the sun." He slipped the silver sun from his pocket, the half moon setting it aglow.

Evie ran her finger along the silver smile. "So you bought your little sister her very own sun."

He nodded. "She saw the jewelry set at a local craft fair that summer but couldn't afford it. We didn't have money growing up. Dad died in a car accident when we were young, and Mom worked in the office at our elementary school. I'd been working odd jobs since I was twelve, saving up money to get out of a dark and dying town, but I dipped into my savings and bought the jewelry set for Abby. She loved the necklace and earrings, swore she'd never take them off. She even used a version of this sun on her signature. She was an artist. Worked mostly in oils. Lots of landscapes, many of oceans and beaches. She was wearing the jewelry set the day she died."

When his throat tightened, Evie said softly, "Ice cream."

He breathed in the two sweet words. "On the way home from the grocery store with that pint of ice cream, the sun came out. Abby was giddy, literally bouncing in the seat. She begged me to drive down to the river where the sun set the ice on fire. I'm not an artist, but I knew what she meant. That part of the river was beautiful when the sun came out." And deadly. His eyelids closed.

"And being the doting older brother, you said yes?"

"Being the doting older brother, I said, *No*." His lips curved in a humorless smile. "Technically, I said, *Hell no*. The road to the river was covered in ice. It was too dangerous, especially in my old, beat-up pickup truck with shoddy tires. So I took her up Welton's Hill, one of the highest spots in town where she could see the river below. For an hour I ate ice cream while she sketched fire on ice. She looked so happy and content, I wish we could have stayed there for hours. But the wind picked up and we had to pack up. We got back in the truck and started down the hill. On the first turn the tires lost traction, and we skidded toward the shoulder. Those few hours of sun followed by the cold wind had turned the road into a solid sheet of ice.

"I corrected, but we slid farther and faster. I had no control." The memory still had the power to ice his veins. "We careened off the road and plunged into the river. Water and debris rushed below the icy surface, pounding the truck. I yanked on the door, but it wouldn't budge. I got the window down and climbed out, expecting Abby to follow, but she couldn't move. It was like she was frozen. I grabbed her and got us both out of the truck.

"The cold, it was shocking. And the sounds." Echoes of the past pounded his ears. "The water was a freight train. Sheets of ice moaned and cracked. My hands got so cold, so quick, I lost hold of Abby. The current pulled her to the back of the truck, where she was able to grab the tailgate. I went after her. It was surreal. Her hair swirling about her, her hand reaching out to mine, her mouth frozen in a scream I couldn't hear."

Evie slipped her hand into his. Warm. Soft.

"I caught her hand. The current pulled, but I hung on. At that point, someone from the surface grabbed my legs and yanked. Abby slipped out of my fingers. I kicked the hell out of whoever was pulling me and lunged for my sister and caught this." His fingers curled around the sun pendant. "And I never let go. Even when Abby stopped kicking, even when those last few bubbles of air trickled out, and even when I saw the light go out from her eyes, I never let go."

When he was working the final hours of a deal, when he was bone tired and had given everything he thought he had to give, he always managed to find a place with more. More insight, more energy, more will. He sought that place now. "Now there were two people at the surface pulling on my legs. The chain snapped. I tried to go after Abby, but the rescuers pulled me back. I watched as she floated away, limp and lifeless." He brought the fisted pendant to his lips. "And I never let go."

"I'm so sorry, Jack, so, so sorry." A long, thready breath rushed from Evie's mouth.

"Me too." Jack set the sun on the dash. Even without the metal touching his palm, he felt the heat. That sun, that moment, had been branded into his flesh. "By the time the rescuers got me out, police and search crews were at the scene. They wouldn't let me go back in for Abby's body, not that I could have done much. Hypothermia had set in. I was dropping in and out of consciousness, but I had to give them credit. For hours police, firefighters, friends, neighbors, and strangers searched for Abby. They sent divers into the screaming waters. They walked up and down the shore and checked every crevice and soft spot that had formed in the ice, searching for her body. Even when darkness came, they searched. Her body was never found, and she was presumed dead. In my mind, there was no presumption. I saw the light go out of her eyes. She was dead."

The pronouncement brought him no peace. "Four days later we had a funeral and said our good-byes. Our mom took comfort that Abby was in a place with more light." The muscles along his throat constricted, cutting off words and breath.

"But there was no comfort for you." Evie's hand cupped his knee, the pressure firm and steady.

"Abby hated the cold. I wanted to find her body, to get her out of the cold." He shook his head. "When I made my first million, do you know how I celebrated? No cake. I hired a recovery crew to look for her body. For two weeks they searched the river and the reservoir but found nothing. Twice since then I've had the best search-and-rescue teams using the newest and most sophisticated equipment to locate my sister's remains, and two more times they came up empty."

Evie shook her head in commiseration. "Unknowns are a bitch."

"Yeah, so when I saw the photo of the earring in the wreckage from the second bombing, I was drawn to it, couldn't stop thinking about it. The rational businessman in me knew the earring the victim wore had nothing to do with Abby. It was unique, a custom piece of jewelry, but the artist could have made dozens, maybe hundreds of pieces using that sun."

"But the big brother…" Evie prompted.

"…couldn't let go. If that was Abby's earring—and it would be the longest of all long shots—then I had to assume someone found it. Which meant someone found her body or the place where her body may be. Really, that's all I ever wanted, to find her body and get her out of the cold. That's when I called you in."

"To help you put your sister to rest."

"But then as I was going through the photos from the third bombing, I spotted a piece of wreckage, a piece of the woman's robe that had the same curve and angle as one of the sun's rays. And you understand that, right? It was only a half-inch curve, but it was enough to make me wonder why a sun my sister treasured was popping up in artwork created by a mad bomber."

For the first time since they arrived at the ocean lookout, Evie's eyes lost some of their softness. "Why didn't you mention the sun to anyone?"

"Because when I first discovered the connection, it wasn't a judicious use of limited resources. The aim is to find the bomber and stop the murder of a woman and child and who knows how many others, not look for the remains of a girl who had a pair of silver sun earrings that matched one of the victim's. And that was a major factor, Evie, the earrings could have simply been the ones the victim was wearing when she was abducted. There was no tie to the bomber."

"Until now." Evie jammed her seat belt in place and started the car. "Not only does he use a sun motif important to your sister, he painted her. This bomber is linked to your sister."

Jack's hand curved around the sun Abby wore so close to her heart. "I know."

CHAPTER THIRTEEN

Saturday, October 31
9:35 a.m.

At five-foot-two, Evie was closer to the ground than most people, which meant she could get a better look at their feet, and this morning, her world revolved around feet.

Captain Ricci stood at a podium set up on the scarred earth of the Central Branch of the L.A. Public Library. At his elbow was a six-foot blowup of Carter Vandemere's signature.

"Anyone who has seen or purchased artwork by an individual using this name should contact the Angel Bomber hotline," Ricci was saying to the group of fifty-plus journalists gathered in the courtyard. "This individual may also go by the initial *V* and use the same angled slant to the letter."

Behind Ricci stood Jack along with representatives of each of the law enforcement agencies working the case. Cho was representing the FBI, a good call because Evie needed to be on the streets looking at feet.

The man who'd taken a shot at her and Jack was still on the loose. If he had anything to do with the bombings, it was possible he showed up at the press conference to watch the chaos he was creating. Bombers weren't overly social, so she was looking for a man set off from the crowd. She strolled past the library's fountain area where mothers sat with baby strollers.

She rammed a wayward lock of hair out of her face. Hell, he could even be here looking for his next victims, a brown-haired woman and a blond infant. She wound through Saturday-morning joggers, checked out the bus stop, and poked her head into a sandwich shop.

When she reached a coffee shop, she jammed her hands on her hips. "Dammit, Freddy, stop following me."

"Man, you're good," a voice from behind her quipped. "You got eyes in the back of your head?"

She turned and aimed an arched eyebrow at the tabloid journalist who'd been on her tail all morning. "I smelled you." She fanned away his sickly sweet breath. "What is that?"

"Wacky Watermelon." He slicked a wad of neon green gum over his tongue and blew a bubble that looked like nuclear waste. "It's supposed to keep my mouth occupied so I give up the cigs. Doc says I'm a few sticks away from stroking out."

"Unless the toxic gum kills you first."

Freddy leaned in and said under his breath, "You're looking for him, aren't you? You're thinking he may be here getting a boner over all this attention."

She pushed him away. "Shouldn't you be out shooting cheating celebrities or strung-out rock stars?"

"I belong right here at your side, and you know it." He nudged his shoulder against hers and waggled his eyebrows. "Ask me; I know you want to."

Freddy was smarter than he looked. "Okay, Freddy. Does anyone in this crowd look like anyone in the crowd outside the library when Lisa Franco was killed?"

He stopped blowing bubbles. "No, and I've been looking." He dug into his man purse and took out a small photo album. "Here are some shots of the crowd from the third bombing. I isolated the onlookers who fit your profile, blew them up, and cleaned up their features."

As she flipped through the photos, she had to give kudos to Freddy. Ricci had an LAPD uniform shooting the crowd for facial recognition and comparison, but Freddy's doctored shots could be useful. "Good move. Can I keep these?"

Freddy put his hand on his heart. "For you, *mi corazón*, anything."

She jabbed the album into her bag and took off, the photographer keeping pace alongside her. In little doses, he wasn't *that* bad. While she searched for big feet, Freddy snapped photos. On her second loop around the fountain, Jack finally took to the podium.

"I'm Jack Elliott, and I live and work downtown," Jack started. Every eye, every ear in the plaza turned to him. "An evil has invaded my neighborhood, destroying lives and property and peace of mind. People are afraid to shop and dine and meet with friends. Small businesses are feeling the fallout from the bomb. I'm encouraging all of my neighbors, employees, and colleagues to work with Captain Ricci's team. Be watchful and report any suspicious characters and activities. Residents have set up…"

Authoritative. Earnest. Compelling. And from the heart. Because Jack's heart was very much involved. His private art collection was being used as the basis for the bombings, and his sister, at the time of her death, had been wearing custom jewelry that ended up in the bomber's portfolio.

Freddy pointed to the dais where her colleague, Steve Cho, now stood and was saying, "In each previous bombing, the improvised explosive device has been encased in a fanny pack with the ignition fully visible."

"Why aren't you up there, Lady Feeb?" Freddy asked.

"I don't have the right temperament."

Freddy waggled his eyebrows. "You hit someone once, didn't you?"

"Not during a press conference."

"After?" A grin, more impish than smarmy, slipped onto his lips.

"I'm not the kind of girl to hit and tell."

Freddy laughed, then cradled his lip with his hand. The swelling had gone down, but the skin was blackish purple.

"How's your lip?" Evie asked.

"Still attached to my mouth."

At the dais, Ricci took over at the podium. "And now we'll take questions."

A reporter with a handheld recorder hopped to his feet. "Do you have any indication when and where he'll strike next?"

The press conference had been carefully scripted up to this point, each participant playing a role in disseminating specific information. Ricci would tread carefully here. He couldn't tip off too much to the bomber. At this point they were holding back the connection to the *Beauty Through the Ages* collection. "We don't know when, but we're assuming it will be sometime next week and that he will continue to work the downtown area."

"What are you doing to safeguard area residents?"

The questions and answers flew, and Evie shifted from shoes to heads. She scanned the area for faces. No one with barely contained glee. No one with a smug smirk of superiority. No one with a marked emotional release. She checked her watch. And no more time. In four minutes she and Jack would head to LAX. While most of the team would be working the streets of downtown L.A., she and Jack would be flying to southwestern Pennsylvania.

"Listen, Freddy, I'm heading out of town for the day. Let me know if you get any matches on the faces. And there's one more thing." She dug into her purse and took out a wad of bills and counted. "Here's two hundred fifty-six dollars and"—she reached into the front pocket of her jeans—"twenty-six cents."

Freddy waved off the money. "Don't even try and back out on our deal, Lady Feeb. You promised me an exclusive once we find Bomber Boy."

"We're still on. Consider this a tip for service above and beyond." She patted her bag where the photo album was stashed. "I want you to find a fast horse and play one on me. If you win, pay Skip that next installment."

"You're fuckin' serious?"

"I need you in one piece, Freddy." A guy who had all those pictures of his nieces on his dresser couldn't be that bad. "Anyway, I had someone in my life who took a chance on me when no one else would." She smoothed the wild hair over her right ear.

He wiggled his fingers in front of his chest. "Ooooo, I sense a juicy story."

"It is." She took his hand, opened his fingers, slapped the money on his palm, and took off to get Jack.

* * *

9:41 a.m.

The bitter, black brew scalded Carter Vandemere's throat. Just the way he liked it.

"Want me to top that off?" The woman behind the counter held up a coffeepot.

"I'm good," he said. He was beyond good. He was notoriously good. A giggle jiggled the seared flesh of his throat.

On the television in the corner of The Bean Thing where he'd spent a beautiful Saturday morning watching the sun, people were lining up to talk about him. This. This was what he wanted, dreamed of for the past decade. People seeing his art, acknowledging his masterful work. His art, while certainly not traditional, made people feel, and good art—no, great art—did just that. The stronger the emotion, the more powerful the art. The more powerful the art, the more masterful the artist. For the past three months he'd incited shock, horror, and bone-chilling fear. But until now, he hadn't received the adulation he deserved.

He credited the little FBI agent, the one with the red boots and eyes the color of steamy espresso. When she exploded onto the scene, things changed; most important, things with Jack Elliott changed.

He took another long, blistering swig. The big-shot businessman and art collector had ignored him. Stupid, stupid man. Hot brown liquid sloshed over the rim and splashed onto his hand, leaving a brilliant scarlet streak. Another beautiful shade of red. But now, he finally had Jack Elliott's attention, and he couldn't wait until Jack saw his latest installation, the one he'd personally set up and displayed in Jack's desk drawer.

CHAPTER FOURTEEN

Saturday, October 31
5:11 p.m.

*R*umble. *Craaaaack.*

Lightning spidered the sky as Jack straightened his tie tack, then held open the door to the art boutique.

Always the gentleman. Always in control. But Evie knew better. On the flight from L.A. to southwestern Pennsylvania, Jack had been in business mode, taking comfort in what was familiar and known, business. With Evie, he'd determined goals, identified strategies, made an action plan, and prepared to execute. He'd been singularly focused on the investigation to identify how the Angel Bomber was connected to his dead sister, Abby.

As for what was simmering under his purposeful work, Evie had seen the whitening of his knuckles when they touched down and a flash of sadness in his eyes when they walked out the jet's door and into the cold, gray windy day. He was visiting his hometown for the first time in fifteen years, the place where his sister had died after slipping through his fingers.

Squeezing Jack's hand, she walked into the boutique in search of a killer. The shop smelled of pine and candle wax and was filled with artisan batik quilts, grainy wooden bowls, handblown glass, and jewelry.

A white-haired woman waved from behind a counter where she was ringing up a set of large glass goblets. "Be with you in a minute, dears."

Jack took Evie by the elbow. "Custom jewelry is over here," he said.

The muscles along the back of her arm tensed, but she didn't pull away. Nor did she jab him in the gut, a not-so-gentle reminder that she didn't like being led around. Jack had taken some hard blows lately, but unlike Freddy, he didn't sport a fat lip. Jack had been slammed in the gut.

The bomber clearly knew Abby. He'd painted her portrait and in all of his artwork had used the sun motif that was so important to her. He could have been one of Abby's friends, the bagger at the grocery store where Abby bought vanilla ice cream, the kid in the back row of art class, or the artist who created the sun jewelry.

"Does anything look familiar?" Evie asked.

Jack studied the tiny boxes of rings and pendants and earrings. "Nothing stands out." His jaw squared and tightened. She could see the frustration welling. Jack wasn't used to dealing with unknowns.

"Good afternoon, kids." The woman with the white hair slipped behind the jewelry counter. "Looking for wedding rings today?"

"Wedding?" Evie could barely get the word out. Jack looked equally aghast.

He was the first to recover. "No rings today. We're not looking for a specific piece but a particular artist, someone who works in silver and makes items like this." He held out the silver pendant from his key ring.

"That doesn't look familiar."

"I purchased this piece at a local art fair about fifteen years ago."

"Fifteen years?" She held the pendant up to the artificial light. "You know, this might be one of Harris Kerr's. He works with mostly large metal pieces now, but I think when he was first starting out, he might have done some jewelry work."

"Do you know how we can get in touch with him?" Evie asked.

"He doesn't have a phone. No Internet. He's one of those brooding artist types. Just leave him alone and let him create, but I think I may have his address as a few years ago I had to mail him a commission check for a piece of his we sold."

* * *

6:42 p.m.

"I've never seen so much barbed wire in my life." Jack pulled the rental car up to the gate of Harris Kerr's property, a few wooded acres off the Monongahela River, lit up tonight like the outer perimeter of a maximum security prison.

"Technically that's concertina wire." Evie pointed to the top of the eight-foot chain-link fence. "That's barbed wire, and that one along the side is a lovely little piece of art called razor-ribbon wire."

"Since he probably doesn't have any executive assistant we can tap, any plans to get us into his fortress?" Jack asked.

"He knows we're here." She pointed at a camera mounted on a post at the front gate. Then she took out her shield and held it up to the camera. The camera whirred, zooming in. "Let's hope he chooses to do this the easy way."

Nothing had ever come easy to Jack, which was fine. He'd worked since the age of twelve, mowing lawns and shoveling snow. He didn't mind working hard. Just the opposite. He loved pouring himself into a project. He loved racing to the finish line and notching the win. But this project, the investigation into his dead sister's ties with a bomber, was eating at his gut. Had his sister known the bomber calling himself Carter Vandemere? Had he been warped and twisted back then? Had Abby sat for him? Had he hurt her?

A hand settled on his arm. Evie's. She nodded to the gate swinging open. "Looks like he's going to play nicely."

Jack threaded the car along the pocked driveway. The wind had picked up, and lightning continued to streak the inky sky. "Do you really think this could be Carter Vandemere?"

Evie was quiet a moment. These bits of quiet from the fiery FBI agent at first surprised him, but he was learning that Evie wasn't all fire and brimstone. She had a contemplative side, when the hair atop her head tilted to the right and her big brown eyes narrowed. "The location concerns me," Evie finally said. "Vandemere knows L.A., and unless this Kerr fellow has some West Coast property, I'm not sure if I can buy into his involvement."

The first thing Jack noticed about Harris Kerr was his eyes. They refused to meet his. In a business deal, that would have sent Jack out the door. Then Jack noticed the hands. Three fingertips were missing from the left hand along with the pinky on his right.

"The things we sacrifice for the sake of art." Kerr held up his hands, gazing at them as if they, too, were works of art. Jack only saw the hands of a possible killer.

"Please show us your workshop," Evie said with a bluntness he'd come to expect, not because she was rude but because time was of the essence. Tomorrow was the first day of November.

The first icy raindrop fell as Kerr led them to a garage behind the small trailer that was his home. There Jack saw stacks of steel sheets, pyramids of pipes, saws, grinders, and cans of paint. Next to him Evie sent a sweeping gaze through the shop. Did she see traces of a killer? Bits of a bomber?

She walked slowly around the room, her boot heels tapping the cement. She stopped at the workbench holding coffee canisters full of nails and screws and wire. "Do you make jewelry?"

"Ahhhh, the commercial cash cow." Derision dripped from Kerr's voice. "Yes, I was guilty of sucking on that teat once in my career."

She handed him the sun pendant. "Is this one of yours?"

Kerr plucked a loupe from the desk and held the pendant under a lamp. "That's one of mine. I also made a matching pair of earrings."

"Only one?" Jack asked, the question as sharp as the wire that lined this place. If the answer was yes, the earring used in the second bombing belonged to Abby.

"All of my pieces are one-of-a-kind originals. Where did you get this?"

"I bought it for my sister at an art fair in town fifteen years ago."

"The blonde with the pretty blue eyes."

"You remember her?"

"Super fans are good for an artist's ego. She loved my work, fell head over heels with the sun set, but was crushed when she found out the price. I wished I could have cut her a deal, but I was doing the whole starving artist thing and couldn't let the piece go."

Evie poked through the coffee canisters, metal clinking and clanking. "Have you ever been to Los Angeles?"

"California? Never. Why do you ask?"

Because I want this to end here, Jack thought. *I want you to be the Angel Bomber so we can put an end to the death and destruction of human life. And so you can tell me where to find Abby's body so I can lay her to rest.*

"When was the last time you flew on a plane?" Evie continued.

"I've never flown. I'm quite happy right here."

Evie pulled out the mangled earring from her bag, a one-inch piece of twisted silver that sent Jack's insides quaking. "Is this one of yours?"

Again, Kerr settled the loupe on his eye. "Absolutely. This is from the same set as the pendant. There's a hash mark on the back where I soldered the sun to the loop."

Abby's earring. The one she'd worn in death. Which means someone had found her body. Jack's fist tightened. Because while Harris Kerr was not the bomber, he'd dropped a bombshell.

Sheets of icy rain fell from the sky as they left Kerr's shop, but Jack didn't feel the biting bullets. "Carter Vandemere found her body," Jack said when they got into the car. "He touched her and took the earring."

"We don't know that for sure."

"You do, Evie." He spun on her, daring her to call him

wrong. "You're like me. You work from the gut. You trust what's in your core. Tell me, what's your gut telling you?"

Her hands were in her lap, fisting and flexing. "That the bomber was obsessed with your sister, he knew her before her death, and he somehow got his hands on her earrings. And that right now we need to find out who your sister was hanging around with before she died."

He jammed the keys in the ignition and twisted hard. "I know where to start."

"Where?"

The one place whose black, gritty dust he'd wiped from the soles of his shoes and swore he'd never see again. "My home."

* * *

7:55 p.m.

Jack secured the parking brake. The roads in this neighborhood were hilly, pocked, and strewn with loose gravel. They hadn't changed much in fifteen years. "Zoe lives in the blue house on the right," he said as he reached for the keys in the ignition switch.

"Which means you grew up in the yellow one." Evie squinted through the windshield where the wipers blasted at full speed. "That's a great tree in the front yard. Bet you had a ball climbing it."

His hand hovering over the keys, he studied Evie, who was in turn studying the rows of tiny dilapidated houses and him. She was in bomb tech mode, checking out the landscape, looking for anything that might go boom. In other words, she was worried about him.

"I did." Jack rested his wrists on the steering wheel.

"For the record, we didn't have a horrible childhood. I don't remember much about Dad, other than he loved to work with wood. On the weekends he'd go out in the garage and build things, chairs, cabinets, picture frames. That's where Abby got her artistic ability. As for Mom, she worked hard and never complained about going without. Abby, when she was in her sunny place, she could light up a room."

"But you wanted to get out of here? Like Abby, did you need more sun and light?"

"I needed more life. This is a dead town covered in black dust." He scrubbed his hands along his arms. "It's called coke and settles into everything, the sidewalks, the rain, your skin."

"Not a beautiful place."

"Definitely not." He switched off the car. "I tried to talk Mom into leaving, but she refused. She died two years after I left. Pancreatic cancer. No one knew because she didn't have insurance and didn't see a doctor."

Before he reached for the door handle, Evie grabbed his arm. "You don't need to go in. This could be headed to some pretty dark places."

"I know." Dark thoughts had been slamming his skull. Was the person now calling himself Carter Vandemere watching Abby at the river? Did he have anything to do with the accident? Was he one of the searchers? Did he find Abby's lifeless body? And most important, if he did, what had he done with it? "That darkness is the reason I need to be here."

"You do realize that I have the power to bar you from anything to do with this case, don't you?"

"You won't."

Her mouth quirked in irritation. "What makes you so confident?"

Evie wore her heart on her sleeve for all the world to see. "You'll do just about anything to find the Angel Bomber, and you'll use any means and resources, including my pains and past, to get him."

Guilt washed across Evie's face.

He settled his finger under her chin and brought her gaze back to his. "I'm the type who appreciates and admires that kind of passion and drive."

Craaaaack.

Another bolt of lightning split the sky.

They ducked through the rain, which was on its way to sleet, and knocked on Zoe's door. Zoe Sobeski grew up in the house next to his and had been Abby's best friend, and unlike him, she'd never been able to shake the old neighborhood, first caring for her ailing mother, then taking over the house when her mother died. Zoe knew Abby's friends, dreams, and fears.

The door swung open, framing a woman with a bulging midsection and a little princess in her arms. The corners of his lips turned up.

The woman's eyes widened. "Jackie? Jackie Elliott?" She put the princess on the floor and wrapped Jack in a bear hug. Then Zoe held him at arm's length and turned him as if inspecting a coat for possible purchase. "Man, Jackie, you grew up good, and you smell good, too." A hand smoothed the side of her hair while the other tugged the baggy shirt over her very pregnant midsection. "I'm a mess. Dan and I have been at a Halloween carnival with the kids all day."

Today was Halloween? He hadn't even noticed. Next to him, Evie looked equally surprised.

"You look beautiful, Zoe," he said.

"You must be having eye problems." She pulled him into

the house, where in addition to the little princess, there was a little clown and an even littler hobo. With her toe, she nudged away a toy fire truck and four Barbie dolls. "Who's your friend?"

"*Agent* Evie Jimenez." Evie took out a thin wallet, and with a snap of her wrist, showed Zoe her badge. The movement was so natural, the badge could have been an extension of her hand.

"Cool costume," the little hobo said as he tugged at Zoe's oversized T-shirt. "Mom, can I be an FBI agent for Halloween next year?"

Zoe kissed the top of his head. "Of course." She turned the warm smile on Jack. "What brings you back home?"

"Abby."

Zoe settled a hand on the little hobo's head and pulled him to her side. Jack knew this wouldn't be easy for Zoe. She'd taken Abby's death hard. After the accident, Zoe wouldn't talk about Abby, and she stopped coming over, even after his mom begged Zoe to remain a part of their lives. *It's like I've lost two daughters*, his mom had said.

Jack dipped his head at Evie. "It's important."

"Of course. Let me get the kids upstairs. My husband is getting the bathtub ready now."

The little princess was staring at Evie. "You look like a cowgirl, not an FBI agent."

"Don't be stupid," her little brother said. "She has the badge. She's an FBI agent."

The princess nibbled her bottom lip. "You're a cowgirl, right?"

Evie squatted so she was eye-level with the little girl. "I'm a cowgirl *and* an FBI agent."

The child's eyes widened. "A girl can do that?"

Evie didn't blink. "A girl can do anything."

The princess smiled smugly, stuck her tongue out at her brother, and spun on her sparkly slippers. For the first time that day, Evie grinned.

It didn't last long as Zoe returned to the living room without the kids. She swept the blankets and blocks and scattered Cheerios from the sofa. With her hand at the small of her back, she lowered herself onto a rocking chair. "We have about twenty minutes before they're done."

Evie took a seat on the sofa. "Did Abby have any friends who considered themselves artists? Particularly any who painted portraits?"

"There wasn't a big art crowd at school, and I don't remember Abby talking about anyone like that."

"Did she ever sit for a portrait?"

"She liked to be behind the canvas, not on it."

"Did she ever complain about anyone watching her, maybe even stalking her?"

"Never. This is a small town. Everyone pretty much knows everyone's business."

"You were at the river the day of the accident searching with the volunteers, correct?"

Zoe rested her hands on the top of her belly and rubbed, long slow strokes. She nodded.

"I know that was a tough day for you, Zoe." Evie leaned toward the other woman. "But I need you to think hard. When you were searching the riverbanks for Abby's body, did you ever see anyone who didn't belong, a stranger or someone who looked out of place?"

"It was dark and cold so everyone was pretty bundled up, but no, I don't remember anyone out of the ordinary."

Zoe finally turned to Jack. "What's going on? Why is the FBI asking about Abby after all these years?"

Jack locked gazes with Evie, and she gave him a quick nod. He was not a trained investigator, but he knew how to deal with people, and Zoe had been like a sister to him.

"Have you heard of the Angel Bombings?" Jack asked.

"Of course. How awful. I had to turn off the television news after the last bombing. Those photos, especially of all those children outside the library." She shuddered. "God, they were horrible."

"We believe Abby may have known the bomber."

Zoe stopped stroking her belly. "What?"

"We found some artwork belonging to the bomber, and in that artwork was a portrait of Abby."

Zoe gripped the sides of the chair. "No."

"Yes, Zoe, and there's more. You know the sun earrings and necklace Abby always wore, the ones I gave her? She was wearing them the day she died. One of the earrings was found on one of the bombing victims."

Her nails dug into the padded arms of the rocker.

"We're looking for a young man who was between the ages of fifteen and twenty back when Abby knew him," Evie added. "He was socially awkward or shy. He may or may not have known Abby, but he must have watched her."

Zoe shook her head.

"I know it's hard to think about these things," Jack said. Upstairs the water stopped running. "But try, Zoe."

"No, you don't know." She stood, her hands kneading her lower back.

"The thing you need to realize about bombers," Evie said, "is that they grow their skill set over time. Fifteen years ago when he knew Abby, he wouldn't have had the knowledge or the confidence to do what he did to the women in those bombings."

Zoe's chin trembled. "But now he does?"

"Well yes, and we're trying to stop him before anyone else dies."

Her body swayed. "Oh, God."

Jack turned to Evie, but her gaze was locked on Zoe, eyes hot and sharp. The hairs on the back of his neck stood on end. "What's going on?"

Zoe sank back into the rocker and wrapped her arms around her belly.

"What's wrong with her?" Jack asked. When neither Evie nor Zoe moved, he started for the stairs. "I'm going to go get Dan."

Evie grabbed his arm. "No." She pulled him to her side. "Zoe is fine. She just needs to tell us the truth, and that will be much easier if it's only us."

"What truth?" Jack asked. Something had just happened, and while he was in the middle of it, he had no idea what was going on.

Zoe's hands knotted in the fabric of her T-shirt.

Evie looked up at him. "Your sister did not drown in the river. Someone pulled her out."

Zoe nodded.

The words hit him as hard as the rushing river ice fifteen years ago. "Carter Vandemere?"

Evie shook her head.

Zoe finally spoke. "I did." Then the silent sobs rocked her entire body.

CHAPTER FIFTEEN

Saturday, October 31
8:09 p.m.

Sit." Evie pointed to the sagging sofa, and when Jack didn't move, she reached up, placed her hands on his broad shoulders, and pushed. The man looked like he was about to topple over. Zoe Sobeski, Abby's best friend, had just admitted that Jack's sister had survived the crash into the frozen river fifteen years ago. Zoe sat in the rocking chair, convulsing with silent sobs.

Upstairs the splashing had stopped, and giggles poured down from the steps. "Listen, Zoe," Evie said, taking the woman by the shoulders. "I need you to get it together and tell me exactly what happened the day Abby got swept down the river."

The pregnant woman continued to rock and sob.

"Your kids will be down in a few minutes." She gave

Zoe's shoulders a soft shake. "They don't need to see you like this."

Zoe wiped her nose with the back of her hand. "No, they don't." She let out a series of short, fast breaths. She cast a glance at Jack, then turned quickly. "I, uh, arrived at the river about a half hour after the crash, and like everyone else was searching the riverbank on foot, hoping to find her on the shore or, God forbid, see her through the ice. The sun was setting, and I knew we didn't have much time." The woman squeezed her hands so tightly her fingertips turned purple.

Evie unknotted Zoe's hands and placed them on her stomach. "What happened?"

Zoe flattened her palms on the bulge. "Everyone was on the main river, which seemed odd to me. Abby never went with the flow." A shaky laugh tumbled from her pale lips. "Abby always did her own thing. So I started down a side creek. Lots of snow and rocks, but the water wasn't as deep, so there was less ice. I started running, chasing the sun, which was going down, and that's when I saw her. Stretched out on the bank. Yellow jeans, green jacket, white boots."

Jack didn't move but for the blood draining from his face. Evie tried to catch his eye, but he was totally focused on his sister's childhood friend.

"And when you found her?" Evie prompted.

"I took her into my arms. She was so cold and still. I couldn't see her chest moving. I felt for a pulse and found one, just barely."

"She was dead," Jack said. "I saw her die."

Zoe nodded so quickly, tears fell from her eyes. "She did die, Jackie. She told me all about it. About her lungs that felt like they were imploding, the world fading to black, and you refusing to let go of her necklace. Then she told me about the light, a brilliant golden light at the end of a tunnel with gold bricks, but when she got to the tunnel, she said she couldn't get through, that she pounded on those bricks until her hands were bloody. And finally, she stopped fighting. Abby said the next thing she remembered was me grabbing her around the chest and pulling her up the riverbank."

Evie watched for Jack to crack, to explode and shatter. He swallowed twice. "Are you telling me Abby was alive and you never said anything to anyone?"

Zoe pushed aside Evie. "Yes, Jack, I said something. I said one word. *Yes*." That single word was wrapped in steel. "I got Abby back to my car, and it was clear she was going to live. She was smiling and talking about the light. Jack, she looked so happy, I mean ecstatic. She said she wanted to go to the light."

Jack's hands balled into fists. "You helped her die?"

"No, Jack. I helped her *live*." Zoe heaved herself out of the rocker, her stomach throwing her off balance as she waved a hand at the picture window where sleet slashed at the glass pane. "She wanted out of this place, and for the past year she'd been planning on going to L.A."

"Los Angeles?" Evie asked because Jack looked like he'd just taken a blow to his jaw.

Zoe nodded. "Abby had talked about moving to California for years, living and working in a place where the sun shone three hundred days a year, where there was no snow and sleet and steel mill dust. It wasn't just a dream. She made plans. She was saving money and found this place in downtown L.A. where a bunch of artists stayed in an old warehouse. She said it was a dive, but cheap. A week before the accident, I loaned her the rest of the money for a bus ticket."

Jack found his voice. "She was only sixteen. She hadn't even graduated high school."

"Like that was important to her," Zoe said with a snap. "Come on, Jack. You knew Abby better than anyone. When she wasn't down, she thought she could take on the world."

"But she wanted Los Angeles?" Evie had to keep this on track.

"Yes. So after I pulled her from the riverbank, she begged me to help her escape." Zoe crossed her arms over her chest and turned to Jack. "She knew you would never let her go. God, Jack, you were her brother, father, and bodyguard all rolled into one. She said if she stayed in this place any longer, she'd die. She didn't use the word suicide, but she was talking about getting out of this place one way or another." Zoe took a deep breath. "I gave her clothes and drove her to the bus station in Pittsburgh and that night watched the bus take off."

Color crept back into Jack's face. A raging red. "You let my mother, a woman who loved you like her own child, think Abby was dead!"

"I made a promise to a friend!" Zoe's cheeks pinkened. "Abby said she loved you and your mom and would come back. She just …. she said she'd come back eventually."

"She didn't!" Jack's voice was so loud the giggling on the floor above stopped.

"I know, Jack. I think about it every day. I loved her, too, and that's why I let her go." Zoe's calm, steady gaze landed on Evie. "What do you need from me now?"

"Let's all be clear," Evie said. "At no time was a young man in the picture who liked to paint and draw and may have been stalking Abby?"

Feet padded down the steps. "Never," Zoe said softly.

Evie let out a long breath. "Which means Abby must have met Vandemere in Los Angeles."

The tight line of Jack's mouth bent at the corners, and she

could see the struggle. He wanted to say it, but he couldn't bring himself to. He was a man who didn't let go, and for more than fifteen years he'd been hefting a mountain of guilt on those broad shoulders.

She, on the other hand, tasted the words—the hope— perched on the tip of her tongue. She savored the sweetness, the fullness and richness of a time in an investigation when anything was possible. She squatted in front of him, forcing his gaze on her. "Which means..." Jack had to be the one to make the jump, but damn if she wasn't going to give him a push.

His jaw twitched. Then his lips curved into a barely there smile. "Which means my sister still may be alive."

* * *

Sunday, November 1
12:26 a.m.

"Dammit, where are you?" Evie said under her breath.

With only the soft glow from the dimmed cabin lights, Jack watched her dig through the cupboard behind the bar in his jet. After less than twelve hours in his hometown, they were flying back to Los Angeles. He ran both hands through the sides of his hair, still damp with icy rain. It was amazing how your entire life could change in a handful of hours.

Evie swatted at the hair falling across her face and muttered another curse.

He grinned, and Evie had been the catalyst, the spark, for the monumental change. "Second shelf on the right."

Bottles clanked until she finally pulled out a squat bottle of a twenty-five-year-old single-malt scotch. "How'd you know what I was looking for?"

"You strike me as a whiskey kind of girl."

"I am, but right now this girl isn't the one in need of a shot." She slammed two ice-filled tumblers on the table and poured a long stream of the amber liquid into each.

Jack lifted his glass to her. "Well done, Agent Jimenez. You have officially rocked my world."

She settled into the captain's chair across from his. The wind and rain had tangled her hair. Mud clung to her boots. She scraped a fingernail along her jeans, and two dried Cheerios popped off. "Glad to be of service."

Jack brought the glass to his mouth, the icy liquid burning a swath of warmth down his throat and into his gut. "She's alive. Until anyone can give me proof otherwise, Abby is alive."

Evie set her glass aside and reached across the aisle, curving her palm over his hand. "I'm with you all the way on this one."

He rotated his hand so her palm rested against his. Such a small hand. Dirt under two nails. But so powerful.

"I will find her," Evie said with the same conviction she used when promising to track down and stop the Angel Bomber.

This was the woman who had no qualms about defying presidential orders and who carved a spot for herself on Parker Lord's famed team. To say she was formidable was an understatement. He laced his fingers with hers. "I appreciate the sentiment, Evie, but right now you're doing what you need to be doing." With his free hand, he tapped the face of his watch. "It's November first. The bomber could strike at any time. You need to be pouring your heart into finding Carter Vandemere."

"It's a good thing I have a big heart."

Agreed. She poured it into her work and wore it on her sleeve.

She scooted to the edge of her chair, her knees brushing his. "I also have a big team of incredibly talented people, including Agent Jon MacGregor. He is the best missing and endangered person finder in the world. He's on his way to L.A. and will meet with us in the morning."

He shouldn't be surprised. Evie, who knew only one speed, was charging ahead. He brought their clasped hands to his lips and whispered against the intertwined flesh, "Thank you."

CHAPTER SIXTEEN

Sunday, November 1
6:51 a.m.

So what is this place?" Evie asked over the roar of the whisking rotors as she and Jack dashed across the roof of the Elliott Tower. On the overnight flight from southwestern Pennsylvania, they managed to snag a few hours' sleep. This morning Jack no longer looked shell-shocked and in need of a stiff drink. Far from it. Before the plane landed, he'd slipped on a fresh shirt and suit, shaved, and arranged for a helicopter to take them from LAX to the Elliott Tower. He was a man charging ahead to find his long-lost sister.

Jack slipped a hand along her waist, escorting her toward the roof access door. "A rooftop," he shouted.

The wind lifted her hair, the ends slapping her across the face as if to wake her. Oh, she was awake all right, especially the skin at the base of her spine where Jack's fingers set off hot, wild sparks. And of course her own fingers still pulsed with a heat from where his lips had touched last night. Evie grabbed his hand and jogged past the door to the other side of the roof. "I mean this."

The helicopter took off, the *rota-swoosh* and brisk wind fading.

"A garden," Jack said.

"On a roof?" She strolled to a pair of pergolas that housed wooden planters with shrubs and flowers, bronze sculptures, and stone pathways winding through thick grass and along wooden benches.

"These types of enhanced work spaces boost employee morale and give employees a convenient, aesthetically appealing place to take breaks and eat lunch. It's a bottom-line booster."

Evie dipped her fingers into water cascading along a sheet of copper into a koi pond. "It's beautiful."

Jack cast a quick glance at the fountain, then checked the face of his watch. "I guess it is."

"You don't get up here much, do you?"

"No, not on this side of the roof."

"You have beautiful gardens you don't stroll through and beautiful paintings you don't look at." She threw back her arms as if to embrace the sky. "You, Jack Elliott, are missing out on life."

A slow smile curved his lips. "That may be the case, and we can certainly discuss the deplorable situation that is my social life after we meet with Agent MacGregor."

Flinging the water from her fingers, she followed him back to the door. As she had mentioned to Jack on the flight back to L.A., Jon MacGregor, her team's endangered-and-missing-child expert, had flown in to spearhead the search for Abby Elliott. They were scheduled to meet first thing this morning.

At the door to the roof stairs, Jack dug into his pants pocket and frowned. He patted his suit coat and shirt pockets. The frown reached his eyes.

"What is it?" Evie asked.

"I left my key card in my other suit coat."

"No worries." She dug into her bag and pulled out her key card. "I got us covered."

He waved it off. "Visitor badges don't allow roof access."

She swiped anyway. The dot remained red.

Jack dug out his phone and jabbed at the face. He barked an order, then disconnected the call with another jab. "Security will have a man here in ten minutes." He jabbed at the phone again. "Let me call my maintenance team and see if they can get here quicker." His face now sported a full-fledged scowl.

"It's not that big a deal, and there are worse places to be stranded." Evie wandered back toward the garden. Back home in Albuquerque, she had a potted cactus garden one of her nephews had made her for her last birthday, the perfect type of garden for her as it could stand the heat, was small, and didn't need much tending.

"As you keep reminding me, a clock is ticking." More than a hint of irritation edged his words.

She laughed and sat on a bench near the copper-sheeted fountain. "This isn't about a clock, Jack. It's about you making a mistake."

As expected, he strode to her side. "Excuse me."

She propped her boots on the rock surrounding the koi pond. "You're the type of guy who doesn't make mistakes, and it ticks you off that you left your key card in your other coat."

He watched the fish slide in and out of light dappling the waters before shaking his head and sitting next to her. "I take it you know this because you're not the type of gal who makes mistakes."

A laugh ripped from her chest. "Hardly."

"There's no room for error in the bomb business," he argued.

"True. I don't cross wires while at work, but I'm no stranger to messes."

This time he laughed as he reached out and plucked a leaf from her hair. "So you get a little ruffled." He held up the leaf.

She plucked it from his fingers. "Oh, no. I make full-on mistakes."

"Like?"

"I think we'll need more than ten minutes."

"Like?" He kept that intense gaze on her, a man who commands attention and answers. But she didn't have anything to hide.

She cupped her hands behind her head. Where to start? "Like having an egg hunt with my nephews last Easter in my mom and dad's house and not being able to track down all the eggs. For three months the house stank until my mom unearthed the last of the rotten eggs, which six-year-old Tommy had hidden in a vent in the laundry room."

"I call that unbridled enthusiasm."

"And there was the time just last month when my teammate Finn Brannigan asserted his motorcycle was faster than my truck. Of course I had to prove him wrong, and I did until a cop pulled me over just as I got the speedometer past one hundred. Definitely a mistake, and for the record, we both got speeding tickets."

"And that's team bonding."

She could see why Jack Elliott was so successful in business. He could put a twist on anything he wished. She unlaced her hands and let them fall in her lap. Did he even remember kissing her fingers? Did he sense the jolt his lips had sent through her entire body? "And then there's last night."

A vertical line striped the center of his forehead. "What mistake did you make last night?"

She grabbed his hand and twined her fingers with his. Last night he'd been vulnerable when he admitted his hope, his bone-deep desire, that his sister was still alive. Looking at him over their clasped hands, she said point-blank, "I should have kissed you back."

Jack's eyes sparked, and she knew he remembered the touch of his lips to her fingers. His shoulders, so wide they blocked the rising sun behind him, bounced in a soft laugh. "You're fearless."

"Does that bother you?"

"No, not at all. I like strong, courageous, independent women."

"Is that the type you take to your bed?"

"I..." He tilted his head, not a single wave of hair falling out of place. "Yes, it is."

"That's good to know." Because knowns were always so much easier to work with. She was about to open her mouth, when the roof access door opened, a harried security guard rushing at them and apologizing for not getting there sooner.

For a solid five seconds, Jack stared at their clasped hands before turning to the guard. "No worries," Jack said as he pulled her to her feet and walked her toward the stairs, their fingers still intertwined.

* * *

7:22 a.m.

"Pull over," Evie said as Jack turned onto Sixth Street in the Arts District. "There's Jon." This morning her teammate Jon MacGregor could have passed for a well-turned-out artist type. Black trousers, mock black turtleneck, and a gaze so intense, Evie could feel the razor-sharpness as they pulled into the parking lot of a seafood warehouse.

After a quick greeting, Jon handed each of them a stapled batch of papers. He was all business, and despite the moment on the rooftop, she and Jack were back to the business of finding his sister. "Here's the hit list. I checked classified ads and real estate publications from fifteen years ago and came up with twelve leads of low-rent spaces targeting the artist crowd. If Abby came to this area, it's likely she stayed in one of these buildings. This morning I'm going to visit all of the warehouses and talk to property management companies and see if I can get a bead on Abby, and especially for you, Evie, I got the name of a street cop who's been working with runaways down here for twenty years."

Evie's dad had worked his entire life as a beat cop for Albuquerque PD. He never wanted to make detective, never wanted to get into vice or homicide. He wanted to be on the streets because according to him, that's where it all started and ended. Evie nudged Jack in the stomach. "I told you he was good." She skimmed through the papers. "When I'm done with the cop, I'll help you tackle buildings."

"Sounds good." The serious set of Jon's eyes softened. "And stay safe."

Damn that shooter for taking a potshot at her in the alley. First Hayden and now Jon was concerned about her. *Her.* She clapped her teammate on the shoulder. "Sure, Jon. You too."

Downtown Los Angeles wasn't a war zone, but this morning it reminded Evie of her days in Afghanistan, the days she watched the skies for incoming rounds and checked carefully around corners for things that went *boom*. The air hummed, as if charged by a low-voltage current of expectation. Today was the first of November, and the Angel Bomber could strike anywhere at any time.

On their drive to the Arts District, they'd passed three patrol cars and a patrolman on foot. In Little Tokyo a K-9 walked the streets with his handler. At this hour as dawn made way for day, the streets were empty and quiet, but soon people would gather for Sunday-morning services, coffee, and playdates at the park.

She pictured infants in swings, strollers, and their mothers' arms. *Stay safe.*

* * *

8:59 a.m.

The Paz de Cristo warehouse smelled of roasted turkey and unwashed bodies. Evie and Jack wound their way through row after row of picnic tables and benches to light spilling from a door leading to an industrial kitchen.

A woman with plastic gloves and a potato peeler in her hand waved them in. "Excellent! So glad you're here. A youth group from Pasadena was supposed to help, but their bus broke down on the One-Ten Freeway."

Evie took out her shield. "We're looking for Officer Alfred Nunez? We were told he volunteers here every Sunday." Paz de Cristo was one of downtown's many outreach programs that served the hungry and homeless.

"Yep. Great guy. He's getting the last tier of the wedding

cake." The woman pointed her potato peeler at a two-tiered cake on the counter with red roses and gold piping. "He should be back in a few minutes."

Jack put on a pair of gloves and picked up a potato peeler and began to peel potatoes. Evie wasn't surprised. He was a man most comfortable at work. And she liked that about him.

"Someone getting married?" Evie motioned to the wedding cake.

"The couple who bought the cake was supposed to get married yesterday, but the bride called it off right before she walked down the aisle," the kitchen manager said. "Literally. She was watching her two little flower girls toss petals as they made their way toward the altar and realized she didn't want to have kids with the man waiting at the end of the aisle for her. Heartbreaking for everyone, but I'm grateful they thought of us. The cake will easily feed two hundred of our guests."

As Jack started on his second potato, Officer Nunez, a twenty-year veteran of the streets of downtown L.A., walked in with more wedding cake. "You from Captain Ricci's team?"

Evie nodded. "Thanks for meeting with us."

"Hope I can be of help. This guy's messing with my streets, and I want him stopped." He set the cake on the counter. "What can I do?"

Evie took Abby Elliott's junior-year school photo from her bag. "Do you recognize this girl?"

Officer Nunez rubbed at the stubble on his jaw. "She's a sweet-looking young woman but sad."

"At the time this picture was taken she was very sad," Jack said.

"She would have landed in the downtown area about fifteen years ago," Evie added. "She was tall, about five-ten and thin. She was an—"

"—artist," Officer Nunez said with a snap of his fingers. "Yeah, I remember her. She was a painter. Used to sit outside on sunny days and paint. Luz was her name."

A spike of heat ran up Evie's back. "That's Spanish for light. Have you seen her recently?"

Officer Nunez shook his head. "Not for years. She was one of the more talented artists and was working regularly down at one of the beaches. I figured things must have taken off for her and she got to a better place."

A place of light and laughter, Evie prayed. "But she lived down here?"

"Yep, the Twin Citrus building off Santa Fe. It was one of those places with cheap rent, but a developer came in a few years ago and turned it into fancy lofts. No street kids hanging out there these days."

"Did the girl you knew as Luz have any friends?" Evie asked.

"She was well-liked, always laughing, the kind of person who drew others to her."

"Any boyfriend?"

"Not that I remember, but I only knew her for that one summer."

"Do you remember any young males, between the ages of fifteen and twenty, who may have been interested in her or maybe who she sat for as a model? A loner type. Also an artist who may have a bit of a darker side."

"Nothing comes to mind."

Evie handed him her card. "If you think of something, let me know."

Officer Nunez handed the photo back to Evie and tilted his chin at Jack who'd peeled the potato down to a stub. "Did you know her?"

"She was my sister." Jack's throat convulsed. "I mean, is."

It was heartbreaking to watch Jack's face. She couldn't imagine being in his place, thinking one of her brothers long-dead but then having a sliver of hope lodge in her heart.

Officer Nunez must have had a lurch in his own heart. He took off his apron and gloves. "You know, I can't help you find Luz, but maybe I can help you find a piece of her."

The street cop took them to the Twin Citrus Lofts, which were five stories of half-million-dollar flats. "The developer spruced up the building, but he also wanted to stay true to this place's roots." Officer Nunez patted the smooth, white trunk of an orange tree. "He put the citrus trees out front to commemorate this place's origins as a citrus-packing plant, and in a nod to the artists who once lived here, he maintained the original stairwell. Kind of cool. Even for an art-dud like me."

The on-site property manager let them in and showed them the stairwell. Evie stood on the bottom floor and looked up, a crazy kaleidoscope of color and shapes stretching above her. On the bottom floor were dozens of art pieces: a mural of the downtown skyline, a giant blue eyeball made with spray paint, and portraits in every shade of the rainbow.

As they walked up the stairwell, Jack searched for Abby's artwork, squatting low to the ground and standing on tiptoe. Evie looked for any art that spoke killer because it was possible this was the place Jack's sister met Carter Vandemere. There were plenty of twisted faces, hopeless faces, lost and hurting faces, but none filled with terror that marked Vandemere's work.

On the fifth floor, Jack finally grew still. He stood in front of a chest-high landscape with a group of sea turtles swimming in a crystal-blue lagoon.

"It's one of hers." Jack traced the tiny signature at the bottom, *Abby*, a smiling sun tucked in the loop of the *Y*, his finger tentative, as if not sure if the image existed or his eyes were playing tricks on him.

Evie made no attempt to rush him. A clock was ticking, but he needed this time to remember what was and what could be. He pressed his hand into that sun, color and a smile flooding his face. "She's alive."

She would never argue otherwise. As an Apostle, she couldn't. Like Jon MacGregor, she would need proof positive of death before she'd ever give up hope that Abby Elliott was alive and painting in a place filled with sun.

When Jack finally turned away, he got as far as the adjacent wall where he stopped again, this time before a portrait of a girl with a cat in her arms. The entire thing was done in black and white and oddly somber. It had a powerful pull, and Evie had stood before the image a good ten minutes before dragging herself away.

"One of Abby's from her darker days?" Evie asked.

Jack shook his head. "She didn't paint on her dark days, but I've seen something like this before."

"At one of the downtown galleries?"

He took a step back, the lines around his mouth disappearing with realization. "No, it was at the Abby Foundation."

"A piece from one of your artists in residence?"

"No, but someone who wanted to be. The foundation receives about five hundred grant applications every year, and once the selection committee narrows the applicant pool down to forty or fifty artists, I see the portfolios."

"Are you a judge?"

Jack laughed. "No, I'm a control freak, as you would say. I want to be kept abreast of who we're supporting." He tapped his finger on the cat's forehead. "I remember something very similar to this. Talented artist, but he didn't make the cut."

Evie searched for a signature, but another artist who'd created a mural of a parking lot with spray paint had smudged the bottom of the girl and cat painting. "So, it's possible this artist knew Abby."

"And the good news for us is that we have contact information on all Abby grant applicants."

* * *

11:07 a.m.

On the second floor of the Abby Foundation, Jack hauled a storage box from the archive room and set it at Evie's feet. Eight more followed. "There we go. Every grant application the foundation has received in the past five years." He slapped the top of a box, a flurry of dust rising about them. "And every application includes a portfolio and written application, including an address and phone number." Which could be key in finding an artist who may have known his sister.

Evie slipped off a lid and thumbed through the folders. "You guys ever hear of computers? Amazing little things. So good at storing and organizing information."

Jack sat on the floor next to her. The storeroom was warm and stuffy, and he'd discarded his jacket and rolled up his shirtsleeves. "All of our applicants are required to send hard copies of portfolio pieces so we get a true representation of their work. Digital files, by the nature of computer screens, don't."

Evie's hands stilled on the files.

"What?" Jack asked.

"Your sleeves."

"What about them?"

"You rolled them up."

"And this is significant?"

Her teeth dug into her bottom lip as she studied him. It was the same look she gave the bits of bomb debris. "It's different. You're different." With no further explanation, she dug back into the file folders. Dust floated around them. Already Evie wore a smudge of gray on her forehead and another on her right cheek. Because she was a woman not afraid to get dirty or ask tough questions, like about the women he took to his bed, who were strong, independent, and wildly successful in their chosen fields. Evie to a *T*.

"Here we go," Evie said as she pulled out a folder thirty minutes later. "Here's another sad girl in black and white, but this time she has a bird clutched in her hands."

Jack peeked over her shoulder; her hair, which smelled of berries, tickled his nose. "I'd say that's the same artist. What's the name?"

Evie flipped to the application page and sucked in a breath. "Vandemere, Carter." She flipped through the rest of the portfolio. "But how could that be? These aren't as graphic as the images on his online portfolio."

Jack swung his body so he sat next to her, his shoulder pressing into hers. He could feel the tremor. Was it him, her? "Work like his online art would have no chance in getting a grant from the Abby Foundation."

"But these definitely have an edge." She paused at a portrait of a woman leaving bloody footprints in a garden."

Jack dug through the papers and pulled out the first page of the application. The fist clenching his heart let up. "Here's his address. It's in a low-rent area off Seventh."

Next to him Evie had once again grown still.

"Did you hear me, Evie?" He gave the paper a victorious shake. "We have his address. Right here."

Slowly, she raised the final page of the application package, which included notes from the applicant jury and a large red *REJECTED* stamp. "Look at the date," her voice wavered.

"August eighth of last year," Jack said, his forehead scrunching into a series of sharp folds. "Is it significant?"

"That's exactly one year from the first bombing." Evie's hand shook, the paper rustling. "This rejection—from the Abby Foundation, from *you*—was the seminal event that tripped his wire and pushed him over the edge."

Jack reached for his phone.

"Who are you calling?"

"Ricci. We need to get a team out to this address. We've got him." Then they would get Abby.

Evie took the phone from his hand and slipped it into his shirt pocket. "*We* are not doing anything. Jack, this rejection date is one more link between you and the bomber, and I sure as hell am not going to take you to his front door. I want you back in your office and behind your desk where I know you'll be safe."

CHAPTER SEVENTEEN

Sunday, November 1
1:37 p.m.

The warehouse building Carter Vandemere listed as his residence sported seven boarded-up windows, four chunks of missing awning, and one stray pug peeing on the cracked front steps.

They'd been watching the building, which had initially been used as a tire warehouse, for the past two hours. Except for the peeing pug, Evie had seen no signs of life.

Cho was on the roof next door, and a half dozen squad cars were posted within the square block. Jack was tucked securely in his office. Evie knew because she'd deposited him on the marble doorstep and watched him walk through the etched glass doors. When it came to these bombings, everything kept coming back to Jack: the *Beauty Through the Ages* collection, the connection to his sister, and now the date of the first bombing coinciding with the day Vandemere was rejected by the Abby Foundation.

Evie flexed her fingers. "It's time."

Ricci settled mirrored sunglasses in place, looking even more Hollywood than usual. Evie scrubbed the cuff of her denim jacket on the grimy window of the bottom floor. The single vast room was empty but for a pair of broken chairs, a pile of sun-rotted tires, and stacks of what looked like empty meat and cheese tray holders.

Ricci pointed to the flight of stairs crisscrossing the back of the building. On the top floor they found an entrance to four apartments. She checked for pressure-sensitive boards, trip wires, and packets of irritants. None. She unholstered her Glock and inched toward the door with a handwritten number three.

Rap, rap, rap.

Refrigerated trucks at the Asian foods warehouse across the street hummed.

Rap, rap, rap.

Blades of light slipped through the barred window at the far end of the hall. A lock clicked. Her pulse spiked. The door opened a crack. An eye blinked.

She held up her shield. "Agent Evie Jimenez, FB—"

The door slammed. Something on the other side crashed.

"Got us a runner!" Evie took two steps back. Ricci opened the door as far as the chain would allow. She landed a kick square on the chain. A chunk of door frame groaned and splintered.

They rushed in, leading with their firearms. A bare white ass disappeared down a hall. She hurdled over an upended table and pounded down the hall and into a small bathroom where she found him trying to climb out the window.

"I am packing a gun, and you are not. My gun is pointed at your lily-white ass. What I do with my gun and how it affects your ass are up to you."

* * *

1:40 p.m.

Evie flicked the driver's license onto the table. Edward Lagos. California resident. Male. Age twenty-five. The guy was unmarried, lived alone, and had some serious antisocial tendencies. He hadn't once looked her in the eye.

"So why'd you run?" Evie asked.

"I thought my landlord sent you. I'm two months behind on rent."

"Since when do sworn agents of the federal government go door to door to collect rent?" She leaned her shoulder against a metal shelving unit covered in flowering plants.

"Give me a break," Lagos said. "You woke me after forty-eight straight hours of work."

And from the looks of this place, Lagos didn't work with circuit boards, switches, reels of wire, batteries, or propane cylinders. Not a whiff of PVC glue, sulfur, or gunpowder. The man liked *flowers*.

She pushed away from the sugary plants and walked to a three-foot canvas perched on an easel in the center of the room. "You don't have anything with, say, people in it?"

"I don't do people."

"Nothing with beautiful women?"

"I prefer the beauty of botanicals."

Evie poked at the canvases behind the sofa and stacked on the kitchen table. She had to try. "Do you ever use a pseudonym?"

"No."

She placed the knuckles of her fists on either side of the chair he was sitting in and looked him in the eye. "Ever hear of Carter Vandemere?"

One twitch. One blink of an eye. That's all she needed to nail this guy. Her palms itched.

His face remained as flat and soft as the flowers on his canvases. "No."

She pushed off and went back to the window. If this guy was a bomber, she was a beauty queen contestant.

"How long have you lived here, Mr. Lagos?" Ricci asked.

"Skylar. My name is Skylar Lake, and I moved in six months ago."

"Did you know the former occupant?"

"No. He was long gone by the time I got here. Landlord kicked him out. Even sold off a bunch of his stuff." He frowned at Evie. "That's why I was worried. The guy who owns this place is a money-grubbing capitalist pig."

After wrapping up the interview with the flower guy, Evie and Ricci headed down the steps to hunt down the landlord who might have references, next of kin, or something on Carter Vandemere. It was like those dot-to-dot puzzles her nephews worked. One dot led to another. She just had to keep chasing damn dots.

On the bottom floor of Lagos's apartment building, Evie spotted movement at the far end of the alley. She spun on her boot heel.

Ricci raised an eyebrow. "You want to check it out?"

A matted black cat slipped out from behind a garbage bin, and she shook her head. "Let's go talk to a money-grubbing capitalist pig."

* * *

3:09 p.m.

James Horvath III was the owner of Jimmy Ho's Wash & Go coin-operated car washes. In addition to the car washes, he owned three rental properties, including the old warehouse building Carter Vandemere had listed as his residence on his Abby Foundation grant application.

They found the self-professed king of car washes in a cinder-block office behind the original Wash & Go in East L.A. off Whittier Boulevard. For a guy who made his living with soap and water, Jimmy Ho was a dirt bag. He wore enough gold chains around his neck to pay for two nephews' orthodontics.

"Yep, that's my place," Jimmy Ho said when Evie asked him about the warehouse property off Sixth Street. "Old pile of shit, but you wanna know something? There are plenty of people who want to rent old piles of shit. Had a film production company last month that rented the bottom floor for two weeks. Made some serious green. Green's everywhere, even in old piles of shit."

"Carter Vandemere," Evie said. "What can you tell us about your renter named Carter Vandemere? He was an artist."

"Don't remember the name, but those artsy-fartsy types, some of 'em just go by initials. Had a renter named *Z* who tried to pay his rent with an original piece of *art*. Piece of shit is what I called it, and not the kind that leads to green."

"Carter Vandemere," Evie said again. This guy was starting to piss her off.

Jimmy Ho rolled his chair across the filthy floor to a row of metal file cabinets on the back wall. "What property did you say again?"

"Warehouse off Sixth. Loft number three."

She stretched her fingers. Damn, Vandemere was so close she could picture her fingers wrapping around his neck.

The landlord poked through a file drawer and eventually took out a single piece of paper. "Yep. Carter Vandemere. Deadbeat low-life. Lived there seven months total. Paid the first four months. All on time. All in cash." He pounded a fist to his chest two times. "Love those renters. But looks like the guy turned into a real slacker. Got three months behind. Gave him the boot last December."

"The current renter says you sold off some of Vandemere's stuff."

Jimmy Ho squirmed. As he should. There were very clear laws about how and when to sell off goods tenants left behind.

"Vandemere did this." With her phone, Evie showed him a picture of the third bombing victim's right foot. "And this." A snapshot of the first victim's right thumb. "And this." A jogger who got too close to the second bomb and had her right leg severed at the knee.

Jimmy Ho blanched, a nice creamy white tinged with green. "Okay. Okay." He pushed back the phone. "At the beginning of last December, I phoned Vandemere and told him to pay up or he'd be on the street. He told me he'd have the money that evening. I popped over to the warehouse in the afternoon 'cause I know these deadbeats. They think they're smart, but they're the ones who don't have nothing, no brains, no property, no pot to piss in. So I get there around noon and find him loading up his car."

"What kind of car?"

"Hell if I know." The landlord shrugged. "Then he takes off."

"Where was he going? Was he alone?"

"I have no idea, 'cause by that time, I was seeing red." Jimmy held up both hands. "Hey, stop looking at me like that. I'm not the criminal here."

"Any forwarding address?" Evie asked. "List of references?"

"I ain't running no Ritz-Carlton. People come and go, and they leave enough money behind to keep everything running."

"What did Vandemere look like?" Ricci asked with the same level of irritation nipping at the back of her neck. "Race? Big guy? Little guy? Old? Young?"

The landlord picked at his teeth with the sharp tip of a letter opener. "Is there any kind of reward money involved?"

Evie's hand shot out, her wrist slamming into Jimmy Ho's hand. The letter opener flew across the room and clanked into the file cabinet. "Think harder, Mr. Horvath. You met Carter Vandemere at least once. What did your renter look like?"

Jimmy dipped his head as if deep in thought, then shrugged. "Green, Agent Jimenez." He smiled, a gold tooth on the side of his mouth glinting in the dirty light. "All I saw was green."

On the way to their cars, Ricci said, "Man, that guy is slime."

Evie ran her hands along the arms of her jacket and shimmied, trying to shake off the ick. "Yeah, and we just rolled around with him."

"The pisser is, the guy genuinely doesn't remember a thing about Vandemere."

"Yeah, he's too blinded by all his shiny riches."

They reached Ricci's car. "I'm going back to the warehouse lofts. I'll talk to the other renters and see if we can get a visual ID. You want to come?"

Evie rapped the top of his car. "I'll be there later."

After Ricci left, she turned in a slow circle. "My nephews love this game. I'll play." She put her hands to her mouth and called, "I spy with my little eye...Jack."

CHAPTER EIGHTEEN

Sunday, November 1
3:09 p.m.

How'd you know?" Jack stepped out from behind a car wash bay near Jimmy Ho's Wash & Go corporate office.

Evie stood with her arms crossed, her boot tapping the cracked concrete. "I smelled you."

He arched an eyebrow and picked his way through potholes to where she stood near her little red Beetle. The boot kept up a steady beat, like a ticking bomb ready to explode. Still, he walked toward her. He'd been following her all day, and he was surprised it took her this long to call him out.

"I'm serious," she said. "During a deployment in Afghanistan, I was at the site of a roadside bomb detonation. I didn't have any ear protection and suffered irreversible hearing loss in my right ear. The interesting thing is when one of your senses starts to crap out, others get better. I have a wonky right ear, but I have eyes like an eagle and"—

she tapped the side of her nose—"a nose like a bloodhound. But enough about me. You're supposed to be in your office. Dammit, Jack, you don't belong here. This man we're hunting isn't just dangerous. He's deadly."

"All the more reason for me to help."

Evie's lips pinched. "I get it. This is about Abby. You want to find this guy to find your sister. And I get the whole guilt thing and the control thing. But I also know you're a really smart man, Jack, so what I don't get is why you are acting like an idiot!"

Jack scrubbed a hand across his jaw. "The woman who deals with bombs wants to know what makes me tick?" He hadn't even tried to go to his office when she dropped him off at the Elliott Tower this morning. The last thing on his mind was business. "Fine. Abby's part of it. So's the guilt and control, and like you, I want to save the baby and the woman and anyone else within range of that bomb. But the biggest part is I know I can make a difference."

"You already have, Jack."

"I can do more. I know his home turf. I know the art world he's skirting, and like you, I know this guy has a beef with me."

He watched the worry slide across her face. Worry for him. Worry for an unknown woman and child. Worry for a city gripped by terror. She was the kind of law enforcer who cared for everyone she was charged with protecting. "Eventually his path and mine are going to cross, and this entire city will be better off if you are at my side. You, more than anyone, know how to defuse this guy." He kept his words calm even though he was simmering inside. "So if you think I'll be of more use in my office making deals with Japan and Seattle, I'll go back to the office. If your gut tells you I won't be of use, send me away."

Evie jammed her hair from her face, her fingers tangling in the mass of curls. She pressed her fingers into her skull as if massaging away an ache. Seconds ticked. The heat and steam in the center of his chest expanded. She was smart. The best. That's why he brought her on board.

At last Evie's hands dropped to her sides. "Here's the deal, Jack. I am the CEO and chairman of this investigation, and you"—she flicked her fingers at his handkerchief—"can be my chauffeur."

"Your chauffeur?"

"Can't handle the job?"

He almost laughed. He'd made the power play, and she'd come at him with a counteroffer. She was letting him in on the investigation but with a very limited and subservient role. Parker was right, Evie was damn good. He took the keys to her Beetle. "Where would you like to go, Agent Jimenez?"

"Let's head back to Vandemere's former loft. I want to talk with neighbors and nearby merchants. I want to see if anyone remembers him." Evie made her way to the passenger side door and dipped her head toward the door handle.

Jack let out a soft laugh, bowed his head, and reached for the door.

Just as she ducked in, Jimmy Ho, his gold chains jangling around his neck, came running out of his office.

"Have a change of heart?" Evie asked.

"After your pictures, Agent Jimenez, I almost had to change my pants," Jimmy Ho said. "Listen, that bomber guy's bad news, bad for business, and just plain bad. So I did some digging and got a name for you. When I put the press on Vandemere to pay back rent, one of his buddies forked over the rent payment. Here's a copy of the bank deposit with the check."

Evie snatched it out of the landlord's hand. "Rene Masson of the Masson Gallery in Venice. The notation reads: *Advance on Fall Show.*"

* * *

5:01 p.m.

Jack unfolded his body from the front seat of Evie's Beetle and straightened his suit jacket. "Next time there's a congressional vote to increase the FBI's budget, remind me to tell my representative to vote yes."

Evie dug a handful of coins out of the front pocket of her jeans. "The car suits me and my budget just fine."

He cocked his head looking from her to the red car. They really were a good fit. "Tiny and attitudinal."

She plinked the coins in the parking meter in the lot just off Venice Beach. "You have a problem with tiny and attitudinal?"

Right now Jack wasn't having a problem with much of anything. They were closing in on Carter Vandemere, which brought him one step closer to Abby. That tiny bit of hope that had sparked to life when he learned his sister hadn't died in the river fifteen years ago had turned into a glowing ember, fanned by Evie's all-out push to find the bomber. "Not at all."

Locking the car, they hurried down the boardwalk to a shop with a black awning and a giant skull and crossbones painted on the window. A bear of a man with a glassy expression and a bird's talon tattooed across his face stood in the doorway.

Jack frowned. "Are you sure this is the right place?"

"This is the address on the check of the art gallery dealer who paid Vandemere's back rent," Evie said.

"Why would Vandemere have an art show at a tattoo shop?"

"Vandemere's art is edgy, and this place has edge written all over it."

"This place has already leaped off the edge," Jack said under his breath as Evie pulled open the door and charged into the shop that smelled of green soap and cigarette smoke from the last millennium.

"I'm looking for Rene Masson," she told the tattoo artist at the closest workstation who was outlining a pinup girl on a customer's biceps.

"The pretty lady wants a dude named Masson," he called over his shoulder. "Anyone here named Masson?"

"I'm Masson," a skinny man with braids hanging to his waist said from another workstation.

Another tattoo artist, who looked like his mild-mannered accounting manager, said, "I'm Masson."

"They're fucking liars." The man getting the pinup tattoo on his biceps winked at Evie. "I'm Masson. Wanna spend some alone time together?"

Jack's spine stiffened notch by notch, but Evie wasn't fazed. She walked up to the man in the second workstation and flashed her badge. "Does Rene Masson work here?" She used her I'm-a-busy-don't-take-no-bullshit-FBI-agent voice, which was exactly what she was at this moment.

The chuckling died down, and the artist in the first station asked, "He a freelance inker?"

"Not sure. He's involved in the art community down here."

The tattoo artist turned back to the giant boobs. "Ask Tink. He's the owner. He's working a full body tat in the back."

In a small room off the back, they found a man who could

moonlight as a Mac truck. He had wide shoulders and metal plates in his head that looked like the grille of a truck. On his right arm was a winged Pixie.

"You must be Tink," Evie said.

The man sniffed the air. "You must be pork."

"Chorizo," Evie said.

The skin around the Mac grille wrinkled.

"I got a helluva kick," Evie explained.

Tink's chest rumbled, like an engine warming up. "Okay, I'll bite. What do you want, Officer Chorizo?"

"Agent Chorizo." She flashed her shield, then tilted her head at the naked woman. "Would you like to do this in private?"

Tink lifted the needle from the woman's backside where he was adding green pigment to rows of dragon scales inked across her right butt cheek. "Nessa won't mind, will you?"

"Just don't make him color outside the lines," she said with a grin.

"I'm looking for a man named Rene Masson. He could be an art gallery owner or broker. This is his last known address."

"Masson ain't here no more, and he wasn't into skin art."

"You know him?"

"Never met him personally, but I heard of him. He rented this space up until last year."

"Do you know where I can find him?"

"Six feet under."

Jack saw more than heard the groan rattling around Evie's chest and over her downturned lips. "What happened?"

"Shot last year in a robbery attempt. Sad, but it's part of doing business down here."

"Did Masson leave behind any office materials?" Jack asked. If Vandemere had a show scheduled in Masson's gallery, there had to be a record of it. "Office files or even items like boxes of promotional material?"

"Nope. By the time I moved in, the place had been emptied."

They needed to find Masson's next of kin. Best-case scenario, they would have his work files in storage somewhere, which would include items like artist profiles and photos. A photo of Vandemere would be a huge break at this point in the case. He could see Evie pinning that photo to the wall in her temporary office at LAPD where she'd started a gallery of sorts.

After she finished interviewing Tink, Evie hovered at the table. The dragon, outlined and partially colored, covered two-thirds of the woman's body, its chest rising and falling with the woman's as if it were a living, breathing beast.

"Does it hurt?" Evie asked.

"Only when the needle touches skin." Nessa let loose a laugh, and the dragon scales rippled, catching light and taking on an iridescent glow. Evie lingered, as if mesmerized by the dragon.

Once outside the shop Jack arched an eyebrow at her. "You're not thinking of getting a full-size body tattoo, are you?"

Evie shuddered. "I don't need to make that kind of statement."

"Statement?"

"Tattoos are very much like bombs in that respect, a way of shouting to the world, 'Look at me and see my message!'"

True. Someone like Evie made a loud enough statement without any added adornment. She was strong, powerful, and full of so much light and life. Abby would have loved to have painted her.

Side by side, they headed back to the public parking lot near the beach. This time of evening street artists were packing up tables full of ragdolls made of bandannas and seascapes painted on shells the size of his palm.

"If you must know," she said, "I always thought I'd like to have a beaded chain tattooed around my ankle. Each bead would include the initials of each of my nephews. I figure if I'm going to make a statement, it needs to be something I will never, ever waver on. Although, the rate my brothers are going, I might need a double strand."

When they reached the parking lot, Evie paused to stare at the dipping sun setting the water on fire, the sand glistening like millions of sugar crystals.

"Beautiful, isn't it?" she said. "Doesn't it make you want to kick off your shoes and dance?"

"I don't dance." Even at the galas and fund-raisers he attended on a monthly basis, he never took to the dance floor. He was too busy doing business.

Evie raised her face to the fire-streaked sky. "Maybe you should."

"Maybe I shouldn't." He unlocked the car door. And right now, his business was Carter Vandemere. "A serial bomber is on the loose."

"Exactly. When things are dark and ugly, the world needs a little beauty." She plopped down onto the hood of her rental car and lifted her boot. "It'll be quicker if you help. Easiest way is to straddle the boot and pull."

For a moment he stood stock-still in the middle of the sidewalk. The world needed beauty, and Evie was standing before him, red cowboy boot extended. He shook his head. How could he turn away from that?

Facing away from her, he straddled her calf and cupped her boot heel, the soft leather pressing against his thighs. A surge of blood rushed to his midsection. How long had it been since he'd been with a woman? A few months? Closer to a half year? The German deal had sidetracked him. He was getting turned on by a red cowboy boot.

Evie's other boot touched his ass. "I'll push. You pull."

Or he could just stand here fantasizing about her wearing only red leather cowboy boots. He pulled, and the boot slid off. He straddled her other foot. This time her bare foot sank into his ass as she pushed off. He stood, holding a boot in each hand.

She peeled off her socks and dug her toes into the sand, making a soft little humming sound at the back of her throat. She didn't even realize how sexy she was, her bare toes burrowing into the beach. "Now you," she said.

Who was he to argue? This week he was the chauffeur. He slipped out of his oxfords and socks.

She grabbed his hand and dragged him to the sand. "Well?" she asked. "How does it feel?"

"Like warm sand."

A growl erupted in her throat. "Close your eyes."

He'd rather watch her, her face lit by the sun's last grasp on the sky.

"You are such a stick in the mud." She stood on tiptoe and reached up, her palm sliding his eyelids closed.

"Does Parker know you act this way in the middle of an investigation?"

"Shut up and keep your eyes closed."

This was borderline ridiculous, standing on a beach and playing in the sand when his city, his past, and his future had been upended by a serial bomber. But Evie, whose job right now was catching a serial bomber, deemed right now was the perfect time to dig her toes into the sand. Crazy.

"Now what do you feel?" Evie asked.

"Sand between my toes. Warm sand."

Next to him Evie made a soft grumbling noise. Sand rained gently on the tops of his feet. "Now what do you feel?"

This woman wasn't going to let up. With a deep breath, he tilted his head back and let the thoughts drain from his mind. No bomber. No destruction. No work. No digging into his past. No worrying about the future. The only thing that existed was this moment with a barefoot woman on the beach. Again, a shower of powdery sand fell on his feet. "I feel rain without water. Tiny bits of sky falling on my feet."

"Beautiful!" A hand slipped into his and led him across the sand, the warm granules growing cool. "Now what?" A soft hitch, one of wondrous expectation, edged her words.

"I'm walking through frosty sugar."

"And what do you hear?"

He rolled his head along his shoulders. "Waves. Whispering to one another. Telling secrets."

She grew silent, and he opened his eyes. She stood next to him, her gaze transfixed on the ocean set afire by the setting sun. At last she inched up on her toes and landed a kiss on his lips, a hot and fleeting spark. "Thank you."

He was about to ask for what, when he remembered what she'd said. When one of your senses falters, the others take over. She couldn't hear the soft sounds, the hush-hush whisper of the ocean that he and most other people took for granted.

CHAPTER NINETEEN

Sunday, November 1
6:44 p.m.

Here are the photos you requested, Agent Jimenez, and as soon as Rene Masson's brother calls, I'll patch him through."

"Thank you." Evie took the three massive binders from the LAPD clerk who worked the records section of the Pacific Community substation that served Venice. She handed them to Jack. "You know, I could really get used to having an extra set of hands around, Mr. Chauffeur."

Jack set the folders on the table and held out a chair for her. "Anything else?"

"A second set of eyes?" She slid one of the binders his way.

Together they searched through hundreds of pages of records in the investigation of Rene Masson's murder following a B&E last year: witness statements, diagrams, reports from latent, and hundreds of crime scene pics.

"What exactly did the shooter steal?" Jack asked.

Evie flipped through the property report. "Looks like he busted into the petty cash drawer and emptied it. According to Masson's records, he kept about three hundred dollars in there."

"Interesting that he'd take the petty cash but leave behind an eight-thousand-dollar Rolex." Jack pointed to the watch on the victim's right wrist.

Evie looked at the timepiece. A nice work of art in gold and diamonds. "So the shooter's deadly *and* dumb."

Thumbing through the final binder, Evie studied Masson's autopsy pictures. Single GSW to the back of the head. Smart shot. Experienced shooter. No defense wounds. Multiple contusions to the face upon impact with the floor. Upper right shoulder—

"Oh shit," she said on a rush of air.

Jack snapped his gaze from the binder.

She pointed to a red patch of raw flesh on Masson's shoulder. A perfect square, as if someone had taken an X-Acto knife and stripped away a two-inch piece of skin.

"Hey, Campo," she called out to the homicide detective investigating Masson's murder. "We need a bit of illumination. What's up with Masson's shoulder?"

"Yeah, we wondered about that," Campo said. "We thought maybe he had some medical work done, but we checked and didn't find anything."

"Could it be gang related?" Evie asked. She was about to make a big jump, and she needed debris cleared. "I know some initiation rites for new members include bringing home proof from victims."

"Haven't seen any of that around here."

"But I've seen it before," Jack said.

So had Evie. A ripple of gooseflesh cascaded over her

body. In the pages of pictures she viewed every night before bed: "Lisa Franco, the bomber's third victim, had a patch of skin like this taken from her right shoulder. These things are most likely souvenirs, little mementos for the killer to take out at his leisure and enjoy. Helps him reminisce and remember the good times."

The homicide detective took a seat at the table. "You're thinking your bomber killed my vic? What's his motivation?"

Her mind whirred through all the things she knew about Vandemere. "Masson agreed to sponsor an art show for Vandemere but didn't get many, if any, interested buyers. The gallery owner, needing his valuable real estate, gave Vandemere the boot."

"A rejection," Jack said. "We're starting to see a pattern."

"Exactly, and I'm beginning to think Vandemere had a series of rejections that sent him over the edge."

Campo put both hands behind his neck and squeezed. "You just flipped my investigation on its ass."

"Mine, too." Because Vandemere's canvas just got bigger. "He's not afraid to kill beyond his art and with weapons other than bombs."

* * *

9:54 p.m.

"Take a right and pull up to the Mexican food place," Evie said.

"Interesting choice," Jack said. Everything about Evie was interesting. That knot of hair. Her bare feet in the sand. Where she chose to eat a late-night dinner.

"I like spicy food," she said. "Reminds me of home."

Jack squeezed out of her rental and rested his hands on the hood. "And you just happened to pick the restaurant where Lisa Franco, the Angel Bomber's last victim, worked as a waitress?"

"It's a business dinner. We'll eat, and I'll get a little business done on the side."

A woman after his own heart.

Inside the restaurant, they sat at a corner booth where Evie had a full view of the restaurant. One by one she studied the staff members and tables full of customers. He picked up a chip and dabbed it into a bowl of salsa with bright orange chunks.

"Wait!" Evie grabbed his hand. "That one has habaneros in it." She dipped her chip into the salsa and bit. "Definitely habaneros. You might want to try that one." She pointed to the other small bowl with pale green chiles.

Jack dipped his chip in the habanero salsa and took a bite. "Not bad."

She stared, then reached across the table and tapped his forehead. "Not a drop of sweat. You've been full of surprises today. First poetry on the beach and now spicy salsa. What else are you hiding under that fancy suit?" Her gaze was bold.

He'd love to face Evie in a boardroom. And a bedroom. He scooped up another mound of salsa. He blamed that random thought on her boots against his ass, not to mention the kiss she'd landed on his lips. "You know about chiles?"

Evie took another chip and dipped. "I grew up in New Mexico surrounded by chiles and horses."

"You ride?"

"Some. My folks couldn't afford a horse, so I worked out a deal with a woman who owned a stable in our neighborhood. The deal involved a shovel, mountains of horse crap, and a sweet little old appaloosa named Noggin."

"So the boots are legit?"

Evie's chip paused above the salsa bowl. "'Scuse me?"

"The boots, jacket, and jeans, they're not part of some act to position you in a more authoritative role with the people you work with on both sides of the law."

"An act?" She laughed. "As a girl I never played dress-up. For better or for worse, I'm the real deal, Jack. What you see is what you get."

* * *

11:25 p.m.

Evie held true to her word and did business through much of dinner. She questioned the bartender, two waitresses, and the busboy who'd worked with Lisa Franco the night she disappeared. No one reported noticing anything unusual or disconcerting about Lisa or any of the patrons that night. A good thing for her, her dinner companion didn't seem to mind. She loved that Jack wasn't intimidated by her work.

After dinner, the waiter brought them the check, and when he placed it in front of Jack, Evie tried to snag it.

Jack's fingers tightened around the paper. "I'll take care of it."

"I invited you to dinner. I will take care of it."

Jack didn't move, as if he didn't understand the language she spoke. She didn't budge. At last he let go of the check. "Thank you."

She knew this was some kind of power play. Being with Jack was like being in a boxing match. Jabbing and ducking and occasionally touching. Like that moment on the beach when she'd risen to her toes and kissed him. The action had been spontaneous, surprising even her, but she didn't regret it. She was attracted to powerful things, and this man was all about power.

They waited at the table until the busy manager finally had a moment to talk.

"I don't remember anyone but regulars that night," the manager said. "Like I told the police, I don't remember anyone acting odd or particularly interested in Lisa."

"What time did she leave?" Evie asked.

"She closed the place. So it was probably around eleven thirty or so."

"Did she leave alone?"

"I walked with her. We keep the street parking for customers, so we went to the parking lot on the corner."

"You escorted her to her car?"

"Not that night. Lisa stopped to talk with the cat girl."

"Cat girl?"

"Young homeless woman who has a bunch of cats. Lisa had a soft spot for the street kid and used to take her and the cats leftover fish tacos."

Outside Jack didn't question where they were going or why they didn't take her car. Her boots needed to be on the street. The night was crisp and cool. Jack's suit still looked like it came straight from a magazine ad. He was clearly out of place among the street people, but as she was finding out, he had his uses. Like straddling her leg and slipping off her boot. She could still feel the taut muscles of his thighs.

She found a quartet of men sitting on milk crates in an alley. "We're looking for the cat girl," Evie said.

"Do I got four-one-one written on my forehead?" one of the men quipped.

Evie took out her shield. She had to try. "Would you care to rethink your answer?"

Another man scratched the beanie slung low over his

forehead. "Wasn't she over at the dining hall off Second tonight?"

"Nah, that was Bat Man. I last saw Cat Girl at the hot dog stand in Gotham City."

The men snickered. Evie turned to Jack and held out her hand, and with a straight face he pulled a bill from his wallet.

She waved the hundred-dollar bill in the air. "There's one more if I actually find the girl at the location you give."

The men grumbled among themselves, and a skinny one with a sore oozing on his left arm pointed behind them. "Try the alley behind the second produce warehouse. There's a little space with an awning where she sometimes hangs."

As they took off down the alley, Jack settled his hand at her back. "He's a tweaker."

"Yep, and every one of those dollars is going straight into his arm."

Behind a row of produce warehouses that smelled of overripe melon, they picked their way through uneven pavement and wooden pallets. Light from the street didn't reach this far, and shadows huddled and shifted.

At the second building under an awning, a pair of yellow, slitted eyes stared at her. Something at the back growled, a sound too low to be a cat. Evie slipped under the awning and found a young woman sitting against the wall, a tabby in her lap.

"I'm Special Agent Evie Jimenez, and I'd like to talk to you about Lisa Franco. She worked at the Mexican restaurant on the corner." She squatted. "Four weeks ago you spoke with Lisa over by the car park. She gave you a bag of fish tacos."

The girl edged back. She was so bundled up in layers, it was hard to tell her age and build.

"Your friend died the next day. You were most likely the

last person to talk to her before she was abducted. Do you remember seeing anyone following her?"

The girl hissed and spat at Evie's hand.

Jack sat on a stack of pallets. "Your cat is beautiful. What's her name?"

The girl with the cat in her lap snapped her gaze to his shoe. "Bella."

"Bella," Jack repeated, his voice wrapped in the same softness of the sugary sands of Venice Beach. "Who are the others?"

"Simon, Topper, and Crook. They're feral." She leaned toward Jack but still didn't meet his gaze. "They don't like most people."

"Your friend, Lisa. Did the cats like her?"

"Bella did. Lisa used to bring us stuff from the restaurant." She scratched under the cat's chin. "Bella loved the fish tacos."

"I bet she did." Jack stared at his shoes. "I bet Bella misses Lisa."

"She does." The cat girl dug her fingers into the scruff of the feline's neck. "She really does."

"I bet you do, too."

The girl shrugged.

"He's a bad man," Jack continued. There was a simple rawness to his words, and Evie knew a part of him was thinking about Abby. Had the bad man done anything to his sister?

The girl hugged the cat to her chest.

Jack remained where he was but his words grew softer, drawing the girl closer. "The man who took Lisa could hurt Bella."

The girl and the cat started to rock. "He...he hasn't been around since that night."

Thank you, Jack. Thank you. Thank you. Evie sat on the pallet, wooden splinters digging into her butt, and forced her lips to stay closed.

"Do you know his name?" Jack continued.

"No, but I've seen him around a few times."

"Does he live around here?"

"I don't know."

"Does he live on the streets?"

"No. Definitely not."

"How can you be so sure?"

"He doesn't smell like the street."

On the streets of Albuquerque, Evie's dad had worked with those who called the streets home. On workdays he'd come home smelling of sun, ripe sweat, dust, oil from the asphalt, and a dash of despair.

"What does he look like?" Evie asked. "Hair color? Eyes?"

The young woman buried her face in the scruff of the cat's neck.

"What kind of shoes did he have?" Jack asked. "Work boots? Tennis shoes?"

The girl rocked faster. "Dress shoes. He wore shiny dress shoes."

"Big? Little?"

"Medium. Kind of skinny. Brown."

Evie pictured the giant tennis shoe of the man who took a shot at her and Jack.

"If you ever see him again, can you call me?" Evie held out her card. The cat girl turned away.

Jack took out one of his cards and set it on the curb. "To keep Bella and the others safe."

As they walked away, the cat girl picked up Jack's card and slipped it between her layers of clothes.

* * *

11:53 p.m.

"You gonna tell me you learned that at Harvard?" Evie asked when they reached her rental car.

"No."

Evie stopped in front of the driver's side door, blocking his way. He could try to physically move her, but given the fiery glint in her eye, that would most likely lead to a scorch mark or two on his suit. He could tell she wanted answers and wasn't backing down.

He slid his hand in his pocket, his fingers tapping the keys. "I learned it on the streets of New York," he said.

"Spent a lot of time there?"

"A bit."

She rested her butt on the car door. "Who are you, Jack?"

"Haven't we been down this road before?"

"Yep, and it looks like you took me on a little detour." She crossed her legs at the ankles. "So how did you end up on the streets of New York?" For someone who looked so relaxed, she was holding on tight. She wasn't about to let go.

He settled back against the car. "After the accident, my mother couldn't look me in the eye. She didn't say it, but she blamed me for Abby's death. I picked that spot on the river. I was driving the car. And I let go."

"More importantly, you blamed you."

"Yeah, I did. I was beating myself up, and it got pretty bloody. A few months after the accident I finally took off. New York was close and big, the perfect place to get lost."

"Did you get lost?"

He rubbed at the center of his forehead where life had handed him a few hard knocks. "For a while. I spent some time in some pretty ugly places, saw a lot of ugly things, did a few, too. Got in more than my share of fights. It's not a part of my past I'm proud of."

A cloud passed over Evie's face as she stood and reached for her car keys. "We all have parts of our pasts we want to forget."

CHAPTER TWENTY

Monday, November 2
6:02 a.m.

Why, there you are, Evie!" Mrs. Francis, the night clerk at the EZ-Rest Motel, set a fresh batch of muffins on the front desk counter. "I was getting ready to send out the hounds for you. You must have gotten in pretty late last night. Everything okay?"

"Everything's great," she said. Her teammate Jon MacGregor was in town hunting down Jack's missing sister, she and Jack had tracked Vandemere to the Abby Foundation, and last night they got a visual lead from a girl who liked cats.

"You let me know if you need anything for your room," Mrs. Francis continued. "I asked housekeeping to leave you two bottles of shampoo for all that beautiful hair of yours, and I made another batch of blueberry muffins. I saw how much you enjoyed them the other morning. I take it you're not one of those girls who's afraid of fat and sugar and gluten, are you?"

"I adore fat and sugar and gluten, especially when they taste like this." Evie picked up an oversized muffin.

"The secret to a good blueberry muffin is lemon zest. All that sweetness needs a bit of tartness for balance."

As Evie ducked into her car, she took a giant bite of muffin. She wasn't good at the whole balance thing as she tended to skew hard, but Mrs. Francis was clearly onto something. She'd have to get the recipe for these.

When she reached LAPD, she stopped first by the evidence room. "Got a big shoe for me?" Evie asked the clerk behind the desk.

He poked through a series of totes on a counter along the side of the wall and pulled out a plastic bag with a large blue tennis shoe, the sneaker of the man who'd taken a shot at her.

"Any fingerprints?" she asked as she signed for the evidence.

"A partial, but no matches so far," the clerk said. "We should have DNA results back by next week."

Little good that would do her. This was the first week of November. The bomber would strike this week.

"Thanks." With the bagged shoe tucked under her arm she went to her office, where she found Hayden sitting on one side of her horseshoe-shaped desk and Smokey Joe on the other.

She held up the shoe. "Big or little?"

Hayden looked up from his laptop. "Big."

She set the shoe on Smokey Joe's lap. "Big or little?"

The old man slid his gnarled fingers over the leather, laces, and sole. "Definitely big."

She grabbed the sneaker and glared at it. "So it's likely the guy who took a potshot at me, the guy wearing this shoe, was not the same one the homeless woman, the one known as Cat Girl, saw the night Lisa Franco was abducted. She said he had medium-sized, narrow dress shoes." A growl gurgled at the back of her throat. "Which means it's possible that the shooter has nothing to do with the Angel Bombings."

"Think the guy shootin' at you was a mugger?" Smokey took a bite of his cinnamon roll and washed it down with a swig of coffee. "Or maybe one of them druggies. These big cities are filled with muggers and druggies."

"The shot occurred the first day I joined the investigative team. I asked a lot of questions that day, met with a lot of people. It would make sense that the shooter was someone not too happy about my presence on the Angel Bombing task force."

"What about that Jack fella?" Smokey asked. "Someone want to take a piece out of his hide?"

"Not that I know of." And after last night, she understood so much more about him, especially his involvement in the case, probably one he didn't even understand. He had spent some time in dark, cold places, which was why Abby's sun was so important to him.

A head popped into the doorway. "Hey there, Smokey Joe. The line is set up, and your computer's good to go."

Smokey hopped up and grabbed his cane. "Gotta get to work. You kids holler if you need anything."

Evie sunk into the chair vacated by the old man. "Smokey is *working* here?"

"Two months ago Ricci set up a hotline dedicated to the Angel Bomber, and they received thousands of calls," Hayden explained. "Smokey suggested he listen to see if he could pick up anything others may have missed."

Because when one sense goes, others usually sharpen. "It can't hurt."

"Yesterday Smokey listened to almost one hundred calls, and he says he's not leaving until he listens to them all or you catch the bomber."

Evie smiled. Smokey was the type to never give up. Like all of her team. "He'd make a good Apostle."

"I'm sure Smokey Joe would agree." Hayden pushed back his laptop. "We should probably get Berkley to talk to the homeless woman you spoke with last night to see if she can get a sketch of Lisa Franco's abductor. Right now, the girl with the cats is our best lead."

"Honestly, I don't think even Berkley could get something out of that girl. Not once did she look me or Jack in the eye. It was the oddest thing, holding a conversation with someone who refused to look at you. Frustrating, too, because it felt like I was missing out on part of the conversation."

Hayden nodded. "When it comes to communication, words are overrated. Most communication is done through face and body movement. I'm not surprised she wouldn't make eye contact. It's not an uncommon behavior for people who live on the streets."

"But why? Why couldn't I get through to her?"

"Could be a matter of societal distrust or fear, lack of confidence or low self-esteem, or a symptom of a mental disorder. Or it simply could be she decided to put on a pair of blinders last night. People very much choose what they want to see."

Evie fired up her computer, wondering if Jon had made any inroads in finding what happened to Abby when she landed on the streets of L.A. When she looked up five minutes later, Hayden was still staring at her. "Okay, Hayden, what do you *see*?"

"Your hair. The up-do looks very nice on you."

"It's been getting in my eyes."

"I see." With a half smile he turned back to his computer.

"I hate it when you do that."

"Do what?"

"*See* things that aren't there."

"Exactly what am I not seeing?" Hayden asked with a smile. She was still getting used to seeing her uber-serious teammate smile so much. Evie blamed it on Kate, his fiancée.

"Nothing."

"The same nothing that has you wearing lipstick."

"Lip balm. The air's much drier here." Her cheeks warmed with a blush. What the hell? She never blushed. "Really, Hayden, I don't have time to talk about cosmetics with you. A clock is ticking and I have..." She tossed the shoe on her desk with disgust. "A big shoe."

"And you're questioning if this shoe belongs to the bomber?"

"Cat Girl swears the man who was with Lisa did not have big feet."

Hayden closed his laptop. "Time for a field trip."

Hayden's job as a criminal profiler was to get into a killer's head and become the monster, or in this case, a shooter with big feet.

They drove the few blocks to the alley where the shooter took the first shot at her and Jack. Hayden stood just outside the mouth of the alley. "I'm standing here and spot you and Jack talking in the alley."

"We were *arguing* in the alley."

"Fine, arguing. It's after seven and dark. Why am I in the alley?"

"You're following me, possibly looking for a place and time to ensure I'm no longer on the case."

"I stand here more than a minute. It's a clear shot, but I

don't shoot. I'm sweating. My hands are shaking. You and Jack continue to argue. Still I don't shoot. Why?"

"You're afraid."

"Of what?"

"Getting caught."

"Or?"

"Actually killing someone." Evie pinched her bottom lip. "But the bomber has no problem with murder. He shot that gallery owner in Venice."

Hayden extended his arm with an imaginary gun. "Finally, I shoot. The shot goes high and wide. Why?"

"Because you're a lousy shot."

"Or?"

"Because you don't want to kill. You just want to scare us away." Evie slipped her hands in her back pockets. "This doesn't sound like the bomber. His bombs are designed to kill, to hurt, to maim. The carnage is part of his emotional satisfaction."

"So?" Hayden asked.

"So maybe my shooter wasn't Carter Vandemere, just someone trying to scare me off."

"That's one scenario. Know anyone like that?"

She pictured a wall of good words to live by, including, *Thou shalt not kill.*

* * *

6:45 a.m.

"Good morning, Mr. Elliott." Claire set a six-inch stack of papers on his desk. "Here are all of the items that need to be signed or have your direct authorization."

He hadn't stepped foot in his office for four days and

hadn't done a lick of Elliott Enterprises business. Shocking to anyone who knew him. But right now, he needed to be focused on the bomber. And Abby. It was a good thing that during the past ten years, he'd managed to surround himself with the best: the best executive assistant, the best financiers, the best legal team, the best executive team. For the past four days, they'd kept the machine that was Elliott Enterprises running smoothly. He'd power through this paperwork and get back to the station. Today Evie planned to hit the streets and scout out possible locations for the bombing, and he planned on being at her side.

"The items requiring your signature are already dated and notarized where needed," Claire added. "The German deal is in triplicate, so use a good pen."

He reached for his desk drawer. Footsteps pounded in the hallway, and Brady jogged into his office. "Hey, good to see you. I was starting to think you and the FBI agent came to blows."

"Are you insinuating that she knocked me out?"

"That or you popped her, which would have landed your ass in jail."

"We're playing nicely."

"How nicely?" Brady asked with a grin.

Jack held out his hand, motioning to the folder Brady carried. "Status on the Seattle project?"

Brady sat in the chair across from his desk. "I put a push on the planning and zoning commission, and we should get the nod next Monday, Tuesday at the latest."

"Good work." He opened the folder. More ducks exactly where they needed to be. "I also want you to talk with some of Matsumoto's suppliers and find out what his track record is. Then give Mats a call and ask him point-blank if he's talking to other venture firms."

"You want *me* to talk to Matsumoto?" Brady's eyes grew bright, then clouded with wariness.

"You know our position." Jack curled his fingers around the drawer pull.

Brady cocked his head. "You sure Agent Jimenez didn't cuff you on the head. I've seen her in action."

There were moments Evie left him dazed, but not in this case. Brady could handle the Matsumoto deal because Jack needed to get these papers signed and then get to the police station. He jerked open the top drawer.

Click.

He reached for a pen but froze when his knuckles brushed against the small plain brown box.

Pop. Riiiiiiip.

The box shuddered.

"Down, Brady!" Jack yelled as he dived to the ground.

CHAPTER TWENTY-ONE

Monday, November 2
7:14 a.m.

Jack's office, a sea of black and white, now sported a new color: red.

Evie ducked under the crime scene tape stretched across the door and went directly to the desk where Jack and Brady stood, Brady's face ash white and Jack's flushed in anger. An officer stood at their sides, taking statements.

"That son of a bitch," Jack said, his lips barely moving. "He got in here, right under my nose."

Evie assessed. No blood. No abrasions. Not a single thread snagged on his jacket. Likewise, Brady was uninjured. She picked a red tissue paper heart from his ginger hair.

"There's plenty more." Brady jabbed a hand at Jack's desk.

Hundreds of little red tissue hearts were scattered on the glass-top desk and black marble floor.

"Exactly how did it go down?" Evie asked.

A vein in Jack's neck thickened. "I opened the desk drawer, heard a click, and the box burst open."

In the drawer were the remains of a small brown box. The anti-movement switch must have triggered some kind of firing train inside, but lucky for Jack and Brady, the box didn't hold shrapnel, nails, or bits of barbed wire, just red, fluttery hearts.

Jack rested a knuckled hand on his desk. "What the hell was he trying to pull?"

"It's always about the message." Evie pinched the red tissue heart between two fingers and spun it. "This is Vandemere's way of showing us some love, the cocky SOB. It's also a message for you, Jack, that he has the power to get into your inner sanctum."

"It'll be the last time. Claire, get security on the line."

"Yes, Mr. Elliott," Claire said. Today Claire wasn't beige but a ghostly white.

"What I don't get was how he got in," Brady said. "With you gone, Claire's had the office buttoned up tighter than a duck's arse."

"Get a record of who's been through this door or using my elevator."

Brady headed for the door, but Evie waved him back. His hair was an array of ginger spikes. "You okay?" she asked.

Brady's normally affable face remained somber. "I can honestly say that was the first time my life flashed before my eyes."

She blamed it on the unknown. In the split second after that click, Brady knew something was coming at him, but he didn't know what and with how much force. In that sliver of moment, he didn't know if he was going to live or die. "What did you see?" she asked.

The corners of his mouth quirked. "A guy who needs to stop working weekends and get a life. Maybe a girl. Definitely a stiff drink."

She thumped him on the back. "I'm going to get him, Brady."

"When you do, it's okay if he loses a testicle or two."

"I'll keep that in mind."

The crime scene techs arrived, and one motioned to Jack. "We'll need your suit, Mr. Elliott." Good. Every member of the team knew the danger behind those paper hearts. This was no prank.

"Of course," Jack said. "I keep a spare change of clothes in the closet."

"I'll get it." Evie's heart had settled back in her chest, but her blood was still amped. Like Jack, she needed to do something. The closet smelled like Jack. Rich leather and that hint of citrus. She thumbed through the silky suits.

"The dark blue one," Jack said. "Red tie."

She picked out the dark gray with a light gray striped shirt. No tie. She handed him the clothes. "Here you go."

His eyes narrowed, but just as she hoped, a hint of a smile curved his lips. "At least I know what to expect from you," he said.

Evie had told him, What you see is what you get. No surprises. No hidden agendas. She was worried for Jack's and Brady's safety and mad as hell at the bomber for slipping in under her radar.

In the reception area, Brady, who was sitting at Claire's computer, waved them over. "Just called up security records. Your office has been accessed five times in the past four days, all times by Claire."

"True," Claire said. "I had to get papers or file things."

Evie motioned to the badge at Claire's waist, this one

with a reprint of a painting of a child holding a dove. "Anyone have access to your badge?"

"I keep it on all the time at work."

"And when you leave work?"

Claire's upper body bristled. "I leave it in the console of my car, but my car's always locked."

"And so was Jack's door," Evie said. "I'll need a list of people who've been in your car or have had access to your keys."

The woman had aged ten years. She was thinking the same thing as everyone else in the room. If that brown paper box had been filled with one of the bombs used on the Angel victims, Jack and Brady would be dead. "Of course, Agent Jimenez."

Jack rolled his head along his neck as if he was trying to shake off the tension.

"Come on," she said, dipping her head toward his private elevator.

"I need to stick around until the police finish their sweep of the building."

"No, you need to come with me. I need your eyes."

"Where are you going?" he asked.

"To church."

* * *

11:11 a.m.

The gates of the True North compound stood wide open. A sandwich board sign on the shoulder of the twisting mountain read, *Healing service today!*

For a moment Jack gave thanks that Evie, Brady, Claire, and no one else in the Elliott Tower was in need of healing.

A bomb had gone off in his office. At his desk. Brady said his life flashed before his eyes. Jack had seen only fury.

"Looks like we won't need to invoke the name of the all-powerful executive assistant," Evie said as he pulled onto the compound drive. She'd been casting surreptitious glances at him on the drive to Topanga Canyon as if he were about to explode. She might be onto something. After having hundreds of paper hearts explode around him, something was simmering low in his gut, at the back of his head, and center of his chest.

The faithful had gathered to pray, and by the number of cars in the parking lot, the faithful were many. Jack found a spot in an overflow lot in a dirt field. Evie had explained on the drive over that after her teammate Hayden had walked her through the shooting, she sensed the shooter wasn't their bomber, just someone trying to scare her away, and that was the same day they'd visited North.

The True North church was a big cinder-block building with no windows and a vestibule filled with stained walls instead of stained glass. Jack held open the door for Evie, and it took a few moments for his eyes to adjust to the low lights of the main room. Inside row after row of folding chairs faced a raised stage that stretched across the width of the building, backed by a black floor-to-ceiling drape. Probably two or three hundred people, mostly senior citizens and a few students and young families, raptly watched the stage.

North stood center stage, his shirtsleeves rolled to his elbows. "For here in His name, the blind receive sight, the lame walk, the deaf hear, the dead are raised, and the good news is preached to the poor. And who are the poor?" He pounded his chest. "I am the poor. You are the poor. And only one can bring riches. Only one can heal."

Evie and Jack slipped along the back of the building

through the standing-room-only crowd and stopped near the side aisle.

"And that is the almighty savior who is right here, right now." North held out his hands, palms facing upward.

"He thinks he's God," Jack said against Evie's ear.

"More like one of his instruments. I went to one of these things with my great-aunt Louisa when I was in high school. She was a former opera singer having issues with her throat."

"Was she healed?"

"She never complained again." Evie stood on tiptoe. "Do you see him anywhere?"

Him. Their shooter. Jack despised violence, especially after his street days, but fight surged through his veins. He'd love to get his hands on the man who'd taken a shot at Evie.

"I'm sensing someone here," North continued. "A soul in need of healing. Something to do with the chest. No, the lungs."

A gray-haired woman cried out and jumped to her feet. A man in a white smock, one of North's lackeys, jogged down the aisle with a microphone and held it under her chin. "I was just diagnosed with COPD."

A murmur swept over the crowd.

North held out his hands. "Come, sister, come."

The crowd roared. Someone cried out, "Alleluia!"

The woman, steadied by the man in the white robe, joined North onstage. North placed his hands on her shoulders. "In His name you are healed."

She collapsed to the ground. A cheer tore from the crowd. Two men in white smocks stepped out from the wings.

Evie grabbed Jack's thigh. "Guy in the smock to the right of the curtain. Brown hair. Build is right. What about the face?"

A good thirty yards away, Jack tried to get a good look, but it was too dim on that part of the stage. They hurried up the side aisle and ducked through a slit in the drapes. A trio stood around the woman with the lung disease, hands clasped in prayer. When the man with the brown hair looked up and saw them, he took off out the back door.

This time Jack didn't interfere. Evie took off and got Brother Big Shoe on the ground in less than seven seconds.

CHAPTER TWENTY-TWO

Monday, November 2
1:21 p.m.

Evie propped her boots on the table of interrogation room number two. "You know, Brother Trujillo, the silent routine is really making me wonder about your soul. Silence indicates a man who may have something to hide, something the divine might frown upon."

James Trujillo, a former gangbanger from East L.A. who found the way, the truth, and the light thanks to Gabriel North, shuffled his big feet. He'd been holed up in an interrogation room saying the same line over and over. "Is Brother North here yet?"

When North finally arrived, Evie left Brother Big Shoe and met with the pastor in a room next door. "No attorney?" Evie asked.

"Brother Trujillo doesn't need one," North said with an arrogant lift of one eyebrow.

"This is serious, North. We're ninety-nine percent sure your man took a shot at a federal agent."

"Round that up to one hundred," North said. "He told me about it the night he did it."

She slapped her hands on the table. "You kept that little nugget to yourself?"

"Brother Trujillo shot at you to *frighten* you," North said with the exaggerated calm and patience her oldest brother used with his four-year-old son. "He was concerned that you were a threat to my ministry. I don't agree with what he did, but I am certain he won't do it again."

"Why's that?"

"Because I told him not to."

"And he'll obey?"

"He has blind faith."

"That's a hell of a burden you're carrying." And power.

"I take it seriously. My job is to shepherd my followers to eternal salvation. I listen to their trials and guide them through tribulations."

Evie rubbed at the back of her neck. "What do you know about Trujillo?"

"He's not your bomber, Agent Jimenez."

"Why don't you let me decide?"

For about an hour, Evie grilled both Gabriel North and James Trujillo, and by the end, she knew North was right. The overzealous believer was not the Angel Bomber. Trujillo had been in Mexico on a mission with some of North's followers during the second bombing, and he didn't show any signs of resentment, the emotion that usually fueled serial bombers. And according to Cat Girl, he had the wrong size feet.

As she left the interrogation room, North fell in step beside her. "You know we're very much alike, Agent Jimenez."

"How's that?"

"We're both in the business of saving souls." They reached the elevator bank. "I hope you catch him."

"I will."

"Sounds suspiciously like blind faith, Agent Jimenez?" A devilish glint lit North's eyes.

She believed in herself, her team, and justice. She couldn't do what she did without such rock-solid faith. "Absolutely."

As Brother North's shiny shoes tapped down the corridor, she checked in with the officer who'd been recording her interview of the Wrong Way Brothers. "Where's Jack?"

The officer checked his watch. "He left an hour ago."

"Did he say where he was going?"

"Home, I think."

Odd, that Jack would go home. But maybe not. Facing off with an IED, even one filled with hundreds of tiny red paper hearts, was enough to make most people want to curl up with a stiff drink or in a soft bed. She could go check on him. No, she *should* go check on him.

"Speaking of Jack," the officer said. "Your teammate Jon MacGregor was looking for you earlier. He found something on Jack's sister."

* * *

2:07 p.m.

A man's vehicle of choice told a good deal about him.

Carter Vandemere's dad had driven a half-ton pickup truck. "Now that's a real man's truck, son. Can haul your tools and a horse trailer, and if you got a girl you're wanting to poke, throw a couple sleeping bags in the bed and you're ready." Nudge. Nudge. Hah. Like Carter had ever needed to haul tools and a horse or take a girl out for a drive. But the pickup truck had come in useful when he'd had to haul materials to the construction site where he blew up his father. That had definitely been one of his better explosions. Windows had shaken for a city block, and his father had been blown into golf ball–size pieces.

His mom drove a minivan. Good for hauling groceries.

As for the little FBI agent, the Beetle rental car suited her. Red, small, and full of sass. Plus it had all those nice curves. Agent Jimenez had nice curves, too. Not too big, not too little, a perfectly proportioned landscape of peaks and valleys. When he was growing up, he had a special sketchbook, the one that held all of his drawings of beautiful girls. He rated them with tiny red hearts. Evie would have received five hearts.

Carter slipped along the back of the lower level of the Elliott Tower parking garage.

Now Jack Elliott, he was a man with many different cars. Carter slid his hand over the black Audi. This was the car of a man who liked speed and had great style.

He slipped off his backpack and set it on the ground, taking out the bundle of dynamite. It wasn't one of his better designs, more function than form, but it would do exactly what it needed to do. He dropped to the ground and shimmied on his back under the car, this one a Mercedes CLA-Class. Affordable luxury. So telling. He pressed the bundle against the wheel well, the click of the magnet against metal truly a beautiful sound.

* * *

2:08 p.m.

Evie pulled her rental car up to the bronze statue of two children holding hands. Her teammate Jon was parked two spaces down in front of a blue and pink giraffe.

"Fun times ahead," Evie said as she hopped out of her car.

"I hope so." Jon had spent the past few days tracking down artists whose work appeared in the Twin Citrus stairwell in hopes of learning about the young artist calling herself Luz. He finally found one, an artist named Greta Antony who ran a fine art gallery for children in Malibu.

A bell tinkled overhead as they walked into a sunny room filled with giant colored blocks covered in drawing paper and long, low tables piled with scraps of fabric and pipe cleaners and fuzzy balls. While Jon went to find the owner, she watched a preschooler making a flower garden out of waxy pieces of string. The child looked up and asked, "Do you know how to make a caterpillar?"

Evie squatted. "I think I can work something out." She coiled six waxy sticks into different-sized circles and set them side by side, adding curling antennas.

"Blue eyes or green?" Evie asked the kid.

"Green."

She added green eyes and a smile, when a throat cleared behind her. She lifted her gaze.

"The owner's in her office and ready to talk," Jon said.

Evie hopped up from her tiny chair and followed Jon down a hallway.

"I'm surprised you didn't bring Jack," Jon said. "You two have been spending quite a bit of time together this week."

Because Jack had control issues not to mention knowledge and a skill set that was helping her investigation. "He skipped out at the station after I collared North's guy. I think he's had enough explosions in his world today."

"Pretty shaken?"

"More angry than anything. Vandemere pulled a power move on him."

When they reached the office, a woman in a paint-smudged apron greeted them. After introductions, Jon asked, "You knew the young woman who painted this." He showed her the photo he'd taken in the Twin Citrus stairwell of the frolicking turtles.

The woman's eyes brightened. "Yes, that's one of Luz's. She was one of the more talented kids at The Colony. The Colony. That's what we called it. Sounded so much more bohemian than low-rent warehouse space. Luz worked mostly in oils but would occasionally paint in watercolors and sketch with colored pencils. She had such a fun signature."

"What do you remember about her beyond her art?" Jon asked.

"She always slept with the light on, drank tea, not coffee, and when she had a few dollars to spare would go down to Little Tokyo and buy yakitori."

"How long was she at The Colony?"

"Just that spring and summer. I must have been eighteen or nineteen, so that was about fifteen years ago."

"Do you have any idea where she may have gone after she left The Colony?"

"I have no idea. She never talked about going any place else. She loved it there. We were all shocked when she just up and left."

"Up and left?"

"She packed up all of her art supplies and took off to paint one morning. She never came back. Left everything behind in her room, not that any of us had much of anything back then. A few T-shirts and a toothbrush."

Evie met Jon's gaze, and she noted the deep creases on either side of his lips.

"Any friends?" Jon asked.

"Everyone loved Luz. She was always so happy and bubbly. I remember her sitting on the back loading dock one day hugging herself. She said she had to hold herself together or she'd burst with happiness. She loved it here, the place, the people, the sun."

"Did she have a boyfriend?" Jon continued.

"No, she was having a love affair with art."

"Was anyone interested in her?" Evie asked. "Another artist, possibly one who didn't get on well with the crowd."

The woman nodded. "That would be Dougie. He followed her around like a lovesick puppy. Offered to clean her brushes. Used to leave little gifts on her bed and in her dresser drawers. It freaked her out. I think he was one of the reasons she left."

Jon's eagle gaze sharpened. "Did Dougie by any chance reveal his last name?"

"None of us had last names at The Colony."

"Do you remember anything about his art?" Evie pictured that gruesome online portfolio and the tame but somber works submitted to the Abby Foundation.

"I think he did mostly portraits."

"Do you recall what he looked like?"

"Oh, yes. Dougie was very memorable."

Evie pressed her palms against her thighs to keep from jumping up and hugging the woman. "Could you work with our sketch artist?"

"I can do better." The woman reached into a desk drawer and pulled out a sketch pad. With a thin piece of charcoal, she drew a face. Ten minutes later, she gave the face to Jon. "This is a very good representation. Hair and eyes are brown."

Evie studied the drawing. Heavyset boy, unkempt hair to his shoulders, long, narrow nose, deep-set eyes. An itch stole across the palms of her hands.

After the interview, Evie and Jon stood at her car. "This is him," she said on a half-whisper-half-prayer. "I'll need to get an age progression, but I finally have something other than unknowns."

"While you get an artist on the progression, I'm going to talk with some outreach groups and agencies that dealt with teenage runaways and the mentally ill. Jack said Abby had highs and lows, and it's possible she hit a low and fell into a dark place."

Evie rubbed her palms on the sides of her jeans. "You still believe she's still alive?"

"You know me, Evie." Jon opened her car door. "I always believe."

She took in those words, pushing out what she knew of bombers, and this one in particular. "I'll give Jack a call and give him an update."

Jon laughed. "Don't bother."

"Come on, Jon. This is Jack's sister. He'd give away every billion he had to find her."

"Trust me. I know exactly how much Jack Elliott wants his sister found. He tells me every afternoon when we have our daily conference call."

"Conference call?"

"That also includes a private investigator he hired along with one of his contacts at LAPD."

Evie shook her head. Of course Jack was on the case. He was Jack, wheeling and dealing, moving and shaking.

* * *

2:20 p.m.

Mondays were dead. Nothing worth shooting ever happened on a Monday, which meant Freddy should be at home in bed dreaming of his beachfront condo in Maui or even working out with the jump rope one of his nieces got him for his birthday last month.

"It's good exercise, and fun," his niece had pronounced with way too much joy when he opened the gift. In his world, jumping rope didn't happen on Mondays, either.

All day he felt as if his skin was jumping off his bones. He kept looking over his shoulder and sniffing. For what, he had no idea. What did a bomber smell like? Freddy ran his hand along his greased-back hair. The bomber was due to strike any day, and Evie was still stomping through the streets in those red cowboy boots trying to sniff and snuff him out.

On this sunny Monday afternoon, Freddy poked his head into a half-lit art gallery. He liked shadowy places because they often hid folks doing shadowy things.

"Hey, Freddy." A young man in baggy pants and a bulky sweater one step removed from a goat waved from the top of a ladder where he was changing a lightbulb. "You got some shots for us today?"

Rudy B's was a hole-in-the-wall gallery off Fifth that specialized in photography installations. Most of it was artsy stuff, the human body in motion, architectural shots, extreme close-ups. Last year during his downtime, Freddy had taken some shots of L.A. prostitutes. Raw and gritty. More character study than sexy. Story up the wazoo. Made himself a nice little chunk of change. "Not today. I'm looking for Durant."

The man atop the ladder waved to a door. "In the base-ment. Give him a triple buzz."

And basements were especially dark places.

Freddy gave the buzzer three short jabs and called out, "Hey Durant, it's your favorite photographer of the starz."

The heavy metal door whooshed open, letting out a belch of cool air that reeked of bleach and wet cigarette butts. Durant sat in front of a small canvas superimposed with a digital image of a couple embracing. The artist must have gotten himself some new high-tech equipment because the brush marks on the digital image had been sharpened and defined.

"Who are you today?" Freddy asked as he stood over Du-rant's shoulder and watched him apply a thin layer of bright blue to the woman's dress. Having gone to art school some-where in New York, then having studied in Paris, Durant was a damn good painter.

"Chagall. Early years. Easy to replicate because he didn't use many colors." With a frown, Durant lifted the brush and made feathery brushstrokes. "But getting the right texture has been a bitch."

Durant was an even better businessman. When he got tired of *frijoles* for dinner every night, he started re-creating works by masters. Not surprisingly, there were a number of folks in this town willing to pay big bucks for fake masters. These were *legit* fakes. People knew they were buying fakes. Freddy wagged his head. Only in L.A.

With another frown, Durant tossed his brush into a glass of clear liquid and wiped his hands on a towel at his waist. "Got a buyer for me?" Durant asked.

"Not today. I'm looking for a particular artist, and since you know some folks on the darker side, I wanted to get your take."

Freddy showed him printed screen shots of Carter Vandemere's art, which Evie had so graciously provided. His
Lady Feeb was getting antsy, rattled enough to ask Freddy
to check with his downtown contacts.

Durant studied the printouts. "You don't strike me as the
dark and twisty type."

"It's for a lady friend of mine."

"Must be an interesting lady."

"She is." Freddy had never met a cop like Evie. She'd
given him a fistful of bills and every last penny in her pocket
to bet on a horse so he could duck Skip's fist. He shook
his head. She tried to come across all hard-ass, but Agent
Jimenez was a softie.

Durant handed Freddy the papers. "I haven't seen this
stuff in any of the storefront galleries, a bit too edgy for most
art buyers, but once in a while we get stuff like this at the
pop-ups."

Downtown L.A. had dozens of established art galleries,
and artists who hadn't yet found a place in those galleries
would often get retailers or businesses to set up short-term
or pop-up galleries displaying their work. Some even set up
their art in parking lots and on sidewalks.

"Got any names or locations for me?" Freddy asked.

Durant stroked the tip of his goatee. "What's in it for me?"

Freddy pictured that Angel Bomber award, compliments
of Jack Elliott. "A quarter mil."

"Let me do some asking around."

Good, 'cause Durant knew who to ask. The smile on his
lips fell away. "Be discreet, Durant. This guy could be dangerous."

Durant turned back to the fake Chagall. "Discreet is my
middle name."

On the way back to his car, Freddy's phone buzzed.

Someone on the tip line. Good. He could use a big, juicy Hollywood scandal right now. "Freddy Ortiz, photographer of the starz."

"Hello there, Freddy, I'd like to invite you to my next show."

"What's playing?" Freddy reached for his door handle. Man, he hoped this was an invite to a comedy show. He could use a few laughs.

"Something wonderfully explosive." The voice was fast and breathy. "It's debuting this Friday."

CHAPTER TWENTY-THREE

Monday, November 2
3:43 p.m.

I need to see Jack." Evie stood before Claire, who was tucking fat reports into three-ring binders with the EE logo.

"You mean Mr. Elliott?"

"No, I mean Jack. Is he in?" She'd tried his penthouse, but he hadn't answered. Nor did she spot one of his cars in his private parking space at the Elliott Tower. Carter Vandemere had just phoned Freddy Ortiz, and while they weren't able to get a trace, they got an important known: The next bomb would go off this Friday. Evie wanted to know if Vandemere had reached out to Jack. She gripped one of the empty binders. Or heaven forbid he'd found Jack.

Claire snapped closed a binder. "No."

"Do you know when he'll be in?"

"He's out for the day."

"I tried calling, but he didn't answer." Which was so un-

Jack-like. This investigation had been the focus of his life the past few days. "Do you know where I can reach him?"

"No."

"Bullshit." Evie let go of the binder and rolled one shoulder, then another. A tightness had settled in, bunching her muscles. "You know everything about him, including which hand he uses when he pees."

Claire dropped a report, and papers went flying. "Agent Jimenez!"

Evie squatted to pick up the papers. "Okay, that may be a stretch, but don't you dare pretend you don't know if he wears boxers or briefs because I'm sure you've either routed his laundry or bought him a pack or two of *chonies*. So where is he?"

Claire said nothing as she dropped to the floor to pick up the papers, but Evie saw the smile. She also spotted a wide, rippled length of flesh that crept up Claire's forearm as she reached for papers under a chair. Evie had seen enough victims of bombs to know that was a scar from a third-degree burn, and she wondered about this woman who seemed to want to blend in with the world. Whatever her past, she was loyal to Jack Elliott, and as his executive assistant knew his schedule.

"So where is he?" Evie asked again as she finished picking up the papers.

Claire attempted to straighten the papers, but they remained catawampus. She tapped and tapped and tapped. "I genuinely don't know. He checked in around two and said he was taking the day off."

Evie took a deep breath, relief loosening the knots in her shoulders. So he hadn't just up and disappeared, but something still wasn't right. "Taking the day off? Are you talking about our Jack?"

Evie started to put the papers in order, but Claire waved her off. "Yes, *our* Jack, and I can get it from here. I believe you have more important things to do than collate, and as soon as Jack calls in for messages, I'll tell him you stopped by."

Evie set the papers on top of Claire's desk. "Boxers or briefs?"

Claire laughed out loud. "Agent Jimenez! That is hardly an appropriate topic of conversation."

"Sometimes appropriate is overrated." Evie spun on her boots. She still needed to find Jack and give him the good news that they finally had a sketch of Vandemere's face as a teen, which was being age-progressed at this very moment.

Just as she was about to get back on the elevator, a streak of ginger flashed down the hallway. She poked her way through a maze of offices and found Brady Malloy on the phone.

"I'll have marketing send you Jack's and Heinrich's mug shots along with a high-res logo for each company. If you need anything else before the story goes to print, give me a call."

Evie balled her fists on the edge of Brady's desk. "Where's your guy? I have news about Abby."

"I'll have him give you a call when he checks in." Brady pulled back the sleeve of his jacket and checked his watch. "Which should be in about an hour."

"Did you hear me, Brady? I have info on his sister."

"Loud and clear. I don't want to disturb him today."

"You know where he is?"

Brady settled back in his chair. "Jack is taking some time off this afternoon. No work. No bomb investigation. Even no Abby. He needs a break."

Another loyal pit bull. "Who is he to you?" Evie asked.

Brady ran his fingers along the cuff of his jacket sleeve.

"Jack Elliott's my savior. Literally. He scraped my ass up off the streets."

"New York," Evie said.

Brady's eyebrows folded into two checkmarks. "Jack told you about New York?"

"A little. He said it was a dark, ugly time."

Brady nodded. "For both of us."

Evie ground her boot into the plush carpet. "It's about to get dark again. I need to talk to Jack, and not just about Abby. The bomber has set the date for his next *show*."

* * *

6:09 p.m.

Evie rolled down the car window and stared at the keypad. Flexing her index finger she punched in four letters: *ABBY.*

The gigantic iron gates with the scrolling initials EE swung open. She'd known Jack Elliott less than a week, but she knew a good deal about him. At times. Other times, like now as she drove her Beetle down the dusty ranch road, she could honestly say Jack had thrown her for a loop. Mr. Uptown and Uptight owned a forty-acre spread in Ojai, a small artist and agriculture community northwest of Los Angeles. From what she could see in the glow of her headlights, the ranch was well-maintained, and not to her surprise, in the business of making money. To her right stretched row after row of citrus trees and neat stacks of plastic crates. Jack was making money off his second home, a ranch with a large mission-style house made of adobe the color of the sun.

An older woman with wide hips and a wide smile waved at her as Evie walked through the courtyard.

"What do you think?" The woman handed her an orange.

The fruit was heavy and dimpled and smelled of summer and sun. Evie tore off a section and took a bite. Juice dribbled down her chin. "Perfect."

The older woman laughed. "Good. You're getting them for dinner."

"I am?"

"You're here to see Mr. Elliott?" Even here he was *mister*.

"Yes." About a ticking bomb.

"He's around the back at the barn," the woman said. "Be careful. There's been quite a ruckus back there today."

* * *

6:11 p.m.

Jack slipped the bolt in the paddock gate. A burst of wind sliced down from the mountain and cooled the sweat along his forehead.

"You wanna get him inside now, Mr. Elliott?" Manny asked.

Jack slipped off his gloves and tucked them in the back waistband of his jeans. "Let's give him a little more time."

"Okay, he's doing fine here in the paddock. We'll give him a chance to stretch his legs a bit," his new stable manager said. "I'm going to head on over to the Dawsons' place and see if the vet's done. I want her to come out and take a look at that hind leg. The abrasion doesn't look too bad, but I'm sure you want to take care of your investment."

As Manny took off in the truck and trailer, Jack rested his arms on the top rung of the railing, a tear in his jacket gaping open and catching wind. An investment? He almost laughed. The chestnut Thoroughbred nosed cautiously around the paddock, lit this time of evening by a pair of security lights attached to the barn. Business had been the furthest thing from his mind when he bought this horse this afternoon. He'd been thinking about one thing, the bomb in his desk.

An Ojai neighbor of his had been boarding the horse for the owner who'd been trying to sell him off for the past year. Jack had heard about the horse and occasionally got a look at him, a wild thing with fire in his eyes.

"He's beautiful." The voice, low and throaty, was barely audible on the wind.

Jack hadn't heard Evie approach, but he wasn't surprised she was here. Nothing she did surprised him.

"What's his name?" Half of Evie's hair had escaped its knot and whipped about her face.

"Sugar Run."

Evie stood on the bottom rung of the fence so they were the same height. "Sounds familiar."

"Thoroughbred out of Kentucky. Three years ago he won the Derby and the Preakness. Didn't make the last leg of the Triple Crown because of an injury."

She climbed to the second rung. "And you've added him to your collection?"

Jack laughed. "He is my collection. You're witnessing the first day of my first acquisition. So now you can't accuse me of having a barn with no horse."

Evie slung one dusty boot over the top rung and then the other, settling her butt on the railing. More faded blue jeans. She had obviously never received the memo about standard FBI dress. Or more likely, she got the memo and chucked it in the garbage.

Evie nudged his shoulder with hers. "What's wrong with him?"

"He's blind."

"You bought a blind racehorse?"

"I bought a beautiful horse that can still run like the wind."

She fell silent for a moment as Sugar Run continued to edge his way along the far rail. "Do you plan to hire him out for stud fees?"

"Not sure. After taking him off the racing circuit when his sight started to go, his previous owners tried that route, but he's been too aggressive."

"What do you plan to do with him?"

"Watch him run."

Evie rested her shoulder against his. Beneath her denim jacket he felt the taut muscle. There wasn't much soft about Evie, except those rolling waves of hair.

"This has something to do with the bomb in your office," Evie said.

He laced his fingers. "Brady saw his past flash before his eyes, but me, I saw my future."

"Didn't like what you saw?" She kicked her legs, her boot heels softly tapping the metal railing.

"I saw a few things that needed changing."

"Change starts with a new horse?"

"Change starts with an old dream." He aimed his laced fingers at the Thoroughbred. "When we were kids, Abby loved the sun and I loved fast horses. I loved watching them run, seeing their power and grace. I always wanted a race-horse, but I've been too busy."

"Until the bomb in your desk drawer."

"Until the bomb in my desk drawer." He looked at her out of the corner of his eye. "But you're not here to see my new racehorse, are you?"

Evie's legs stilled. "We got a lead about a young artist who was obsessed with your sister when she got to L.A. We have a sketch that's being age-progressed."

Jack's face broke open in a full-fledged smile. It was a huge break. "I knew you Apostles wouldn't let me down."

Evie nodded but didn't smile.

"And..."

"Freddy got word from Vandemere. He's set a date for the next bombing. This Friday."

Another gust of wind sliced through the paddock, picking up dirt and dry grass. "It's a known," Jack said. "And that's good."

"That's how I see it. One more dot gets us that much closer." Sugar Run's nostrils flared, and he sidestepped, his rump banging into the railing. Jack unlaced his fingers. "We should get him inside."

Evie whipped her collar over her ears and ducked another peppery gust. "How's he do on the lead line?"

"Fine once you get him moving."

Evie took the leather line hanging over the top rung. "Do you mind?"

Sugar Run danced nervously, kicking up dust.

"Do you dare?" Jack asked. Although that was a stupid question. Evie always dared.

With a grin, Evie hopped into the paddock. "Approach with caution." She made soft nickering noises and kept her steps steady and even. "Hey, sweet baby." Sugar Run's ears turned. "It's okay. We're going to get you inside." She ran her palm along his neck. The horse stutter-stepped. "Clear debris." She quietly snapped the lead line to the halter ring, all the while keeping up a soft, steady chatter. She aimed her chin at Jack. He slid the bolt and opened the gate, barely making a sound.

Pulling on the line, Evie led the horse toward the barn. Jack matched their steps. The horse was clearly keying in on sound and wind. Another gust of wind blew down from the mountain. Sugar Run charged forward, but Evie checked him with the line. When they reached the barn, Jack unlatched the lock and swung open the door. The air was warmer and still. A bird in the hayloft screeched.

Sugar Run's nostrils flared. His gaze grew wild. He veered to the side, and Evie went with him, her shoulder crashing into a stack of hay. Her boot heels slipped on the newly washed floor, and she landed on her butt.

Jack reached for the line and steadied the horse as Evie picked herself off the ground. "It's okay, old boy," she said. "It's a good place. A safe place."

"Set hot charge." She opened the stall and put the feed in place. Sugar Run slipped into the stall. Jack shut the gate.

"Detonate." Evie slid the bolt into place.

"Impressive. A bomb specialist who can also defuse horses. Does Parker pay extra for that?"

"He should."

Jack picked a piece of hay from her hair and a leaf from her collar.

"I'm a mess," she said, swatting at the mud on her sleeve and jeans.

"Seems to be a rather common state with you."

She slipped her hand to his chest and plucked off a long piece of straw. "At least I'm not the only one today."

With Sugar Run happily munching in his stall, Jack led Evie to the back of the barn and the hose and spigot. She slipped off her jacket and ran a stream of water along her arms. Droplets scattered on her tank and beaded on her hair, reminding him of a hundred tiny diamonds catching fire from the light overhead. He reached out and caught one of the drops. At that moment she turned, and his palm brushed her cheek. The touch was unexpected but not unwanted. The heat of her skin chased away the chilly wind. Her eyes grew smoky.

He moved first, but she wasn't far behind. He pulled her to his chest. She ran her fingers up his arms, ten tiny lightning rods. He pressed his mouth against hers and breathed in her spicy scent. Droplets of water trickled from her hair, and he swore he heard the sizzle as they landed on his skin.

A truck rattled up the drive along with a whiff of diesel. Manny hopped out, followed by the vet. Jack pulled himself away but couldn't take his eyes off her lips, now red and swollen, and for a moment his. "I need to go."

Evie placed both hands on his chest as if to steady them both. "I understand." She took a step toward him, those wide, full lips curving into a smile. "But when you're done, I want to finish what we started."

* * *

7:22 p.m.

"And in the latest news from the Angel Bomber case..."

Evie, who'd been hunched over her computer at Jack's Ojai kitchen table for the past hour, grabbed the remote and turned up the volume of the small TV sitting on the counter. This afternoon Ricci had released Greta Antony's sketch of the young man who'd been overly attentive to Abby Elliott at The Colony fifteen years ago.

"Police are looking for a Caucasian male in his early to midthirties," the newscaster continued. "He's approximately five-ten and has brown hair. He may be overweight and wear his hair long. Here's a sketch of him in his mid- to late teens." Greta's sketch of the heavyset boy flashed onto the screen. "Here's the same man progressed in age fifteen years."

Evie edged closer to the TV. Was this Carter Vandemere?

Was he lurking in downtown L.A.? Bent over a workbench wiring his latest murder weapon?

"If you've seen this individual, contact LAPD immediately on the Angel Bomber hotline."

And most important, would anyone recognize him and report his whereabouts?

When the newscaster finished, Evie switched off the TV and stretched her arms and shoulders. She'd spent the past hour studying street plans, building schematics, and event listings for downtown, zeroing in on those hosting events this Friday in churchlike settings. With the sketch released, maybe they'd snatch up Vandemere before he set up his next *show*, but in the meantime, they were scouting possible locations and warning potential victims. They were closing in on this guy.

She closed her laptop. Just an hour earlier, she'd been closing in on Jack who was still in the barn with Sugar Run and the vet. Was he avoiding her? Did he regret the kiss? Was he shocked at her bold pronouncement that she wanted to finish what they started? Or had she scared him away?

She knew nothing about seducing a man. Growing up, most of her close friends had been boys, and ninety percent of the people she worked with these days were men, not that she'd ever tried seducing any of them, which wouldn't have worked anyway because she'd always been one of the guys. A cop in work boots and work jeans who could swear and sweat with the best of them. She had few curves and a hard edge, hardly desirable. At times like this she wished she had a sister, someone to ask about things she'd never understood, like how to make herself desirable to a man like Jack, a man who collected fine, beautiful things. She wouldn't dare ask her mother who'd hop on a plane with the talk of grandchildren, which would scare a man like Jack away.

Jack wasn't the commitment kind, because he was committed to his work. And when he did make time for a woman, she guessed he didn't go for the type who wore more dirt than perfume. She needed help. She pushed aside her laptop. And in the past she'd always turned to her team. She stretched her fingers, popping her knuckles, and picked up the phone.

"Hey, Sugar and Spice." Her teammate Hatch had a thing for nicknames. He also knew about the fine art of seduction. Before he reconnected with his ex-wife this past summer, he had women coming in and out of his bed like a toy store at Christmastime. "How's your bomber?"

"In my sights. I need your help."

"Got a reluctant witness you want me to chat with?" Hatch asked. He was the team's crisis negotiator. He could talk bombers into giving up their IEDs and two hundred rioting prisoners into ditching their shivs and heading back to their cells.

"I have a reluctant man I want in my bed."

"Reluctant? Is he intimidated by you?"

"Not this guy. He's got an ego the size of a skyscraper."

"Straight?"

Evie's belly warmed where Jack's arousal had pressed into her as they kissed behind the barn. "Um...everything points in that direction."

"Another woman in the picture?"

"Nope, but I guess you could say he's married to work. The guy doesn't know how to turn off."

"Hmmmm. And he knows you want him in your bed?"

"I communicated that quite clearly."

"You sure he's into women?"

"Yes, but I'm guessing he prefers those not so messy."

Hatch made a soft clucking noise. "Then show him another side."

"There is no other side. I'm one of those what-you-see-is-what-you-get kind of girls."

"Exactly, you're a *girl*, Evie. Maybe you should let him see more of that."

But she wasn't girly. She didn't own blingy things or perfumes and powders. She pictured her brothers' wives. One was a teacher, another a paramedic, another a cop, and another a restaurant owner. They were all strong women. They had to be to be married to her brothers, but they still had softer sides. One wrote poetry, another grew roses, one played guitar in a church band.

Show him another side.

Her mother had taught her to bake. *If you want to catch a man, Evie, you don't need womanly wiles. You need this.* Her mother had held up a wooden spoon. Evie hadn't been too concerned about catching a man, but she'd loved the cooking lessons.

Rosalee, Jack's housekeeper, had put dinner, a black bean lasagna, in the oven. There was also a green salad with oranges and jicama. But no dessert. Evie poked around the pantry and found a few staples and powdered cocoa. And oranges. Oranges were everywhere.

Show him another side.

After thanking Hatch, Evie set her phone on the kitchen counter where she could see incoming e-mails and slipped out of her jacket.

An hour later she popped a pan of chocolate sponge cake into the oven and rinsed the orange cream from the mixing beaters, when boots sounded on the back steps followed by the sound of scraping.

"How's Sugar Run?" Evie asked.

"Calm. The vet said his leg is fine. We just need to get him acclimated to his new surroundings. Right now he's pretty jittery anytime he's out of his stall." Jack hung his jacket on a hook by the door. It was so strange to see him out of a tie and those shiny platinum cuff links and tie tack. "How'd it go with you?"

"Also calm. Nothing new on Vandemere."

Jack sniffed. "Rosalee's black bean lasagna?"

Evie nodded. "Rosalee assumed I'd be staying for dinner."

"Are you?"

"Is that an invitation?" *And does that include your bed?* Evie nibbled on her bottom lip. She could still taste him, and she wanted more.

"Yes."

"Good." Evie let out a long breath. "You may want to go shower. You smell like a horse."

Jack laughed. "It's been a while since I've been around horses."

He headed up the winding wooden and wrought-iron staircase. She breathed deeply. She liked a man who could wear sweat and still be sexy. Check that. She liked Jack Elliott.

Fifteen minutes later, Jack was back in the kitchen with freshly washed hair and wearing clean jeans and a soft plaid shirt. He sniffed. "What's that?"

"Chocolate cake with orange cream. I made it."

"To celebrate?"

"To use up some of the oranges around this place. Really, Jack, there is such a thing as too much of a good thing."

She took Rosalee's lasagna out of the oven while Jack started a fire in the kitchen's beehive fireplace. It was so domestic. She bit back a snorting laugh. If her mother could see her now, she'd be sending out wedding invitations. Hah. Both she and Jack were married to work, which meant they'd make great lovers. No expectations. No strings. No worries.

She set the lasagna on the table, when Jack's phone rang. He answered it, his face leaching of all color. Tearing off her oven mitts, she grabbed his arm as he looked like he was about to topple over. "What happened?"

"A bomb just went off outside the Elliott Tower parking garage. Brady's been hurt."

CHAPTER TWENTY-FOUR

Monday, November 2
10:51 p.m.

There she is!" Evie pointed to the woman standing near the coffee machine in the waiting room at Good Samaritan Hospital.

Jack ran to Claire and grabbed her by the shoulders. "Where is he?"

"Bed number fourteen," Claire said. "The doctors are just finishing up."

"Is he okay?"

"Don't let him fool you. He's pretty shaken up."

Jack found Brady stretched out on a hospital bed with a rakish patch across his forehead. His lips were deathly pale but smiling. "You know, I should get blown up more often. I've had two very beautiful nurses attending to my every need. One brings me Popsicles, and the other wraps my feet in heated blankets."

Jack sank into the chair. He had no words.

"What happened?" Evie asked.

"I got in my car after work. It was parked where it always is. Lower level parking garage, space twelve. As I pulled out of the garage and onto the street, I heard a loud pop, and then boom! The glass on the passenger side shattered, and then there were flames." Brady's smile wobbled. "Everywhere. Which is about the time I bailed."

"Before the explosion, did you see anyone in the garage, on the street, or even on a nearby roof watching you, possibly aiming something that looked like a remote at your car?" Evie asked.

"No." Brady ran a hand through the hair spiking up from his head. "Is that what happened? Someone flipped a switch and torched me?"

"That's usually the case with these kinds of vehicle-borne IEDs. Have you talked to Captain Ricci yet?"

"Yep, and from what it sounds like, he's got half of LAPD on the streets right now."

"As he should." Jack's fingers fisted and unfisted, and he finally picked up the chart hanging from the end of Brady's bed. "What did the doctors say?"

"I'm fine, Jack. Just a few cuts and bruises." He pinched his chin and cocked his head. "I kind of have a nice rough-and-tumble look going on, don't I? Might help me with the chicks. What do you think, Evie? Would you kiss a mug like this?"

Evie planted a kiss on his forehead. She turned to Jack. "Listen, I, uh, need to go. I'm going to have a busy night."

"I know." His gaze slid over her. "I'm going to stay here until the doctors release Brady, and I'll take him home."

"I'll check with Ricci and make sure someone swept Brady's place. Just in case."

A chill stole across Jack's chest, icing his words. "You think this was Vandemere?"

"I'm thinking a lot of things right now, mainly that I need to take a look at what's left of Brady's car."

Because Evie dealt with bombs and the sick minds that used them for destruction. He reached for her hand, and they stood dusty boot to dusty boot. If it weren't for that terrified call, those boots would be parked next to his bed in Ojai, or more likely, in the middle of the kitchen floor because he wanted her that much.

He opened his mouth. He wanted to say more, but this wasn't the time or place. With a squeeze of his hand, he turned away.

"Jack!" Evie dug through her bag. "The cake would have made a mess in my purse, so I brought you this." She handed him an orange.

* * *

11:17 p.m.

Inside the Elliott Tower parking garage, Evie poked through the plastic tub that held the remains of a PVC housing and a single blasting cap. "Doesn't look too sophisticated, and it certainly doesn't have the firepower of Vandemere's other IEDs."

"No, but we're pretty sure it's his." Ricci took her into the lower-level parking garage, and in the parking spot marked for Jack Elliott were a hundred tiny red tissue-paper hearts.

"You know what he's doing, don't you?" Evie didn't let Ricci answer. "He didn't want to kill Brady, he wanted to rattle Jack. He's a resentful SOB. I'm guessing it has something to do with being rejected by the Abby Foundation, but it may go back even further to his sister, Abby."

"Any news on her?"

"My teammate Jon MacGregor is beating the streets."

As Evie was about to leave the garage, Jack pulled his car into the lower executive level. He looked as tired as she felt. "Did you get Brady home?" she asked.

Jack nodded. "And he's snoozing thanks to some very good drugs."

"By the way, this is a crime scene. You shouldn't be here." He should be safely tucked in his penthouse condo where she had an officer posted.

Jack tipped his head to the uniform at the guard station. "The officer let me in."

"Did you slip him a fat check?"

"No, I told him I have a lead on who did this." Jack ran a hand down the tired folds of his face. "I just got a call from Callie Portillo, the homeless girl with the cats. Around four thirty today she saw the man with shiny brown shoes who'd been following Lisa Franco the night she disappeared."

Evie clasped her hands to the front of her chest and closed her eyes as if deep in prayer. "Please, please tell me she got a look at his face this time."

"Unfortunately, no. But she got a good look at his shoes as he was climbing down the stairs with a backpack on his back."

Evie's eyelids popped open. "Stairs?"

"Yes. Callie had been sitting with some of her cats behind an old building down by the L.A. River, and she saw this fall from the bottom of his shoe as he walked down the stairs." He held up a red tissue-paper heart.

Any ounce of tiredness she'd been feeling swept away with the wings sending her heart racing. "And we have a location on these stairs?"

"It's the old canning warehouse." Jack's eyes brightened

to the color of cobalt glass and were just as sharp. "I'll show you where."

"This isn't your sandbox." She sounded like a broken record.

Jack jabbed his fingertips at his chest. "He's aiming sand at me and people I care about."

"Exactly, Jack, and sometimes that means you can't see what you need to see."

* * *

Tuesday, November 3
12:02 a.m.

When she was a kid taking religious education classes, Evie had learned about stairways to heaven. Right now she was looking at a stairway to hell.

According to Cat Girl, the man who'd abducted Lisa Franco was leaving this building with a backpack a few hours before a vehicle-borne-IED went off, injuring Brady Malloy, Jack Elliott's best friend and right-hand man.

Outfitted in body armor, she and two men from Ricci's team made their way up the stairs. On the fourth floor their handheld spotlights illuminated a large room with two doors leading to what must be two smaller rooms. The main room was empty. Both doors were closed. A shiny new padlock hung from the door on the right. The muscles along the backs of Evie's legs tightened. Shiny new locks on old abandoned buildings were usually hiding things.

She took in a deep breath. The air smelled of dust, old rubber—her nose twitched—and solder. Aiming her light at the padlocked door, she studied the area. "Bulge on the floor. Looks like a pressure-sensitive device, and on the door is a trip wire." This place was designed to warn the occupant of anyone approaching and slow law enforcement entry. "Okay, men, let's get this place cleared."

* * *

10:04 a.m.

Black dust was everywhere. Smudged across door handles. Streaked on the wooden arms of the futon. Peppered on Evie's boots. They'd cleared Vandemere's workshop late last night, and crime scene technicians had just finished processing.

After she snagged a few hours' sleep back at the station, it was time for Evie to get her hands dirty. She clapped the crime scene tech's shoulder. "Thanks, Ronnie. I appreciate the thoroughness."

"Let's hope this is the last time my guys need to do this."

"I'm always full of hope." That's why she poured herself body and soul into her work, why she joined Parker's team. "How many good prints?"

"At least a dozen unique."

"Let's get those run through IAFIS. I also want them checked against the last victim, Lisa Franco. If we get a match, it's one more nail in Vandemere's coffin."

She snapped on a pair of gloves and with Cho went straight to Vandemere's workbench. Time to get a handle on the bomber's construction process and a look into his crazed mind. There was a soldering iron, wire, timers, electrical tape, pipes, and a wicked-looking jar of nails and rods.

"And lookie here," Cho said as he hauled out two boxes below the bench. "RDX and sodium chlorate."

There was no glee in this discovery. Only horror.

As she was poking around the trash can, she found a paper coffee cup with a generic label and *AM-NF-CN* written in grease pencil on the side. There was also a wadded-up sketch of a woman with large breasts. However, the shining star in the trash can was a receipt from an art store in Whittier for the purchase of stretcher bars and more than one hundred dollars in oil paint. It was a cash deal, but it was possible a clerk might remember him, especially with the prompt of Greta Antony's sketch.

Evie knew the moment Jack entered the room, and it had nothing to do with her heightened smell or vision. She felt him. After his best friend almost being blown to shreds, Jack was a teakettle about to blow.

"Everything okay with Brady?" she asked.

Jack nodded. "Ricci wants me to take a quick look around."

She turned to Ricci, who nodded. "Since all this stuff keeps coming back to Jack, I want to see if anything strikes him as familiar or significant." Abby Elliott was linked to Vandemere. Was it possible that Jack shared a past with the twisted bomber?

At some point the room grew silent. She looked up. Every eye in the room was on Jack, who stood at her side holding a large sketch pad. A single vein pulsed thick and ropy along the side of his neck.

She took the sketch pad from him and almost dropped it. The drawing was rough, a series of pencil scratches, but she knew the face. Big brown eyes, wide mouth, thick eyelashes and brows, all framed by a crazy knot of hair. She saw it on those rare occasions when she looked in a mirror. But the body was wrong. Those weren't her curves and swells.

"Holy shit," Cho said. "He's got Evie sitting on a wooden bench and holding a rosary and baby."

"That's enough." Jack's words were as loud and sharp as the crack of a pistol. "I'm having you pulled from this case."

Evie tugged at her ear. Now that the initial shock of finding a sketch of her in Carter Vandemere's workshop had faded, she could think clearly. "I told you about my little hearing issue, right? Did I mention that sometimes I have a ringing in my ears? Kind of jumbles up sounds, and things don't make sense. Like now. Surely I didn't just hear *you* say you're having me pulled from my case."

"Stop being a smart-ass, Evie."

"But I am smart, Jack, and I'm good at what I do." She forced a calm despite the crazy spewing from his mouth. "I'm not getting out of this investigation."

"Look at that!" He aimed a hand at the sketch.

She turned away. She knew what was going on in his head. Crap like having your best friend almost blown to pieces played with your mind, and not in a good way.

He cupped his hand around her jaw and forced her gaze on the sketchbook. "Look at that." Jack's lips barely moved. "Tell me what you see."

"Me."

"Exactly. Artists create preliminary sketches like this for larger, more complex works. Vandemere plans to use you in the fourth bombing."

With little gentleness, she extricated herself from his hand. "Ain't gonna happen, because there's no way in hell he'll catch me. I'm a trained law enforcer."

"You're stepping down." Jack's command struck her squarely in the chest.

She took a step toward him. "And what gives you that right?"

"I brought you into this investigation, and I can take you out."

"Oh, yeah?" One more step and she was inches from his face. "Is your name Parker Lord? Do you currently serve as president of the United States? Because unless you can say yes to either of those questions, you have no control over whether I stay in this investigation or not. Got that? You don't control me." Her voice came out in a lethal whisper.

He grabbed her wrists. This time she didn't let that touch soften her.

"Officer Hawes." She dipped her head at a uniform standing in the doorway. "Please cuff Mr. Elliott and take him downtown."

She turned back to Carter Vandemere's workbench of terror but not before she caught a glimpse of the molten fire of Jack's face.

CHAPTER TWENTY-FIVE

Tuesday, November 3
3:32 p.m.

Four dots of dried blood coated one side of the tiny rectangle of metal. Evie held the razor blade up to the sunlight streaming through the window of Carter Vandemere's *art* studio. Did the blood belong to Mexican restaurant waitress Lisa Franco? Gallery owner Rene Masson? Some other nameless victim?

She was still meticulously going through every item in the workshop when the uniformed officer standing guard at the door called out, "Hey, Evie, you got a visitor downstairs."

She slipped the razor into the plastic bag. Four dots of blood. Four more dots that drew her that much closer to Vandemere.

"He says it's urgent," the officer added.

Yeah, she knew about urgent. Evie snapped off her gloves and booties and tossed them in the box just inside the door.

"You want to head out to the art store in Whittier with me?" Cho asked. They'd found the store receipt dated two months ago, and with any luck, a clerk might ID the buyer of the art supplies.

"No, I need to take care of some stuff down at the station." Namely Jack. She'd told Officer Hawes to release him after an hour, giving them both time to cool off. The meticulous work of combing through Vandemere's tools had refocused her energy, and she hoped that Jack had found a redirect for his. When she'd had him hauled away from the crime scene, the cool, collected businessman looked like he was ready to blow more than a few buttons on his pin-striped vest.

It was possible he was waiting for her below. Her boots pounded down the back steps of the warehouse. If so, was he ready to apologize? Ready to go another round? When she reached her car, her boots skidded to a stop. A wide ass was leaning against the hood.

"You don't look too happy to see me, Lady Feeb. Were you hoping to see someone else?" He waggled both eyebrows and patted the hood.

A serial bomber or billionaire in a buttoned-down suit would have been at the top of her list. She took a seat next to Freddy. "You got something for me?"

"I got some interesting pictures earlier of Mr. Jack Elliott being escorted out of here by the police. Could make me some serious money 'cause there's a story there."

"Don't even think about it."

"I can think about it all I want, but don't worry, I'm holding back until we get Bomber Boy." Freddy nudged her knee with his. "So what's up between you and The Suit?"

"You must be fabricating things again."

"I'm a news guy at heart, an observer, remember? I've seen something sparking between you and Guthrie Got-bucks."

"That would be the cataclysmic clash of our personalities and lifestyles. I don't like suits, and he likes women who have a bit more skill with a hairbrush."

Freddy tugged at a curl that had escaped the chaos on her head. "I kind of like the hair. Reminds me of a few of my nieces when they get out of bed and watch Saturday-morning cartoons."

She smacked away his hand. "Why are you here, Freddy?"

His face grew serious. "Got some intel. A friend of mine who's—shall we say—familiar with the darker side of the L.A. art scene did some nosing around, and he found a woman who posed for an artist around here. The woman told my buddy the artist was into some pretty bad shit that's right up Bomber Boy's alley."

"You got a name and address?"

"Better. I got us an appointment with her that starts"—he checked the clock on his camera—"in seven minutes."

* * *

4:01 p.m.

Zelda had no last name. She also had no lower teeth, and as far as Evie could tell, no bra or underwear under the gold tube dress clinging to her skinny frame. She wore bright red lipstick that bled into wrinkles at the corners of her mouth and combat boots, perfect for walking the streets.

Zelda, along with a whiff of old cigarettes and dollar-store perfume, climbed into the passenger seat of Evie's Beetle, which was parked at Union Station.

"You must be Durant's friend," Freddy said from where he was crammed in the backseat.

The woman winked a heavily caked eyelid. "I'm everyone's friend."

According to Freddy's friend, Durant, who knew about the darker side of L.A.'s art scene, this woman might have met Carter Vandemere. "You posed for an artist six months ago?" Evie asked.

"Art?" Zelda took a long drag on a short cigarette. "I don't know what he was creating on that canvas, and I don't want to know, but, yeah, I posed for this guy. He offered to pay double my going rate if I agreed to a little kink."

"What kind of kink?" Evie asked. Hayden said Vandemere didn't have much success with women, so it was possible, even plausible, that he employed the services of prostitutes.

Zelda tugged the zipper down the back of her dress, the two halves of gold parting and revealing a two-inch scar on her shoulder. "Hurt like a mo-fo," Zelda said, "and after the first cut, I made him quadruple the payment."

Evie's stomach twisted and she closed her eyes, but she couldn't blot out the sick horror of Vandemere making the cut and a world where a broken woman was desperate enough to sell her skin. She flexed her fingers and cleared her throat. "Did you get his name?"

"John." A crackly cackle slipped over her lips. "Just another John."

"What did he look like?"

"He was wearing a hat and sunglasses when he picked me up. Didn't want to be seen. Get that all the time. Back at his whacked studio, I had my back to him the entire time, but I remember he was a skinny guy, brown hair, nice shoes. That kind of struck me as odd, given that he was squattin' in the old canning factory."

"The one by the canal?"

"Yep, that's the one."

Evie stretched her fingers. She could almost feel this guy, he was so close. "Any distinguishing characteristics? Scars? Accent? Jewelry?"

"No, nothing like that, but I remember his car. Blue Honda Accord. Pretty plain Jane, but I got his license plate number."

Every once in a while a blue bird, a bit of unexpected goodness from an unexpected source, landed in her lap. *Please, God, let this be a freakin' bird.* Evie cleared her throat. "You got a license plate number on this guy?"

"Yeah, a little security. I take down the license, text it to a friend. She does the same with me. Us gals on the street, we kind of look out for each other. You know, in case something happens."

Hell, yeah, something was about to happen. Evie's hands shook as she took down the license plate number from Zelda and hauled out her phone to call California DMV.

Before the aging prostitute left she jutted a veiny hand into the backseat. Freddy took a hundred-dollar bill from his wallet and slipped it onto her palm.

Twenty-eight minutes later Evie was stroking that blue bird. She had a name. The blue Honda Accord was registered to Adam Wainwright, the director of the Abby Foundation.

* * *

5:38 p.m.

Claire was gone for the evening, and the door to Jack's office was shut, but Evie had seen his car in the lower-level executive parking spaces. The last time she'd seen him, a sworn officer of the LAPD was escorting him out of Carter Vandemere's art studio. Jack had gone peacefully and without cuffs, but he'd been livid.

The inside of Jack's office was lit but empty. Damn, she must have just missed him. She was about to rush to the parking garage, when a door on the far wall opened. Jack stepped out, his hair damp and jaw cleanly shaven. He wore another suit, but not one of his three-piece jobs. This one was solid black, with a narrow jacket and trousers. Beneath the jacket he wore a black shirt and black tie. Monochrome done right. The man could wear a loincloth and look like he belonged on a Hollywood red carpet.

"Nice duds," she said as he made his way toward her. She breathed deeply. And nice, nice smell. Two of her nephews, the sons of her second-oldest brother, had a pet Weimaraner, and when the boys left for school, the dog would roll around on the boys' blankets and clothes as if he couldn't get enough of their wonderful little-boy smell. Guilty. She loved Jack's big-boy smell and would love to roll around the blankets of his bed.

He straightened the cuff links at his wrist. She straightened her hair.

"Jack—"

"Evie—" they said at the same time.

Evie took a step back. "Go ahead." What she had to tell him was going to punch him in the gut.

Jack sat on the edge of his desk. He stared at his hands, then lifted his gaze to her, those denim eyes as warm as the jacket she wore over her heart. "I'm sorry, Evie. I overstepped my boundaries this morning."

"Yes, you did." She took a step toward him.

"I should not have interfered or questioned your ability to do your job."

"Also correct." Another step.

"But sometimes around you, Evie"—he tugged at the hem of her jacket, pulling her into the V of his thighs— "I don't think." His head dipped, and he brushed his lips against hers. Soft and sweet but powerful enough to warm her to the tips of her toes.

She slid her hands along the lapels of his jacket. "That's a bad thing?"

"I'm not sure." The admission was raw and delivered on a shaky breath, and so unlike the Jack Elliott she'd met a week ago. That man had been sure of everything.

She released his lapels and stepped back because she was about to dial up the number on his personal Richter scale. "I got a new lead."

"Something on Abby?"

She shook her head. There was no way to soften this one. "A man we believe to be Carter Vandemere picked up a prostitute six months ago in a blue Honda Accord. The car's owner is Adam Wainwright."

Jack stood and buttoned the top button of his jacket. "Adam is not the bomber." Mr. Confident was back.

"He fits the bomber profile. He's a failed and frustrated artist working at a desk job launching other people's art careers."

"He looks nothing like the heavyset kid who lived with Abby at The Colony."

"It's been fifteen years. People change."

"Dammit, Evie. I handpicked Adam. He's part of my executive team."

"Bad guys, the really good ones, have a talent for hiding what they don't want others to see."

"I'm a successful businessman. I see past the bullshit."

"People see only what they want to see." She grabbed his hands. "Listen, Jack, whether you like it or not, I have to follow up on this lead. I called Wainwright's phone, and a unit stopped by his house, but we can't find him."

Jack rolled his head about his neck as if his thoughts were too heavy to hold his head upright. He checked his watch. "In fifty-two minutes Adam will be with me. We're having an exclusive preview for VIPs of the *Beauty Through the Ages* exhibit, which is being boxed up this week and sent to the museum where it will be officially put on exhibit."

She looped her arm through his. "Excellent. I'll be your date. Will there be cake?"

The pinched skin around Jack's mouth smoothed. He took her hand, giving it a squeeze. "Probably." Looping his arm over her shoulder, he led her to the elevator and stopped. "You can't go like that."

"Like what."

He ran his finger down her nose, the tip of his finger coming away with a black smudge.

CHAPTER TWENTY-SIX

Tuesday, November 3
6:21 p.m.

Hold this." Jack handed her the stuffed Chihuahua.

Evie backed away. "I am *not* carrying around a stuffed dog."

"Just hold it while I get the dress off the mannequin. It's the only extra small in the store."

Jack had taken her to one of the boutiques on the bottom floor of the Elliott Tower to shop for something appropriate to wear to an Abby Foundation VIP dinner. The shop had already closed for the night, but Jack, being Jack, had *associates* who apparently wouldn't mind the late-night sale. After a thorough search of the store, he'd decided on the red sweater-y thing in the display window. She decided to avoid another argument so they could get going and she could get her hands on Adam Wainwright.

In the dressing room, she slipped the dress over her head,

the fabric gliding over her skin like melted butter. Jack really did have exquisite taste.

Back in the boutique, he handed her a pair of black heels.

"Holy crap, Jack. Those heels are five inches high. I could kill myself."

"Says the woman who handles bombs for a living."

She poked her feet into the heels, which were surprisingly comfortable.

Near the cash register, Jack slid his fingers over a necklace with glittery black beads.

"I do not need any jewelry." This was taking too much time. She needed to grill Wainwright.

Jack tilted his head and studied her. "You're right, Agent Jimenez, no jewelry. You have enough sparkle already."

As she left her credit card information and the tags at the cash register, she spotted a display of silk scarves, her eye drawn to a pretty beige square with swirls of teal and purple. It reminded her of peacock feathers. She snapped off the price tag and added it to her pile. Slipping the scarf in her bag, she turned to Jack. "Let's fly."

Jack, who'd been leaning against the register counter, his arms crossed, shook his head. He took her hand and led her to a freestanding oval mirror. "What do you see?"

"Jack, I don't have time for this."

He spun her so she faced the glass. "What do you see?"

"A woman in a red sweater."

"Exactly." He slid his hands along her sides where the silky cashmere clung to her waist and swished in drapey folds below her hips. His gaze settled on the soft folds of the deep V brushing the swells of her breasts. His lips touched down along the bare slope of her shoulder. "A woman."

* * *

7:17 p.m.

"Pretty swank," Evie said as Jack escorted her past the string quartet stationed outside the Abby Foundation's front door and into the bottom-floor gallery, lit tonight by candles in handblown glass. Waiters carrying trays of champagne flutes and steaming hors d'oeuvres threaded through the standing-room-only crowd. "How many people are here tonight?"

"About fifty." Jack nodded to the president of the Abby Foundation board and one of the art critics for the *L.A. Times*. "All VIPs who've supported the Abby Foundation over the years."

"So where's Wainwright?" She kept her voice low, but he could hear her impatience, feel it. Her body thrummed with energy.

Jack ground his back teeth. Evie was hardheaded and unyielding. Arguing with her was like...like arguing with himself. Especially since she wasn't one bit intimidated by him. He was still having a hard time with that one. Few people in this world were as fearless. "Adam is giving tours of the third-floor exhibit."

She headed for the stairwell. "*Vámonos.*"

On the third floor, a dozen people mingled, some talking with Brandon Brice, the Abby Foundation's current artist in residence and others trickling in and out of the *Beauty Through the Ages* gallery. Adam stood at the door to the exhibit like a loyal sentry, and Evie zoomed in on him like...like a federal agent hell-bent on capturing a serial killer.

As Evie escorted Wainwright to one of the studios, Jack positioned himself at the door to the gallery. While she looked like a federal agent, Evie also looked like a beautiful, intelligent, passionate woman, and it wasn't just the dress.

He ran a hand along his forehead. She'd look even more beautiful, intelligent, and passionate out of it.

"Intriguing little thing." A pair of rose-lacquered nails landed on his arm.

He kissed the cheek the woman offered. "Good evening, Reggie. You look beautiful, as always."

Reggie's lips curved in a pout. "Beautiful but on the back burner."

He supposed he had this coming. Last year he'd met Reggie Thurston, the owner of a string of wildly successful shoe stores, across a boardroom table, and within twenty-four hours of that first meeting, they were partners in business and occasionally in bed.

"You missed the fund-raiser for the orphans," Reggie went on.

"I've been busy."

She tilted her head toward the door where Evie had taken Adam. "With the little firecracker?"

"With business."

Reggie laughed.

"What?"

She patted him on the cheek and slipped into the gallery, adding over her shoulder, "You are so blind, Jack."

* * *

7:30 p.m.

Adam Wainwright looked like a man whose necktie was too tight. Red face. Veins popping up along his temples. Odd. He wasn't wearing a tie.

"I have a room full of important people out there, people who have the power to make or break the work I do with the foundation," Wainwright said with a snip. "So you better make this quick."

Evie pictured the scar on the prostitute's shoulder, the one taking the place of a two-inch square of flesh. Did the sick mass of humanity who sliced it from her body take his time? Did he savor each cut? Or did he rush through the process? But more important, was Adam Wainwright that sick mass of humanity?

She took out her phone and showed him the picture she'd snapped in the parking lot fifteen minutes ago. "Do you recognize this car?"

"It's mine."

"You drive it regularly for both work and pleasure?"

"Yes." A snap joined the snip. "What's this about?"

"Ever pick up a prostitute in it?"

Adam rubbed at the veins along his temples. "That's not my scene."

"Are you sure? I have a female prostitute who claims a man driving this car picked her up on June third of this year."

"I already told you, Agent Jimenez, I don't swing that way."

"Did you loan your car to anyone that day?"

"No."

"Does anyone else have keys to this car?"

"No."

"Mr. Wainwright, I'll need you to come down to the station so we can let the witness see for herself."

"No."

She tugged at her bad ear. "'Scuse me?"

"That won't be necessary. I was doing something else on June third of this year, and it had nothing to do with picking up a prostitute." He took a series of deep breaths and slipped off his jacket.

"You have witnesses that can vouch for you?"

He hung the jacket over an easel. "Quite a few. All very credible." Slowly, he unfastened the buttons on the cuff of his left sleeve. "I was at a hospital on Wilshire Boulevard. As a patient. My partner left me on June second, which is the day I did this." Adam pushed back his shirtsleeve and rotated his forearm, displaying a thin pink scar that ran two inches above his wrist. "Pathetic, huh? I wasn't really trying to kill myself, just get the attention of the man who I thought was the love of my life. Didn't work. He never showed up, called, or sent a get well card."

The scar wasn't red or angry, but she could see it was still raw. Evie had never experienced that kind of pain, probably because she'd given her heart to her career. She shifted her gaze to Wainwright's face, etched with pain. Her heart went out to the man, who clearly could not have been driving his car. Jack was right on this account. "I'll need to know who had access to your car and keys that weekend."

"Just Mr. Elliott."

"Jack Elliott?"

"After I attempted my pathetic little cry for attention, which took place here in my office, I got wise and called nine-one-one. An ambulance took me to the hospital where I was under suicide watch for forty-eight hours. I was worried about my car sitting on the street in this neighborhood, so I called Mr. Elliott and told him about my monumental screw-up. He had my car moved to the Elliott Tower parking garage, which has better security."

Evie could see Jack taking control and taking care of everything. She pictured Claire's scars and heard Brady's words: *Jack Elliott's my savior*. A man who pulled people out of dark places because he'd been there himself. A man who refused to let go.

Adam tugged his sleeve over the scar and tried to smooth the lines on his face. "Do you still need me to go down to the police station?"

"No." Because if Adam Wainwright wasn't driving his car that weekend, he wasn't Carter Vandemere.

* * *

9:49 p.m.

"My job would be so much easier if you'd just admit you're the bomber." Evie slipped her arms around Jack, who stood in front of the glass wall of his office on the thirty-sixth floor of the Elliott Tower.

He cupped his hands around hers. "I wish it were that easy."

Right now nothing was easy. After leaving the VIP gathering at the Abby Foundation, Jack brought Evie back to his office, where he checked his calendar and verified that he had one of the garage parking attendants pick up Adam's car and leave it in the parking garage. The keys had been dropped off and kept in Claire's desk.

"This is the second time a security breach has been connected to Claire," Evie pointed out. The first being that her security card had been the only one to access Jack's office in the days before the paper heart bomb exploded.

Jack turned around and faced her. "Claire is not the bomber."

"No, she's not, but it's possible the bomber is using her to get access to you."

He was a dark silhouette against the L.A. skyline. She couldn't make out his face, but she felt the anger rolling along his body, tightening and tensing his muscles.

"He's not going to win," Jack said. Confidence was so damned sexy on this man.

"I know." She slid her hands along his chest.

His hands pressed against hers. "He is not going to hurt the people I care about." Jack's heart thundered against her palm in a message stronger than words. He cared. About his staff. About her.

His head dipped, a slow, calculated movement, giving her a chance to back away from the deal.

A laugh bubbled up her throat, and she threw her arms around his neck, capturing his lips with hers. His hands slipped around her back, and he drew her against the solid wall of his chest, a groan—one she felt more than heard—ripping low in his gut, across his chest, and against her lips. She welcomed it with a soft groan of her own. His hands slicked across the buttery folds of the dress he'd chosen for her, slipping it from her shoulders and past her hips, where it fell to the floor like a brilliant spill of paint.

His fingers fanned through her hair, lifting it, then splaying it across her shoulders and chest. He stepped back as if to admire his handiwork. "Beautiful," he said around a smile.

With less gentleness, he tore off his jacket, shirt, and tie. In the moonlight his skin was molten gold. She ran first her eyes, then her fingertips along the dips and mounds of his chest, smiling as his skin rippled and gleamed with heat.

Her fingers froze just above the skin peeking out above his right hip. She stepped back and blinked. "You have a tattoo."

He pulled her to him, his lips sliding along her neck. "Yes."

"When did you get it?"

"Discuss later," he said against the hollow of her throat.

She pushed him away. "Discuss now."

His breath came out in ragged puffs. "This is another power struggle, isn't it?"

"Probably."

Jack eased back but kept his hands around her hips. "I got it in New York."

She unlatched his belt and tugged down the waistband of his trousers, exposing an elongated four-pointed star. "What is it?"

"A compass. To remind me that I am the master of my fate and captain of my soul."

She traced the tip of the star. "I've heard that before."

"From the poem 'Invictus.' My brooding seventeen-year-old self loved it."

She ran her index finger along his waistband. "And you chose to tuck it away and not share your message with the world."

"It was a message for one." His entire body stilled for a handful of endless seconds before he unfastened the button of his dress pants, the fabric falling and exposing the full tattoo with a curving letter *N* and arrow. A compass from a man who knew exactly what he wanted in this life and how to get it. And he'd chosen to show it to her.

She threw herself into his arms, his hands exploring every heated inch of her, pausing only when he found the piece of raised skin on her thigh. "And you have a scar," he said. "Recent."

"Houston. Falling glass." She pointed to the tiny white scar dissecting her eyebrow. "Same place I got this."

He kissed her from the tiny scar through her eyebrow to the one on her thigh and every place in between, and she melted into him, wondering how she could ever have thought him cold.

CHAPTER TWENTY-SEVEN

Wednesday, November 4
6:12 a.m.

Evie stood at the kitchen counter, a knife in her hand and a frown on her face.

"Personally, I thought sex was pretty damned incredible last night," Jack said. After making love in his office he brought her to his penthouse and made love to her again in his bed, and if he had his way, he was very much looking forward to repeating the act in his kitchen.

He crossed the room and nuzzled the side of her neck. She tasted sweet and salty. He slipped his hands under the black shirt she'd thrown on and ran his palms up the silky curves along her waist and chest.

"It was." Evie pushed him away and aimed the knife at his chest. "Where's your juicer?"

"My what?"

"Citrus juicer." She stabbed the knife at the counter, and

for the first time he noticed a small mountain of sliced oranges on the counter. "I was craving fresh-squeezed orange juice this morning, so I went to the store and bought oranges, but now I need a juicer."

Jack ran his hand along the stubble of his chin. "I don't have one."

"You own twenty acres of citrus—"

"—but don't own a juicer. I know, Evie, I'm in serious need of help."

She tossed the knife in the sink and wound her arms around his neck, the sweet, sunny smell of oranges engulfing him. His hands cupped the soft swells of her hips.

"It's a good thing you have me." She landed one more kiss on his lips, then patted his butt. "Back in a flash."

The tails of his shirt flying out from the faded curve of her blue jeans, she darted out of the kitchen, and with her went his breath. While a bomber was rocking all of Los Angeles, one tiny bomb investigator was rocking his world. He stared at his hands, empty but for the lingering heat of her skin. She'd slipped away from him so fast, so easily. Because she had juice to make. Work to do. Serial bombers to stop. His fingers curled into his palms. And in the staccato tick of a clock or the single beat of a heart, she could be gone.

He flattened his palms on the cold granite of the kitchen counter. There was nothing he could do to stop her. As she reminded him yesterday in her blistering speech, he wasn't Parker Lord. He wasn't the president of the United States. He was a crucial part of her current investigation and her *chauffeur*. When the case was over, she'd move on to the next pile of smoldering wreckage. Away from him.

The front door swung open and seconds later, Evie charged into the kitchen with a small, round electronic appliance. "Voilà!"

And he was also the guy whose compass shook every time she walked into a room. Pushing himself up off the counter, he crossed his arms over his chest. "Where did you get that?"

"Mrs. Simmons two floors below. She told you to keep it. She has two others."

"You know Mrs. Simmons?"

"I do now. Nice woman." She nudged him aside and plugged in the juicer. "She invited us to a potluck at her place a week from Saturday."

But would Evie be around a week from Saturday? Would she have already slipped out of his life? "A potluck with my neighbors?"

"I told her we'd be there." She grabbed two orange halves. "With cake."

Jack couldn't help it. He forgot about next week and people who slipped out of his hands and laughed, because now was a good time to laugh.

As she squeezed the oranges, he scrambled eggs and made toast. They ate breakfast, neither reaching for their phones or computers, because when that happened, the magic of fresh-squeezed orange juice would end.

Evie set down her empty glass. "I have work to do."

"Me too."

"Ready to play chauffeur?"

"I'm going to check in with Agent MacGregor on his search for Abby." Last he heard from Agent MacGregor, no one had seen or heard from Abby after she disappeared from The Colony. But she was alive. He refused to let that bit of hope slip from his hands. "Then I need to take the helicopter out to Ojai." The horse wasn't just part of a collection. It was a living, breathing thing, and according to his new stable manager, the living wasn't easy for the blind racehorse.

"Problems with Sugar Run?"

"Manny texted this morning. Sugar Run isn't adapting well to the new environment."

"Good. You go take care of your dream." She leaned over the table and gave him a sweet, orangey kiss.

* * *

8:09 a.m.

"How old is he?" Evie asked the woman standing at the bottom of the playground slide. At the top of a jungle gym stood a little boy with stick-straight blond hair and a dirty face. He was banging a stick on the plastic roof of the slide, the metal rail, and the nine plastic tic-tac-toe squares.

The woman smiled. "Two and a half. Not quite a terror, but close."

Evie took out her shield and showed it to the woman. "Keep your eye on him, okay?"

The woman wrapped her arms around her chest even though the sunshine flooded the little park off Grand this morning. "I heard the police on the news say the Angel Bomber's next victim might be a blond-haired child."

"We're doing our best to make sure there are no more victims." Evie smiled at the kid banging away like a drummer in a rock band. "But in the meantime, keep him close."

Carter Vandemere was scheduled to strike in two days, and if he hadn't done so already, he was probably on the hunt for a brown-haired woman and a blond infant.

It was impossible to think she could talk to every parent with a young blond-haired child, but any she saw as she was cruising downtown had been getting a personal warning from her. She'd already stopped by neighborhood day care centers and school bus stops where mothers with infants waited for their older schoolchildren. She'd been to fast-food restaurants with play gyms and jogging tracks where parents ran with baby joggers.

Save the baby!

* * *

8:25 a.m.

Smokey Joe waved off the steamy cinnamon roll. "Thanks, Katy-lady, but I'm not hungry."

"We need to talk," Kate said. She'd surprised the snot out of him when she showed up last night. Said she missed his cranky old butt, and he missed her, but he had work to do.

"Need to git back on the phone calls." Smokey Joe ran his hands along his desk until he found his headset. They had two days before Evie's bomber would strike again, and calls were pouring in to the Angel Bomber hotline. L.A. coppers were taking the calls, which were being taped, and one by one he was going through 'em, listening for anything that might prove useful. Evie said bombers usually kept their distance. They didn't like to get too close, but it was possible the bomber would insert himself in some way into the investigation. Right now Smokey was interested in a pair of calls that sounded like they came from the same man using different names. "We'll talk on my lunch break, okay?"

"Not okay." Kate sat in the chair next to his, the sigh from the chair cushion just as loud as the one that came from her mouth. This morning she sounded tired and a little peaked. Probably her new job. She was heading up some public relations stuff for a real nice nonprofit group in Reno. He was so damned proud of her, getting back into the world of the living.

Smokey slipped the headset around his neck. "Then talk fast because this crazy fella is about to strike again. A woman and a baby. What kind of screwball kills little babies with bombs?"

She let out another long breath. "I talked to Fran yesterday."

He fingered the headset cord. "Fran? Who the hell is Fran? Does she know something about the bomber?"

"Fran Watland, your cousin, the one who lives in Key West."

"Franny? Why, I ain't seen her for fifty years. We used to go blackberry picking together on the Rim. How is the old girl?"

"Great. She said she'd love to see you."

"Did you give her my address? She can visit me on my mountain as soon as I help Evie get this Angel Bomber business taken care of. So you'll need to excuse me, Katy-lady; Evie needs me."

He settled the headphones over his ears and pushed Play. Someone clicked Stop.

"Why the he-ell did you do that?"

Kate took the headphones from his head. "You're not going back to your mountain."

"What?"

"Over the past six months you've run off every aide your caseworker has arranged to live with you. You have refused my repeated offers to move in with Hayden and me. So Fran said you're welcome to move in with her and her daughter."

Smokey chuckled.

"I'm not joking, Smokey."

"Me neither, so you can tell Franny and everyone else I ain't leaving my mountain."

There was a long pause. Smokey counted the ticks on the clock somewhere near the door. He counted to a hundred before she said, "At this point, what I say doesn't matter."

"What are you talking about, Katy-lady?"

"After you drove your car off the mountain, your case-worker set off to track down your closest living relative and found Franny. She explained to Franny that you're a danger to yourself and others. Franny agreed." Kate's voice cracked. "Franny also agreed to serve as your legal guardian if you are unable to make sound choices. If you choose not to go live with your cousin, Franny will seek a court order giving her conservatorship. Don't you see, Smokey? I'm no longer in the picture."

CHAPTER TWENTY-EIGHT

Wednesday, November 4
3:51 p.m.

Evie poked her head into her office. Hayden was staring at a computer, and Smokey Joe was staring at the wall.

"Meeting starts in two minutes," she said. Neither Hayden nor Smokey Joe moved. She banged on the door frame. "Wakey-wakey. Ricci called an all-hands meeting and needs status reports."

Hayden pulled on his jacket and headed out the door. Smokey didn't so much as move an eyelash.

"Come on, Smokey. Ricci will have donut holes."

"Not going." The old man knotted his arms across his chest.

Evie fell in step with Hayden. "Someone wake up on the wrong side of the bed this morning?"

Hayden nodded. "I'll fill you in later."

On the conference room walls, most of the beautiful

women wore smiling faces. The same could not be said for the group gathered around the conference table. They had two days to catch a bomber out to kill two people, including an infant. Every hair on Evie's body stood on end.

Ricci sat at the head of the table. "Just got the fingerprint report from latent. One set of fingerprints in Vandemere's studio matched Lisa Franco's. Blood type found on the futon was also a match."

Knox's hands fisted. He'd been working the homicide case and just got the evidence he needed. He knew his killer; now they just needed to find him.

"Cho, anything new with stuff found in Vandemere's workshop?" Ricci asked.

"I followed up with the art store in Whittier. No one remembers the purchase or a customer who looks like the man in our sketch. I've also been visiting home improvement and hardware stores that sell the items we found, and again, no hits. And no hits so far on the coffee cup we found."

"Anything on the hotline, Hayden?"

"More than five hundred calls came in after the sketch aired. So far nothing solid."

"What about Abby Elliott?" Ricci's questions came at a rapid-fire pace.

"I tracked her to The Colony where she had an unwanted admirer named Dougie," Jon MacGregor said. "I haven't been able to find a trace of her or her art beyond that. Right now I'm looking into cold cases from fifteen years ago and checking into unidentified bodies of young women."

"She's alive," Evie said.

Jon's eagle-eyed stare didn't waver. "I agree."

Ricci turned to her. "What about the folks who have access to the *Beauty Through the Ages* collection?"

"Still nothing. Adam Wainwright, Brandon Brice, and

Claire Turner have no direct ties to the bombings. I'm following up on who could have stolen Wainwright's car and have some guys beating the streets to see if any other prostitutes were picked up by Vandemere. Since the security breaches occurred with Claire Turner, I'm digging into who has access to her Elliott Enterprises security key card."

"What about Elliott?" Knox asked.

"He's no longer a suspect," Evie said.

Knox's jaw twitched. "Because he saw your Saturday panties."

With the evidence linking his homicide victim, Lisa Franco, directly to Vandemere, Knox's intensity had shot up a few degrees. He was ready to blow. One of them needed to keep cool. "No, Knox. Because Elliott spends sixteen hours a day chained to a desk in a glass-and-chrome tower, and he has the phone records and e-mail trails to prove it."

"Yeah, right." Knox rested his elbows on the table and leaned toward her. "Why don't you tell us the real reason? Tell us about your new crime fighting tool. The one between your legs. Dip your wick and—"

Evie flew across the table and slammed her fist into Knox's jaw. The homicide detective's head snapped back. Perfect position for Evie to grab the collar of his shirt. She drew his face to within inches of hers, her breath heating the air between them. "Care to rephrase that?"

Knox's lip curled. Evie twisted the fabric in her fist, tightening the chokehold. Hayden and Cho must have bolted from their chairs. They stood on either side of her like bookends.

"Knock it off!" Ricci said. "All of you."

Just as fast as the molten fire erupted, Evie put a lid on it. She released Knox's collar and held up both hands, fingers splayed wide. "'S okay."

"No, it's not okay." Ricci jammed a hand through his hair, which looked anything but Hollywood slick. "Knox, that kind of talk can get you booted off this investigation. Hell, it could get you a few weeks of serious R-and-R not of your choosing."

Knox wiped his mouth with his sleeve, the fabric smearing with blood.

"What the hell is wrong with you?" Ricci continued.

"You wanna know? You really wanna know what's eating me?" Knox jabbed a finger at Evie. "A hotshot bomb specialist blows in and takes over. For a moment let's forget about her and talk about the other girl, the one who really matters, Lisa Franco." He walked across the room and spit at the trash can. He missed, the wad of blood and saliva hitting the wall. "Yesterday I saw a futon mattress covered in Lisa Franco's blood." He swiped the spittle from his chin. "For almost a month I've been busting my ass on this case because I owe that girl and her family a fair and thorough investigation, and I don't want it clouded by a cop who's nailing the guy at the middle of all of this."

"We're on the same team, Knox." Evie raised her hands in the air and waggled her fingers. "Wearing matching T-shirts and waving the same fucking pom-poms. No one, including Jack Elliott, is clouding my judgment. I got my eyes wide open, and God help Carter Vandemere when he finally gets within my sights." Her heart crashed against her chest to the beat of the ticking clock.

After a full minute, Knox wiped his mouth with his sleeve again and sat in a chair near the door.

"Okay, everyone." Ricci banged his palms on the table. "Two days."

"Two days," everyone said in unison like a circle of football players breaking from a huddle. Two days.

"You coming, Evie?" Hayden asked from the doorway. "Maybe you can talk Smokey Joe out of his funk."

"Yeah, I'll be there in a minute." She waited until the room emptied out of everyone but Ricci.

Ricci stared at his splayed fingers, then at her. "You gonna report Knox for harassment?"

"Nah." She picked at a new stain on her jacket sleeve.

"You'd have a case."

That would get them no closer to putting an end to the case that mattered. She shrugged. "We're all stressed." She studied the dirt under her right index fingernail.

She was living Houston all over again. One of the officers on guard in the Houston disrupt, a man on her team, hadn't trusted her to do her job. When the toddler who was being evacuated bolted from his mother's arms across the court-yard where the IED had been planted, she dived instinctively at the kid, leaving her post. The officer on guard, bigger and stronger and more capable—at least in his own mind—pushed her aside, deciding he'd go for the grab, but his clumsy actions and complete lack of knowledge of the IED set off the explosive, injuring the child, her, and himself. The president had been right. She was responsible in part be-cause it was her crime scene, and for a few seconds, she'd lost control of one of her men.

"You gonna report me for belting him?" Evie asked.

"Nah." Ricci flashed her a bit of Hollywood bright. "We're all stressed."

"You probably should," Evie said. "Knox could squeal like a pig." And if he did, the president would come down on her.

"Not Knox. He doesn't want it anywhere on paper that anyone got the jump on him, especially a woman."

Because women were softer, weaker. She stood, cradling

a fist in the palm of her hand. Not in her world. "I'm not sorry I decked him."

Ricci clamped his hand around her shoulder. "Which is why I'm glad you're here. Knox, too. He's one of our best. I specifically asked for him to be assigned to these bombings." He escorted her to the door. "You two are very much alike."

"I'm so going to try and forget you said that."

"I'm serious. You're both good at what you do, and you both know it."

* * *

4:06 p.m.

"Hold it right there, Manny." Jack popped the post in place. "I think we're good." He gave the fence a hard shake. Not a budge. "You get the post hole digger, and I'll pick up the extra wood. We need to keep debris or anything else that will spook him at a minimum."

Sugar Run stood at the far end of the pasture pawing at the ground. This morning Manny had introduced Sugar Run to the pasture, going through careful precautions to get him safe and acclimated, but the fiery horse got skittish, bolted, and broke the fence. Lucky for all of them, the horse wasn't hurt, although he looked sorely agitated.

Jack rested a dress shoe on the bottom rung of the fence. "What do you need?" Jack aimed his words at Sugar Run. "You're mad at the world and taking it out on a wooden fence post. It's not working for you, my friend. You're going to end up a cold, lonely old man."

Like him. Until now. Until Evie came into his life he hadn't realized how cold, how lonely, he'd been. She was feisty but people flocked to her. And fiery. Oh, yeah, she had plenty of fire. He'd told Evie that he was involved with this case because he felt responsible. Then he admitted he was holding on to hope that finding the bomber would help him find his sister. All true. But the past few days he'd found life beyond the office, in things like cake, and sand between his toes. All thanks to Evie.

"Is that what you need, big guy? A little filly to chase away the dark and cold?" But Sugar Run had been violent with the mares. "Then how about a friend." He pictured blind Smokey Joe and Evie. Evie was fond of the old man, bringing him muffins, helping him find his way. Maybe that's what Sugar Run needed, someone to help him find his way.

Jack jogged across the pasture. "Hey, Manny. I need the vet's number."

An hour later, Jack hopped out of the truck and walked to the pasture gate, unlatching the lock and pushing it open. Sugar Run's nostrils flared, and his ears swiveled. Jack flipped the latch on the trailer and swung open the door. The lone inhabitant flicked her tail and sauntered off the trailer and into the pasture.

"Mr. Elliott, are you sure this is going to work?" Manny asked.

Unlike most of his business dealings, Jack was very much out of his element. "No."

Sugar Run danced from one hoof to another as the visitor pranced through the pasture.

Manny joined him at the fence. "I've heard of buddy horses before, but not this."

"I couldn't find a buddy horse on such short notice. The vet said this was the next-best thing."

"But a goat, Mr. Elliott?"

Jack placed one dusty dress shoe on the gate rung. "Our

Boy has made a pretty strong statement this past year. He's been aggressive with other horses and acts out against humans. Yet he's still lively and wants to run. I think he's saying he's frightened and not sure how to find his way in his new, sightless world." Jack watched the goat picking her way across the pasture. "Maybe Miss Alfalfa can help."

CHAPTER TWENTY-NINE

Wednesday, November 4
8:53 p.m.

Jack's Audi looked out of place in her motel parking lot next to an old Impala and minivan with missing hubcaps. The driver, on the other hand, looked very right.

Evie hitched her bag on her shoulder and climbed out of her Beetle. She stepped into the circle of Jack's arms, leaning into a cloud of air that smelled of Jack, although tonight's version had a dash of dust and sweat.

"How was your day?" she asked. Such a mundane phrase, one she'd heard thousands of times from her parents and her brothers and their wives. She had no idea how good asking this of someone could make her feel.

"Got a new goat," Jack said. "And you?"

She held up her hand, one of her knuckles still swollen. "Got in a fistfight."

Jack took her hand and brought it to his lips. "Tell me about it."

"I'm fine."

He pulled her hips to his and leaned against the car. "Talk."

She ran the knuckles of her good hand along the front of his shirt. "Not much to talk about. The homicide cop popped off, and I popped him. Won't be the first time cops took a swing at each other in the heat of an investigation, and it won't be the last."

Jack tucked her hand into his arm and escorted her out of the parking lot. "Hayden said Knox deserved it."

Evie pushed him away. "You know about the fight?"

"I'm keeping abreast of things."

She shook her head in awe. "Have I mentioned lately your issues with control?"

He drew her to his side. "Have I mentioned I'd like to take a crack at Knox? Hayden said he's been yanking your chain since the day you arrived and that there wasn't a person in that conference room who wasn't cheering you on."

"Now you're acting borderline stalkerish. You realize that, don't you?"

"From the way it sounded, it's a good thing you got to Knox before Hayden did."

"My team has my back. Always have. Always will." She ground her boot heel into the loose asphalt. Unless the president booted her from the team. "The whole thing should have never happened. I swear it's Houston all over again. I'm tired of having to prove myself."

"So stop."

"Says the person with the Y chromosome."

"I'm serious. You're the best, Evie."

She tucked her arm in his and headed for her motel room. "You're just saying that because you've seen my Saturday panties."

"I'm saying it because it's true."

"Okay, I'm one shade shy of wonderful. So let me get a fresh set of clothes, then we'll go back to your place and I might let you see my Wednesday panties."

Jack coughed out a laugh that turned into a smile. She loved that smile, and she could seriously get used to seeing it every night as she drifted off into sleep.

Inside her room, she tossed her bag on the bed and dug out a clean pair of jeans and two T-shirts and pairs of underwear. In the bathroom, she reached for her toothbrush and froze. A card was perched next to the tiny coffeepot. Someone had scrawled, *Evie*, on the front and placed a heart over the *i*. Red ink.

She tore open the envelope, and silvery confetti poured out. No, not confetti. Twisted bits of metal. A razor-sharp sliver speared her palm. Plucking out the metal shaving, she ignored the trickle of red oozing from her hand and took out the card, which was a photograph of a brown-haired young woman holding a blond-haired child. Both were wide-eyed and terrified.

The earth tilted. She grabbed on to the bathroom counter with both hands. Her stomach heaved, and she swallowed sickness brought on by a sick man. The sick, twisted son of a bitch.

"Evie, what happened to your h—" Jack's gaze shifted to the photo, and he rested a knuckled fist on the bathroom counter. "He has his next victims."

Evie pulled in one breath, then another. "This is good." Another breath. "This is good because right now we know that this woman and this child are alive, and they will be for at least another day." She grabbed a washcloth and pressed it into her palm. "Call Ricci. I need to talk to Mrs. Francis, the night manager. Her office window faces the parking lot, and she pays attention to who's coming and going." Yes, this was very, very good.

She sprinted to the manager's office. "Mrs. Francis!" Evie pushed open the door to the motel's front office so hard the door handle dented the wall. Yeah, she was fired up. The desk was empty. "Mrs. Francis?"

Evie took a deep breath. Mrs. Francis was already baking. Banana nut muffins. She flipped open the desk gate, her boot heel sliding on something slick and shiny red.

"*Mierda*!" She dropped to her knees next to Mrs. Francis. Mouth still. Chest still. The only movement was the blood trickling from a hole on the side of her neck. Evie slid her fingers to the older woman's wrist. No pulse but still warm.

A shadow sliced across her. She recognized the smell.

"Get down here," she told Jack. "Press your handkerchief against her neck."

Evie straddled the older woman and started compressions. "Come on, Mrs. Francis. Come on."

"What happened?" Jack asked.

Push. Push. "GSW compliments of Vandemere."

"How can you be so sure?"

Without stopping compressions, she aimed her chin at the older woman's torn sweater, a square patch of raw flesh showing on her shoulder.

Within four minutes, the first squad car arrived. In eight minutes an ambulance pulled into the pocked parking lot, and only then did Evie step away, dragging Jack with her. Like her, his arms and knees were streaked with Mrs. Francis's blood, and his face was deathly white, as if his blood had spilled onto the cracked tile of Mrs. Francis's office. Regardless of what he saw during his street years, there was nothing compared to this ugliness. A world where white-haired old ladies who needed to supplement their Social Security income worked as motel night managers and got shot for being in the wrong place at the wrong time. Her bloody hands fisted.

Another car with flashing lights turned into the parking lot, this one with the word *Detective* written on the door.

Like Jack she believed there were pockets of beauty. Of goodness. Of justice. And she was grateful for men and women who fought for justice with passion and force.

Evie met Detective Knox at the door of Mrs. Francis's office. "You see her, Knox? That's Dottie Francis. She has fourteen grandchildren and bakes the world's best blueberry muffins. The secret is lemon zest in the batter. She is Our Girl, Knox. You hear me?" She thumped Knox on the chest. "Our. Girl."

Knox's jaw tightened, along with his fist. "You're damn right."

* * *

11:47 p.m.

Ding.

The elevator doors leading to his penthouse slid open, but Jack couldn't bring himself to step into that small, brightly lit box with its mirrored walls and creamy white Italian tile. He stared at the congealed blood on the side of his shoe. The knot in his stomach lurched.

"You want to take the stairs?" Evie asked.

Twenty-four flights of stairs is exactly what he needed:

the singular task of putting one foot in front of the other, the pounding echo, the narrow upward chamber with no distractions. "Do you mind? I missed my workout this morning. Not that I'm complaining." Had it only been this morning that he and Evie shared a bed and fresh-squeezed orange juice? Jack tried to smile, but it never reached his lips.

Evie opened the door to the stairwell. "Let's go."

As they headed up the stairs, he forced himself to walk, but by the third floor he was jogging, and at floor six, he took off at a sprint. At the tenth floor he finally slowed and Evie, who'd stuck with him, said, "You can never outrun it."

A deathly pall. A sickly odor. The ugliness continued. Dottie Francis, the sixty-eight-year-old manager of the EZ-Rest Motel, was pronounced dead upon arrival at Good Samaritan Hospital. He wore the stain of that death, a stain that sickened and angered him.

He slowed, and they took the next two floors at a slow walk until Evie stopped and held up her hand. "Did you hear that?"

"Hear what?"

"Listen," she said. "This place is like an echo chamber. Someone's on the stairs below."

He pulled himself out of the deathly fog. Evie pulled out her gun and flattened herself against the wall.

Footsteps sounded below, slow, almost plodding. Heavy breathing. The air in the stairwell thinned. A shadow appeared on the floor below.

Evie extended her arms. "Get your hands in the air."

The footfall stilled, but not the huffing and puffing. "Whatever you say, Lady Feeb."

* * *

Thursday, November 5
12:07 a.m.

Evie jammed her sidearm back in her holster. "Dammit, Freddy. I'm going to take your camera and throw it down the stairwell."

Freddy came around the corner, sweat pouring down his face, hands raised. "No camera." Huff. "Just me." Huff, puff.

No slickster grin. No sickly sweet smell of watermelon bubble gum. He sank onto the landing and clutched his chest. "I bequeath my camera to my niece, Lilliana, and you, Evie, can have my superhero lunch box and thermos."

Evie took a seat next to him.

"Man, you stink, Lady Feeb."

Of blood and sweat as she'd tried to bring a dead woman to life. "You too," she said. Sweat soaked Freddy's shirt, but there was no camera hanging there. "What the hell are you doing here?"

"My landlord locked me out of my place. I was hoping you could loan me a few bucks."

* * *

12:29 a.m.

When she was a little kid, Sabrina hated the dark. At night she'd huddle under the covers, trying not to think about the monsters lurking under her bed, behind her curtains, and in her closet. The worst ones lived in the closet. Really bad ones with sharp fangs and red, bulging eyes, always ready to pounce on her and tear her apart with claws as long as her fingers.

Her mom finally gave her a bottle of pink glitter body mist to keep by her bed.

"Monsters are afraid of the color pink and anything that sparkles," her mom had said.

Stupid, but at the time, she'd fallen for it. The body mist with its pretty pink pump and swirly label still sat on her dresser in her bedroom even though she didn't believe in monsters anymore, at least not the kind that lurked in closets. Her chin trembled. The real monsters lurked outside of closets. Right now she wanted that bottle of monster spray. She wanted her mom. A cry lodged in her throat. Today she was in a dark closet, and a monster stood outside the door.

Her throat spasmed, but the duct tape across her mouth stopped the cry rushing up her throat. The bundle in her arms whimpered.

Angela. Her baby.

A baby raising a baby. That's what everyone said. That she was too young to raise a kid.

Despite what they said, Sabrina was trying to do things right, like this whole thing with Angela's ear. Her baby had been up all night last night, tugging at her ear and fussing. This morning the fusses had turned into screams. Her mom was working and so was her grandma. She could have waited for one of them to get off work, but she'd done the responsible thing. She'd bundled up little Angela and took the bus to the pediatric urgent care clinic, the affordable one downtown where she'd waited patiently for the doctor to see her baby. The doctor said Angela's ear was red and bulging and gave her medicine that smelled like bubble gum. She'd done the right thing.

Until she got to the bus stop.

The man driving past the bus stop had offered them a ride. He didn't look like a monster. He was in a nice shirt and shiny shoes. Little Angela was exhausted and still fussy, and Sabrina was tired and fussy because neither of them got any sleep the night before.

That was the problem. She'd been too tired to see the monster behind the man, but she heard him now outside the closet where she was trapped. Metal against metal. Clinking and sawing.

Angela, her beautiful angel-headed daughter, cried out, and Sabrina held her to her chest and cried like the baby she was.

CHAPTER THIRTY

Thursday, November 5
6:55 a.m.

"Y̶ou know, I could really get used to the good life." Freddy pulled the lever, and a cloud of milky foam plopped into his coffee cup. "Maybe you and The Suit can adopt me after you get married."

Evie bulleted a croissant at Freddy's head, but he snagged it in the air. "Fast hands," he said with a chuckle as he tore off a bite. "So where's The Suit this morning?"

"Running up and down the stairwell."

"Why?"

"Because it's an efficient use of his time." Evie understood so much more now about Jack. He didn't have time for gym memberships or hobbies that netted him exercise, so he ran stairs. Those tight stairwells also helped him think or rather corral and control his thoughts, feelings, too. She'd seen that last night as he'd dealt with Dottie Francis's death.

She curled her fingers around the gold-rimmed coffee cup and pictured the plain Jane paper cup she'd found in Carter Vandemere's trash. So far they'd had no luck in tracking down the shop where the cup had come from. Today she planned on hitting more coffee shops.

"Didn't you two get enough exercise last night?" Freddy leered at her.

Evie took a long draw of rich, steamy gourmet coffee. "This is so not a good way to wake up."

"Don't blame me, Lady Feeb. You invited me."

Evie had been around controlling Jack too long because last night she'd insisted Freddy crash in one of Jack's spare bedrooms. He'd been booted from his apartment, and she was worried about him staying in a cheap motel because clearly Carter Vandemere could get in and out of cheap motels. She grabbed another croissant and was about to dunk it in her coffee. She frowned. Since when did she have croissants and gourmet coffee for breakfast? Since Jack. She dunked and took a bite. Delicious.

At her elbow, her phone lit up with a text. "Looks like we're tied." She clicked on the photo accompanying the text and showed Freddy. "My youngest brother and his wife had their first child last night. That makes eight nephews."

"Congratulations, Evie." Freddy's smile was genuine. "Everything go okay?"

"Everyone's healthy and happy." Her phone buzzed with another text. She groaned out a laugh. "Except my mother, who felt compelled to remind me that I am now the only one of her children who has not blessed her with a grandchild or ten."

Freddy spread raspberry preserves on another croissant and topped it with a sliver of dark chocolate. "You and The Suit would have some good-lookin' kids."

She pictured a collection of little people: all with Jack's denim-blue eyes, his royal jaw, and really great hair. They'd also have his drive and intelligence but her sense of humor and spirit of adventure. Everyone needed to get a little dirty once in a while. The pictures were shockingly clear. A breath froze in her lungs because they shouldn't be. She'd never wanted children. Ever. She was dedicated to her career and to being the doting aunt. Hell, she was going to have her nephews' initials tattooed on her ankle, that's how serious she was.

People change. That's what she'd been saying about the obese image of young Carter Vandemere.

A wave of something warm—something that had nothing to do with Jack's coffee—settled in her midsection.

The bronze door of Jack's penthouse opened, and he jogged in, a towel looped around his neck. No sweat. Prince of his world. And hers?

He dropped a kiss on the top of her head. "Let me grab a shower, and I'll be ready to go."

Freddy took a sip of his espresso. "Did you feel that, Lady Feeb?"

She wrapped her arms around her midsection. "Feel what?"

Freddy licked the foam from his lips. "The ground shifting beneath your feet."

* * *

7:11 a.m.

Hayden Reed reached across the bed and hugged air. His eyelids flew open. The right side of the bed was empty. He threw off the covers and poked his head into the bathroom. Also empty. Pulling on his trousers, he checked the adjoining living room. A door on the other side of the room opened, and Kate walked in.

"He's gone," Kate said around a frown. "Smokey Joe is not in his room."

Hayden slipped his arms around his fiancée's waist and pulled her to him. He'd gotten very used to waking up with Kate in his arms. He planted a kiss on her irked lips. "Did you check at the coffee machine in the lobby?"

"Yes. I also checked the hotel's exercise room, garden, smoking area, and the little bakery around the corner."

"Maybe Smokey took a cab and went to the police station early. He's been poring through those phone calls for days. Really, he's been impressive, Kate."

"Not this morning." Kate pulled her phone out of her back pocket and jabbed at the keys. "He could have let me know where he's going."

"Yes, he could have, but he's mad at the world about being forced off his mountain. Let me make a few phone calls and see if I can track him down."

* * *

8:22 a.m.

With a fat marker Evie wrote on her white board: *1*. She had one day to catch a killer.

Freddy pushed himself back from the desk in Evie's LAPD office and squinted at the image on his laptop. "You think Ricci will put me on payroll for this?"

"No," Evie said. "But maybe you'll earn yourself a get-out-of-jail pass or two." She stood over his shoulder and stared at the face he'd been working on all morning.

An artist LAPD regularly used for age progression had modified the sketch of young Carter Vandemere, but they weren't getting any hits. Since Freddy was so well versed in altering images, she'd asked him to do some of his Photoshop magic.

"What do you think?" Freddy asked.

Evie stared at the altered image. Fifty pounds thinner, fifteen years older. *People change.* "Jack, come take a look at this."

Jack, who'd been studying the portrait of the woman in the red dress, joined her. "He doesn't look familiar, but send it and any others to me, and I'll forward them to the office for Brady, Claire, and Adam." All people who could have ties to the bomber.

Ricci popped his head in the doorway. "Just got a call from Huntington Park PD. A teenage mother and her baby were reported missing this morning."

The air rushed from Evie's lungs. She'd been expecting this call, but that didn't soften the blow. "Got a picture of them?"

"Check your e-mail."

She spun toward her computer. Until she joined the army, Evie had struggled with patience, but working with military ordnance taught her a good deal about taking her time. Jack could use a lesson or two from her army days. He paced back and forth before the portrait, his jaw so tense, she could see the contour of bone.

Part of his agitation had to do with finding the bomber, but he was also waiting on word from Jon about his sister.

A file appeared, and Evie enlarged the image. A woman, more like a girl who couldn't be more than sixteen, popped onto the screen. She held a blond-haired baby in a christening gown. Evie took the photo she received with the metal shavings and set it next to the photo of Sabrina Delgado and her six-month-old daughter, Angela.

Next victims confirmed.

Jack let out a growl. She grabbed her purse. At this point she no longer expected Jack to stay put.

* * *

10:47 a.m.

Screaming babies were everywhere.

"It's that time of year," Vivian Becker said as she led them down a hall to an office at the pediatric urgent care clinic on the east side of downtown Los Angeles. Becker was a physician's assistant and presumably one of the last people to see Sabrina Delgado and baby Angela before they went missing. "Kids get germs and share germs. The office was jam-packed yesterday from the time we opened our doors."

"What time did Sabrina and Angela arrive?" Evie asked.

The woman sat behind a desk and clicked on a computer. "Our registration clerk has her checking in just after noon. The child presented with irritability and tugging at her left ear. We had a few broken bones, a concussion, and lacerations with higher urgency, so I'm afraid to say she waited a number of hours before we were able to get to them. I personally examined Angela at four in the afternoon."

Evie couldn't imagine holding and trying to comfort a fussy baby for that long.

"But we got the little thing fixed up," Ms. Becker continued. "Antibiotics to fight the infection and acetaminophen for pain and fever."

"What time did Sabrina and her daughter leave?"

"A little after five. I'm sure because the receptionist had already locked up and left for the day. I had to unlock the door for Sabrina."

"Was there anyone waiting outside for her? Did you see where she went?"

"No ride. I believe she was walking to the bus stop." This made sense, as the girl had no car.

"Did you see her get on the bus?"

"No. I had one more patient to see, but you may want to ask the people at the insurance office next door. A few employees from there take the bus every day."

As they left the urgent care clinic, Jack settled his hand at her back, and she moved closer to him, not because she needed his protection but because she liked the feel of him, solid, steady, and anything but cold.

A trio of women from the insurance office next door who took the bus yesterday was soon gathered in the reception area.

"Yes, we saw them," one of the women said. "Poor little baby. Screaming its lungs out. Honestly, we were all a little relieved when the man drove up and offered her a ride."

"Are you sure the driver was a man?" Evie asked.

"I think so. I didn't get a good look at him, but I remember his voice. Definitely male."

"Did you notice anything about him? Hair color? Ethnicity? Clothing?"

"He didn't get out of the car, so we didn't see him."

"What kind of vehicle was he driving? Make? Model? Color?"

The woman frowned. "I...I...I have no idea."

"Wait a minute," another woman said. "Wasn't he driving a minivan?"

"I'm not sure." The first woman knotted her hands at her waist.

"Yeah. I'm pretty sure it was because I remember thinking, oh, good, he probably has one of those child safety seats that come with minivans."

"Is there anything else you can remember about the man or the vehicle?" Evie asked.

"You know, there's one more thing, Agent Jimenez," the third woman said. "I noticed a badge thingy clipped to his car visor. I remember because it was really pretty. It had a painting of a pretty ballerina with a ribbon around her neck and flowers in her hair. I think they were yellow and..."

"Orange," Jack said softly.

"Yes, orange!"

"It's a replica of a work by Degas." Jack's skin was the color of his snow-white shirt. "The person we're looking for works for Elliott Enterprises."

CHAPTER THIRTY-ONE

Thursday, November 5
11:11 a.m.

I want a list of every employee on payroll and every person who's been issued a visitor's pass in the past year," Jack told Claire.

His words came out calm and measured, but Evie saw the rolled-up cuffs and thin line of sweat along his hairline as he paced in her office at LAPD. From the very beginning Evie knew they were looking for someone with intimate knowledge of the *Beauty Through the Ages* collection, so she wasn't surprised that the person calling himself Carter Vandemere was most likely an employee of Elliott Enterprises.

Giving Jack some privacy, she ducked into Hayden's office down the hall and let out a squeal. "Kate!" Evie threw her arms around Hayden's fiancée. "Here to help catch another serial killer?"

"I'll leave that up to the experts." Kate returned the hug.

Evie held Kate at arm's length. "You look fantastic, positively glowing. Is it the new job or the shine from your new engagement ring?" She grabbed Kate's hand and held the giant rock up to the light and whistled.

"Probably a bit of both."

Hayden ran into the room, his jacket off and tie folded back over his shoulder. "The beat officer near the bus stop hasn't seen anything, either."

Kate's teeth dug into her bottom lip.

"Seen what?" Evie asked.

A looked passed between Hayden and Kate.

"What is it? Something to do with Vandemere?"

"Nothing to do with the case," Hayden assured her.

She looked from Hayden to Kate, her boot tip beating a tattoo on the floor.

"It's Smokey Joe," Kate finally said.

"He's missing," Hayden finished for her.

Evie's boot stilled. "And you planned to keep this from me?" she belted out.

"I didn't want to distract you from the investigation," Hayden said.

"Distract me? That's ridiculous. Where was Smokey last seen?"

"The front desk clerk at the hotel reported seeing him sitting on a lawn chair near the pool and gardens early this morning."

"And then?"

"Gone." Kate's voice cracked.

"Are you saying he just walked out onto the streets of downtown Los Angeles?" Evie asked with wide eyes.

"This is the sightless man who thinks he can drive a car," Hayden reminded her.

"I'll say something to Ricci. He has dozens of men combing the downtown area, and we'll have them keep their eyes open for a cranky old blind man with a burr up his butt."

* * *

1:04 p.m.

Evie rested her chin on her fisted hands and stared at the envelope. Carter Vandemere had dotted the *i* on her name with a heart. On a sketch pad in his art studio of terror, he'd drawn her body, or at least his perception of it, in lush, curvy detail.

"You're thinking," Ricci said. They'd just finished the daily task force meeting, but no one was eager to leave the room.

"I've been known to do that on occasion." She tossed the envelope to Ricci. "Jack's right. I'm involved on a very personal level, compliments of Carter Vandemere. So I've been asking myself, why me?"

"And?" Ricci asked.

"Jack. It always comes back to Jack," Evie said. "Vandemere used Jack's prized art collection as the basis for mass murder and destruction. He set the paper heart bomb in Jack's desk, and he placed the IED in Brady's car. Vandemere wants to cause Jack pain." The clock ticked above the door, but she couldn't hear it. Too much whirring in her mind. "So maybe it's time to give him the power to hurt Jack even more."

Ricci stared at her over the tips of his fingers. "I'm loosely following this. What's your plan?"

"We make a deal with Vandemere. In this deal, he gives us Sabrina and baby Angela, and we offer to give him someone he values more." Across the room, Jack stiffened, but she refused to look at him.

Ricci angled his hands, aiming his fingertips at her. "You."

"I don't think so." Jack shot up from the windowsill.

"Unfortunately, what you think in this situation doesn't count," Evie said.

"Jack's right," Cho said. "That's dangerous at best, stupid deadly at worst."

Hayden quieted the murmurs by lifting a single hand. "But Evie is far from stupid. What do you have in mind?"

"The switch is just a ruse to flush him out of the shadows and get him within *our* sights, and when that happens, we'll have our sharpshooters in place."

Ricci tapped his fingers against his chin. "We have a half dozen crack shots in SWAT."

"Exactly," Evie said. "Parker can even send our guy, Brooks."

Jack opened his mouth. Evie glared.

Knox, who now had the blood of Dottie Francis on his hands, asked, "How would we get word to Vandemere?"

"He craves media attention, gets off on seeing his name in the papers and hearing his name on television. The media would be quickest and easiest."

"You think he'd fall for it?" Ricci asked.

Everyone turned to Hayden, the criminal profiler who'd been poking around Carter Vandemere's head. "He's driven by an almost insatiable need for attention. But we're dealing with a serial killer who works with bombs. He causes destruction from afar and will be wary of any situation that puts him at risk. He won't bite."

A heat rose up the backs of Evie's legs. "So we make him a risk-free deal."

"How?"

"We tell him we'll let him strap a bomb to me before the switch."

"No!" Jack banged his hand on the table, and papers and coffee cups jumped.

On the heel of her boot, she turned toward him, pushing down the urge to throw him bodily out the door. "You don't get a vote, Jack."

Ricci tapped his pressed fingertips against his lips. "I'm head of this investigation, Evie, and I say no. Unequivocally no."

They didn't get it. She ground a fist into the center of her forehead. They just didn't get it. Jack stood with his arms across his chest, his stare cold and unyielding. But she'd seen him change over the past week, seen him walk barefoot in the sand and celebrate with cake. Time for others to change their attitudes. Her hand dropped to her side as she took off out the door, calling over her shoulder. "Back in a flash."

She ran to her office and picked up the bomb components she'd been tinkering with. Running back to the conference room, she set the IED on the table. Cho sat up straighter. Knox jumped up from the table.

"That's not live, is it?" Ricci asked.

She flicked the switch. "Now it is."

The rest of the world disconnected. No movement. No smells. No sweat trickling down her back. No rush of air from the overhead vent. Oddly enough, the only sense she was aware of was sound.

Tick. Tock.

Tick. Tock.

Her fingers flew over the wires. Steady. Sure.

Tick. Tock.

Tick. Tock.

Before the ticks reached thirty, she threw up her hands. "Done." A breath rushed over her lips.

No one said a word. They all stared at her with wide eyes, a few with mouths gaping open. She wasn't sure if they were shocked that she'd set the IED in motion or rendered it safe in less than thirty seconds.

"I'm his girl," she said. "I know my stuff, and I know his bombs."

Ricci unlaced his fingers, blood flooding back to his white knuckles, and he aimed a finger at her. "Don't you ever, *ever* do anything like that again under my watch."

"Come on, Vince," Evie said with a half scowl. "Did you really believe I couldn't disarm that thing?"

He didn't say anything, and she turned to Hayden next to her. "And you, Hayden, you didn't move an inch because you, too, knew that I could handle this. That I can handle Vandemere."

Hayden said nothing because she was right. Frustration bubbled in her veins.

Knox finally sat back in his chair. "Everyone in this room knew you could do it," he said. "Including me."

She wanted to hug the man. Each of the task force members around the table nodded. Only one man didn't. Jack was stone still.

Ricci let loose a sigh. "Evie can do it. I've seen her render safe IEDs like this and others that are twice as sophisticated."

Jack's granite visage cracked. "What if Vandemere changes things up? What if he uses a different device?"

Everyone turned back to Hayden. "It's unlikely. A bomber's signature, especially over a period as short as a few months, stays pretty much the same. If we were looking at an IED created in a year or two where he had more time for research and development, we could be looking at a higher level of sophistication."

"Not likely," Jack said. "But it's *possible*."

"Anything is possible," Hayden admitted.

"The odds are in my favor," Evie said. "The reality is, I'm damn good at handling things that go boom."

"What about the *baby*?" Jack asked.

Evie pictured a bald head, flat eyes, rubbery skin. An image from her past, one that haunted her every day since she'd walked out of the Albuquerque Police Academy. "We can use a doll."

Ricci pushed back from the table. "You think your boss would go for it?"

Evie opened her mouth, but Hayden spoke first. "Parker trusts her implicitly."

Evie swallowed the scratchy thickness inching up her throat. Her boss also trusted her to keep her nose clean on this one. With a shaky nod, she stood and walked away, ducking her head so she didn't see her face reflected in the window.

CHAPTER THIRTY-TWO

Thursday, November 5
4:04 p.m.

Kate ran a comb through Evie's hair, the tines tangling in the tips.

"Is this really necessary?" Evie asked with a wince.

"No," Kate said as she untangled the comb. "But you will be less distracting this way." Kate, a former broadcast journalist who'd spent thousands of hours in front of a camera, whisked the comb through the handful of hair until it landed in a soft, smooth wave over Evie's right shoulder. Then she fisted a handful on the left side and went on the attack. "In broadcast news, viewers should be focused on what you're saying, not on"—she waved her fist—"this."

"It's called hair, and I swear it was washed, combed, and fully submissive when I left for work this morning."

Kate battled the attitudinal locks. "Ever thought about cutting it off?"

Evie had never been a fan of dresses, never wore nail polish, and owned only a handful of jewelry. "It's my one nod to my girly side."

"Good. It's absolutely beautiful." Kate smoothed the left side of Evie's hair and let it fall down her back. "Does Jack like it?"

On his chest, across his back, down his thighs. In the mirror of the vanity, Evie watched red creep up her neck and across her cheeks. She cleared her throat. "Did you hear from Smokey Joe?"

The tines of the comb bit into Kate's fingers. "Not yet. He doesn't know this area, and there are so many cars here."

"I'm sure Smokey's fine. He survived the Viet Cong, prostate cancer, and a serial killer. He can survive L.A. traffic." Evie unclenched Kate's fingers from the comb. "As soon as he's done pitching his fit, he'll show up and stick his tweaked nose right back in the middle of the investigation."

"I'm sure you're right." Kate unfolded her arms and took a bag of cosmetics from her purse. "You worry about those you love."

Evie regularly worried about her nephews, her brothers and teammates while they were on duty, and Jack. She worried about his safety as he nosed his way into her investigation, about his health when he worked without play, about his heart when something happened to those he cared about. Yes, she worried. She wrapped a lock of hair around her finger. Because she loved him. He was controlling and stubborn but underneath it all, a man of passion and power.

Kate dabbed a puff into a compact of loose powder. Evie wrinkled her nose, bracing for the blow, because unlike Jack, she sweated. About her job. About those she cared for. About young mothers and little babies abducted under her watch. But not about going on television and issuing an invitation to a serial killer. This time she wanted to be in the spotlight.

"There," Kate said as she spun Evie from the mirror. "Beautiful."

Jack had said the same thing, and under his gaze and hands, she felt beautiful. She felt womanly. And it all felt right. She'd come to L.A. to catch a bomber, and instead a man had caught her, and the funny thing, one-track Jack didn't even realize it. She did. Because make no mistake about it, she chose to get caught.

One of the producers waved her over. "We need you on set, Agent Jimenez. Are you ready?"

After the Houston bombing, Evie had been running from the media who'd crucified her, and just a week ago, she'd ducked behind broadcast reporters in Bar Harbor. Oh, how things changed. "*Vámonos.*"

In the course of SCIU operations, she rarely worked with the media. Hayden took care of most of that, except when it had to do with the president. Then it was always Parker at the commander-in-chief's side. The producer had Evie take a seat in the chair and hooked a small battery pack to her waist and clipped a microphone to the collar of her jacket. Ricci had opted to not go with a press conference, as they needed a controlled environment. They wanted to keep the interview focused on a few scripted questions and answers.

The camera swung toward her and the broadcaster. "Today I'm here with Special Agent Evie Jimenez of the FBI's Special Criminal Investigative Unit and one of the leads on the Angel Bomber investigation." The broadcaster turned from the camera to her. "What can you tell us about the current status of the investigation?"

"We would like to assure the citizens of Los Angeles that our multi-jurisdiction task force is out in full force, keeping the streets and people of Los Angeles safe." Not too much. Vandemere needed to think he still was steering the ship.

"Where is the next bombing likely to take place?"

"We're focusing on the downtown area, no specific district yet. We don't know when he'll strike on Friday, but it will most likely be at a time and place with a high concentration of people."

"What should everyone be looking for?"

Evie suggested, and Ricci agreed, to focus on the woman and child. Behind them an image of Sabrina and baby Angela appeared. "We're looking for this woman and child who may be dressed in clothing very similar to this painting." A photo of the fourth portrait popped onto the other side of the screen.

"Is there anything else, Agent Jimenez?"

"I have a message for Carter Vandemere or for anyone with the ability to get Mr. Vandemere a message." She looked directly into the camera. "Call me on your favorite *tip* line." Vandemere considered Freddy an ally and had already used his tip line. It was their best shot at direct contact.

The reporter squirmed, and she could tell he wanted to ask more questions but simply nodded. "Thank you, Agent Jimenez."

When the cameras turned off, the broadcaster helped her unclip her microphone. "Thanks for playing by our rules," she told him.

"Thank Jack Elliott." He tossed the mic on the chair. "Next time you talk to him, tell him we're even."

She continued to marvel at Jack's connections, at his wheeling and dealing, at him.

"Think you'll nail him?" the broadcaster asked.

She blinked. "Excuse me?"

"The bomber."

"Absolutely."

"You sound rather confident."

"I am."

The broadcaster removed his mic. "I'm done here after seven. Any chance you can get away for an hour and grab some sushi?"

"No." A hand landed on her arm, a monogrammed cuff link glinting under the hot, bright lights overhead. "She's working."

As Jack escorted her from the production studio, she leaned in and asked, "Jealous?"

"No, because unlike most women, you don't play games."

Evie didn't understand relationship games. If she liked a man and wanted him in her bed, she let him know, and there was only one man she wanted in her bed right now. "True."

"So what now?" Jack asked.

"We wait for Vandemere to call."

His face clouded with doubt. "And you're just going to sit around and do nothing?"

"Of course not. I'm going to go get a cup of coffee." She slipped her arm into his. "You're coming with me."

* * *

5:27 p.m.

"Good evening," the woman behind the coffee counter at The Bean Thing said. She wore a bright green nametag that read, *Margot*. "What can I get for you?"

"A serial killer would be nice," Jack said.

Evie dug her elbow into Jack's stomach, then fished out a business card from her purse. This was the fourth coffee shop they'd hit in her quest for a match of the paper coffee cup found in Vandemere's trash can. For a man who was supposedly cool and in control, Jack had been agitated the entire time, as if he'd had a double-shot or two of espresso. "I'd like to speak to the manager or owner?"

"That would be me. I'm also the cashier and chief coffee cup washer."

Evie took out Vandemere's used coffee cup. "I'm interested in a customer, possibly one of your regulars who buys a lot of coffee to go." Evie wished she had the age-progressed image from Freddy, but he was still waving his Photoshop magic wand. "I'm looking for a man wanted in conjunction with the Angel Bombings. Are you familiar with the case?"

"Of course." Margot ran her finger along a stain on the wooden counter. "He's down here, isn't he?"

"Yes."

"And you'll get him?"

Her job was to catch killers, but being an Apostle required more. She also gave people hope. "He doesn't stand a chance."

Margot wiped her hands on her apron. "What can I do to help?"

"We're looking for a male between the ages of thirty and thirty-five. A loner. He wears polished brown shoes. He considers himself an artist, and he drinks this." She held up the coffee cup from Vandemere's trash.

The woman took the cup. "The cup's not one of ours, but the order's familiar." She pointed to the grease-penciled letters. *AM-NF-CN.* "One of my regulars drinks Americano with non-fat milk and cinnamon."

Jack's arm, pressing into hers, tensed. Or was that muscles along her arm? How a man drank his coffee seemed insignificant, but it was another dot in the image slowly taking shape. Evie took the age-progressed sketch from her bag and handed it to the coffee shop owner. "Does he look like this?"

The woman squinted. "A little in the eyes, but the shape of his nose is wrong." She tapped her chin. "And there's something off about his chin and mouth."

"Would you be willing to look at some photos for us and a sketch we're working on?"

"Sure." A bell over the door tinkled, and Margot handed back the sketch. "Can we wait until closing? It's just me most of the time, a little fish trying to compete with the big guys, and I always get a post-dinner crowd. A few espressos and plenty of decafs."

Before Evie could say a word, Jack whipped out his checkbook. "I'm sure that will cover your evening receipts." Jack set a check on the counter. "I'll go get the car."

Margot picked up the check. "Is he for real?"

Evie craned her neck. Ten thousand. "Very real."

The coffee shop owner tucked the check into the cash register and whipped off her apron. "Is he single?"

"No." Evie seriously loved this man.

* * *

7:03 p.m.

Bang. Bang. Bang!

Jack scrolled to the next page of the massive security report of people who were issued security passes into the Elliott Enterprises buildings within the past year.

Bang. Bang. Bang!
Whirrrrrrrr!

"Dammit, Claire," he called through the open door of his office. "Can you put an end to whatever is causing that racket?"

"Night crew working on the floor below. Do you want me to have them hold off until you're done here?"

He had new tenants, an advertising and public relations firm, taking over the entire thirty-fifth floor after the first of the year, and a construction crew was retrofitting the space for them. The investment now would earn him long and hefty lease payments in the near and not-so-near future. He rubbed at the center of his forehead. At one point he'd defined himself by the deals he made, but now it was all about lives to be saved.

Sabrina Delgado and her baby, Angela, would be strapped to a bomb, a living, walking weapon. How many would die? How many would suffer under the fallout?

He swiped his palm down his face. This is the type of stuff Evie dealt with daily. How the hell did she live with it? And how the hell could he live with it? With her? With the idea of everything he cared for blowing up in his face?

Bang. Bang. Bang!

"That's okay, Claire. I'll go elsewhere." His executive suite was closing in on him. "By the way, that's a beautiful scarf."

His assistant fingered the length of blue, purple, and beige silk at her neck. "A gift from Evie."

Evie. Bright and colorful. Wreaking havoc with his staff. With him. But in the best way.

He checked his watch. "Speaking of Evie, have you seen her? She was supposed to stop by after she rounded up Freddy Ortiz." In one of her more sound moves, Evie was going to have the coffee shop owner talk to Freddy Ortiz and help him manipulate the age-progressed image of Vandemere. That had been over an hour ago. Evie was supposed to be back in his office to go through the names and photo IDs of people with Elliott Enterprises security ID badges.

"She's here," Claire said. "But she needed to run a quick errand. She told me to tell you she'd stop by when she was done."

"Where is she?"

"I'll let her tell you about it when she finishes."

* * *

7:05 p.m.

Evie pulled her jacket around her and stepped onto the roof of the Elliott Tower. The air was dry and cool up here, clearer, too. No whiffs of exhaust fumes, hot asphalt, flower bunches, or hot dogs wrapped in bacon. Quiet, too. Just the faint echo of a bus on the street below.

She strolled to the copper fountain area and called out, "Come out, come out, wherever you are!"

A shape shifted near the fountain.

She took a seat on one of the benches, propping her boots on the fountain.

At last a head with sprigs of gray hair stepped out from the shadows. "How'd you know I was here?" Smokey Joe asked.

"Women's intuition."

"You don't do that girly stuff."

Evie ran a hand down the controlled curls of her hair. "I have my moments. The truth is, Claire, who knows everything about this place, let me up here, same as you."

"Go away."

"Sure. After I boot you in the butt." Evie banged one boot, then the other on the concrete ledge. "Would you prefer me to do it with my right foot or left foot?"

"Put a cork in it, Evie."

"I don't think so. Captain Ricci has had people running around looking for you all day, and Kate is worried sick. Literally. I caught her throwing up."

"She'll get over it."

Evie patted her hand on the bench, but Smokey Joe continued to stand. "What are you doing up here?" she asked.

"I needed to get away."

"You chose the roof of the Elliott Tower?"

"I chose a place without a bunch of yapping idiots." He glared in her direction.

Evie chuckled. "I work with bombs, Smokey. It'll take a lot more than that to singe my eyebrows."

Smokey reached behind him until he found the bench. "I came up here because this is the closest thing to my mountain." He sank down as if his tired old legs couldn't hold him anymore. "I can't do it, Evie. I can't go live with a bunch of strangers. Franny may be my cousin, but she's not my family."

"I know," Evie said. She'd been with Kate and Smokey Joe five months ago when they'd all been hunting for the killer known as the Broadcaster Butcher. "Kate's your family. So why not move in with her and Hayden? They'd love to have you. Except for the times when you're acting like a stubborn old mule."

"Can't do that, either. At least not yet. They're still trying to figure out how to live with each other. Beginnings are hard, like with you and your Jack fellow."

"I'm not sure he's my fellow yet."

"Oh, he is. He just doesn't realize it."

"You know this because?"

"I heard it." Smokey Joe pointed to his ear. "I have more than seven decades in this old skin. I've seen plenty of folks find that special person, and when they do, they change. The things they say and how they say it change. I hear it in your voice."

And she felt it. The quickening of her heart when Jack walked into a room, the heating of her blood when her skin brushed his. For more than a decade she'd been content with her job, her teammates, her duty to protect and serve, but now she wanted more. She wanted Jack. "You're a cagey old thing, aren't you?"

"How's that?"

"Steering this conversation to me and Jack when we are supposed to be talking about you."

"There's nothing wrong with me."

"Says the man sitting on the roof of a thirty-six-story building and hiding from everyone because you don't want to face the truth."

"What truth?"

She didn't have time for this. "You can't live alone anymore."

"Don't you tell me what I can and can't do," Smokey said with a roar that sent a ringing through her ears.

"Do you really want to go this route?"

Smokey crossed his arms over his chest.

"Fine." She cleared her throat. "You *cannot* live alone. You *cannot* drive a car. And you *cannot* keep distracting people and taking away resources from my bomb investigation."

"You don't need to yell." Smokey rubbed the side of his head.

"Good, because I'm only going to say this once." She pressed the tip of her index finger onto his thigh. "I have one lousy day to catch a serial killer before he straps another woman to a bomb and blows her body to bits, and this time, the woman will have a baby in her arms. A baby. Do you want that to happen?"

Smokey Joe's bushy gray eyebrows met at the bridge of his nose. "Course not."

"Then why the hell did you take off? We need all the help we can get at this point."

His gnarled old fingers picked at the armrest of the bench. "That sculptor guy, the blind artist you've been checking out. Did you know he lives alone?"

"No, I didn't."

"Gets to the studio every day by taking the bus. Has a little grocery store near his apartment that he goes to a few times a week."

"Mr. Brice has a Seeing Eye dog."

"I'll get me a dog."

Her patience was growing thin. The clock was ticking. "He's also half your age and in good physical shape. He hasn't had a recent bout with prostate cancer, nor has he driven a car off the side of a mountain, which, by the way, more than hints at a suspect mental state."

"Why don't you just throw me off the side of the building?"

"Because that would devastate Kate and Hayden, two people I care about." Evie took Smokey's hand. "And I care about you. I don't want you living on that mountain alone. Something has to change, and once you get over your little hissy fit, you'll admit it."

Smokey scratched the stubble along his chin. "One day? You're saying we got one day to catch a killer."

"One day."

He hopped up from the bench. "Well, you need to stop your yammering and get back to work."

"Sounds like a plan." She tucked her arm through his. "But after we catch him, we're going to talk."

Smokey grumbled.

CHAPTER THIRTY-THREE

Thursday, November 5
7:59 p.m.

Jack tore off the check for a half million dollars and slipped it into an envelope.

Evie was a grown woman and a highly skilled FBI agent. He jammed his checkbook back in his pocket. She was also a woman who did things at her speed, within her time frame, and her way. He put away the pen and straightened the blotter on his desk. He finally checked the clock on his office wall. Which means he *shouldn't* be worried that she was more than an hour late.

Claire had said Evie had to *run an errand.* Was that a euphemism for defusing a bomb or tracking down a lead on a serial killer? He hopped up from his chair.

Down the hall to the right of the foyer, light spilled from the door of the marketing and public relations offices. He found Freddy Ortiz behind a large computer screen. At a table nearby sat Brady, the jaunty bandage on his forehead still in place, and the owner of The Bean Thing.

Brady said something soft, and the woman laughed.

"Hey, boss," Brady said when he tore his gaze from the pretty blonde. "I told Freddy he could use our art department's equipment."

"Of course," Jack said.

"I want a Christmas bonus. A ham would be nice." Freddy smacked his lips. "Nah, I want a whole pig." He pushed back from the computer. "Okay, Miz Margot, *ándale*. I have the photo file loaded, and we're on the big screen. Tell me if this one is any closer to Mr. Americano-Nonfat-Cinnamon."

Jack watched Brady watch Margot walk across the room. "So what's up with you and the coffee lady?"

"We're going out for a beer when she's done," Brady said.

"Since when do you go out for beers with pretty blondes on Thursday nights?"

"Since a few bombs convinced me that there's life outside the office."

For the past week Jack had been out of the office and at Evie's side. No eighty-hour workweek. No business meetings masquerading as meals. The world kept spinning, and he continued to make money.

"For the record," Brady said, "I kind of like beer on Thursday nights with pretty blondes."

And Jack liked whiskey with attitudinal brunettes. He checked his phone. Still no word.

"Is everything okay?" Brady asked.

Jack drummed his fingers on the table. "Do you know what she's planning?" She. Evie. "To offer herself in exchange for the woman and child Vandemere has already abducted."

"There's no way LAPD or the FBI would go for something like that. It would be suicide."

"In theory, the switch would never take place. It's just a bluff."

"So what's the problem?"

This was the piece that no one else seemed to get. "Evie doesn't do anything halfway." With a low growl, Jack left the marketing department offices.

Back in his office, he found Evie sitting on his desk and waving the check for half a million. "You're upping the Angel Bomber reward. Very, very impressive, Jack. Should we hand-deliver to Ricci tonight?"

"He said to drop it off in the morning. He knows I'm good for it."

Evie crooked a finger at him, and he was a missile locked in on her. He planted himself between her legs. The warmth of the *V* of her thighs surged through him.

"You're a good man, Jack," she said as she pulled his head toward hers. Her tongue slid along his lips. "A very good man."

And she was safe. For now. He lost himself in the sweetness of her lips, pressing her body against his. Close. So close he didn't know where he ended and she began.

She put her hands on either side of his face. "I love you, Jack Elliott."

His lips stilled.

She laughed. "Why do you look so shell-shocked? I'm not shy about letting anyone know my feelings. So let me get everything off my chest." She slipped off his jacket and tossed it on the floor. "I love your power and strength and success." She detached his tie tack and loosened his tie. "I love that you use your money for good." One by one she unbuttoned his shirt buttons. "I love that you hear rain tin-

kling in falling sand." His shirt fell open, and she slipped
her hands under his T-shirt. "I love eating cake with you."
Her fingers pressed against his heart. "I love the thought of
spending the rest of my life with you and having children."

Jack pressed her hand to his chest. Could she feel the hammering of his heart? The steam raging through his blood-
stream? He ran a hand through his hair. Before Evie he had
such clarity. Where he wanted to go and how to get there. Now
there was this haze. A beautiful, warm, steamy haze.

* * *

8:18 p.m.

Freddy shaved off the sideburns, then leaned back in his
chair. "What do you think?"

"The face still isn't the right shape," Margot said. "Make
it even narrower."

"Is he anorexic or something?" Freddy popped a piece of
gum in his mouth.

"Could be. He drinks a lot of coffee." She pressed her lips
in a hard line. "The nose is still not right. Make it flatter."

Freddy reached for the mouse. "Okay, let me dink around
with this some more." Because he wanted to nail this guy.
The guy who'd blown up Lisa Franco before his eyes and
who now had his sights set on Evie.

He punched up the cheekbones and was taking more flesh
off the neck, when his phone rang. "Freddy Ortiz, photographer of the starz."

"Hello, Freddy."

The wad of gum dipped and lodged in his throat. He
hacked until the gum popped out and landed on the table.
He'd talked to Evie about this. He knew what to do when

this creep called the tip line. First, he had to stop panicking. Cops were on the call because last week Evie tapped the line. He needed to get Bomber Boy talking so they could make the trace. Sweat rolled down the sides of his face. "You, uh, got Agent Jimenez's message."

"What does she want?"

"To be in your next exhibit."

"I already sent the invitation."

"No, not at, *in*. She wants you to use her in the mother and kid piece."

"Why would she want to do that?"

"To save the mother and kid."

"She's just going to show up and say, 'Here I am. Strap a bomb to me'?"

"Yep. That's what she had in mind."

Vandemere let loose a long, twittering laugh. "She must think I'm an idiot."

Freddy nibbled the side of his cheek. He needed a whopper of a story here. "Evie thinks you're a smart guy. Talented, too. She's been studying your work, looking at your canvases, digging through the debris. Called you a master. She's your biggest fan."

"My biggest fan." A breathy echo fanned his words.

"Um, yeah, and she knows you. She said you want your work seen, and you'll get a hell of a lot more publicity if you use someone like her."

"And she's willing to die?"

Freddy gnawed on his lip. "Now this is where the story gets really good. She said like you, she's a master at what she does. She knows your work and can get out."

"This is some kind of trap, isn't it?"

"She said she's willing to give you some assurance."

"Assurance?"

Freddy told him about the crazy plan Evie and the boys in blue hatched. No sane person would believe it. No sane person would walk into it. When he finished, there was silence. Had Vandemere run like the wind?

"Uh, you still there, Vandemere?"

"Yes. I'm here."

"So, are you in?"

More silence. "Hell, yes."

* * *

8:31 p.m.

Evie took the hair band from her wrist, tied it around a wad of curls atop her head, and ran from Jack's office, her phone to her ear and Jack on her heels. While she and Jack had been making love on his desk, Vandemere had called Freddy and agreed to the switch.

"Did you guys get a fix on the phone?" Evie asked Ricci, who was on the other end of the line.

"Pay phone in Glendale," Ricci said. "Got a few sets of eyes searching down there now, but nothing yet."

"So where and when are we meeting Vandemere?"

"Freddy couldn't pin him down. Vandemere said he'd call tomorrow with details."

"No surprise there. Holding off on that information would make it presumably harder to set a trap."

The elevator dinged and the doors opened. Evie ended the phone call with Ricci and hopped on. Time to get to LAPD and set the trap. She pushed the Lower Level button, while Jack stood in the foyer, frowning.

"Hey," she said with a wink. "I thought sex tonight was pretty damned great."

Jack didn't smile. Nor did he get on the elevator. "Don't do it."

It would be so easy to let the doors close, to end this all-too-familiar conversation before it got started. A clock was ticking. She jammed her finger on the Open button. "This is my job, Jack. This is what I do. This is who I am."

"Please, Evie." Soft words. Soft blue eyes. "Please don't even pretend to offer yourself to this guy. There's always another way to broker a deal."

No commands. No demands. *Please*. She scrubbed at the side of her head. He was so much easier to ignore when he was a control freak. "Jack—"

"I love you." Jack didn't move, as if stunned by his own words.

Her heart swelled and threatened to leap from her chest. *This*. This is what she wanted, what she needed. But shitty timing. "Look me in the eye, Jack, and listen because I don't have a lot of time, and I'm only going to say this once. We're not making any deals with Vandemere. It's just a bluff." She held out her hand. "So come here, Mr. CEO and Chairman. You have me in your arms. I promise you, I'm not going to slip away."

* * *

9:29 p.m.

Jack had never seen an assassin. The ponytail surprised him.

Evie grabbed the man's hand and pulled him to her in a one-armed hug. "Hey, Brooks. What the hell took you so long?"

Brooks, Parker Lord's sharpshooter, hugged Evie, then

aimed his chin at a tall man with shaggy blond hair. "Hatch took a detour."

Hatch lifted his shoulders in a what-can-I say shrug. "I wanted to see the ocean."

Laughter rumbled through the conference room, the loudest from Evie. These men were her teammates, the best of the best. Like Evie. Jack kept reminding himself of Parker's words. *If it were anyone I cared about strapped to one of those bombs, I'd want Evie working the scene.*

The best were in the room. In addition to Evie's teammates, there was Ricci's bomb squad and an LAPD SWAT team.

The tall blond man held out his hand. "Hatch Hatcher."

Jack shook. "Jack Elliott."

"I know." Agent Hatcher leaned forward and added in a loud whisper, "How was the cake?"

"Hatch!" Evie popped her teammate on the back of the head.

Agent Hatcher clapped Jack on the shoulders with both hands, then took a seat at the table.

Evie's other teammate wasn't as friendly. Brooks, the assassin, stared at him with the cold, black eyes of a man who knew how to kill. And Evie thought *he* was protective of her? Jack ran a hand through his hair. Meeting her brothers and father should be interesting.

Jack stood in the background as plans were made, and to Evie's credit, never at any time did they discuss an actual switch. On paper this was strictly a ruse to get Carter Vandemere out in the open.

Midway through the discussion on road closures, Brady skidded into the room, huffing and puffing. Right behind him was Freddy Ortiz, covered in sweat. Freddy held up a flash drive. "Got him. Got a face and a name on the bomber."

CHAPTER THIRTY-FOUR

Thursday, November 5
10:12 p.m.

That's..." Evie scratched the side of her temple. She'd seen that face before.

"One of the clerks in the coffee kiosk," Jack said.

"Yes!" Evie's pulse spiked. "He's the one who drew the bow on the slice of German chocolate cake."

"Name's Douglas Woltz." Brady had finally caught his breath, but a flush still covered his pale, freckled face. "Here's his file from personnel." Brady handed Jack a folder, but Evie snatched it from his hand and whipped out a fistful of papers.

"But what's his connection to Jack?" Evie asked. "How would a guy who works at a coffee cart know about the *Beauty Through the Ages* collection?"

"He's a friend of Claire's," Brady said. "They eat lunch together."

The almighty executive assistant. She smacked the folder against her palm with a whoop. "Our boy has a name and even better"—she waved a paper in the air—"an address." She grabbed her bag and aimed her index finger at the tabloid photographer. "You, Freddy, are amazing."

"What? No lip action?" Freddy asked with pouty lips.

Evie thwacked him with the folder on the butt.

* * *

11:07 p.m.

After getting evicted from Jimmy Ho's slum warehouse last December, Douglas Woltz moved into a one-room apartment over his mother's garage in Whittier. According to parking records from Elliott Enterprises, he drove his mom's Dodge minivan, which was conspicuously missing from the parking spot behind the garage apartment this evening.

"I haven't seen Douglas for a few days," Ruthann Woltz told Evie. She was a big woman with three chins. "But that's not unusual. He works long days and spends most of his weekends away from the apartment."

"Did he ever say where he stayed on weekends?" Evie asked.

"No. I just assumed he...he...had friends he was staying with." Her chins trembled. "Young men do that all the time, don't they? Stay with their girlfriends? And friends?"

"Have you seen any women coming or going recently?"

She gnawed on her bottom lip. "No."

Evie took a deep breath. "Mrs. Woltz, I want you to think very carefully before you answer my next question because lives are at stake. Do you understand me?"

Her lips were white. She nodded.

"Have you seen or heard a baby crying over the past twenty-four hours?"

"Nothing like that. Absolute silence from up there."

Absolute silence. The state of the world right before an IED blows. "We need to go inside."

The older woman clutched Evie's arm. "He's a good boy, Agent Jimenez. He's smart and talented and hardworking. He's a good boy."

She held out her hand. Rock steady. "The key."

Ricci's team evacuated Mrs. Woltz and neighbors on either side. They brought in an infrared and heat-seeking machine, then the bomb dog. No wires. No pressure-sensitive devices. And when Evie ran her hand along the door, she found only dust.

Bang. Bang. Bang!

"Police!" Ricci called. "Open up."

She tried the key. No fit.

"He must have changed the locks," Ricci said.

"No problem." Evie lifted her boot and kicked. The door splintered.

Inside was a typical garage grunge apartment. Plaid couch from the seventies, plastic chairs and table, orange tweed curtains. No explosives, electronics, or laboratory apparatuses. But his *art* was everywhere. Life-size nudes with varying degrees of mutilation crowded a short hallway, and she could almost hear their screams echoing through the narrow space. Pastoral scenes with women far from peaceful were affixed to the ceiling above a small twin bed, the first thing he saw upon waking, the last thing he saw as he drifted off to dreamland. Evie shivered.

"Hey, Evie, take a look at this," Ricci said.

Evie drew up in front of the refrigerator, her blood chilling. Six canvases, made of a smooth, leather-like material, hung from small magnets on the door, each about two-inches square and each featuring a single image: a sun. Five of the six suns were so bright, they almost hurt her eyes. Brilliant yellows, fiery reds, molten golds, and blistering white-blues. The sixth sun was on a lighter, more brittle canvas and featured a simple dark outline with a smiling face and curved rays. A tattoo.

"It's Abby."

Evie jumped. There were few things that could make her jump, but the sound of Jack's voice—raw and ragged and just inches from her ear—was a stab to her gut. He'd been in a squad car down the street during the sweep and entry, but Ricci must have given him the green light. She took his hand in hers. Because everything kept coming back to Jack.

His fingers tightened around hers. The muscles along his throat convulsed. Was he holding back a string of curses? A cry of gut-shredding pain?

"We don't know for sure that the tattoo belongs to Abby." One of them had to hang on to hope. "I'll get Parker to flex some muscle and get a rush DNA test done. We'll know in less than twenty-four hours, but until then, Jack, don't let go."

He finally tore his gaze from the squares of human flesh. "Do you think that belongs to Abby?"

She wanted to hang on to hope, to believe that his beloved sister was alive and living someplace where the sun shone three hundred days a year.

"No bluffing," Jack said around an attempt at a smile.

But she also knew bombers. They selected weak and vulnerable victims. Fueled by rejection, they seethed with rage and resentment. And they always had a message. That tattoo screamed, *I finally captured the sun.*

Her own neck convulsed as a single barbed word rose up her throat. "Yes."

* * *

Friday, November 6
12:31 a.m.

LAPD had put out an APB on Douglas Woltz and his Dodge minivan, and Jack had made a few phone calls of his own. An employee in his building was the Angel Bomber. Brady and Claire and his head of security were contacting other employees at the coffee kiosk to see if anyone knew where he could be.

The hunt was on, and Jack was damn well at the front of the pack on this one because they were looking for one of his employees. Who collected two-inch squares of human skin. Abby's sun.

He closed his eyes, blotting out that sun. For now.

Evie crawled out from under Vandemere's bed, swatting dust from her jacket. "*Nada,*" she said. Which had been the case with the entire garage apartment. They'd found nothing that hinted at where Vandemere may be hiding.

They left the apartment and found Hayden sitting on the top step of the front porch and taking a long swig of coffee.

"Did you get anything?" Evie asked.

"The mother's a nervous wreck," Hayden said. "I'm sure she doesn't know where her son's at right now, but I'm having Hatch have a go at her." He pointed his coffee at the front room of the main house, the windows ablaze with light.

"If anyone can dig something out of her, it will be Hatch."

Evie sat on the step next to her teammate. "Any other relatives?"

"No siblings. Dad's dead. Died in a construction accident ten years ago. Explosion gone wrong at a job site." He took another swig of coffee. "I'm getting the case reopened."

Evie ground her boots into the dried leaves gathered at the base of the steps. "Was Mom able to give us the names of any friends?"

Hayden shook his head. "Not a one. He's the quintessential loner with poor social skills."

"Did you get any of his story?" Evie asked.

"You had him pegged," Hayden said. "Vandemere's father is ex-military. Ran a construction company in West Covina. The company's specialty was demo work. They took down old buildings, blew up old stumps, and blasted holes in mountains to make room for roads. He spent his childhood surrounded by guns and explosives."

"And a pretty explosive dad," piped in Agent Hatcher, who'd just stepped out the door and onto the porch.

"You got Mom to talk?" Evie asked.

"Got a little more out of her," Hatch said. "There's a high level of dysfunction in the family. Unlike his father, little Douglas showed no interest in sports, hunting, guns, or any other violent activities. He preferred much quieter pursuits, most notably drawing."

"And Good Ol' Boy Dad didn't like it," Hayden said.

Hatch nodded. "Called his son Pantywaist and Faggot Boy."

"Homosexual?" Evie asked.

"Definitely not," Hatch continued. "Woltz has always been interested in the ladies. Even his earliest drawings were of the female form, but according to his mother, few girls were interested in him."

Jack pictured the sketch of Woltz in his teens. "He had weight issues."

"Morbidly obese from age five on," Hatch said. "Food soothed him, Mom said, and she was right at his side, handing him the spoon. Which led to socialization issues, playground bullying, low self-esteem. You name it."

Hayden swallowed the rest of his coffee and held up the take-out cup. "The easiest way to understand a person like Douglas Woltz is to picture him as this cup. At a young age, he didn't fit his dad's ideal of what a son should be." Hayden ripped a gash down the back of the cup. "Dad forced him to play Little League and Pop Warner and dragged him on dove hunts and to the target range. Douglas, of course, did dismally." Hayden dug into the inner pocket of his jacket and took out a pen. "Dad was disappointed, which was manifested in anger." Hayden jabbed the pen into the cup. "His mother couldn't make peace so she made him brownies and pies." *Jab.* "His weight increased. Neighborhood kids laughed and taunted. Classmates shunned him and threw peas at him in the lunchroom." *Jab. Jab. Jab.* "Douglas turned increasingly inward and spent hours drawing and painting. Those were very lonely and dark hours. Until something triggered a change in his teens."

Hatch nodded. "When Douglas was sixteen, the senior Vandemere took a shotgun and shot up his son's sketch pads, paints, and easels."

Hayden set the mutilated cup on the step. "About that time, some unsettling things began to happen."

"Explosions," Evie said. "Bottle bombs going off in an empty field near his house. CO-two cartridges filled with smokeless gunpowder and lobbed into the school gym."

It was amazing, almost frighteningly so, listening to Evie

and her teammates paint this picture. They intimately knew this bomber because this was the type of person they dealt with daily.

Hatch nodded. "Woltz was a boy ravaged and raging. He ran away at age seventeen and lived in downtown L.A., but after a year he came back, pretty shaken."

"Daddy Dearest let him back home?" Evie asked.

"After beating the shit out of him," Hatch said. "Broke his nose and jaw."

"Thus rearranging facial features." Evie sighed. "People change."

Hayden jabbed the empty cup a dozen more times. "This is what he's become. A shell of a man with holes."

"And he's spent a lifetime trying to fill the emptiness," Evie said.

"First with food," Hayden said. "Then with art with increasing violence. He's a very wounded individual."

"Agreed," Evie said. "But hundreds of thousands of children suffer abuse, some far worse, and they don't become serial killers."

Jack couldn't take his eyes off the mutilated cup.

CHAPTER THIRTY-FIVE

Friday, November 6
6:19 a.m.

Evie was in full battle mode. She stood at the bathroom mirror in Jack's condo fighting with her hair. The hair was winning, but Jack couldn't laugh. He couldn't even smile. Today was the first Friday in November, the day a sadistic bomber, a man under his employ and inspired by art Jack handpicked, had every intention of strapping a bomb to a woman and blowing her up in a twisted expression of art.

Evie untangled her fingers from her hair and caught his gaze in the mirror. "Any chance you know how to braid?"

They'd fallen into his bed well after midnight, and she'd snatched a few hours of sleep. He had lain awake the whole night, watching the moonlight sifting through her hair and across her skin. Before dawn, he got up and made a single phone call.

Do you ever stop working, Jack?

That call had nothing to do with work.

He slid his hands along the sides of her rib cage and around her waist. He pulled her backside to him and kissed the slope of her neck. He had to try one last time because one way or another, this thing was going to blow today. "Don't do it."

She turned, wrapping her arms around his neck and pulling his lips to hers. "Stop worrying."

"Impossible."

Landing one more kiss on his lips, she tapped his butt and pulled him out of the bathroom. "Gotta go."

Today he wouldn't be allowed to play chauffeur or sit in a parked car down the street. Today he would be in his office doing deals and making money while she planned to meet up with a serial bomber.

"Have a great day at the office, honey," she called with a silly wave.

He waited until the door closed behind her before he said ever-so-softly, "You too."

* * *

7:22 a.m.

Sunshine and no fog. *A great day to catch a killer*. One of Parker Lord's favorite sayings. Evie agreed.

She poked her head into Ricci's office. "Any word on the time and location for our little bomber meet and greet?"

Ricci set the phone in the cradle. "Have a seat."

Impossible. There was too much fire racing through her veins today. She paced back and forth before his desk. "Have Brooks and the SWAT team arrived?"

Ricci stared at his hands.

"Is the hazardous devices unit ready to go?" The clock had ticked down. Today was the day. She was going to catch a killer.

"The plan's off."

Evie spun on her boot heels. "Did he strike already?"

"No." Ricci flattened both palms on his desk. "The plan is off because you've been pulled from the case."

Evie jammed her hair behind her ears. "Excuse me?"

"The plan where we offer to switch you for the girl and pick off Vandemere with a sharpshooter is off because you are no longer on the multi-jurisdiction task force to find the Angel Bomber."

Evie's hands tightened into rocks. "It's Knox, isn't it? He squealed about me belting him, and I've been suspended." *Damn. Damn. Damn.* She pictured Jack, the consummate deal maker, calm and always in control. She could learn a thing or two from him. She slipped her hands behind her back. "I lost my temper. I was wrong. So slap my hand, write up a report, but *please*, Vince, do it after the day is over."

"This isn't about Knox."

She knotted her fingers. "Then why did you pull me from the investigation?"

"I didn't pull you."

A cloud moved in front of the sun, and the room grew dim, then dark. Or maybe that was just the thunderheads rolling through her head. There were only two people who could pull her off the job, Parker Lord and—

"The president." She flung her hands in the air, then landed a finger on her nose. "Who needs me to keep my nose *clean* on this one." She aimed that finger at Ricci. "This is bullshit. This is not about his administration or an election but a woman and child living or dying."

"Parker pulled you." Ricci rubbed at the center of his forehead. "And for the record, Evie, I don't agree."

Boom! Both her palms landed on his desk. "What the fuck is going on?"

"Parker said he was concerned about your safety."

"My safety!" The thunderheads rumbled and tumbled, smacking her skull. "Didn't you tell him it's a bluff? That I'm not going to get near a bomb?"

"In writing and verbally. I even told him about every piece of Kevlar and blast plate you'd be wearing under your dress."

Evie pushed her hair behind her ears. "No. No. There's something wrong here."

"Yeah, Evie. There sure as hell is because anytime now Carter Vandemere is going to call and set up a date between him and you, and I'm gonna have to find a way to make it happen without you."

"No. No!" Evie bolted out the doorway and ran down the hall to her office where Smokey Joe was drinking his morning coffee and eating a cinnamon roll. "Where's Hayden?"

"With Brooks. Your sharpshooter got hold of today's weather report and wanted to talk to the SWAT guys about wind and visibility. I think they're in the war room. Man, that Brooks is one intense—"

Evie took off, running at high speed until she landed in the conference room with all the beautiful women on the walls. "What the hell is going on, Hayden?"

Hayden and Brooks looked up from a giant map of Los Angeles. "Good morning, Evie," Hayden said.

She parked herself six inches from his nose. "Dammit. How could Parker do this?"

"Do what?"

"Pull me."

"He pulled you from the Angel Bomber case?" Hayden asked, his eyes wide.

"Now?" Brooks added with equal incredulousness.

"You don't know about it?" Evie asked in a voice edged with panic. Bullshit. There was no edge. It was full-on panic.

"I have no idea what you're talking about," Hayden said. "Parker never said anything to me about pulling you. Are you sure you heard correctly?"

She nodded. But maybe Ricci's hearing was going to hell. Maybe the bomb squad captain had been around one too many explosions.

Evie punched at Parker's phone number but missed. She forced her fingers to stop shaking. Parker believed in her, trusted her. She finally dialed his number, and the phone rang and rang. "Damn you, Parker, where are you?"

Every eye in the conference room was on her, including the eyes of Sabrina and Angela Delgado. She took her phone to her office and tried again. This time Parker answered.

"What the hell is going on?" Evie asked.

"Evie? I— " His voice became garbled. "I'm on the jet headed to L.A."

"What the hell is going on?" Evie repeated.

"You and I are going to talk about that when I land."

"No. Now. I want to know now." Silence. "Parker, you there?"

"Jack called me this morning."

"Jack? My Jack?"

"Yes, *your* Jack."

"Why would he call you?"

"To tell me about the problems with your right eye."

"No, Parker. That would be my right ear."

"No, Evie, your eye, the one that was damaged in the Houston bombing."

"What are you talking about? The eye doctor cleared me two weeks after the explosion. Said I was good as new."

"He also advised you to be mindful of any blurriness or obstructed vision for the next few months."

Despite a fire raging in her chest and wicking her throat, she kept her words cool. "I have had absolutely no issues with blurriness or obstructed vision. My eyesight is perfectly fine. So would you please call Ricci and tell him I'm back on the case?"

More garbled words.

"Parker?"

"Jack said you were hiding it from everyone, including Hayden and Ricci."

"You believed him?"

"I believe this man knows a hell of a lot about you." Parker's voice, normally smooth and modulated, grew choppy. "Probably even more than me at this point. He told me about every single scar on your body."

She squeezed the bridge of her nose. "So some guy knows what my Saturday panties look like. You're going to believe him over me?"

"I get the distinct impression he's more than just a *guy*."

Evie swore in both English and Spanish. "He told you I told him that I loved him, didn't he?"

"He told me you wanted marriage and kids. Kids? Evie, something is clearly going on with you. You are not yourself."

Because she'd changed. She jammed her hands into the sides of her hair. But Jack hadn't. He was still the calm, collected businessman, still in control. The puzzle pieces fell in place. "He bluffed. He fucking bluffed."

Silence. "I'm sorry, Evie. I didn't hear you. I'm on my way, and you and I are going to talk."

The line went dead. Now was the time to talk, but not to Parker Lord.

* * *

7:57 a.m.

Evie took one of the Elliott Tower elevators to the top floor, staring at the Picasso and seriously wanting to further rearrange the face, sticking the woman's nose on her chin. She slammed a palm on the elevator door, trying to release a smidgen of the pressure building in her chest. Didn't help. Steam rose. All she saw was red.

Claire was a blur of beige as Evie stormed into Jack's office. He sat behind his desk, his royal throne. His computer was dark. He was waiting for her. A prince giving her a fucking audience.

"Parker Lord," she belted out as she slapped her hands on the great glass desk. "He's your *associate*."

Jack didn't deny it because he couldn't. Nor did he blink. That gaze, the one that had become as comfortable as her favorite pair of faded jeans, pierced her.

"Parker is the individual you met in the course of doing business." *Slap.* "The one who got you the crime scene photos." *Slap.* "The one you called this morning and told to take me out of the investigation." *Slap, slap, slap!*

"Yes." That single word was a gunshot to her chest.

Her boots backpedaled until the backs of her knees slammed into a thick, glass coffee table. She pressed hard into the glass, focusing on that pain, not the pain crushing her chest as Jack walked toward her.

"I met Parker ten years ago." Jack lowered himself onto the edge of a black leather chair, his knees just inches from her. "He had some investment money, and a mutual friend introduced us."

More space. She needed more space between her and this guy. She slipped away, moving to the other end of the table. "You're Parker's *finance* guy?" She shook her head but not too hard. She didn't want the tears gathering in her eyes to fall. "I always wondered how he could afford the great glass house on a cliff, the yacht, the private jet. And all this time I thought the director just gave him an extra-large expense account because he's the greatest fucking FBI agent in the history of the agency."

Jack interlaced his fingers. "Parker and I have made a good deal of money together."

"Good deal?" She wrapped her arms around her chest. So cold. The room was so cold. How could that be when she wanted to blow? "You know about deals, don't you? You know when to hold, when to fold, and when to bluff." Her fingers dug into the dusty, wrinkled sleeves of her jacket. "You told Parker I had vision problems, and you wrapped it in my declaration of love." Her vision blurred. She jammed her dirty sleeve against the damn tears. "You used my words, my love, against me."

"I used it to save you."

"From what?"

"Yourself."

"That's bullshit!"

"That's the truth." Jack stood. He wasn't shaking or crying, and his damn suit was clean. Damn him! "You were offering yourself in exchange for a woman who will be blown up today."

"We weren't going to go through with it! Dammit, how many times do you need to hear that?"

"I don't need to hear anything, Evie, because I know you.

You're all in. You don't do things halfway and never will. If the chance presented itself, if there was no way to save that woman and child, you'd throw yourself out there. You'd strap on the bomb." He shook his head as if in awe. "Because you're that dedicated to your work. You're *that* good."

She couldn't argue because on a gut level, the level that wasn't connected to words she *should* say and backed by years of *training*, she knew he was right.

Save the baby!

"And the irony of it all, Evie, is you don't realize how good you really are. You're as blind as Sugar Run and Smokey Joe. You've spent your entire life trying to prove yourself. To that testosterone-filled family of yours, to the Albuquerque PD, to the army, and now to Parker Lord and the president of the United States."

"You don't know what you're talking about. You don't know me."

"I know you shot the baby."

Evie's body rocked, as if slammed by an iceberg.

"Why do you look so surprised?" Jack asked. "I'm a businessman. Before I go into any deal, I do my due diligence. I wanted the best on this case, and I dug deep, and when I did, I found you. I also found out about your time in the Albuquerque Police Academy, and yes, I learned you shot the baby during firearms testing, and because of it, you walked away."

"It didn't break me."

"No, failing that test lit a fire under you and made you what you are. The best." He looked at the ceiling and shook his head. "The absolutely asinine thing is you don't seem to buy into it. You spend every hour of every day trying to prove that you belong in a world where you are clearly at the top of the heap. Your obsession to prove yourself is going to get you killed." He thumped a finger on the thick slice of glass. "I'm putting an end to this here and now."

"You controlling, manipulating son of a..."

"And loving, Evie." He jumped up and grabbed her shoulders. "Don't you dare forget that, because that's where this all comes from."

Steam and smoke swirled through her head. Two men she trusted, two men she loved—Jack and Parker—betrayed her. Big, important men playing with her little, pathetic life.

She swept her arms up and out, breaking Jack's grip. Her right hand landed on something smooth and glossy. A vase, most likely old and worth twice her annual salary. Her fingers curled around the glass. It would be so easy to throw the vase across the room, to create chaos and destruction with the beauty Jack collected.

Her hand shook. Sweat slicked her palm. Blood throbbed in her fingertips.

But that would make her no better than the sick man calling himself Carter Vandemere. He was a bomber. A serial killer with holes in his cup. A destroyer of beauty.

She set the vase on the table and left Jack Elliott's cold, beautiful kingdom.

CHAPTER THIRTY-SIX

Friday, November 6
8:01 a.m.

Shut. It. Up!"

Sabrina held the infant to her naked breast, but Angela turned her head and screamed louder. "I...I'm trying," Sabrina said on a choked cry.

"Try. Harder." The man's hand fisted at his side. His hand was skinny, all bone and angry knuckles.

"She's...she's hurting. Her ear, it's hurting."

The man who'd imprisoned her in a storage room in one of the big, tall buildings downtown—for hours, days, she didn't know—shook, his bones rattling as if he were coming undone. Exploding. Like the bomb. She could see it on the table behind him. She knew who this was and what he was going to do.

"She needs her medicine," Sabrina said. "It's in my bag.

Please get my bag. I'll do anything you want. Just help me help my baby."

His hand twitched as did his arm and leg. Like something was sparking inside him, something he couldn't control.

Angela cried out, and Sabrina rocked. "The bottle of pink liquid. In my bag. Please. It'll make her feel better. She'll be quiet."

The man reached for her diaper bag, the one with happy, hopping rabbits, his bony fingers tossing out Angela's diapers and pacifiers and little socks. At last he pulled out the bottle of antibiotic. *Oh, no!* Was this kind supposed to be refrigerated? She couldn't remember. But it didn't matter. It was something. She was doing something for her baby. She held out her hand, and the skeleton man settled it on her palm. "I need the syringe."

His body twitching, he dug again and pulled out a small plastic tube. Angela screamed, the sound making the man shake harder. Sabrina calmed herself, calmed her hands, and stuck the syringe into the medicine bottle, pulling out the exact amount as indicated on the label. She could do this. She could make her baby well.

She held the syringe to Angela's mouth and squeezed. Her baby girl grimaced and spit.

"Shut. It. Up."

Sabrina swiped her finger along Angela's chin, shoving in the medicine. "Take it, sweetie, please, please take it."

Angela spit and screamed louder.

Calm. Be calm. She'd been reading parenting magazines and online baby websites. She was trying to be a good mom. Trying. She set Angela on her legs and squirted in another drop of medicine. Angela opened her mouth to scream, but Sabrina blew on her face. Her baby swallowed. Another squirt. Another blow. Yes! It was working.

He started to shut the door, and she stuck out her foot. She had to get it together. For her baby. "She needs a diaper." Her baby had been in the same diaper—for hours, days, she didn't know—and it was soiled and dripping wet.

He dipped back into the bag with happy, hopping rabbits.

"And a blanket," she said, her voice growing louder. "Angela is cold, and she needs a blanket."

* * *

8:37 a.m.

Evie made it down twenty-two flights of stairs before she succumbed to the inevitable. She couldn't outrun the tears.

Her cowboy boots skidding to a stop, she pressed her back against the stairwell wall and slid to the ground. Jack had bluffed. He'd lied about her having vision problems, and Parker had believed him, at least long enough to hop on his private jet and demand an in-person audience.

Tears—the kind her oldest nephew called big, fat, sissy tears—slid down her cheeks. She could no more stop the tears than stop the air rushing through her lungs. Two men she respected, and loved, had betrayed her.

She rested her head against the wall and tried to get her mind wrapped around Jack's words. *You have spent your entire life trying to prove yourself.*

That was true. She'd spent her childhood keeping up with, and at times, barreling ahead of, her three older brothers. Same thing in the army and in her training at Quantico. And even on Parker's team, she refused to be the little sister happy to tag along behind the boys.

As for Albuquerque? She jammed her hands into her hair,

digging her fingers into her scalp and trying to push back the memories but failing.

Right out of college, she'd applied to the Albuquerque Police Academy, on fire and ready to save the world, like dozens of men and women in her family. Unfortunately, she'd been unable to save the baby. One baby. One second. One moment that changed her life.

During her final round of firearms testing at the academy, she'd been placed in a number of simulations where she had to decide when, where, and how to use her service revolver. During the first four simulations, she nailed it, scoring an academy class–high of ninety-nine percent. One more simulation, one more test, and she'd be golden.

Her recruit class had been warned about this particular simulation, the one called Save the Baby, where a bad guy abducts a baby and police are charged with tracking him down and rescuing the child. The problem was the bad guy was using the baby, a bald doll with flat eyes, as a shield.

Recruits had to use their senses, their training, their gut, and patience. Most times, the recruits didn't fire for fear of shooting the child, and the bad guy got away. On the rare occasion, a sharpshooter recruit managed to pick off the bad guy and save the baby. And in the history of the Albuquerque PD, nine recruits fired and shot the baby. Every single one of their names was written on that baby's arm, including hers.

Evangelina Jimenez. A last name with a storied history with Albuquerque PD. The one black mark.

For almost a decade that doll's face haunted her. She dreamed about those flat eyes and for years saw them in the faces of people she served while on Parker's team.

Her heart slowed. She pictured Sabrina Delgado and little Angela. She pictured the child in the Houston bombing.

They had real eyes, eyes full of life and light. Jack was wrong. This had nothing to do with Albuquerque. Just like the bomb disrupt in Houston, this was about saving a real child. She pictured her nephews, Freddy's nieces, and children that someday she would like to have, because—oh, Lord, her mother was going to fall to her knees in praise and thanksgiving—she wanted more than ticking bombs. She wanted children, and if she could ever stand to be in the same room again with him, she wanted Jack's children.

Jack. The man who'd betrayed her to Parker Lord. Her boss. Her mentor. Her savior. But he was also the man who didn't trust her to do the right thing. And dammit, it was time to do the right thing. She took out her phone and texted two words to Parker Lord. *I quit.*

CHAPTER THIRTY-SEVEN

Friday, November 6
10:14 a.m.

Here you go, Evie." Freddy handed Evie a stack of business cards. "Do you think twenty will be enough?"

"One will be enough." Evie tucked a single card into her back pocket.

"I've been thinking about a tag line. You know how I got that catchy phrase, Freddy Ortiz, photographer of the starz? I'm thinking you need one, too. How do you like Bombbusters or Bomb Babe?" The right side of his mouth inched up.

"Freddy."

"Yeah, Lady Feeb?"

She reached over and landed a kiss on his cheek. "Thanks."

"I knew you had the hots for me." Freddy waggled his eyebrows.

Evie couldn't laugh. She didn't have it in her. Not today. "Are you ready?"

Freddy's face sobered. "Let me get my phone charger."

Today was the first Friday of November, and sometime today Carter Vandemere would call Freddy Ortiz's tip line and leave the time and location of the switch, which really wasn't going to be a switch, but first Evie needed to get the ruse back on track.

Freddy squeezed himself into Evie's Beetle, and they drove to LAPD, where she found Captain Ricci and a handful of task force members in the case conference room. Evie handed Ricci the business card.

"What's this?" Ricci asked.

"If you're as smart and creative as I think you are, it'll be my ticket back to a live performance featuring the artwork of Carter Vandemere."

Ricci set the card on the table and laced his fingers. "Parker give you the green light?"

Evie forced down the lump in her throat. "Parker is no longer in the picture. I quit the team. I'm an indie bomb consultant, and I'm offering you my services. We can work out payment later."

Ricci closed his eyes and rested his chin on his steepled fingers.

Long ago, about the time she was sixteen, Evie had accepted and made peace with a higher being. *Please, God, please.*

Ricci nodded. "Let's get ready for an art show."

* * *

10:44 a.m.

Claire slammed an inch-thick report of the Matsumoto deal on Jack's desk.

"What?" Jack asked.

She slammed another folder. This one Seattle. "I didn't say anything."

"But you're thinking it."

Claire balled her hands on her hips. "Exactly what am I thinking?"

Jack shifted his gaze to Brady, who sat across from his desk, a line dissecting his forehead. Both of his colleagues had been glowering and stomping around his office all morning. "The same thing Brady is."

And it all had to do with Evie. Jack pushed back the reports and hopped up from his desk. This morning with a single phone call, he'd convinced Parker Lord to put the wasn't-going-to-happen switch on hold. Jack straightened his cuffs. It had been for Evie's own good.

Claire took her hands from her hips and reached across his desk. She picked up a pen and scribbled on the top of the Matsumoto report. *I quit.* She spun and headed out of his office.

"Wait!" Jack said. "What the hell is this?"

"My resignation."

"For trying to save the life of the woman I love?" There. He'd put all his cards on the table.

"No." Claire's normally placid face lit with fire. "For stripping a strong, competent woman of the confidence and power that is rightly hers." Claire jammed back the sleeves of her suit and aimed a pointed finger at him. "You may be a brilliant businessman, Jack Elliott, but you're a real dumbass when it comes to women."

Claire stormed out of his office, the door slamming and rattling the Murano glass on a nearby shelf.

He turned to Brady, who tucked the report under his arm and headed for the door. "Don't look at me. I'm afraid of both of them."

Jack opened the report on the Seattle deal, but he couldn't see the words. He thumbed through the notes on the project with Matsumoto, but it may as well have been written in Japanese. He bolted up from his desk, his chair rolling and crashing into the credenza. He stood in front of the wall of glass. Below him thousands of people walked and talked and went about their business.

Business wasn't on his mind. Evie was. She crowded every inch of his head and heart. Claire had accused him of taking Evie's power. A laugh caught in his throat. Impossible. The only person able to put out the fire in Evie was Evie.

The sharp tap of footsteps sounded behind him. Red cowboy boots? He spun, trying not to frown. Shiny black loafers. "Good morning, Agent MacGregor," Jack said.

"My apologies for interrupting, but your executive assistant wasn't at her desk," Agent MacGregor said. "Do you have a moment?"

Jack had all day because he wasn't getting a damn thing done thanks to his thoughts about Evie. "Of course."

"I have news about Abby."

Jack braced his hands on his desk. "You got DNA results from the sun tattoo?"

"No." Agent MacGregor held up a manila envelope and motioned to the small table and a pair of leather bucket chairs near the window. A place to share a cocktail and chat about the Los Angeles Lakers. A place to do business. "I have some photos I need you to take a look at."

A place for answers. Knowns, Evie would call them. Jack took the seat across from Agent MacGregor. Fifteen years ago, Abby had slipped out of his hands. His fingernails dug into the flesh of his palms.

"I've been following up on some cold homicide cases,

Jack, and came across this one." Agent MacGregor pulled out a thin stack of papers. Five, maybe six pages.

Jack's jaw spasmed. He had deal memos longer than that.

"The victim was a teenage girl discovered fifteen years ago in a park in Orange County."

Jack stared at those pages. Squiggles on paper. Letters. Words. A story. He motioned for Agent MacGregor to continue.

"Police worked the case for months. No trace evidence. No witnesses. No leads." Agent MacGregor reached into the envelope again.

"But you have photos."

"From the coroner's office. We need you to verify if the deceased young woman found in the Orange County park is your sister."

Jack closed his eyes. He pictured the bits and pieces of flesh left behind from Vandemere's bombs. Had the sick, broken artist tortured Abby? Had she felt pain and terror and the deadly chill of darkness with no hope? His gut tightened. Evie was right. Unknowns were a bitch. He opened his eyes and nodded.

Agent MacGregor placed a single photo on the table, one of a beautiful girl in a flowing white dress lying on the grass, face lifted to the sun, golden hair spread out like a halo. "The homicide detective working the case called her Angel Girl," MacGregor said.

Jack traced the flawless curve of her cheek, the smooth slope of her arm, the tips of her toes painted with pink nail polish. No, not just a girl. Not a nameless angel. A warm rush of blood rocked his fingertips.

"It's Abby." Despite the tightness in his throat, the words flowed with ease. Maybe because he'd started this journey seeking only her remains. He slid his finger to the center of her chest where her heart had once beaten with deeply felt sorrows and joys. "How?"

"Asphyxiation." The single word, drummed from cold, hard facts, was softly delivered. "Bruising on the neck indicates manual means. Lack of trauma to other body parts and no defense wounds lead us to believe she went quickly."

A matter of seconds? Minutes? Jack pressed his lips together. "The missing skin?"

"From her right shoulder, taken post-mortem." Agent MacGregor nudged the envelope toward him. "There are additional photos if you need to see them and a detailed report from both the coroner and the investigating officer." He rested both forearms on the table and leaned toward Jack. "From what I've been able to learn, Douglas Woltz fell in love with your sister, but she didn't return the feelings. Abby was too much in love with the world back then. My guess is she rejected Woltz. She told him no more little gifts, no more paintings, no more stalking. Woltz snapped, choking her in a fit of rage that probably surprised them both. He regretted his actions and placed her body where it would be found and tended to, because he wasn't a killer, not back then. Before he let her go, he took a piece of her, the sun she loved so much."

Jack stared at his hands, just inches away from the envelope that contained the proof positive he'd been searching for of his sister's death. Page after page of reports. Dozens of photos. But did he want to see it all? Did he *need* to?

"I also found this." Agent MacGregor reached into his briefcase and took out another envelope, this one fatter. "It's Abby's artwork from her time at The Colony. I tracked down one of her roommates who'd kept them all these years. Her friend said she couldn't get rid of the drawings and paintings because they were too beautiful." He placed the fat envelope on the table.

Jack stared from one envelope to the other. One of death. One of life. Business was all about choices. Choosing the right people, the right numbers, and the right timing. For the first time in fifteen years, he had Abby within reach, just inches from his fingertips.

With rock-steady hands, he picked up the fat envelope and opened the flap. The contents spilled out, like the sun on a cloudless summer day in L.A.

* * *

12:37 p.m.

The Los Angeles Toy District, a couple of squarish blocks between Little Tokyo and the Fashion District, had hundreds of dolls. Pocket-size dolls bundled by the gross. Dolls that took a bottle and peed. Dolls that burped. Dolls that could say *mama* and *bye-bye*.

Evie picked up a doll that could reportedly give hugs. She flicked the switch on the back, and two hard, plastic arms jerked, the metal grinding. Not a good choice. The doll looked more robot than human, and right now, Evie needed a lifelike doll because Carter Vandemere was an artist, a visual guy. She needed a baby with blond curls and soft, fleshy skin, a baby that looked real.

Making her way through a crowd queued up before a vendor selling sizzling hot dogs wrapped in bacon, she crossed the street to another toy wholesaler with stacks of bulk hula hoops and cases of yo-yos. She poked through a table display of leggy dolls with big boobs and tiny waists and a box of baby dolls with plastic hair.

A small Asian woman waved a doll with red pigtails. "Baby for five bucks."

"Not quite what I need," Evie said.

"What you need?" The woman curled her finger at Evie, inviting her closer. "Tell me, and I find you something special."

Evie pictured the doll in Murillo's *Mother and Child* portrait. "I need a beautiful baby with soft skin and hair the color of the sun."

The Asian woman's face wrinkled, like an apple left too long in the sun. "Don't have that down here. Mostly cheap overseas crap." She tapped her chin. "But I help."

Her tiny feet, outfitted in purple satin slippers with gold thread, slipped through the busy sidewalks of the Toy District, Evie at her heels. Even though it was noon on a Friday, bodies thronged the sidewalks. Evie ran to keep pace with the small woman as they threaded their way through the crowd.

"Shu-Shu help," the woman said as she ducked through a forest of scooters and plastic suitcases into a toy shop.

A small Hispanic man with no teeth grinned and took her to a bin at the back where stacks of baby dolls with clumps of polyester hair and painted pink cheeks were stacked. He dug into a cabinet under the display and pulled out a doll made of soft, flesh-toned fabric. It wore a pair of footed pajamas like her baby nephews wore and had soft, sun-colored wisps of hair and an angelic face.

Like little Angela Delgado's.

Maybe, just maybe, if the light was right and Carter Vandemere wasn't looking too closely, this would work.

"Or maybe this one," the man next to her said. "The eyes are more lifelike."

Evie took the doll, which was much lighter but made of hard plastic. The eyes had long lashes, the kind that fluttered up and down depending on the position. She brought the doll upright.

Her blood froze. The doll eyes, glass blue marbles, had been crossed out with a thick black marker.

She spun, searching for the man who'd handed her the doll. Not the one called Shu-Shu, the other one who'd been at her side.

Him. Carter Vandemere. Douglas Woltz.

Evie grabbed the shopkeeper. "The man standing next to me looking at dolls, where did he go?"

Shu-Shu pointed to the front door.

Evie pushed through bins of plastic balls in every color of the rainbow. She shoved aside a woman looking at pails of colored chalk and buckets of beads. She burst onto the street. Shoppers with giant black bags crowded the sidewalk. "Thin man, buzz cut," she said to the people in front of the toy shop. "Have you seen him?"

They shook their heads.

She grabbed the vendor selling iced fruit. "Man running out of the shop. Which way did he go?"

"Don't know."

Evie stood in the middle of the street, turning in a slow circle. Carter Vandemere, the Angel Bomber, had been at her side. He'd handed her a baby with hair the color of the sun and eyes marked for death. Now he was gone. She brought the baby, the one with the crossed-out eyes, to her chest and hugged it.

CHAPTER THIRTY-EIGHT

Friday, November 6
1:02 p.m.

He was at my side, breathing against my neck." Evie rested her fists on the top of Ricci's car. "All I needed to do was look up. Then one kick to the groin or a hand to the throat, and he'd be down. He'd be in our hands."

"He will be," Hayden assured her.

"Do you think this affects the plans for the switch?" Ricci asked.

Hayden shook his head. "If anything, it shows his level of investment in Evie. He wants her in that painting, and he's following her, ready to make a move."

"No phone call?" Evie asked Freddy, who'd been tucked into the backseat of Ricci's unit.

"Nothing yet."

But she'd had something. She'd had *him*. She popped her fists on the hood. She'd been so focused on finding a lifelike baby that she'd failed Cop 101: Be aware of your surroundings. He'd been there. Close enough to smell his roasted coffee breath.

She pushed off the car as a black limo pulled up to the police barricade. *No, God, please, please no.*

The limo stopped and less than a minute later took off, revealing the one man she didn't want to see, didn't *need* to see. For a moment, she considered ducking into one of the winding alleys, but she couldn't hide, not from this man.

"Good afternoon, Evie."

She clasped her hands behind her back. That way he couldn't see them shaking. "Hey there, Parker."

Her former boss nodded to Ricci. "Excuse us, please."

Ricci turned, and she grabbed his shirtsleeve. "No, it's okay. Everyone can stay."

"Everyone can leave." Parker nodded once. Every person near the barricade jumped to attention and left: Ricci, Hayden, Knox, three uniforms. Only Freddy Ortiz didn't budge.

"Everyone," Parker repeated.

Sweat beaded on Freddy's forehead as he studied the cracks in the sidewalk. She almost laughed. From the moment she'd met him, he'd been like a sticky piece of gum she couldn't get from the bottom of her shoe.

"Give us a minute, Freddy." Evie gave his shoulder a squeeze. "I'll be okay."

Freddy looked from her to Parker, giving her boss a tilt of his chin—apparently permission to engage with Evie—before he walked to the end of the barricade where he parked his wide butt, his gaze pinned on them.

"You have an admirer," Parker said.

"Business partner. We're bomb consultants. Have something that goes boom? We're in the room." She tried to smile, but her lips spasmed.

Parker took a yellow legal notepad from the right pocket of his wheelchair. "Status?"

When Parker asked questions, people answered. Termination of employment didn't change a thing. "Vandemere is still expected to plant the IED sometime today," Evie said. "Probably after sunset given the dark background of the portrait and possibly in an area with Christian symbols. We're waiting for him to reveal time and location for the switch. In the interim, tactical is on alert, and Ricci has doubled patrols in the downtown area."

Parker jotted a few notes, then tapped the tip of the pen on the pad. "No attempts from the Hostage Rescue Team?"

"Hayden doesn't think Vandemere is the type to go for a talk-down, but Hatch will be on site and try to engage him when he calls Ortiz."

"And you?" *Tap. Tap. Tap.*

"As soon as we get the call, I'll head in with the doll. The goal is to catch sight of him and pick him off. I'll grab the girl and disarm the IED. Each device has had a thirty-second delay, and I'll have no issue rendering it safe."

"I have no doubt you will." *Tap. Tap. Tap.* "You think he's going to go for the doll."

She scratched at a stain on her sleeve. "I pray he goes for the doll."

After taking a few more notes, Parker tucked his pen in his pocket and looked her squarely in the eye. "I made a mistake, Evie."

A feather of something light and warm tickled her chest.

"I should not have doubted your ability and judgment for any length of time," Parker continued. "I should not have pulled you from the task force."

She wanted to have a hard heart, to turn her back on this man who turned his back on her, if even for a moment, but she couldn't. "Then why did you?" The words came out with a soft waver. Yeah, it hurt like hell to admit how much this man's opinion meant to her.

"A man I know and respect and trust tells me you are in love and talking about marriage and *kids*. To say I was shocked was putting it mildly. Simply put, Jack Elliott dropped a bomb on me."

Evie's knees finally gave, and she plunked onto the barricade so she was eye-level with Parker. "You're not the only one."

Parker's hand settled on her shoulder. He squeezed, and she put her hand over his. "In that moment, Evie, I had a sliver of doubt about you, about your mental and emotional and physical state. In that moment, I decided to fly out and see with my own eyes what kind of state you were in, and after seeing you, it's clear you're healthy and capable. I'm sorry, Evie."

Evie didn't play games; she didn't know how. Nor did she hang on to anger and resentment because crap like that oozed and festered and filled the void of broken, empty human beings like Douglas Woltz. "I forgive you."

Parker spun his wheelchair and headed for Hayden. "And Evie," he called over his shoulder.

"Yes, sir?" She took off after him.

"I am not accepting your resignation. You are still a member of my team and a sworn agent of the U.S. government. Is that clear?"

"Yes, sir."

"I want a case conference with status reports from every lead, including contingency plans if Vandemere fails to attempt the switch."

"Yes, sir." Her boots made happy sounds as she hurried back to the toy store to buy the doll.

* * *

2:09 p.m.

It was after two in the afternoon, and Carter Vandemere had not yet made contact. Evie knew damn well he could be bluffing, promising the switch but in reality setting up the canvas for his next piece of *art* while she and the Angel Bomber task force waited, which was why she and the team were not sitting around and waiting.

Evie jammed her hands into her back pockets and hurried up the steps to the Paz de Cristo community outreach program, where in three hours the staff and volunteers would be serving up fried cod and coleslaw to more than two hundred of downtown L.A.'s hungry and homeless under the shadow of a wooden cross. All major events in the downtown area had been canceled today, but the good work of feeding the hungry and homeless had to go on.

With the first three bombings, Vandemere had selected locations that closely matched the backdrops in each painting. The wooden bench or pew and rosary led her to believe he may pick some kind of religious center. There were roughly fifty churches, missions, and spiritual outreach centers in the downtown area bordered by the 101, 10, and 110 freeways, and most of them had a wooden bench or two. A holy place for unholy acts.

She found the kitchen manager and members of a church youth group shredding carrots in the kitchen. "Can I interest you in a knife, a beautiful head of cabbage, or a gallon of mayonnaise?" the manager asked.

Despite the hell on the horizon, Evie smiled. "Not today, but when I get this bomber business wrapped up, I'm yours." Her gaze landed for a moment on the teens, caring kids spending a Friday afternoon doing good for others. "Do you have a moment?"

The woman took off her plastic gloves and led Evie into the main hall.

Evie showed her the photocopy of the woman and child. "We're pretty sure he'll place her on some kind of wooden bench, possibly in a church or building with Christian symbols. It's likely she'll be wearing a red dress, possibly with a blue scarf and white shawl. The baby has blond curls. The minute you see them, call us and evacuate the building."

The manager took the photo and raised her gaze heavenward. "I'll show it to the servers tonight, and we'll be on the lookout." As she escorted Evie to the door, she added, "I'm going to hold you to your promise to help, and you're welcome to bring the hunky guy in the suit."

Jack. Who'd peeled potatoes for a soup kitchen. Who'd stolen her heart. Who'd convinced Parker Lord to doubt her ability. She should hate him, but she couldn't. Hate was reserved for killers and those who mocked justice. For men with empty cups and broken, irreparable hearts. And Jack had a heart. She rubbed at the sides of her head. Two of them. His and hers. Unfortunately, he also had a little issue with control.

That, she could deal with. Later. A clock was ticking.

Evie hitched her bag on her shoulder and headed for the next church on her list, a mission near Skid Row. She turned into an alley, when footsteps sounded behind her. They grew faster and louder, and she ducked behind a Dumpster.

A man ran by her, his chest heaving.

"Holy shit, North!" Evie tucked her Glock back in her holster. "Do you want to go and meet your maker?"

Brother Gabriel North dropped his hands to his knees and took a series of deep breaths before turning his head and gazing up at her. "That wouldn't be a bad thing in my world, but I don't think it's my time to go yet. There is still much work in this world to be done."

"Why are you stalking me?"

"I called out to you, but you didn't hear." With one more deep breath, he stood. "I saw on the news that you're looking for Douglas Woltz."

"You know him?"

"Never met him, but his mother has been a member of our community for almost a decade. She joined after she lost her husband. She's always struck me as a kind but lonely woman and dedicated to her son. She was always bragging on him."

Another dot. Another step closer to disarming a madman. "Did she mention something about the bombings?"

"No, but something she said after services a few weeks ago makes me wonder. She told me her son was now going to be a famous filmmaker."

"Why would she say that?"

"Apparently Douglas had just purchased a fancy new camera and lighting equipment."

"And?"

"That's it, Agent Jimenez. It stood out because all of these years she's talked about him being a famous artist, and all of a sudden he's into making movies. It seemed odd."

* * *

2:56 p.m.

"That makes no sense," Ricci said when Evie told the task force members gathered in the LAPD war room about her visit from Brother North. "Why would Woltz's mother say her son is now into filmmaking? Think Brother North is lying?"

Evie pictured the words behind North's desk. *Thou shall not bear false witness against thy neighbor.* And she heard his voice. *We're both in the business of saving souls.* "He's being straight with me. He wants this guy stopped."

"Bombers are plotters and planners," Hayden said. "The film equipment is part of his overall plan."

Evie pressed her hands between her knees, bone pressing against bone as she waited for her colleagues to connect the dots.

"He could be filming the event to share with a larger audience," Ricci said.

"Hell, he could be live-streaming," Knox added.

Exactly what she'd been thinking. "So we're not looking for a public place, but a very private place." Which just turned their search plan on its ass.

* * *

4:27 p.m.

"It's really creepy that you know how to braid," Evie said as she sat in her office chair, Freddy tugging at her hair.

"I told you, I got eight nieces," Freddy said around the comb in his mouth. "I also know how to paint toenails and use a flat iron in case you want to do a sleepover."

"And you're wasting your talents photographing overpaid and over-made Hollywood actors? Maybe you should get out of the paparazzi biz and open a beauty salon."

Freddy yanked on the sections of her hair, folding and tucking. At last he held out his hand, and she slipped the ponytail holder from her wrist and set it on his palm. He secured the braid. "Got a mirror so I can show you my hand-iwork?"

"No." She hopped up from the chair. "I'm sure it's fine."

Freddy didn't let go of her braid. He tugged her closer. "You just make sure you stay fine."

"Stop worrying." She tugged her hair from his hand. "You sound just like Jack."

Freddy tucked the comb in his back pocket. "Where is The Suit? Kind of strange not to see him glued to your side."

"He's in his office." Evie grabbed her bag. Most likely grieving. Her gaze roamed over the photos of Vandemere's victims: seven Los Angelenos from the Angel Bombings, the Venice art gallery owner, motel night manager Mrs. Francis, and now Abby Elliott, who had slipped out of Jack's hands not once, but twice. She walked to the wall and ran her hand along Abby's golden hair. "I'm going to catch him, Abby. He's going to pay." She checked her watch. All-hands meeting in two minutes. "Time to catch a killer."

Freddy grabbed his man purse and headed for the door, adding over his shoulder, "Don't forget, you owe me one phone call. An exclusive shot at this guy."

"Yes. One phone call. After we catch him. Now promise me you and your camera will stay in a safe place until I call."

"No worries there, Lady Feeb. I kind of like most of my body parts." He patted his wide gut. "I'm not too keen on going to a place where a bomb may go off." He paused in the doorway. "I'm serious, Evie. Be careful. We got all these weddings between our nieces and nephews coming up, and I don't want you to miss them."

"The best marksmen in the world will have my back." She pictured her teammate, Brooks. "I'll be fine."

The plan was simple. Identify location. Wait for Vande-

mere to show with the mother and child. Start to make the
switch. Shoot Vandemere. Disarm IED. Save mom and baby.
And they all live happily ever after. The end.

Evie picked up the red dress hanging over the back of her
chair. It was a choir robe from one of Ricci's men, hardly a
match of the dress in the Murillo portrait, but it was long and
red. She jammed the choir robe in her bag and turned to the
door. Her right boot stilled in midair.

Jack. Dressed in a three-piece suit, his jacket unbuttoned
and tie tack crooked. She planted her boot softly on the floor.
"Jon told me about Abby. I'm so sorry, Jack."

He let out a low, long breath. "We have a lot to discuss,
including Abby, but now's not a good time." He pulled a box
from behind his back and handed it to her. "For you."

Jack was a man who collected *things*, who felt comfortable with *things*. She knew this was his way of reaching out.
"Jack, I—"

"It's for the case."

Evie reached in and took out a dress of flowy red silk.

"It's not an exact replica, but close," Jack said. "I told the
seamstress to make sure it wasn't too full, that the woman
who was going to wear this needed to be able to run and
jump and disarm bombs. She made it adjustable so it could
fit over protective gear, and she also used a special fabric on
the arms. It's snug so you won't have any fabric accidentally
hitting any wires or getting snagged on anything."

Her fingers dug into the silk. People change.

He lifted both hands in the air in a surrender of sorts. "I
love you, Evie, enough to let you go, and if you're going to
die, I want you to die doing what you love."

Like Abby.

She pulled the dress to her chest. It had cost him dearly
to have this dress made.

Jack's jaw squared. "I know, I'm being controlling, but it's who I am, and right now this is the best I can do."

"No, Jack. This"—she held up the dress—"isn't controlling. It's perfect." Because it meant he wanted in on the deal and was willing to negotiate. She stood on tiptoe and brushed a kiss on his lips. "We'll work out the deal memo later."

The dress tucked under her arm, she ran out of her office to catch a killer.

CHAPTER THIRTY-NINE

Friday, November 6
6:39 p.m.

Don't you dare say a word." Holding her skirt with one hand, she aimed a finger at Hatch, who was not bothering to hide a laugh. Brooks raised a single eyebrow, and Hayden pulled out a chair for her.

"You look perfect," Parker said.

Like the woman in the four-hundred-year-old painting and like an FBI bomb tech ready to take on a ticking bomb. She sat in the chair; the dress—custom-made by one of Jack's *associates* in a matter of a few hours—rustled.

"Let's go over the final details," Ricci said. "Anything on Freddy's tip line?"

Evie set Freddy's phone on the table. "Nothing yet."

Ricci took out a laser pointer and aimed it at a screen set up on the wall of the conference room. She watched as Ricci went man-by-man through a step-by-step time line. She'd let Ricci and his men worry about location and time. For her, the big unknown was the time delay on the IED. If she had the standard thirty seconds, the girl and her baby would be fine, but it was possible that Brooks or one of the other snipers would pick off Vandemere before he flipped the switch. And of course everything hinged on Sabrina and little Angela being still and quiet. The girl was young, just sixteen years old. Would she be able to remain calm? Could she keep the baby calm?

Riiiiiing.

Evie grabbed Freddy's phone. Call display showed a restricted number. "Agent Jimenez," she said.

"What a beautiful voice you have, Evie."

"Carter." Douglas. Killer.

"Yes, it's me, and I'm looking forward to our little swap. I'll meet you at the long-term parking garage near Union Station in two hours. Just you, Evie. You come alone, or the mother and child will die."

"I need proof of life, Carter. If I'm walking into this, I want to make sure Sabrina and Angela are still alive."

There was a sharp shuffling, a click, and finally a faint cry of an infant.

Her stomach heaved. "Carter?"

The phone went silent.

"Carter!"

The face of the phone darkened.

"We have knowns," Ricci said. "Place. Time. Everyone to their positions."

A clock was ticking.

Evie hopped in her rental car. The government and business offices had emptied out, and traffic was light. As she drove toward Union Station her phone rang. Caller ID showed Freddy, but a different number than his tip line. Must be his private cell.

"Hey, Freddy. This better be important."

"Um, yeah, it is."

"What's up? You get another call from Vandemere?"

"Kind of."

"Kind of?"

"He...he...got to me." A choked sob poured over the line. "Vandemere strapped a bomb on me."

Her heart stilled. "Where are you? Is he there now?"

"N...no. He's on his way to Union Station. Has the mother and kid. He has me tied up in the lower level of the Elliott Tower parking garage, but I managed to get my phone out. I puffed up my big ol' gut while he was tying me up, which gave me a little wiggle room. Pretty good stuff, huh? It'll make a great story." He tried to laugh, but the sound was more of a husky sob.

She banged her fists on the steering wheel. "How the hell did he get you?"

"He called me pretending to have a lead on that old-time Hollywood A-lister boinking his co-star. Anyway, he got to me because he wanted insurance. If you or anyone else tried anything, he'd...he'd..."

"Freddy, you need to calm down. I want you to look at the IED. Is it similar to the one Lisa Franco was wearing that day at the library?"

"Yeah, exact same thing."

"Hang tight, Freddy. I'm a block away."

* * *

7:08 p.m.

"I'm sorry, Evie." Freddy's words tripped out on a jerky breath as she got out of her car in the lower level of the garage. He sat on the ground near Jack's black Audi.

She held up a hand. "Don't move. Don't talk." She pulled out her service revolver and did a visual sweep. Bright security light flooded the entire lower level, and she spotted no bodies, no movement, no suspect objects. Next time she saw Jack, she'd let him know in many different ways that she loved his attention to security detail.

Gun still extended, she backed up to her car. Her cell phone sat in her bag, but she couldn't use it for fear of detonating the IED's ignition device. She had no idea what Vandemere had engineered, but she wanted a closer look. Using the key and not the electronic fob, she opened the trunk and took out a ballistics shield.

Preserve life, Evie, all life, including yours.

Got it, Parker.

She positioned herself behind the shield. She'd prefer her bomb suit, but she didn't have time. When she got to within twenty feet she could see the IED. Same configuration as the device the other victims wore. Thirty seconds. That's all she needed.

"Good news, Freddy. I disarm stuff like this in my sleep."

He didn't move.

She cautiously made her way toward him. Halfway to Freddy, the lights went out, plunging them into a sea of black. She ducked behind a pillar, blinking until her eyes adjusted. Her eyesight was better than twenty-twenty, and she saw dark gray on black shift near the stairwell. Someone had opened the door.

"Good evening, Evie," a male voice said. Rushed and breathy.

Her stomach heaved.

Freddy choked out another sob.

"Calm down, Freddy," Evie said. "You need to be still."

"Good advice," the voice said.

She squinted through the black. A man. Buzz cut, five-ten, but not as thin as she remembered Carter Vandemere. "Good evening, Carter."

"Such a beautiful voice you have, Evie. Everything about you is beautiful, and the truly beautiful thing is you don't even know you're beautiful."

She flattened herself against the concrete.

"I'll never forget the way you looked at me when we first met. Do you remember meeting in the Elliott Tower lobby?" The footsteps grew closer.

"Give yourself up, Carter. Ricci and the team are on their way."

"No they're not. They're headed for Union Station. Probably with a few bomb dogs, heat-seeking equipment, and a sniper or two."

"Ricci's expecting me. If I don't show, he'll come looking, and it will be as easy as putting a locator trace on my cell phone."

"Then we better get a move on things. Tick, tock, like a clock." More footsteps. Louder.

A soiled, sour smell rolled through the garage. Bile rose up her throat. "It's not going to work, Carter. I don't know what you have in mind, but you're the most wanted man in America. You're not going to get out of this city alive. Give yourself up. Ricci wants this thing over, and he's ready to deal."

"I, too, want it over, and it will be. As soon as we paint the final strokes on the canvas, and as soon as Jack loses what he values most."

He turned on a light attached to a band about his head, the kind miners wear underground.

Evie's blood froze. "The baby." Vandemere looked so bulky because he wore one of those soft-sided baby carriers all her brothers used to tote around their kids. Strapped across his chest, the baby reminded her of a rag doll, head lolling to the side, eyes closed.

Oh, God! Dead?

Carter picked up the baby's hand and waved it at her. "Don't worry, Evie. Angela's still alive." He pinched the child's hand, and a soft mew came out. "But very, very sleepy. A few shots of pain medication knocked her right out, but I'm more than willing to completely knock her out if you want to go that route." He pulled his hand from behind his back and aimed a 9mm at the baby's head. "Would you like to see me shoot the baby?"

A cry tore up Evie's throat.

"Decisions, decisions. The baby or your friend, Freddy. One of them will die if you choose to save the other. Like you, Evie, I'm pretty smart. So here's the deal. I will keep everyone alive, but you need to do your part. First, take your gun out of the holster and place it on the ground, and stop looking at the elevator. No one will be riding the elevator. It's conveniently without power right now thanks to a little maintenance memo from Claire." He jabbed the gun at the baby's head. Another weak cry.

Evie set down her gun. "It's me you want. Take me and let them go."

"That's the plan, but first I need to get you where you won't cause any damage. You're such a live wire, Evie. You've done some very brave things in your career. Sometimes I think you use your heart more than your head." He pointed the gun at the door that read, *Stairs*. "After you. But first, slide your phone across the floor."

She hesitated. This was her lifeline with the world. He aimed the gun back at the baby. She slid her phone to him, cringing as he crushed it with his shiny brown shoe.

* * *

7:19 p.m.

Ricci pulled his car onto a side street north of long-term parking near Union Station. Knox's blue sedan was two cars ahead, and Parker and his guys were pulling up behind him. He slid out of his car and waited for the little red Beetle.

CHAPTER FORTY

Friday, November 6
7:42 p.m.

The Elliott Tower north stairwell was pitch-black. Even the emergency security lighting had been snuffed. Vandemere must have shut off the power to this section. Probably not too difficult for a man wielding the clout of Jack's executive assistant.

As Evie climbed the stairs, she counted landings. On the eighth floor, Freddy, huffing and gasping, stumbled. She grabbed him before he pitched forward and got him back on his feet. On the tenth floor, the baby whimpered. On the sixteenth floor, Freddy grabbed the railing. "Can't." Huff. "Go." Huff. "Anymore." Huff. Huff. "Leave here."

"Fine with me," Carter said, "but that would mean leaving a bullet in your head."

And that was Evie's issue. Vandemere didn't need Freddy alive. The photographer wasn't on the canvas. He wasn't part of the show. To Carter, Freddy was as expendable as an empty tube of paint.

Evie slipped her arm around Freddy. "You can do this."

"Can't."

She tucked her shoulder under his armpit. "Unfortunately, you don't have a choice. We're partners and we have all those weddings to go to."

Freddy started up the next flight.

On the thirty-fifth floor, Carter's flashlight zeroed in on the door. "Excellent. We're here. Open the door, Evie."

He waited on the landing until both she and Freddy walked in. Inside was a cavernous room that appeared to be under renovation, mostly dark but for a pair of lights glowing in one of the far corners. Carter waved the pistol at the lights, and they threaded their way through scaffolding, five-gallon buckets of paint, drop cloths, and boxes of light fixtures. "New tenants, due to move in after the first of the year, felt the place could use a new paint job."

Big space. Plenty of places to hide. The issue was Freddy. She had to get him out of the room and then the baby in her arms. They reached the far north corner with the lights. They were the fancy mounted kind of lights, like those used by filmmakers. A camera on a tripod stood between the lights, the Record button not yet powered up. A mound she took for a pile of paint tarps moved and groaned. It was Sabrina, the baby's mother, shackled to a scaffold. With the back of her hand, the girl rubbed the snot from her nose. When Vandemere stepped into the soft pool of light, the girl's whimpering turned into a wail.

"Shut! Up!" Vandemere shouted.

The girl screamed and lunged at Vandemere, the chain rattling and growing taut. "Give me my baby!" She clawed like an animal. The scaffolding shook but didn't budge.

Carter lifted his gun and aimed it at the girl's forehead.

"Calm down, Sabrina," Evie said. Like Freddy, this girl was expendable. Carter didn't care whether she lived or died. "He's not going to hurt you if you do as he says, isn't that right, Carter?"

"Yes. That's the plan." He jerked the gun, clearly tipped with a silencer, in an upward sweep. "Get up."

The girl looked at Evie.

"Get up, Sabrina," Evie said. "We're going to get you to a safe place."

The girl stood, never taking her eyes off the child still strapped to the bomber's chest.

"Get the key, Butterboy," Vandemere said. "It's on the workbench."

Bombers were meticulous planners. The more Evie knew, the better shot she had at getting herself and everyone else out of here. "What's the plan?" Evie asked.

"I'm taking her to the floor below." Carter pointed the gun at Freddy. "Him too."

"Then you'll let them go?"

He shook his head as if she were a child with the wrong answer and he was the second-grade teacher. "Then I'll lock them in a supply closet, and sometime on Monday when the employees of the accounting firm of Marshall and Beck come in for work, they'll find them, earlier if some hard-working stiff decides to clock in some hours on Saturday. Your friends will be thirsty and dirty, but alive."

"The bomb?" Evie dipped her chin toward Freddy's mid-section.

"As long as Fat Freddy doesn't pull any wires, he'll be fine. Captain Ricci or any of his team will be able to shut him down in less than a minute."

"Give me your word."

"My word? Would you take my word, beautiful Evie?"

This man craved attention. She needed to give him strokes. "Absolutely."

His chest puffed, and the baby whimpered. He waved the gun at Freddy. "Now, unlock one of the leg shackles from the girl."

Freddy's hands shook. His fingers glistening with sweat, he dropped the key. The girl let out a cry. Time was important to Carter because he knew that very soon Ricci and company would know she was missing. A simple search of her cell phone's last location would identify her arrival at the Elliott Tower. Freddy fumbled in the gray beyond the pools of light and finally found the key. At last he got the shackle off the mother.

Carter waved the gun. "Now lock it around Evie's ankle."

Freddy squatted at her feet and looked up with huge eyes. When Ricci and the gang got here, they'd send men all over the tower, like ants on a giant wedding cake, and when someone got into the stairwell, they'd see the bits of red silk she'd been dropping like bread crumbs, the final tied to the doorknob of the landing on the thirty-fifth floor.

"Do it," she told Freddy. The metal bit into the leather of her boot.

"Show me," Carter said.

Freddy pulled on the metal. Solid. Locked.

"Same thing. Other side."

Once again Freddy knelt and took the shackle off Sabrina. The girl stood and lunged toward Vandemere and her child.

Evie grabbed her shirt. "Don't! He's not going to shoot your baby, but he won't hesitate to kill you."

"Really, Evie, we're soul mates. You know what's in my head and in my heart." Carter leveled the gun at the girl's head. "To make it very clear, I will blow your brains out if you so much as come within ten feet of me. Got that?"

Sabrina threw her hand in front of her mouth, her teeth digging into her flesh as she tried to hold back the sobs.

"Stop stalling, Fat Ass," Carter said to Freddy, who'd frozen in horror. "Get that on Evie's other foot."

Freddy locked the cuff in place and stood. He dusted his hands and knees. Something silver flashed, and he slipped the key in her hand and she bit back a smile. Despite his size, Freddy was a man with fast hands.

"Bad move, Freddy." And Vandemere was a man with good eyes.

Evie's stomach dropped as Carter, the gun barrel pressed against the baby's head, held out his hand. "Throw me the key. Now!"

He was unraveling. She tossed the key. He pawed the air, but it flew past his shoulder and clattered under the workbench. He waved the gun at Freddy and Sabrina. "Now both of you, that way." He pointed the gun at the door. "I'm taking you downstairs."

"Give them the baby," Evie said on a rush of air. She had to try. "There's a doll in my car."

"Nope. Not part of the deal. It's always been and always will be you for the girl."

"You don't want to kill a child."

"You're right, Evie. I just want to create art." He jabbed the mother in the back of the head with the gun. "Now move it."

"My baby!" Sabrina grabbed Evie's skirts. "You can't let him hurt my baby!"

The mother's scream tore through Evie's head but didn't shake her. "That's not going to happen." Not on her watch.

"Shut her up, Evie." Vandemere ground his hands against his ears. "I can't handle any more from her."

"Sabrina, listen to me," Evie said. "Your baby won't be alone. She'll be in my arms."

"No, she won't be safe there." The young mother wailed. "I need her safe. In my arms."

"First you need to save yourself. You and Freddy are going to a safe place, and I'm going to take care of your baby." Evie untangled the girl's fingers from her skirt. "Show her, Carter. Show her the original portrait you're going to re-create. Show her your masterpiece."

The bony hardness of his face softened around the edges. He picked up a sketch pad, holding it almost reverently. "Yes. The child will soon be in Evie's arms."

"Look at it, Sabrina," Evie said. "I'll have Angela. I'll take care of her. Now do as he says. I can't help your baby until you're in a safe place."

The girl took in a deep breath and shuffled toward the door to the stairwell.

Carter aimed the gun at Freddy. "You, too, Lard Butt."

Freddy didn't move, just like he hadn't moved when Parker had come. BFFs for life. "Freddy," Evie said between clenched teeth, "you're going to do me much more good if you get out of this room to a different floor."

Freddy's terrified gaze shifted to his waist.

"Don't worry about the IED, and don't try to remove it yourself. Let Ricci take care of it."

Freddy wiped the sweat from his face, and Carter jerked the gun at him. Carter's hand continued to shake so hard the gun clacked against his knuckles. Things were definitely not going as the bomber planned, which had him coming undone. If he blew and did something stupid, like shooting and setting off the bomb around Freddy's waist, they could all die.

"He won't kill you," Evie said, her tone calm and factual.

"You have a very specific role to play. You're going to tell Carter's story to millions. You have media contacts all over the world, and you've been taking pictures of all the bomb sites. You're even going to get a six-figure book deal out of it. Tell Carter about it."

"Uh, yeah." Freddy's gaze flicked from Evie to Vandemere. "I'm...uh...calling it *After the Boom*."

Carter blinked, his hand growing steady. "Yes. I need you alive."

Evie almost sank to the floor in a puddle of skirts, her relief was so great. "Get them out of here, Carter." Preservation of life was key. Two down. Two more to go. "And Freddy, I expect fifteen percent, got it?"

Carter pointed the gun at the stairwell, and Freddy and Sabrina shuffled through the paint cans and scaffolding. A single-file line, Carter at the back. With his back to her, Evie scanned the area. She needed a weapon. On the floor near a stack of paint tarps was something long and shiny. A screwdriver. Evie stretched out on her stomach and reached. The tips of her fingers were within a half inch, and her mouth twisted. Why the hell didn't she have long, girly nails?

"Open the door," Carter told Freddy.

She stretched, the shackles digging into her booted ankles, and touched metal. She might even be able to use it to pick the lock.

"Dammit, I said open the door, Porker!"

With the tip of her finger, she rolled the screwdriver closer.

Near the door, someone screamed, "Noooooooo!"

Evie looked up just in time to see Sabrina spring toward Vandemere. "I'm not going to let you hurt my baby."

Carter raised the gun. Even from across the room Evie could see the tremor gripping his arm. *Pop!*

The girl's body froze in midair, her arms wide as if ready to hug. A pool of dampness, more black than red in the shadows, seeped across her shoulder. She collapsed onto the floor.

Freddy teetered for a moment, a giant mountain about to tumble and fall. He grabbed another scaffold as if to steady himself and pulled. Paint cans clattered and splattered. Freddy lumbered toward the door.

Carter turned the gun on the wide, slow target.

"You shoot him, and he'll pitch forward onto the IED," Evie called out. "If he lands on it, we all die."

Pop!

The mountain crumbled and Evie choked out a cry. "Freddy!"

Carter ran to the still mound and leaned over the body, his fingers flying. Seconds later, he held up a black wire. "It's amazing what someone with the right knowledge can do in just a few seconds."

Evie's chin sank into her chest as she bit back a sob.

Carter tucked the gun into the child carrier and wiped blood splatter from his hands on his jeans, unfazed that he'd gunned down two innocents. Were they dead? She listened for breathing. Silence. Damn her ears!

Carter came back to the corner and adjusted both lights so they shone directly on her. "Ready for the show?"

She lowered her gaze to avoid the brightness. Keeping him talking meant keeping him from setting the bomb. She gripped the screwdriver in her hand buried in the folds of her skirt. "What's your gig? Are you streaming live? Got someone from the news media on board?"

"No, not this time. The final show is only for one."

"Jack." Evie's heart plunged to the pit of her stomach. Because everything kept coming back to Jack. Her fingers tightened around the screwdriver.

"Yes, Jack," Carter said. "Who doesn't know good art when it's right in front of him."

"All because the Abby Foundation rejected you for a grant." She squinted through the brightness and spotted him in silhouette. He was six inches from the right side of the camera.

"Because of Abby."

"Abby?" She bent back her wrist.

"My muse. The light and love of my life. The woman I gave my heart to. She said I frightened her, repulsed her." Spit flew from his mouth, the droplets illuminated as they shot across the bright cones of light. "I had to stop those horrible, ugly words." He brought his fingers up to his throat. "And as I stopped the words, she was gasping and calling big brother's name the entire time. 'Help me, *Jack*. I need you, *Jack*.'" He jammed his gun hand at the ceiling. "It should have been my name on her lips. My name!"

The muscles along Evie's shoulder tightened as she lifted her arm.

Carter jerked his gun hand. *Pop. Crack!* A section of the scaffolding behind her shook and splintered. She ducked, but not before a chunk of wood slammed into her upper arm.

He made a tsking sound. "I'm an artist, Evie. I see things most people miss." He aimed the gun at her chest. "Now put down the screwdriver. It's ruining the composition."

Her arm throbbing, the screwdriver clattered to the floor.

CHAPTER FORTY-ONE

Friday, November 6
8:44 p.m.

Ricci checked his watch, then the street.

"Where the hell is she?" Knox asked. "If she doesn't get here soon, this thing could blow up in our faces. You think she got lost or something?"

Brooks, the sharpshooter from Evie's team, drilled him with a glare. "Does Evie look like the type to get lost?"

"Has anyone tried calling her?" Cho asked.

"I did." Every gaze turned to Parker Lord. "She's not answering her phone. I'm getting a trace."

* * *

8:51 p.m.

Evie was so far out of her comfort zone, she would have laughed if she weren't staring death in the face. She had no

gun, no body armor, nothing that went *boom*. All she had
was a red froufrou dress and a baby in her one good arm.
Little Angela kicked her legs and let out a sharp cry.

Evie rocked. "It's not going to work, Carter."

"Of course it will. I've been making bombs for the past
decade."

"Not the bomb, your plan. You are not going to get out of
this alive. The police know what you look like. They know
you operate downtown. There's no way you'll get by the bar-
ricades they have set up."

"I will." Carter affixed a piece of black electrical tape to
a wire. "You look skeptical, Evie, but I have someone who
loves me, who'll do anything to help me and make my hor-
rendous life a little better any way she can. Put ice packs on
black eyes from schoolyard bullies. Wipe tears from my fat
little face. Feed me chocolate cake until I'm ready to puke."

Evie pictured the woman with the garage apartment.
"Your mother."

"Yes, a mother's love is amazing, isn't it? Strong, un-
bending, and never, ever ending."

He picked up the cylinder from the workbench. "Now
take a good look, Evie." He stroked it, a smile twisting his
lips. "Beautiful, isn't it?" He stood partially in the shadows,
but she could see it was the same type of IED as the ones
used on the previous victims.

The bundle in her arms kicked and mewed. Whatever
drug Carter had pumped into baby Angela was wearing off.

Holding the device with two hands, he walked toward her.
Good. Same collapsing circuit, which meant she had thirty
seconds. That's all she needed to disarm it. The flesh of her
upper arm throbbed where she'd been hammered by a flying
chunk of the scaffolding, and she took stock. Blood seeped
through the sleeve of the silk dress, and she had limited

mobility in her shoulder. Not one hundred percent, but that hadn't stopped her before. Her fingers itched to get to work. But instead of strapping the bomb to her waist, he walked past her and placed it behind the bench, well out of reach.

"Wait! That isn't how you do things. The bomb is supposed to be on me." She licked her lips, dry and parched, like her throat.

"You're my biggest fan, Evie, and you know my work. Too well." He smiled a grotesquely wide smile, the planes of his face becoming more skeleton-like. "Anyway, with the increased distance, the trajectory widens, creating a larger mass for carnage." He cocked his head, as if seeing the work from a new angle. "Beautiful."

Angela flailed, and Evie rocked faster. *Calm down, sweet baby, calm down.*

He reached for the timer.

"Wait!"

"No, Evie. It's time." He flicked the switch on the side of the cylinder.

The numbers glowed red. Thirty minutes.

"Bye, bye, beauty."

She yanked on the shackles. "Waaaait!"

Baby Angela screamed.

Carter Vandemere laughed as he slipped from behind the bench and reached for the camera's Power button.

Someone grunted. The tower of five-gallon paint buckets near the workbench teetered, then tumbled. One caught Vandemere in the head. Blood burst from his temple. Beige paint spilled across his body. With a groan, he and the camera crashed onto the floor.

"Freddy!" Evie cried out.

Sabrina, the child's mother, staggered from behind the workbench and ran toward Evie. "My baby!"

"Go back to the workbench. Find the key."

The mother grabbed the child and hugged her to her chest, leaving Evie's arms unbearably empty.

"The key!" Evie shouted. Because of the shackles, she couldn't reach the bomb to disarm it. And with her injured arm, the best option was to free herself and run. "Check under his workbench. Find the key."

Sabrina ran toward the bench but stopped five feet from Vandemere. Her arms drew tighter around her daughter.

"The key!"

"I...I...can't." The girl backed away as if facing a monster. "I can't go near him."

"That's okay, Sabrina. Go to the floor below. Find a phone. Call nine-one-one. Hurry, you need to get Angela out of here."

Twenty-seven minutes.

The girl breathed in the child's scent, her chest expanding as if drawing strength from the baby's essence. Leaning on the scaffolding, she made her way to the door.

* * *

9:04 p.m.

Jack threw his Bluetooth across the desk.

"She's fine," Brady said.

He switched off his computer. He couldn't work. Hell, he couldn't think of anything beyond Evie. "How do you know?"

"She can take care of herself." Brady shut the Matsumoto file they'd been going over for the past hour. "Me and the family jewels have seen her in action."

Jack couldn't smile. He checked his watch. It was past

nine. Had she met up with the bomber? Was the clock ticking? He took out his phone and did the one thing he knew would set off Evie.

"How did it go?" Jack asked.

"It hasn't," Parker Lord said.

"Is Evie all right?"

Parker Lord paused. "She never showed."

"He. You mean Carter Vandemere. *He* never showed."

"No. Evie. She never arrived at Union Station."

"Where is she?"

"I had her cell phone tracked. She's downtown still. We're getting a tighter trace right now."

Had Evie backed out? Did she take herself off the job? Yeah, right. "And Carter Vandemere?" Jack asked. "What did he do when he realized Evie was a no-show?"

Another pause. "Vandemere never showed, either."

The high-rise shifted beneath his feet, and Jack ran for his private elevator.

CHAPTER FORTY-TWO

Baby steps," Sabrina said on a ragged breath of air. "Just ten more baby steps."

Her precious daughter was crying. She was hurting. Scared.

Still holding the wall, Sabrina took another baby step. Nine more until she reached the phone on the desk. The FBI agent wasn't scared. When Sabrina grew up, she wouldn't mind being like her. Strong and smart and beautiful.

Baby Angela's cry turned into a wail, and she clawed at Sabrina's shirt. Her baby was hungry. Sabrina took her daughter's fist and kissed it. This wasn't the time to eat or cuddle or rock.

Eight more steps. She inched her right foot forward. Pain ripped through her right shoulder where the skeleton man had shot her. Her head spun. She doubled over. Another spurt of liquid trickled down her arm.

Sabrina dropped to her knees and set her baby, her healthy, beautiful baby, on the floor. Angela screamed louder. Sabrina knew it was okay for babies to cry. She'd been reading a lot about raising babies, trying to do things right, but right now she needed to do the right thing for Agent Jimenez.

"Seven more baby steps," she said.

Blood slicked her hands, the floor, her arm.

Angela screamed.

It was going to be okay. Six more baby steps to the phone. Five. Four. Three. Two.

Now one.

She reached the desk in the office on the floor below where Agent Jimenez was trapped and raised her arm, grasping at the phone. Too far. She dragged herself to her feet, then fell back to the floor as a blanket of blackness overtook her. Somewhere behind her, her angel baby screamed.

* * *

9:07 p.m.

Absolute silence surrounded her. Even the ringing in Evie's ears had stopped.

She squinted, focusing on the scarecrow of a man sprawled out in front of her, his chest rising and falling to the rhythm of a ticking bomb. She strained her ears. Was that a ragged breath closer to the door? Freddy?

The red numbers on the bomb behind her glowed.

Twenty-two minutes.

The camera and computer lay on the floor in shattered and scattered bits. So much for Vandemere's attempt to stream the bombing and her chances to tell anyone her location.

Her options: get out of the room, disarm the IED with

her injured arm, or get the IED in a containment vessel to minimize destruction. Ricci would have the necessary equipment. And he was on his way. He had to be because Sabrina had found strength to take care of her baby. The young mother had to have made it to a phone by now.

Evie continued to poke the screwdriver at the shackle on her ankle. If the bomb blew here, destruction would most likely be contained to three floors, although building-wide structural damage was always possible. She pictured Jack on the floor above, Brady, too. Maybe Claire. The bomb could hurt them, but it would kill her. Carter, too. And possibly Freddy. Was he alive?

"Freddy!"

No answer.

"Freddy, are you there? Can you hear me?"

A groan wafted through the darkness near the door.

She strained against the shackles. "Freddy. It's Evie. Get up, Freddy. You have work to do."

Another groan.

"We're partners, buddy, and you're not bailing on our first job."

"Ev…Evie?"

Evie's heart lurched against the red silk of her dress. "Near the light, shackled to the bench."

"Vandemere?"

The pile of bones and blood near the pallet of paint had not moved. "He's down." At least for now. "Freddy, I need you to go to Vandemere's workbench and find the key."

Silence.

"Don't you dare die on me, Freddy. You hear me? Don't. You. Dare. Die."

He grunted. "Nope. Not yet. Got too many stories left to tell."

Freddy dragged himself across the room and into the light. His right side looked as if someone dumped a five-gallon bucket of red paint on him. He dropped to the ground next to the workbench and fumbled along the floor. "Can't find it."

"Keep looking, Freddy."

Freddy sat, leaning against a bucket of paint. "Chest hurts. Can't breathe."

"Okay." She steadied her hands on the bench. "You know what, Freddy. Go back to the door. Get out of here."

"No. Gotta get the key."

"Sabrina left a few minutes ago. Ricci and the guys are on the way."

"No. Keep going. We're partners."

"Go!"

He shook his head, his hair falling across his forehead. "Always worked alone. Never had a partner till you. Kind of like it."

Tears—the big, fat, sissy ones—welled behind her eyes. Dammit. She never cried.

"You still there, Evie?" Freddy asked.

She cleared the lump in her throat. "Yeah. Not going anywhere."

"Keep talking. I like the sound of your voice. Turns me on." He sputtered out a cough. "Talk dirty to me."

"You're a sick man, Freddy." But loyal. Damn, he wasn't going until he found the key or someone dragged his ass out of here.

"Tell me a story." He heaved his body past Vandemere's still body to the side of the workbench.

"Story?" Evie scrubbed at her ears. "You want a story? Now?"

"Yeah, it's always about the story." Freddy dug through a

stack of paint buckets. "Tell me the story of how you ended up on Parker Lord's team."

Her hands dropped to the sides of the dress, her fingers digging into the silky fabric. If Freddy needed a story, she'd give him one. "I'd just got out of the army and was amped up to join the FBI. My recruiter was jazzed because in the military, I was kind of a big deal who'd kicked a lot of ass over in the sandpit."

Freddy dug through the tarps. "Gotta love a heroine with confidence and charisma."

"So I marched my kick-ass boots—I think they were brown back then—over to Quantico where the recruiters made appropriate oooing and ahhing sounds. I signed the papers and joined the academy." She checked the ticking clock. Eighteen minutes. "But I didn't even make it to the first day of class."

"What? Were those Feebie guys blind and dumb?" His hands scrambled across the floor, clawing through thick paint.

"I failed the physical."

"You?" He groped along the floor in front of the workbench.

"Hearing impairment. Right ear."

"That's the shits."

"Nope. That's my life."

"You're worrying me, Lady Feeb." He rummaged through paintbrushes and rollers.

Where was the damn key? "After getting the boot for a bum ear, I headed to a nearby bar. I was sitting at the counter just about to hoist my second shot of whiskey when this guy came in and sat on the stool next to me. I didn't know it at the time, but it was Parker Lord, this famous FBI agent who'd started a special investigative unit up in Maine. Anyway, he sat down, ordered a Jimmy B for himself, and told me to march my kick-ass boots back to Quantico, that I was back in. To this day I don't know what he said and why, but I was back in the academy."

"Things went well at Feebie school?" Flat on his stomach, he groped under the bottom shelf of the workbench.

"Things went really well." Evie's voice was about to crack. No, she couldn't let it go there. "Freddy, you find the key?"

More fumbling. More coughing and sputtering. "Not yet."

* * *

9:08 p.m.

Ding.

Jack hopped on the elevator and slammed his palm against the LL button. Down. Down. According to Parker's cell phone locator, Evie was downtown. She said Brother North kept popping up. Jack would head to North's mission, try the soup kitchen, and hunt through every high-rise, every warehouse, and every garage holding toys made from China in his hunt for the woman he loved.

In the parking garage he found his car, but it was not alone. Nearby sat Ortiz's Mustang and the shiny red Beetle. For a second, his entire world went red. He blinked, pushing back the fiery image.

Jack took out his cell phone and called Ricci. "Get to Elliott Tower. Evie and Freddy are here somewhere. Both their cars are in the lower level parking garage."

"We're on our way. Get out of that building, Jack. I want you three hundred feet away."

"Okay." Jack hung up the phone. Not okay. He was about to rush back to his private elevator when he saw a ribbon of red snagged on a piece of concrete near the north stairwell. He fingered the silk. Evie's dress. He burst into the stairwell, a sea of black. He switched on his phone, using the light app as he took off up the stairs.

On the fourth floor, he spotted another bit of red silk. Another on the seventh. Fifteenth. Twenty-first. He didn't stop until the thirty-fourth floor. His foot flew out from under him. Wet. Water leak? No, beige paint and a streak of red. Blood?

He threw open the door. A baby wailed.

He flipped on the light. Blood streaked the floor. A baby lay near the door coughing and hiccupping. Beyond the infant was a dark-haired woman, collapsed on the floor near a desk. He grabbed her. Her eyelids fluttered but didn't open.

He squeezed her arms. "Where's Evie?"

A moan slipped over her lips but no words. Setting her back on the ground, he grabbed a chair, jammed it in the doorway so police would look, and took off up the stairwell.

* * *

9:17 p.m.

Carter woke to pounding, at the back of his head, behind his eyes, and in the middle of his chest.

Then he heard Evie's voice. "So Hatch reached into this hat and pulled out a rabbit. A rabbit!" Silence. "Uh, Freddy, you're supposed to laugh."

"H . . . ha, ha."

So Fat Freddy was alive. Carter ran a hand along the side of his head where his fingers slid across congealed blood.

And so was he despite someone shoving a five-gallon paint bucket at his brain. He dragged himself to his knees and groped around until he found his gun.

Evie's eyes locked with his. In that moment, he saw the truth. She was not a fan. She hated him. But he didn't care anymore, not about the woman. She was but paint on canvas.

He steadied himself on the scaffold. Still time to leave.

Twelve minutes.

"You sit tight, Evie, and keep telling Freddy bedtime stories," Carter said as he headed for the door, his gun hand extended but wobbling. "Nighty-night."

* * *

9:20 p.m.

The door inched open, and Evie held her breath. Ricci? Brooks? Hayden? She'd even take Knox. A man stepped into the room, a halo of light spilling from his cell phone. Dark suit. Pinstripes.

She swallowed a cry of relief. She'd spent the past week telling Jack Elliott he didn't belong at her side and on this case. She was wrong. Jack was a Harvard MBA, but he'd also done some fighting in his life, and not just in the boardroom. On the streets of New York and for his sister.

Before she could call out a warning, Carter fired the gun at the open doorway. Jack dived to the ground and slid behind another scaffold as the door frame splintered.

"Nine minutes," Evie called out.

Carter spun in a circle, gun outstretched. "Show yourself, Jack, or I'll shoot her," Vandemere said, his voice as shaky as the hand holding the gun.

No sound. No movement.

Carter's gun hand jerked. "I grew up in a household with guns. At one time I was a card-carrying member of the NRA. If I shoot, she's dead."

"He's bluffing," Evie said. "He's injured and shaky."

Carter aimed a shot at her, but as expected, the shot went wide. The guy had lost a good deal of blood. He was weak and getting weaker. Plaster rained down on Freddy, who was at the workbench still looking for the key.

A dark shape shifted behind the scaffold. A paint bucket went flying from the right side. Carter spun. Jack darted out from the left side and rammed his shoulder into Carter's back. Carter slammed onto the floor. *Thud.* Blood spurted from his nose and mouth. His body twitched, then stilled.

Jack ran toward her.

"Get back!" She jammed her good arm at the floor behind her. "The bomb's live and has a collapsing circuit."

"How long?"

"Six minutes." She tilted her head toward Freddy. "Freddy can't find the key. Get out of here. Find Ricci. He'll know what to do."

"The key," Freddy said. "Not until I find the key."

"Go, both of you!"

Jack ran to Freddy's side. "Where do you want me to look?"

"She said it flew under the bench, but I can't find it."

Jack dropped to his knees, sliding his hands through paint and dust. Freddy, leaning against the bench, fumbled with his one good arm. They were both fighting for her life. The muscles along her throat convulsed. Because for the first time in her life, she couldn't fight for herself. She'd spent a lifetime scrapping with her brothers, fighting for the country she loved, and waging war on the worst kinds of evil.

Evie could do nothing but stand there motionless. She

took a deep breath. And she could trust in Jack. She had to trust in Jack who was on his hands and knees, searching for a key. Tears swelled in her eyes. The key to her future.

The door swung open, framing Ricci and his team, all carrying heavy beamed flashlights and glowing like angels in bomb gear.

"One minute twenty seconds," she called out.

"Found it!" Jack held up a stick of silver.

Jack pushed Freddy at two of Ricci's men. He ran to the scaffold and dropped to the ground at Evie's feet.

"Dammit, Jack, give the key to Ricci. He's in gear."

Deaf and blind, Jack focused on the lock on the first shackle. Jab. Turn. *Click*. Blood pulsed through her foot as she shook her ankle free.

Jab. Turn. *Click*. The next. She hopped up and tripped on her skirts. Jack untangled her.

Hiking her skirts, she ran toward the door. Freddy, Ricci, and the team had already dived into the stairwell.

Carter Vandemere stirred. One eye opened. Her feet slowed. He was a macabre sight. Paint matted his hair. Blood trickled from his shattered nose. A thick, clear liquid leaked from his swollen right eye.

Jack yanked her toward the door.

"Twenty seconds!" Ricci called out from the door.

Vandemere lifted his hand. He clutched the hem of her skirt with bony, bloody fingers. His mouth twisted in a scream she couldn't hear. No noise. Absolute silence. The moment before a bomb goes off.

Jack kicked off the hand.

"Fifteen seconds!" Ricci.

She pushed Jack in the back. He stumbled toward the stairwell.

"Go!" she screamed. She lunged at Carter and jammed

her hands under his shoulders, her injured arm crying out in pain.

"Ten seconds!"

Evie pulled, dragging Vandemere over tarps and spilled paint. Over Freddy's blood and Sabrina's blood.

"Dammit, Evie, leave him there!" Ricci called.

She heaved again.

Two hands—Jack's—grabbed Vandemere and yanked. They jerked him toward the door. Carter moaned.

Pop. Hissssss. Boom!

Smoke and flames and shrapnel tore through the air. The sky fell. Jack threw his body over her and Carter Vandemere. She knew his intent.

Preserve life, all life.

CHAPTER FORTY-THREE

Friday, November 6
9:59 p.m.

Evie still wore the red silk dress, now sporting a few burn marks, torn hem, paint splatters, and two bloody handprints. Carter Vandemere's latest work of art, and it could very well be his last.

The ambulance took off down the street, lights flashing, siren wailing. Inside was bomber Douglas Woltz, the artist formerly known as Carter Vandemere, and he was being rushed to the hospital where his life would now be in the hands of a surgeon or two. If he lived, his life would be in the hands of a jury of his peers, and Evie had a feeling that would end up very ugly.

"Have a seat, Evie," Jack said. "I want the paramedic to take a look at that arm."

"Do you always get what you want?" Evie asked as she

looked up at Jack, still looking like a million bucks, despite
the streaks of paint and dirt on his suit and face.

He placed both hands on her shoulders, pushed her to the
back bumper of the squad car, and kissed her soundly on the
lips. "Always."

In this case, she had no complaints. She cradled her hands
on either side of his face and returned the bone-melting kiss
with a fire of her own.

"Ah-hem."

Evie tore herself from Jack and nodded to the paramedic
standing behind them. "Don't cut the dress," she warned.

Jack raised an eyebrow as he took a seat next to her.

"The dress has kind of grown on me," she said. "I'm
going to wear it next year for Halloween when I take my
nephews trick-or-treating."

Ricci, now out of his gear and soaked with sweat, joined
them at the car.

"Everyone out of the tower?" Evie asked.

"Safe and sound. We've evacuated the area, and tomorrow morning the structure guys are going in for a look."

Evie rested her hand on Jack's knee and squeezed. "Sorry
about your building."

"It'll be fine," Jack said with a confidence that would
never be shaken. "Plans far exceeded earthquake code."

"Of course. Only the best for you."

"Only the best." He put his hand over hers.

"What about Vandemere's mother?" Evie asked Ricci.
"Did you find her?"

Ricci nodded. "In the parking lot of an office complex
two blocks away, and she was ready to fight for him, too.
She took a swing at the arresting officer."

When it came to their children, mothers of all ages and
shapes and sizes showed formidable strength. Evie had al-

ready received word that Sabrina was in surgery and Vandemere's bullet had missed all major organs. Little Angela had
downed two bottles and was fast asleep in her grandmother's
arms.

Under her narrowed gaze, the paramedic inched up Evie's
sleeve. The wound on her arm needed a good cleaning but
no stitches. It might leave a scar, but that was nothing new.
She pushed the hair from her face and looked at Jack. He'd
taken on a serial bomber and came away without a scratch.
He looked perfect. On the street and in her world.

A flash exploded in her face.

Evie tried to blink away the blind spots. "Dammit,
Freddy. No pictures." She shook her head. No, it couldn't
be Freddy. He'd already been whisked away by an ambulance. When she could see again, she spotted a young girl
with long dark hair.

The girl blew a pink, shiny bubble. "I'm not Freddy."

Evie waved a finger at her. She'd seen that face before.
"You're..."

"Lilliana. His niece. Uncle Freddy told me he'd pay me
fifty bucks for any good shots I got down here."

Evie shook her head. "Why am I not surprised?"

Lilliana blew another neon pink bubble.

"How's he doing?" Jack asked.

"Good. The bullet didn't hit anything too important, but
the doctor said Uncle Freddy would have to stay in the hospital a few days. Now let me get one more." She lifted her
camera.

Click.

As they walked to the sports car one of Jack's people
must have delivered, he pulled her close, tucking her into his
side.

Once at the car, he bowed. "Where to, my lady?"

And dammit, not a single hair moved. She laughed and nudged him upright with her fingertips. "Your chauffeur days are over."

"Or maybe they're just beginning." He opened the door. "So where do you want to go?"

She sank into the lush leather seat. Really, she could get used to having Jack Elliott in her life. "Someplace with cake."

* * *

Saturday, November 7
8:22 a.m.

Evie placed one hand on the desk in Jack's Ojai home office.

"I'm afraid not, Alexi," Jack was saying into his Bluetooth.

She placed the other hand on his desk.

"Six point five won't work on this end."

She brought her knee up and crawled across the expanse of wood the color of browned butter. She spun him from his computer.

"But if you can get your people in Moscow to five and three-quarters, we can open up a dialogue."

She planted a boot on each side of his hips and slipped her hands around his neck.

"Um, Alexi," Jack said, "contact Brady when you get the new numbers."

Jack switched off his computer and tore the Bluetooth from his ear.

"Taking over Russia this morning?" Evie asked as he slid his hands along her thighs.

"Not right now. I have other things on my mind."

"Those will have to wait." She pushed back his chair. "Because you have to see something."

She dragged him outside, and they strolled through sunshine and citrus groves to the pasture. "Look," she said. "Miss Alfalfa spent the past hour herding Sugar Run along the fence. She's showing him where it's safe to go."

"Pretty amazing." Jack nuzzled the top of her head.

And so was Jack, a man who could deal with serial killers and blind horses. A laugh bubbled up her throat. And her. She thought she'd never find a man who could accept the dangers and destruction associated with her job. But then again, she never thought she'd let such a man into her life.

She climbed onto the bottom rung of the fence and rested her elbows on the top rung. Jack slipped his arms around her and nuzzled her neck, much like Miss Alfalfa, who was nudging Sugar Run toward the water trough. "Are you going to collect any more?" Evie asked.

"I think one goat's enough."

She elbowed him in the ribs. "I meant racehorses."

"Do you want me to collect more racehorses?"

"I like horses." She turned. She wanted to see him and him to see her. "Jack, there's something else you should know."

"Full disclosure is fine with me." He slipped his hands beneath her denim jacket.

"I also like kids. I want kids."

His fingers slipped under her tank. "I know that."

"Not just one or two. I'm thinking a few more."

He flattened his hands on her skin, ran his palms along her sides, then dipped his fingers into the waistband of her jeans. "It'll be my favorite collection."

She took his hands in hers, hands that knew exactly what they wanted and weren't afraid to take on anyone and anything. "And I don't plan on giving up my job. I love disrupting bombs and carrying a gun. I love stopping bad guys and making this world a little bit safer for good people."

"I am thankful for that."

"But can you live with that?"

He brought their clasped hands to the center of his chest and pressed her palm against the strong, steady ticking of his heart. She loved the feel, the sound, and the promise of a lifetime with him.

"The bottom line, Evie, is I can't live without you."

EPILOGUE

Sunday, November 8
7:47 a.m.

Evie sat on the porch of Jack's Ojai ranch house, her dusty cowboy boots propped on an overturned orange crate. "Here you go." She tossed an orange at her teammate Hayden Reed. "For Smokey Joe. Maybe it'll sweeten him up."

Hayden caught the orange. "At this point I don't think anything will help."

Even with her less than perfect hearing, Evie could hear Smokey Joe and Kate going at it in Jack's kitchen. Hayden, Kate, and Smokey were leaving Southern California today, and Smokey was not one bit happy about where he was headed: his cousin Franny's house in Florida. For his own safety, he couldn't live alone, and he refused to move in with Hayden and Kate.

"You know what he needs?" Jack asked as he slipped his arm around Evie's shoulder.

"A new attitude?" Hayden asked without a trace of humor.

"A new pasture buddy."

Evie laughed while Hayden's brow wrinkled.

"I'm serious," Jack said. "Smokey needs another horse that has the patience and disposition to put up with him. Goats work, too, if you're in a pinch."

Hayden frowned at the orange in his hand. "Smokey Joe is an old goat, and that's the problem. He's so disagreeable no one wants to deal with him."

Evie peeled the last of her orange before adding, "Kate did."

"She still would, but he refuses to move in with us."

"I don't blame him. You two are madly in love, and he's the third wheel." She pressed her shoulder into Jack's side.

Hayden set the orange on the porch railing. "I don't know what to do."

"Do what you do best, Hayden," Evie said. "Use your eyes. You saw Kate and Smokey together, why did they work?"

Hayden slid his hand along his tie, and she could see the pictures whirring through his head. "For one, she didn't let Smokey push her around. The minute he pulled any crap, like *accidentally* leaving the water on in the upstairs bathroom, she hauled him on the carpet for it. She was tough, but fair. He respected her, and she respected him."

"And..." Evie prompted.

"Kate needed him, and Smokey knew that. Of course Kate never came out and said it, but she did. She needed his isolated place in the mountains. She needed his gumption and passion to start an online jewelry store. She needed his wit and mental acumen. Most of all, she needed his acceptance of her, scars and all. They both considered themselves a little broken. But together, they were whole."

Jack, the consummate deal maker, nodded. "Smokey Joe needs someone not in the mainstream world. Someone with patience, honesty, and toughness. Someone Smokey can respect. Someone a little broken. Do you know anyone like that?"

A slow smile slid over Evie's face. "I do."

* * *

4:31 p.m.

"Does Kate know about your harebrained idea, Evie-girl?" Smokey Joe asked as he groped the air until he found the rail on the stairway leading down from Jack's jet.

"No." Evie grabbed his elbow and started down the stairs with him.

"What about Hayden? Does he know?"

"Nope. Jack and I are the brokers behind this deal." She winked at Jack, who was waiting on the tarmac.

"So you're putting your ass on the line here, aren't you?"

"I like to play with things that go boom."

Smokey scratched at a sprig of hair on the side of his head. "Why?"

"Because time's running out."

"What the he-ell are you talking about?"

"Kate's pregnant," Evie said.

Smokey stopped, his shaky old foot hovering over a metal step.

Evie put her hand on his thigh and pushed his boot onto the step. "The news surprised Kate and Hayden since the doctors told Kate she'd never have kids after the Broadcaster Butcher took all those swipes at her." Evie nudged him forward. "Apparently that's not the case. Hayden finally spilled that she's two months along but hasn't told anyone because she wants to get past the first trimester."

A twinkle lit up the old man's watery eyes. "Katy-lady, she's a tough gal. She'll do right fine."

"Agreed, but with the baby clock now ticking, she can't come running every time you find yourself at the bottom of a canyon after driving off the side of a mountain. The choice is yours. You can make this work, or you can go live with your cousin Franny in Florida."

They'd reached the bottom of the stairs, where Jack handed Smokey his cane. Smokey took a deep breath. "Doesn't smell too bad here. Sea and pines. I like pines."

Evie released Smokey's arm and took Jack's.

"Good afternoon, Mr. Bernard," a voice said.

Smokey cleared his throat and held out his hand. "Folks call me Smokey Joe."

"Excellent, folks call me God, but you can call me Parker." Parker took the old man's hand and shook.

Evie and Jack held back as Parker and Smokey Joe made their way to a black SUV.

"You think this is really going to work?" Jack asked.

"I have no idea," Evie said. "They're both strong-willed and set in their ways."

"Could get explosive," Jack said.

"It probably will." She looked up at him, puffing the hair out of her face. "But there's nothing wrong with a little smoke and fire in a relationship, is there?"

Jack pulled her into his arms. "Definitely not." His lips touched hers, igniting a fire that warmed her to the tips of her red cowboy boots.

He took her life, but left her alive.

Please see the next page for an excerpt from

The Broken

CHAPTER ONE

Mancos, Colorado
Tuesday, June 9
1:48 a.m.

The cry was low and tortured, pulled from the gut of a man who'd been to hell and back.

Kate Johnson threw off her covers and grabbed the box of paper clips she kept on her nightstand. "I'm coming, Smokey Joe," she called even though the old man couldn't hear her. He was too far away, trapped in a time and place known only to his tormented mind. She tore down the steps of the cabin and into Smokey's bedroom.

"Safety pins! Where the hell are my safety pins?" Smokey's hands clawed at the covers she'd tucked around him four hours ago. "Dammit to hell! I need those pins."

Kate took one of his hands in hers and dropped a handful of paper clips onto his palm. "Here you go."

His knobby fingers clamped around the bits of metal, and

he dipped them in a frantic but practiced rhythm. Eventually his cries died off and gave way to moans. Then came the sobs. They were the worst.

As she had done dozens of times over the past six months, she sank to her knees beside his bed and gathered him in her arms. Papery skin over old bones. The sour-sweet smell of cold sweat. Her cheek rubbed against the sprigs of gray hair on his head. As the sobs tapered off and his trembling ceased, she looked at her arms and shook her head. How could a hug, nothing more than two arms, *her arms*, stop a war?

When the old man's breathing returned to normal, he opened his sightless eyes. "That you, Katy-lady?"

She squeezed his bony knee. "Yes."

Relief smoothed the lines of terror twisting his face.

She left his bedside and opened the top drawer of the bureau. "Who was it?"

He inched himself to an upright position. "Never got a name on this one. He wasn't talking by the time ground grunts got him in the chopper. Mortar round blew off half his neck."

"What do you remember about him?" This was another thing she didn't understand, Smokey's need to relive the pains of the past. Yesterday's horrors should be bundled up and tucked away. They had no place in this world. She reached into the drawer for a clean nightshirt.

"He had red hair, color of a firecracker, and he held a picture of his momma in his hand. We lost him before we got to Da Nang, but I made sure the hospital crew got the picture and told them to tell that boy's momma she'd been right there with her son when he needed her, offering comfort only a momma can."

Mommas don't offer comfort. The thought snuck up on her, a jarring uppercut to the chin.

"Katy-lady, you okay?"

The bureau drawer slammed shut. "I'm fine."

She handed Smokey Joe the clean nightshirt and sat on the foot of the bed. That's when she noticed the soft voices coming from the radio on the nightstand. A late-night talk show host was talking to William from Michigan about a school shooting in New Jersey that left two eleven-year-olds dead. "This!" She jabbed a hand at the radio. "What is *this*?"

"Don't know." Smokey raised his gaze to the ceiling. "Can't see."

She snapped off the radio, silencing the voices. "You were listening to the news before bed again, weren't you?"

"You going to start nagging me? I don't pay you to ride my ass."

"No, you pay me to take care of you, and if you don't want to take out any new help wanted ads, listen to me. Your doctor said no news before bedtime. Those stories from the Mideast bring back too many war memories." And trigger nightmares of a time when he desperately tried to save bloody and broken bodies with only a handful of safety pins and a heart full of hope.

His gnarled fingers fumbled with the buttons of his sweat-soaked nightshirt. She reached over to help.

"I wasn't listening to no war news. There was another one of them Barbie murders. This one right here in Colorado. All the stations are yammering about it."

Barbie murders? What an insane world, filled with criminals without conscience, a public fascinated by the gory and gruesome, and media ready to unite the two for the sake of ratings. She didn't miss the crazy world of broadcast news and had no regrets that she hadn't seen a newscast in almost three years, not since she'd *been* the news.

She unfastened Smokey's next two buttons. "So a *Barbie* was killed?"

"Yep. Course the coppers don't call 'em Barbies. That's just my name, but I think that makes six now, all TV gals, all stabbed to death in their homes."

She grew still. "Broadcast journalists? Stabbed?"

"Yeah, not too pretty, either. Each gal had more than fifty knife wounds. Now why the hell does someone need to stab a body fifty times?"

Her hand sought the scar between her right eye and temple. *Because twenty-five isn't enough to kill?*

"I'll tell you why." Smokey jabbed a crooked index finger at his temple. "He ain't right in the head."

Kate slipped the shirt off Smokey's bony shoulders, her own shoulders relaxing. As an investigative reporter she'd seen up close the machinations of the criminal mind. She knew the mean and twisted and evil that perpetuated crimes against humanity. There were plenty of bad people in this world, plenty of knife-wielding crazies, and the twenty-five scars that crisscrossed her body had nothing to do with Smokey's *Barbies*. "Haven't we both determined the world in general isn't right in the head?"

"But this guy's sick, scary sick. He does that creepy thing with the mirrors."

The curtains on Smokey's window shifted with the night breeze, and the hairs on the back of her neck stood on end. "Mirrors?"

"After he kills them Barbies, the screwball goes around breaking every mirror in the house. Shatters every single one. You ever heard of such a crazy thing?"

Sounds ricocheted through her head. The swoosh of a hammer. The crack of glass. The obscenely happy tinkle of falling mirror fragments.

Smokey's shirt, soaked in sweat and terror, fell from her hand.

* * *

Tuesday, June 9, 2:20 a.m.
Colorado Springs, Colorado

Hayden Reed stared at the shards of mirror that once covered an entire wall in Shayna Thomas's entryway. The largest piece was no bigger than two inches square.

Insanity was one hell of a wrecking ball.

He squatted to study the destruction, looking for traces— blood, footprints, hairs, fibers, anything that would lead him to the killer he'd been tracking for five months. All he saw in the broken mirror were distorted bits of his face, a macabre reflection of a man who'd been slammed by a wrecking ball of his own.

Parker Lord's voice echoed through his head. "Hold off on the Colorado slaying," his boss had said. "Hatch can cover for you and bring you up to speed when you get things wrapped up in Tucson with your family."

Hayden stood. His family was fine.

Time to hunt for the Butcher. But first he needed to track down Sergeant Lottie King.

A uniform directed Hayden through the living room and down a hallway where he came face-to-face with a short, round African American woman. Her crinkly gray hair hugged her head in a tight knot, and she wore a simple navy suit and a Glock 22 holstered under her left arm. On her feet were the highest, reddest heels he'd ever seen outside a whorehouse.

"Chief warned me some FBI hotshot was coming in, and you got hotshot written all over you." The sergeant crossed her arms over her chest. "My boys said you're one of Parker Lord's men, a fucking Apostle. That true?"

Hayden noticed the tone. It happened often at the mention of Parker's Special Criminal Investigative Unit, a small group of FBI specialists known for working outside the box and, according to some, outside the law. Some media pundit nicknamed them the Apostles. Like Parker, Hayden didn't care about names, only justice. "Yes."

"Heard you boys play by a different set of rules."

He clasped his hands behind his back. "We don't play."

Her jaw squared in a challenge as she jutted her chin toward the shattered mirror in the hallway. "So tell me, Agent I-Don't-Play, what's your take?"

Shayna Thomas had been found dead in her bedroom four hours ago. Multiple stab wounds. No signs of sexual trauma. Shattered mirrors. All the earmarks of another Broadcaster Butcher slaying. Hayden pointed to a spot three feet down the hall. "The unsub stood there. One strike. Used a long-handled, blunt instrument he brought with him. Carefully positioned his body out of the glass trajectory. You'll find no blood near this or any of the other broken mirrors. You'll also find no footprints, no fingerprints, no trace, and no witnesses." The other Butcher crime scenes had been freakishly void of evidence.

The sergeant locked him in a stare-down. He studied the wide, steady stance of those high heels, the indignant puff of her chest, and the single corkscrew of hair that stuck out above her right ear.

"And your take, Sergeant King?"

The police sergeant's nostrils flared. "I think we got us one fucked-up son of a bitch, and I can't wait to nail his ass to the splintered seat of a cold, dark cell where he'll never see the light of day."

Early in his law enforcement career, he'd learned there were two kinds of people behind the shield: those seeking personal gain—a paycheck, ego strokes, power—and those seeking justice. Like him, the woman in the red shoes was one of the latter. Hayden unclasped his hands. "And I can't wait to hand you a hammer."

A smile wrinkled the corner of her eyes, and he saw what he needed: respect.

"Damn glad you're here, Agent Reed."

"For the record, Sergeant King, I hear you aren't much of a slouch, either."

"Ahh, a pretty face *and* a smooth talker. I think I might be able to work with you." The smile in her eyes dimmed as she motioned him to follow her down the hall.

"Time line?" Hayden asked.

"A man out walking his dog hears breaking glass as he passes Thomas's house. He calls the station at 10:32. Beat officer arrives at 10:37. He makes repeated shout-outs, but no one responds. He looks through the front window, sees the broken mirror, and calls for backup. When the second uniform arrives, they enter and discover the victim in the master bedroom."

"Positive ID?"

"Confirmed. Shayna Thomas. Homeowner."

"Current status?"

"Crime Scene Division's still processing." Sergeant King's red shoes drew to a halt. "This is one mother of a scene."

"Blood." Hayden didn't frame the single word as a question. They'd found excessive amounts of blood at the other Butcher crime scenes, five since January.

"It's the fucking Red Sea in there. You better watch those shiny shoes of yours." Lottie pointed to the door in front of them. "I'm warning you. It ain't pretty."

Wrongful death never was.

Inside the bedroom, blood peppered four walls, striped the white down comforter, and clung to the fan centered on the ceiling. The victim lay on the ground in front of a dresser. Blood soaked her T-shirt and jogging shorts and matted her hair. She was a brunette, slim, probably attractive. Hard to tell. Lacerations decussated her face, arms, neck, and abdomen, but as he expected, the V at her legs was blood- and injury-free.

He saved the hands for last. He always did. It was hard to think clearly after seeing them, hard to stop being the dispassionate evaluator. Drawing air into his tightening lungs, he turned to Shayna Thomas's bloody hands. They rested on her breasts, fingers intertwined as if in prayer, a gesture of peace amidst the chaos of murder.

For a moment he lowered his eyelids and calmed the rage that simmered in a place he refused to acknowledge.

Those bloody hands beckoned him, pulled him in, and wouldn't let go. His boss, Parker Lord, was wrong. Hayden needed to be here.

* * *

Tuesday, June 9, 2:23 a.m.
Mancos, Colorado

Run. Fast and far.

Kate's hands shook worse than Smokey Joe's as she yanked the saddlebags out of the closet and slammed them on her bed. From the bureau, she hauled out the few things she called her own: underwear, scarves, T-shirts, chambray overshirts, jeans, and her leathers. She jammed all but the leathers into the bags and threw in her brown contacts and hair dye. Meager belongings compared to her on-air days, a time when she wore a different face. A face not yet hacked by a madman. A madman who hadn't stopped after the butcher job on her.

The wooden floor creaked behind her. She dropped her leathers and spun. Something shifted in the shadow of the doorway. She reached for the ceramic lamp on the night-stand, then set it down when Smokey stepped out of the darkness.

He cleared his throat with a rough cough. "You taking off?"

Her hand dropped to her side, and she tried not to look into his sightless eyes, eyes filled with confusion and some-thing else. *Oh God, please don't let him look at me like that.* "Yes." What more could she say? *I'm sorry for disappoint-ing you. I'm sorry for leaving because there's a madman roaming the country who vowed to kill me and who has since murdered six other women.*

She yanked the saddlebag zippers closed. How stupid to think she could stop running, stupid to stay in one place so long, and stupid to put an old, blind man like Smokey Joe in danger. She picked up the leather pants and jammed her legs into them. The Shayna Thomas attack had occurred in Colorado Springs, only three hundred miles from Smokey Joe's cabin in southwestern Colorado.

Smokey scratched the stubble on his chin. "That big or-der? You got it done?"

"Order?" She grabbed her helmet from the top shelf of the closet.

"That gal out of San Diego who wants all them angels. You get 'em done?"

Kate couldn't think about their online jewelry store or tourmaline angels. She thought only about getting away. "Order's done. It's boxed and on the table."

"I'll ship it." One of Smokey's slippers, the color and texture of beef jerky, whisked across the floor. "Where should I send your cut?"

"You keep it." She needed no connections to Smokey Joe, no trail that could put him in the sights of a knife-wielding madman.

Smokey nodded and shuffled away. The sound of his ratty slippers on the floor she polished weekly pounded in her head and tugged at her heart.

The past six months with Smokey Joe had been peaceful, and after being on the run for more than two years, she'd needed the rest and recharging. During her time here in the scrub canyons and pine forests of southwestern Colorado, she hadn't thought about the past or the future. She'd been simply living, living simply.

She flung her saddlebags over her shoulder—amazing how little a person needed to live—and rushed down the steps to the bottom floor. She bolted through the kitchen but ground to a halt at the back door.

Turning quickly, she set the timer for Smokey's morning coffee, flicked on the bread machine, and left an urgent voice message with his case manager. Only then did she slip out of the house, dead bolt the lock, and escape into the safe cover of darkness.

Fall in Love with Forever Romance

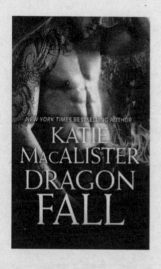

DRAGON FALL
by Katie MacAlister

New York Times bestseller Katie MacAlister returns to her fan-favorite paranormal series. To ensure the survival of his fellow dragons, Kostya needs a mate of true heart and soul before it's too late.

FRISK ME
by Lauren Layne

USA Today bestselling author Lauren Layne brings us the first book in her New York's Finest series. Journalist Ava Sims may be the only woman in NYC who isn't in love with the city's newly minted hero Officer Luc Moretti. That's why she's going after the real story—to find out about the man behind the badge. But the more time she spends around Luc, the more she has to admit there's something about a man in uniform…and she can't wait to get him out of his.

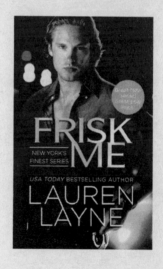

Fall in Love with Forever Romance

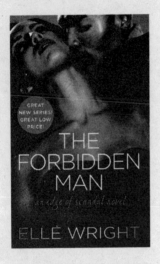

THE FORBIDDEN MAN
by Elle Wright

Sydney Williams has forgiven her fiancé, Den, more times than she can count. But his latest betrayal just days before their wedding is too big to ignore. Shocking her friends and family, she walks out on her fiancé… and into the arms of his brother, Morgan. But is their love only a fling or built to last?

THE BLIND
by Shelley Coriell

When art imitates death… As part of the FBI's elite Apostles team, bomb and weapons specialist Evie Jimenez knows playing it safe is *not* an option. Especially when tracking a serial killer. Billionaire philanthropist and art expert Jack Elliott never imagined the instant heat for the fiery Evie would explode his cool and cautious world. But as Evie and Jack get closer to the killer's endgame, they will learn that safety and control are all illusions. For their quarry has set his sight on *Evie* for his final masterpiece…

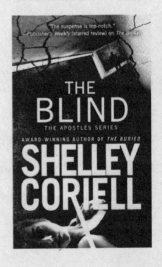

Fall in Love with Forever Romance

THE LEGACY OF COPPER CREEK
by R. C. Ryan

In the *New York Times* best-selling tradition of Linda Lael Miller and Diana Palmer comes the final book in R. C. Ryan's Copper Creek series. When a snowstorm forces together the sexy Whit Mackenzie and the heartbroken Cara Walton, sparks fly. But can Whit show Cara how to love again?

AND THEN HE KISSED ME
by Kim Amos

Bad-boy biker Kieran Callaghan already broke Audrey Tanner's heart once. So what's she supposed to do when she finds out he's her boss—and that he's sexier than ever? Fans of Kristan Higgans, Jill Shalvis, and Lori Wilde will love this second book in the White Pine, Minnesota series.

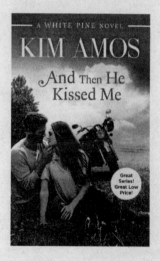